DROLL STORIES

DROLL STORIES

THIRTY TALES BY

HONORÉ DE BALZAC

all now especially translated into modern

English by Jacques Le Clercq, and printed

with illustrations by Boris Artzybasheff

THE HERITAGE PRESS · NEW YORK

TABLE OF CONTENTS

"*A SORT* of medical Molière . . . a museum, in-folio, of pathological anatomy . . . a Saint-Simon of the mob.*" Such are a few of the epithets popularly applied to Balzac in the Paris of his day.

To Sainte-Beuve, who never liked him, he appears as "the indiscreet physician of secret maladies"; to Lamartine, who did, as "the great geographer of human passions." One critic concedes him, like Homer and Dante, his critics and sciolists; another, with unconscious humor, remarks that he has created at least forty characters more celebrated than the forty members of the French Academy. According to Taine: "With Shakespeare and Saint-Simon, Balzac is the greatest storehouse of documents upon human nature that we possess." And Hugo, orating over his grave: "His name will mingle with the luminous trace our period has left for future ages; he surpasses Tacitus and rivals Suetonius, he reaches through Beaumarchais to Rabelais."

What manner of man was he, then? And what of his colossal achievements?

There is, of course, the vast legend, to which he himself contributed, intentionally at times, for he was both ambitious and vain. That statue of Napoleon, for instance, with along the scabbard the written declaration: *"What he was unable to complete with the sword, I shall accomplish with the pen. [Signed] Honoré de Balzac."* The powerful, squat figure emerges, scribbling in an attic or in that miserable apartment in Passy; theatrically arrayed, working by candlelight and by the grace of innumerable cups of strong coffee; eternally dodging his creditors; rushing off to various points of Europe on errands of love; forever

xi

dreaming of huge fortunes and reduced to merciless embarrassment; resisting all pressure to do military duty and languishing in jail for it; laughing bigly and falling upon pyramids of fruit, "superb in his vegetarian pantagruelism"; and day in, day out, page after hurried page, piling up the monument of literature which founds the modern novel.

"I dared write and depict everything," he exclaims somewhere. True enough; even the treacherous reaches of Lesbos and Sodom hold no terrors for him. Though elsewhere, when indulging in interminable orgies of description, he might have remembered, without the least damage to his genius, an axiom of that Voltaire to whom he willingly compared himself: "The secret of boring the reader is to tell everything."

Here is what he wrote in his own hand—the manuscript has been preserved—as advertising copy for *La Peau de Chagrin:*

"Such works bring insomnia to the rich man's mansion and to the poet's garret; they animate the countryside; in winter, they give the crackling logs a livelier reflection. What an author! What verve! What wit! What tireless perseverance in painting and excoriating everything! What an annalist! What passion and what sang-froid!"

True, again; all this simply goes to prove that authors have at all times provided much of their own blurbery, though seldom so convincingly and almost never so accurately.

As for his remark to the sculptor David d'Angers, who was modelling his bust—"Study my nose with special care; my nose is a whole world"—it would be deliberately inimical to take it for an authentic illustration of Balzac's vanity. Wit was essential in him, humor inherent. Vain, Balzac undoubtedly was. Yet there was never anything petty, mean, jealous and smug about him; his was rather a rich, full, lusty, well-conditioned self-conceit, eminently *bon enfant,* eminently *bonhomme,* like himself.

This very buoyancy, it was, enabled him to undertake without terror a labor of such heroic proportions. There is no place for any smallness in a work reared upon this gigantic scale. A man who writes with the pen of Rabelais has neither time nor inclination for the lesser niceties of behavior and conception.

Honoré Balzac was born on the twenty-seventh of Floréal in

the year VIII of the Republic (May 20th, 1799) —it was St. Honoré's Day, too—at Tours, in the street one of his *Droll Stories*
celebrates so exuberantly. Despite his pretensions to nobility,
his origins were humble. The *de*—not necessarily a sign of aris-
tocracy—he adopted in 1830; none of his people ever used it.
Indeed, his father's birth certificate has been found and his family traced back for almost a century. The real name was Balsa;
they were laborers or possibly even farmers in Gascony. This,
Balzac was unaware of; but to his meridional forbears he undoubtedly owes many features of his tumultuous character.

Bernard-François Balzac, director of the military hospital in
Tours, had married Anne Charlotte Laure Sallambier in 1797.
They had four children: Honoré, Laure, another daughter, Lau-
rence, and a son, Henry François. Laure, later Madame Surville,
was always very close to her brother; she has left some stories
and an indispensable study of her brother. From what little we
know of Henry François he seems to have been a thoroughly
objectionable person.

At the age of seven, Balzac was sent to the Collège de Vendôme, where for six years he lived the arduous, severe life of a
boarder, a bitter experience he was destined to turn to advantage in his *Louis Lambert*. In 1813, for a while, he attended the
Collège in his native town as a day-scholar; but the following
year, his father was transferred to a position in the Food Depart-
ment of the Army Commissariat in Paris and Balzac was boarded
with a Royalist schoolmaster, Monsieur Lepître, in the Rue St.
Louis. By 1816, however, his schooling was over.

His father now intended him to become a lawyer; he had
three years' experience in the office of a notary and advocate,
and, in 1820, he actually obtained the degree of Licencié. But
his heart was not in it, as he proves by holding the profession up
to scorn whenever he has a chance. To be sure, few men have
had cause to give attorneys and bailiffs a wider berth.

Having flatly refused to embark on a calling that necessitated
"wallowing in the offal of the courts," Balzac left his parents,
who had moved out of Paris, and began his "garret period." His
father had once written a *History of Rabies,* though this scarcely
predisposed him to favor a literary career for his firstborn. Opposed by his family, virtually without funds, the lad determined to

earn a fortune with his pen. He settled down in a lonely attic in
the Rue Lesdiguières, a stone's throw from the Faubourg Saint-
Antoine. For the next eight years, book followed upon book. He
wrote a tragedy, never published, with Cromwell for hero; he
wrote novels like *C..cqsigrue, Stella, Les Deux Hector, La Dernière Fée, Le Corrupteur,* sometimes single-handed, sometimes
in collaboration (especially with Le Poitevin de Saint-Alme,
later publisher of the *Corsaire* and of the *Figaro*) under such
pseudonyms as Horace de Saint-Aubin and Lord R'hoone, an
anagram. For the most part, they were tedious imitations of the
Gothic novel of horror, leaning very heavily upon Scott, Ann
Radcliffe, etc. All this work fills some fifty volumes; Sainte-
Beuve, one of the few people who has had the courage to read
them, pronounces them utterly without originality or even
promise of talent. As a matter of fact, their author himself considered them futile.

Between 1825 and 1828, Balzac engaged in a series of speculations which were to mar the rest of his life and to give him in-
eluctably to literature. Forever dreaming of making a fortune,
he plunged into a publishing venture, a printing business and
a typefoundry. In the first field, he produced the works of Molière and La Fontaine, in one-volume editions, at a very reasonable price; but his sane, lofty aim was due to fail. The acquisition of the other concerns overwhelmed him. At last, after more
than three years of harrowing struggle, he had practically to
abscond. Eventually his debts were written off, but only ten
years later (1838) and then by a further obligation of ninety
thousand francs mostly furnished by his mother and never
repaid.

"Balzac," Taine writes, "was a man of business and a man in
debt. . . . Harassed and beleaguered, he accomplished prodigies
of labor. . . . Until the very end, his days were precarious and
fraught with apprehension. . . . Money was the tyrant and perse-
cutor of his life; he was a prey and a slave to it through necessity,
through honor, through imagination, through hope. This des-
pot and extortioner bent him over his task, chained him to it,
inspired him in it, pursued him even in his leisure, his meditations, his dreams; it mastered his hand, forged his thought, ani-

mated his characters and cast, over his entire work, the splendor of its jingling streams."

His extravagance by no means eased his situation. The various houses he took, the carriages and curios he bought, the journeys he dashed off on to Switzerland, to Germany, to Austria and Italy. . . . He believed that money calls money, that to be considered rich means to be rich. Meanwhile the bills piled up. He founded two periodicals, one written almost entirely by himself. Both failed. A lawsuit with Buloz, of the *Revue de Paris,* proved successful, but at the price of what time! Goaded by necessity, driven by hope of gain, fame, comfort, peace, urged by his realization of the magnitude of his task, he toiled away like a galley-slave. He would rise at midnight, drug himself with coffee and write sometimes as long as sixteen, as long as twenty hours at a stretch, after which he dressed and ran to the printer's to correct proof. That brainstorm of his in Italy—to melt the silver out of the slag heaps of the Roman mines in Sardinia— was a capital scheme. Riches seemed just around the corner. Unfortunately he was anticipated by somebody else.

Nor, finally, was his mode of writing calculated to facilitate matters. In the light of his extreme laboriousness, of his constant alterations, how much the more admirable still his energy and endurance seem! *Séraphita* and *Le Lys dans la Vallée,* for example, were held up several years, half-printed, even, while he struggled to conclude them. His method of composition, too, was fantastic. It consisted in first sending a sort of vague scenario to the printer, then writing the book itself in the margin of the proofs. His galleys looked like a nightmare battleground with battalions of words, regiments of sentences lying hacked, wounded, maimed, killed, wiped out, blotted out by divisions and armies of new phrases, fresh ideas, elaborations and changes that passed through, over, and beyond them in a torrent of inspiration. Certain volumes required twelve sets, others no less than twenty! His copy was the terror of printers; they would take turns at setting it, for none was willing to do more than an hour of Balzac. His name was proverbial in the business. Publishers refused to defray the excessive costs of composition. These also, ate into the author's earnings.

Between the years 1830 and 1847, no twelvemonth passed without his writing at least three works. The average for this seventeen-year period is six per annum. In 1833 and 1837, six books; in 1839, seven; in 1831 and 1833, eight; in 1830, ten; while in the year 1832, Balzac's output reaches the staggering total of fourteen.

Leaving aside the unsigned and pseudonymous works, if we consider only this period and recall the hallucinating conditions under which Balzac labored, surely here was a record in polygraphy? Surely here was an inferno beside which the existence of Walter Scott fades into the gentle torpor of a garden-party?

In his leisure—one hesitates to write the word—there were certain compensations. Friendship, travel, love. . . . Hugo, George Sand to name but two among literary celebrities; his sister Laure and Surville, her husband; the Comte de Pommereul, with whom he stayed in Brittany to escape Paris and gather material for *Les Chouans;* the de Margonnes, when he visited at Saché, and the Carrauds, at Angoulême. His sojourns further afield were almost all at the behest of love.

Three women exerted a deep influence upon him: the maternal, the wanton, the wife.

The first, Madame de Berny, was the ideal Egeria; for fifteen years, she gave him her unflagging devotion. A friend of Madame Balzac's, and three years her senior, the mother of nine children, she devoted herself to the novelist from 1821 until her death in 1836. She helped him, financially and morally, during the bitter days of his commercial struggles; she was forever inspiring and encouraging him. To a callow youth, the more impressionable because of his curiosity and his love, she opened the charmed horizons not only of a loftier social sphere but also of an entire civilization whose grandeur the Revolution had swept away. It was a perfect association; she gave him her rich experience, the last supreme fires of her passion, her affection, her admiration, her esteem; and when his physical love had cooled, she still remained a loyal friend. In exchange he paid her the tribute of immortality. Did she not sit for the portrait of Madame de Mortsauf in *Le Lys dans la Vallée?*

The wanton was Madame de Castries, a shallow, frivolous, cruel baggage. First they corresponded; soon he was calling upon her. She played with him, cat-and-mouse fashion, for a long time. A Marquise, she must needs look down a little on this stout, exuberant, gesticulating commoner, though she encouraged his high monarchism, put it to political purpose and flattered his vanity. For her sake, he journeyed to Aix-les-Bains, then to Geneva; they were bound for Italy; but before her heartless coquetry, he fled in despair. The Marquise de Castries served as model for some of the less savory of Balzac's ladies, for the Duchesse de Langeais in particular. Their association was very brief.

The wife—in hope and thought at outset, finally in fact and deed—was Evelina, Countess Hanska. As early as 1832, she had written him an admiring letter, piquantly signed L'Étrangère. They corresponded feverishly. What balm for Balzac this romantic communion with the unknown, the lady of exalted station, the mysterious foreigner, a woman of extraordinary culture, of superb taste (did she not read, understand, discuss, and set store by his works?). She was Eve, she was the *Princesse Lointaine,* the Muse and the Madonna. They met for a first time in Switzerland, at Neuchâtel, where she was staying with her husband, in 1833; for a second, at Geneva, in 1834; for a third in Vienna in 1835. She had, from the first, promised to marry him if her husband died; obligingly enough, the latter did so in 1841. But though Balzac visited her in St. Petersburg, then met her in Paris, Wiesbaden, Rome, it was only in 1847 that he went to stay with her in the Ukraine as her official fiancé. They were married on March 14th, 1850, returning almost at once to Paris. Balzac had not been well; his exertions had begun to tell on him. The Russian winter had done nothing to improve his condition. He suffered direly. They reached Paris in April; on August 17th, he was dead.

It had been a full life, expressed chiefly in his works, so many milestones along the road to glory. He was denied what most he desired in order fully to enjoy what he had wrested from fate. He had longed for power; he even stood for the Chamber in two constituencies; but there is no record of his polling a single vote. He had longed for glory; he was a candidate for the Academy several times; once he achieved four votes. He had longed for love; he found the all-desired postponing their marriage until almost too late. He had longed for money, he died a debtor.

But, at bottom, he must have had the consciousness of his own significance, he must have worked for a Balzac in the future. "The historiographer of nature and society"—"the greatest novelist of modern times"—"the vast foundation on which all modern writing rests"—"Dante . . . Shakespeare . . . Voltaire. . . ."

Madame Surville has calculated that from 1827 to 1848, Balzac's writings fill ninety-seven tomes, comprising a total of 10,816 pages, each three times the size of the usual octavo.

What a lesson in humility for a writer!

It is impossible here to give more than passing notice to the *Comédie Humaine.* Already our preface grows lengthy. We must content ourselves with simply citing certain works in order to place the *Droll Stories* in their proper position amid Balzac's encyclopedic production.

The *Human Comedy* is divided into *Scenes of Private Life* (numbering twenty-eight), *Scenes of Provincial Life* (thirteen), *Scenes of Parisian Life* (twenty-two), *Scenes of Political Life* (six), *Scenes of Military Life* (two), and *Scenes of Country Life* (three).

The first category includes *La Femme de Trente Ans,* a character invented by Balzac and stamped indelibly upon the social manners of his age; *La Femme Abandonnée* and *La Grenadière,* searching studies of women and love; *Les Grandes Bretèches,* a trio of harrowing tales of husbandly vengeances; *La Fausse Maîtresse,* an instance of virtue triumphant; *Gobseck,* one of Balzac's greatest studies of avarice; *Béatrix,* an examination of the moral problems of adultery; *Pierre Grasson,* with a plot O. Henry might have invented but characters he could not have drawn, and *Colonel Chabert,* which offers a situation such as the last war has more than once provided.

The second category in many ways includes the best of Balzac. Here are *Eugénie Grandet,* a wellnigh perfect story, hailed by Sainte-Beuve as immortal; *Le Lys dans la Vallée,* marred, no doubt, by a somewhat sickly sweetness but compact with the author's qualities and defects; *Ursule Mirouet,* which deals with the beyond; *Les Illusions Perdues,* in which Balzac has drawn upon his business experiences; *l'Illustre Gaudissart,* a sketch of the commercial traveller; the *Curé de Tours,* with its superb old maid, Mademoiselle Gamard.

The Parisian epos is alive with memorable characters. It was Vautrin, the villain in several works, who closed the doors of the Academy on Balzac. "One convict," Balzac protested, "is not too much in a work which lays claim to daguerrotyping a society with fifty thousand!" Esther, the harlot; Lucien de Rubempré; the Baron de Nucingen; Cotenson—how the characters rise from the pages! *Splendeurs et Misères des Courtisanes* is a life-size canvas of prostitution in every class and phase; *Dernière Incarnation de Vautrin,* a terrific account of the struggles of police and thieves, studded with unforgettable views of lupanar and prison. There are *Cousin Pons* with its grotesque power; and *Cousine Bette,* "an immense work because it depicts vices and horrors without a word of anger or sympathy"; and *César Birotteau,* with its megalomaniac hero. There are *La Duchesse de Langeais,* a story as romantically thrilling as Dumas ever penned and, for good measure, a deal of excellent psychology; *La Fille aux Yeux d'Or,* with its Lesbian lovers and *Sarrasine,* with its comely *castrato.* And, towering over the whole multitudinous gallery, *Père Goriot,* that Lear without a Cordelia, whose death scene surely marks one of the mightiest achievements in all literature.

The fourth category, dealing with political life, is not Balzac at his best. But the *Épisode sous la Terreur* and *Une Ténébreuse Affaire* will never want for readers. *Madame de la Chanterie* relates the triumph of a spy, one of those monsters Balzac excelled in depicting. It is unfolded in judiciary form, which tends to render it tedious. Throughout this series, the author remains reactionary: he is opposed to savings-banks, which only encourage servants to rob their masters; he is opposed to competitive examinations, free speech, democracy. Laws are but spiders' webs through which the big flies pass while the small are caught. Absolute government, benevolent enough to lull the mob in its misery, is the sum of his political ideals.

The Scenes of Military Life, an arbitrary classification, consists of *Une Passion dans le Désert,* a tale of sodomy with a lioness for central figure, and *Les Chouans,* a historical novel whose background Balzac studied on the spot. It is filled with vivid scenes such as the massacre of the Blues, the burning of an old miser, a priest saying mass in a druid forest to an audience of armed peasants. The manners of the Breton peasants, their vigor, their tenacity, their ineradicable vengeance are capitally presented.

The Scenes of Country Life include at least one major work *Le Médecin de Campagne,* spoiled by too much sociological discussion, yet nevertheless realistic and faithful.

Originally Balzac had intended to write one hundred tales, for in 1832 the first ten appeared under the title of *The One Hundred Droll Stories.* . . . The title is modelled upon *Les Cent Nouvelles Nouvelles,* a book in the Boccaccio tradition, written by A. de la Salle and often wrongly ascribed to Louis XI. The second series of ten appeared in 1833; the third in 1837. In 1855, the three dixains were published together in one volume illustrated by Gustave Doré, "an inventor, in his way, just as Balzac was in his, an artist who drew inspiration from Balzac, just as Balzac did from Rabelais and Boccaccio."

"A work quite aside from the *Comédie Humaine* . . . an exceptional work" the *Droll Stories* are. But to regard them as a purely minor, unessential feature in his production is to err grossly. Though fivescore were first planned, he never dreamed of a wide medieval epos like his modern one; but "he considered these tales and prized them as his most difficult masterpiece." Difficult, perhaps. Yet how evenly they flow, how smoothly they read. They seem to hold all the insouciance a writer instills in a work of recreation, of delectation. Repeatedly, Balzac expressed a high regard for the tales. Judging by the welcome they have met with and the numerous editions that have appeared, posterity has been inclined to bear him out.

A highly conservative critic calls them "tales in which all the lusts of the flesh are unleashed, satisfied and left to run riot amid a bacchanalia of flushed Priapi." Professor Saintsbury finds "undoubted genius and not a little art" in *The Succubus.* Lamartine dismisses them as "those futile, somewhat cynical volumes." George Sand called the book indecent—she would!—at which Balzac called George Sand a prude—he too would!

All these judgments are, of course, true, depending entirely upon the point of approach. In the first, the word "lust" sounds a little severe, perhaps because it has come to imply such a very earnest, conscientious, joyless prurience, while the period Balzac treats and the language he writes dictated a naturalness, a guileless directness, an effortless urge. "Lust" seems a very stern term to apply to the Monk Amador, who brought happiness to so many people, or to the Moorish woman, none of whose victims ever complained. True, lickerish lust, when it occurs, as for example in the tale of My Lord of Valennes, usually comes off the worst in the engagement.

In *The Succubus* there is indeed genius. Through the statements of a handful of people, set down in documentary style over a few brief pages, Balzac was able to conjure up the entire social structure of an age. It is as varied and as plausible as *The Canterbury Tales*. This gem alone should save *Droll Stories* from being "futile," if any work which has afforded so much pleasure to its readers could possibly be so.

To George Sand's objection, the answer is: "Yes, these tales are indecent, richly, heartily, jovially indecent in the indecent vein of Rabelais, Verville, Boccaccio, Marguerite de Navarre and all the other purveyors of indecency who furnished the greatest writers of the age."

It is precisely this faculty for identifying himself with the old, honorable tradition that stamps Balzac so unerringly the master and makes *Droll Stories* the unique tour de force it is. We must allow his prefatory challenge: his book is indeed a work of literary archæology. When others were using the Middle Ages as but an additional artifice to enhance the unreality of their writing, Balzac turned to it as to the most natural thing in the world. All the life, all the vividness he brought to the *Human Comedy*, that radiant actuality of character and scene glow in these tales. An interval of six centuries is as nothing to him: he has ease and gaiety on his side. Six hundred years? It means less to him than "the jump of an old flea." Nor does the language (sixteenth-century French, the idiom of Rabelais) hold out the least terrors. It enables him not only to call a spade a spade; it also throws a hedge about the words, softening their crudity. ("Give not this book unto maidens. . . .") But the use of this language goes beyond this. He takes to it so suavely; it fits his thought, it moulds and holds treasures of sly naïveté, of roguish mockery, of tenderness, even, under its very artlessness. Once Balzac declared that only Hugo, Gautier and himself knew the French language. The boast will not hold water. But how many of his contemporaries would have been able or willing to do what he did?

Thus if the *Droll Stories* were but so many bawdy jokes, Balzac's good humor, his verisimilitude and his style would make them worth reading. Yet their ribaldries—the rough-and-tumble jollity of a thoroughly healthy man—should not divert our attention from the genuine pathos underlying more than one tale. The conclusion of *The Venial Sin* has a truly chivalric nobility about it; *The Brother-in-Arms* exalts an ideal of loyalty; *The Unauthentic Courtesan* is high tragedy, for all the manner of its telling; *The Succubus* moves one to compassion for a victim of human superstition; *Perseverance in Love* might, as far as its subject goes, have originated in a Y.M.C.A. tract; and *The Fair Imperia Married* furnishes a touching instance of a woman's sacrifice.

JACQUES LE CLERCQ

Bibliography

*A*MONG the general notices on Balzac, that by Professor Saintsbury in the Encyclopaedia Britannica gives a very fair account of his career and rôle. Sainte-Beuve, an enemy of Balzac's and one of his pall-bearers, deals with him in the *Causeries des Lundis* (vol. 2) and in the *Critiques et Portraits Littéraires* (1836). An indispensable book is that by Laure, Balzac's sister, Mme. Surville: *Balzac, Sa vie et ses Oeuvres d'après sa correspondance* (1858). Other works on him include: G. Densoiresterres: *Monsieur de Balzac* (1851); Théophile Gautier: *Honoré de Balzac* (1859); A. Baschet: *Honoré de Balzac* (1852); L. Gozlan: *Balzac chez lui* (1862); Lamartine: *Cours de Littérature* (1861–1864); Taine: *Nouveaux Essais de Critique* (1865); Paul Flat: *Essais sur Balzac,* 2 vols. (1893–4); E. Biré: *Honoré de Balzac* (1897); A. Cabanès: *Balzac ignoré* (1899); A. Le Breton: *Balzac, L'Homme et l'Oeuvre* (1905); F. Brunetière: *Honoré de Balzac* (1906); F. Wedmore: *Balzac* (1887); Mary F. Sanders: *Balzac* (1904); W. H. Helm: *Aspects of Balzac* (1905); René Benjamin: *La prodigeuse vie d'Honoré de Balzac* (1925). A translation of the last book, by far the most readable biography we have, was published recently in New York by Knopf; Gozlan's *Balzac chez lui* also appeared in America under the imprint of McBride. The lectures and articles of M. Marcel Bouteron, Librarian to the French Institute and Curator of the Balzac Collection, the leading authority on the subject in the world, are both masterly and entertaining.

F THIS book were not a work of art in every sense of a term used perhaps too freely nowadays, the publisher would never have ventured to bring it out. But he believed that the conscientious critics and the chosen readers into whose hands the *Hundred Droll Stories* are destined to fall will remember the illustrious precedents that go to vindicate this courageous attempt. How rash it is, the author realizes; he has reckoned its risks.

None to whom literature is still dear would care to repudiate the Queen of Navarre, Boccaccio, Rabelais, Ariosto, Verville and La Fontaine, those rare geniuses of modern times, each, practically, a Molière, minus the stage. Instead of depicting a passion, most of them depicted their age. So, the further we advance towards that bourn where literatures perish, the more keenly we value these ancient works, redolent with the fragrance of youthful naïveté, strong with the thews of a comedy our theatre lacks, of a vivid, stark, plain, unvarnished expression which no one dares any longer *dare!*

Comprehension, therefore, becomes a duty towards the author who would not accept the vast heritage of our ancestors but merely reconnoitre the field which so many noble geniuses seem to have closed and in which success appeared virtually impossible from the day our language lost its ingenuousness. Could La Fontaine have written *The Amorous Courtesan* in the style of Jean-Jacques Rousseau? The publisher has borrowed this remark from the author to justify the anachronism of the language employed in these tales. Necessarily, the unpopularity of its style increases all the obstacles lying in the way of this enterprise.

There are countless people in France attacked by that British cant Lord Byron so often complained of. These people, whose cheeks blush at a pithy frankness which once moved kings and princesses to laughter, have draped our hallowed physiognomy in mourning; they have persuaded the gayest, wittiest nation in the world to laugh decorously and underhand; they have forgotten how laughter is a naked babe, an infant accustomed to play with tiara, sword and crown, in blissful ignorance of danger.

Thus, as things move today, the author of the *Droll Stories* can be absolved only by his talent, and, justly fearing the alternative, he decided to give his first ten tales only. But we believe firmly in public and author and we hope promptly to publish another series of ten, for we fear neither book nor reproach.

Surely it would be utterly senseless to blame in literature such efforts as the Salon encourages, furnished by men like Delacroix, Devéria, Chenevard and so many artists devoted to the Middle Ages? If the paintings, stained glass, furniture and sculpture of the Renaissance are welcomed, shall its joyful anecdotes and comic fables be proscribed?

Should the appearance of this Muse heedless of her nakedness require hearty protectors and kindly approbation, these will perhaps not be wanting in men whose good taste and virtue are above suspicion.

The publisher owed this foreword to everyone; as for the author's reservations, they form part of the book.

March, 1832.

WE HAVE believed it our duty to reproduce this preface, which the author placed over his publisher's name at the head of the first edition of the first ten tales and which clearly sums up his personal opinion on the moral scope of his work. The creator of the *Human Comedy*, whose genius in the body of his ideas and works exerts so powerful a moral influence, had anticipated such Pharisaic objections as might be raised against a book he rightly regarded as his masterpiece. He had answered them with that profound, peremptory sense which brings light to bear in lieu of discussion.

Balzac's book is not only a work of art in the manner of Don

Juan, Pantagruel and the poems of Pulci, all of them tomes illustrating the first shelf in the libraries of the most squeamish. It is more and unforgettably a book of literary archæology. In an era of renovation which the historians of literature will be called upon to judge, Balzac, youthful, ardent, at an age when men of exuberant fancy are self-intoxicant—the Bacchantes, as it were, of their own faculties—Balzac then resolved to resuscitate a language, to revive the inspiration of the past. He imitated Rabelais as others had imitated Ronsard; he wrote his *Droll Stories* in that marvelous language of the sixteenth century, crisp, bushy, tufted, verdant, radiant in its obscurities, like a Corregio dawn rising through the rich denseness of a sacred wood.

Such was Balzac's thought, such his work. It is literary archæology, done in good faith, without recourse to the Machiavellian strategy of literary archæologists, Macphersons, Chattertons and the rest. One fine day Balzac considered it advisable, either in the interests of his own thought or with a loftier aim in view, to copy certain models upon which people had lately been too apt, perhaps, to turn their backs. And this great linguist, who loved the French language as you love a woman, happened to produce a book of prodigious imitation destined to be no more and no less than an original work. This artist was careless of all save beauty, which he pursued, torch in hand, like a Grecian runner; he poured his young blood, aboil with genius, into the abandoned moulds of Rabelais, Montaigne and Régnier; he transfused its inspired sap. Neither those who love intelligence for its own power, nor those who love it for the pleasure it brings, nor, finally those who love it for its services to language and literary form, can conceivably suffer the *Droll Stories* to perish. That is why we have offered a new edition to the public.

August, 1855.

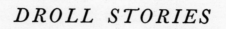

DROLL STORIES

Prologue to First Ten Stories

ERE is a book of the most succulent flavor, a book full of highly attractive diversions, a book spiced to the liking of the same most illustrious tipplers and most precious bibbers to whom François Rabelais, the eternal glory of Touraine, addressed his writings. Not that the Author presumes to be more than a good son of Touraine or to do more than gaily chronicle such high sport as amused the eminent people living in this fertile, pleasurable land. Ah, what a land it is! Richer in cuckolds, in bloods and in jokesmiths than any other on earth, with what a number of famous men it has furnished France! There is for instance the late Courier, of piquant memory, and Verville, author of *The Way to Success,* and what a host of others, equally illustrious! Nor, amid the latter, can we forbear from naming the Sieur Descartes, because he was a melancholy genius; because he cultivated the pale Muse of thought rather than wine and high fare; because the victuallers and pastry cooks of Tours hold him in just horror, refuse to acknowledge him or hear of him, and, if his name be spoken, shrug their shoulders and ask: "Where does *he* live?"

This work, then, is born of the joyous recreations of our excellent old monks; and many vestiges of them there are, scattered about our country, at La Grenadière near St. Cyr, in the borough of Saché near Azay-le-Rideau, at Marmoutier, at Véretz and at La Roche Corbon. And elsewhere, too, in certain storehouses of good tales: old canons and wise dames who knew their fair days when a man could laugh his bellyful and smack his sides without people staring at him as though he were about to bring forth a litter of colts—which is the way of your young

1

woman today as she takes her amusement gravely, in a fashion that suits our blessed France about as well as an oil-cruet sits upon a queen's head.

Laughter is a privilege vouchsafed to man alone; there is cause enough for tears in the present state of our civil liberties, without adding to it in books. I have therefore considered it a downright patriotic act to contribute my ounce of merriment in these times when dullness falls upon us like a vast wet blanket, covers and soaks us to the skin, pierces the very marrow of our bones and dissolves more and more of those ancient customs which made of the Commonwealth a common wealth of amusement. Alas! few are left of those old Pantagruelists who suffered God and King to attend to their own divine and regal tasks, and who, putting no more than an occasional finger in the pie, were content to sit back and laugh. They are dying out day by day; so much so, in fact, that I greatly fear I shall see these noble fragments of ancient breviaries impugned, defamed and turned into a target for the voidance of throat, bladder and bowels. Such a circumstance I would not suffer lightly; I bear too deep a respect for the scraps of our Gallic antiquities.

As for you, O rabid critics, O scavengers of words, O harpies who blight the intent and inventions of all men, remember that we laugh only in childhood; fast as we journey onward, our laughter dies on our lips and gutters out like the flame of an oil-lamp. In other words, laughter is born of innocence and a pure heart; so you, possessing neither, purse your lips, drop your jaws and pucker your brows as men do when they have impurities and vices to conceal. Look rather upon this book as you might look upon a group or a statue, certain aspects of which an artist cannot leave out; in fact, he would be a Simon Pure idiot if he so much as covered them with fig-leaves, since they are not (any more than this book) intended for nunneries.

At the same time, I have been careful, much to my own chagrin, to extirpate from these manuscripts all such old words as, being yet a whit too fresh, might hurt the ear, shock the eye, bring a blush to the cheek and set on edge the teeth of betrousered virgins and of ladies who cultivate true virtue and three lovers. Certain concessions must necessarily be made to fit the vices of the age, and a circumlocution is far more fetching than the word itself! Alas, we are old; we stomach lengthy trifles more comfortably than the swift follies of our youth, when our powers of enjoyment were richer. Spare me your slanders, then, and read this at night rather than by day; and give it not unto maidens (if any there be, nowadays) because this book is highly inflammable. With which advice, I rid you of my presence. . . .

But for the book itself, I fear nothing; I know it derives from a high and noble source, whose every issue has met with signal success, as is conclusively proved not only by the Royal Orders of the Golden Fleece, of the Holy Spirit, of the Garter and of the Bath, but also by innumerable things of note which originated there and under which I find good shelter.

So make ye merry, my hearties, and gaily read the whole with ease of body and in good kidney; and a pox upon you if you disown me after you have read.

These words are from our good Master Rabelais, to whom we all must doff our hats in proof of the reverence and honor we owe to the prince of all comedy.

The Fair Imperia

O N HIS way to the Council of Constance, the Archbishop of Bordeaux added to his retinue a rather pleasing young priestlet of Touraine, whose ways and speech were so particularly charming that he passed for a son of La Soldée and the Governor. The Archbishop of Tours had been glad to give him to his colleague of Bordeaux when the latter tarried in his see: archbishops are used to exchanging gifts for they know how sharply itches the theological palm. So the young priest was included in the household of the southern prelate, a man of sound morals and great learning, and he proceeded to the Council.

Philippe de Mala, as the lad was called, made up his mind to behave properly and to serve his protector ably. But amid this transcendental Council he had occasion to observe many priests who led thoroughly dissolute lives yet earned not fewer, but, on the contrary, more indulgences, gold crowns and benefices than their virtuous, law-abiding compeers. In the course of a night which sorely tried the lad's virtue, the Devil whispered into Philippe's ear and convinced him that he should help himself roundly, arguing that everyone sucked away at the breasts of our Holy Mother Church without these breasts ever running dry—a miracle which proved positively the existence of God. Our priestlet for his part did not disappoint the Devil. Philippe vowed to himself to banquet and batten upon the local roasts, sweets, and delicacies whenever possible—without paying, of course, for he was poor as a church mouse.

As he remained strictly continent, modelling his conduct upon that of the poor old Archbishop, who having arrived at an age when he was physically incapable of sinning, now passed for a

saint, Philippe frequently fell a prey to the most intolerable desires, followed by fits of profound dejection. How many cour-
tesans there were living in Constance to enlighten the understanding of the Fathers of the Council! How beautiful they
were, how shapely, and how cold to the impecunious! Philippe
writhed with rage at the impossibility of meeting these comely
charmers who snubbed cardinals, abbots, commendatory auditors of the Rota, legates, bishops, princes, dukes and margraves
as lightly as they would so many penniless clerks. In the evening,
his prayers done, he would practise speaking to them and teach
himself the blessed breviary of love. He rehearsed every conceivable question they might have put and capped it with an appropriate answer. But next evening, if he chanced to pass one
of these modishly arrayed princesses, lolling back proudly in her
litter escorted by armed pages, Philippe stood gaping at the
lovely face that fired his heart, like a dog snapping at flies.

The Archbishop's secretary, a gentleman of Périgord, had
shown conclusively that the Father, procurators and auditors of
the Rota offered countless presents—not relics or indulgences,
but jewels and gold—to buy their way to privileged familiarity
with the best of these pampered High Church cats. So our poor
lad, in blessed artlessness, hoarded up the coins he received for
his clerical labors, hid them under his mattress and dreamed of
saving enough to view a cardinal's mistress some day for but a
brief moment. As to the rest, he trusted in God.

Innocent, too, of hair, bald from his crown to his heels, he
looked about as much like a man as a goat, clad in a nightdress,
looks like a young lady. But, egged on by desire, careless of his
life and utterly disregarding the pikes of their guardsmen, he
would spy boldly upon cardinals as they went into their mistresses' houses. Then Philippe, watching from the street below,
saw the tapers lighted within the doorways and casements blazing; he heard the blessed abbots and prelates carousing, drinking, revelling in the best of everything, making love, chanting
the privy *Alleluia* and applauding the tunes played for their
benefit. Kitchens performed miracles; the Offices they said were
succulent, rich dishes by the potful; their Matins were little
hams; their Vespers luscious morsels, their Laudes toothsome
sweetmeats. Their tippling done, the good priests fell silent,

while their pages diced in the stairways, and, down in the street, the restive mules stamped on the cobbles. Life moved serenely sweet in Constance—but of course here were religion and faith. Incidentally that was how the Council burned good old John Huss. And why did they burn him? Because he put his finger in the pie without being invited to. After all, why did he try to be a Huguenot before his time?

But to return to the charming Philippe. Often indeed he met with a shower of blows and a sound drubbing; but the Devil sustained him, inciting him to believe that sooner or later it would be his turn to play the cardinal with some cardinal's mistress. His passion made him randy as a deer in autumn; one evening he actually slipped by the horse-block—where he had often seen officers, seneschals, flunkeys and pages, torch in hand, awaiting their masters, the dukes, kings, cardinals, archbishops—and walked into the most beautiful house in Constance.

"Ah!" he mused. "How beautiful, how popular the lady of this house must be!"

An armed soldier suffered Philippe to pass, believing him a servant with a message from the Elector of Bavaria, who had just left. Swift as a greyhound afire with amorous fury, Philippe de Mala darted up the stairs; a fragrant trail of perfume led him straight to the chamber where the lady of the house sat talking to her maids as they undressed her. There Philippe stopped short and stood stock still, like a thief caught in the act. The lady was without petticoat or coif. As they whisked off her clothes and stockings, the women bared her pretty body so deftly and so utterly, that the priest, beyond himself, heaved a cavernous sigh eloquent with love.

"And what do *you* want, my lad?" the lady asked him.

"I want to yield you my soul!" he answered, devouring her with his eyes.

"You may come back tomorrow," she said mockingly.

To which Philippe, flushing to the roots of his hair, blithely countered:

"I shall not fail."

She burst into mad peals of laughter. The lad did not move a muscle. At once aghast and at his ease, he gazed upon her body out of eyes that sparkled and burned with all the splendent fires of love. How beautiful the hair flung back over her ivory white body! And the delicate white patterns of flesh twinkling up between the myriad curly tresses! A balas ruby gleamed on her brow but duller in waves of flame than her black eyes, moist

with the tears born of her rich laughter. Writhing in ribald amusement, she shook off a slim, pointed slipper, gilt like a shrine, and offered to his enchanted gaze a naked foot, slighter than a swan's bill. For she was in high good humor that evening; else why should she not have had the small shavepate tossed out of the window as heedlessly as her first bishop?

"He has pretty eyes, Madame," one of the servants observed.

"Where in the world did he come from?" asked the other.

"Poor child!" Madame cried. "His mother must be looking for him. We must set him back on the right road!"

Our priestlet, without losing his composure, gave a thrill of delight, as he surveyed the bed of gold brocade on which the courtesan was about to rest her shapely form. His glance, saucy and full of amorous intelligence, excited the lady's fancy; half-laughing, half-smitten with the lad, she repeated: "Tomorrow!" Then she dismissed him with a gesture which Pope John himself dared not have disobeyed—especially since he was like a snail minus its shell at the moment, for the Council had just finished unpoping him.

"Ah, Madame," one of the females said, "there's another vow of chastity changed into a vow of love!"

And laughter pelted down again, thick as hail, while Philippe made off, banging his head against the wall, like the young crow he was, blinded and dazed by the sight of this creature, sweeter to savor than a siren rising from the waters. . . .

Having noted the animals carved over the door, he returned to his old Archbishop's with a hundred thousand devils raging in his heart and a new sense of sophistication in his chitterlings. Safe home in his small room, he counted his coins all night long, without once managing to make more than four out of them; but they were his all, and he fondly believed he could satisfy the charmer by giving her all he had in the world.

"What on earth ails you, Philippe?" the good Archbishop asked, uneasy at the hollow sighs and fidgeting of his clerk.

"Ah, My Lord Archbishop," the wretched priestlet answered, "I was marvelling how a woman, though so light and gentle, can yet weigh so heavily upon my heart."

"What woman?"

The Archbishop laid aside the breviary which—worthy man! —he was reading for the benefit of others.

"Ah Jesu! You will scold me, my good lord and protector, but I have seen a lady . . . a cardinal's lady at the very least! And I was grieving because there is much more than one paltry crown between us, even supposing you allowed me to lead her back into the ways of righteousness."

The Archbishop knitted the hirsute circumflex accent above his nose into a frown, but vouchsafed no answer. The humble

priestlet was quaking in his shoes at having given himself away
to his superior, when the latter put in:

"Decidedly, she must be very dear—"

"Ah!" the lad sighed. "She has cleaned out many a mitre and
worn down many a crozier!"

"Well, Philippe, if you will give her up, I shall present you
with thirty crowns out of the poor-box."

"Oh, My Lord, I would be too much the loser!" the lad answered, athrill as he thought of the treat he had promised himself.

"What, Philippe!" the good prelate protested. "Then you
purpose to displease God and to go to the devil, like all our
cardinals?"

Philippe's master, brokenhearted, kneeled down and proceeded to say a prayer to St. Gatien, patron saint of all innocents, imploring him to save his servant. He made Philippe
kneel too, urging him to commend himself to St. Philippe as
well; but under his breath the wretched priest entreated the
saint to preserve him from failing if on the morrow his lady
were to receive him kindly and mercifully. Hearing his servant's
fervor:

"Courage, child!" the good Archbishop cried. "Heaven will
answer your prayer."

On the morrow, while My Lord Archbishop was inveighing
before the Council against the shameless conduct of the apostles
of Christianity, Philippe de Mala was spending his money
(earned at the cost of so much labor) on baths, lotions, scents,
aromatics and other frippery. In fact he doused himself so thoroughly with perfume that he could easily have passed for some
strumpet's pimp. He wandered through the town, found and
identified the house of his heart's queen; but when he asked
passers-by whom it belonged to, they laughed in his face.

"What!" they cried. "Where did this scurvy clod come from?
He's never heard of her . . . never heard of the fair Imperia!"

As the mere name of the lady brought home to him what a
horrible mess he had voluntarily fallen into, Philippe was much
afraid he had sent his crowns to the devil.

For Imperia was the most precious, the most fantastical wench
in the world; she was reputed to be the most beautiful, too; and

none was her match at hoodwinking cardinals or mollifying the hardiest soldiers and oppressors of the people. Doughty captains were hers and archers and lords, all bent on one purpose: to serve her in every particular. She had but to breathe a word and whoever had offended her was incontinently slain. A massacre brought scarcely a light smile to her lips; and often indeed a certain Sire de Baudricourt, Captain to the King of France, called to ask her if there were any particular person she cared to have killed that day. (It was his little way of poking fun at the abbots.) Except the potentates of the higher clergy, with whom Madame Imperia managed to temper her savage whims, she ruled all with a high hand, for her chatter and her technique in amour caught the most frigid and virtuous as in a vice! She was, in consequence, beloved and venerated as much as your genuine ladies and princesses; people actually called her Madame. In this connection, one day, good Emperor Sigismund replied to a genuine —and prudish—lady who complained of it, that they, the respectable ladies, had best cultivate the prudent ways of holy virtue and leave Madame Imperia to the graceful errings of the goddess Venus.

Christian words at which the ladies were quite wrongly shocked.

Philippe, then, recalling the rare sight his eyes had feasted upon the day before, began to fear that things would go no further. The thought saddened him; so, without tarrying to eat or drink, he sauntered through the town, waiting for the appointed hour, the more gladly since he was handsome and gallant enough to find others less difficult to surmount than Madame Imperia.

Night fell. Our handsome priestlet, exulting with pride, caparisoned with desire and whipped on by suffocating sighs glided, slippery as an eel, into the Queen's house. For Queen of the Council she was: all the authority, wisdom and mastery of Christendom bowed down before her.

The majordomo, who did not know Philippe, was about to turn him out, when from the top of the stairs:

"Eh, Messire Imbert," the chambermaid called, "that's Madame's young man!"

And the luckless Philippe, red as a wedding night, climbed up the stairs, aquiver with joy and relief.

Taking him by the hand, the chambermaid led him to the apartment where Madame was waiting expectantly, clad in the lightest of garments amid all the brave show a charming woman puts up with an eye to the immediate future. The radiant Imperia sat by a table spread with a rough goldwork cloth and heaped with all the essentials for the heartiest compotations. Flagons of wine, flanked by thirsty glasses; bottles of hippocras; ewers filled with mellow wine of Cyprus; delicate platters piled high with spices, roasted peacocks, green sauces, diminutive salt hams—how they would have gladdened the gallant's gaze had he not loved Madame Imperia so madly! Nor was she, for her part, unaware that the priestlet's eyes were all for her. Although inured to the roundhead devotions of churchmen, she was delighted. Had she not doted upon the lad all night long? Had not his figure been trotting through her heart all day?

The windows were closed; Madame, in dress and mood, appeared disposed to do the honors to a prince of the Holy Roman Empire. And our rascal, translated to heaven by Imperia's holy beauty, knew that never emperor, nor burgrave, no, nor even cardinal in the process of being elected pope, could possibly prevail this evening against him, a petty priestling with but love and the devil in his pocket.

Affecting a lordly air, he bowed with a courtesy far from foolish, which the lady rewarded with an ardent glance.

"Sit down," she said, "here, close to me. I want to see if you have changed since yesterday."

"Oh, yes, I *have* changed!"

"How?"

"Yesterday," the artful lad said, "yesterday, I loved you; this evening, we love each other. Yesterday, I was but a miserable wretch; now I am become richer than any king."

"Oh, child, child!" she cried mirthfully. "You are indeed changed. For from a young priest, I can see you are become an old devil."

So they sat down side by side before a crackling fire, which distributed their warmth equally everywhere. They sat on, forever on the point of eating, yet never touching a dish because they must keep gazing amorously into each other's eyes. At last, just as they felt content and wholly at their ease, a vast unto- ward clamor rose from the front door, as though people were hammering upon it and shouting.

"Madame," the little maid cried hastily, "here is another of them, I'm sure!"

"What!" said Imperia, haughty as a tyrant suddenly inter- rupted.

"My Lord Bishop of Coire wishes to speak with you."

"The Devil gut him!" she answered, gazing softly at Philippe.

"Madame, he saw the light through the chinks and he's mak- ing a dreadful noise."

"Tell him I'm burning with fever—and it's no lie you'll be telling: I'm sickening for this little priest who dances through my brain."

As she finished speaking and was fondly pressing the hand of a Philippe about to burst out of his skin, the fat Bishop of Coire appeared, breathless with anger. His flunkeys followed, bearing a trout, canonically salmoned, fresh drawn from the Rhine and laid out upon a golden platter; there were spices, too, on all manner of wondrous dishes and a myriad delicacies, liqueurs, for instance, and jams and jellies made by the holy nuns in his various abbeys.

"Ah, ha!" he growled in his harsh voice, "I've time enough to meet the Devil without your bringing him here to choke me, my sweet!"

"Some day your belly will make a fine soft scabbard for a sword!" she answered, with a frown which made her mild, pleas- ing brow suddenly stern and terrible to behold.

"And that choirboy there?" the Bishop said insolently, as he turned his broad red face toward Philippe. "Has he been ad- mitted to the offertory yet?"

"My Lord Bishop, I came to hear Madame's confession!"

"Humph! Don't you know the canons? . . . The right to con- fess ladies at this time of night is a prerogative reserved to bish- ops only. . . . Take yourself off, boy; go herd with simple monks, and don't come back under pain of excommunication."

"Do not budge an inch!" Imperia screamed, more beautiful

in her anger than in love, for now both love and anger possessed her. "Stay here, my friend; you can consider this house your home!"

Then Philippe knew that she really loved him.

"Is it not an elementary theology and a law of the Holy Church that you shall stand equal before God in the Valley of Jehoshaphat?" she asked the Bishop.

" 'Tis the invention of the Devil who adulterated the Bible, but it is so written," answered the great episcopal numbskull, in a hurry to fall to.

"Well, then, let both of you be equal in my sight," Imperia continued, "for am I not your goddess here below? Otherwise one of these days I shall have you delicately strangled between the head and shoulders—I swear it by the might of my tonsure which is every whit as good as the Pope's."

And intending not only that the trout should swell the feast, but also the dish, platters and dainties, she tactfully added:

"Come, sit down with us and drink!"

But the cunning minx was up to a sly dodge or two. She tipped her gallant a wink which told him not to mind this German: the bottle would rid them of him in short order.

The maid seated the Bishop and tucked him up to the table, while Philippe, his song cut with rage as he saw his plans go up in smoke, consigned the Bishop to more devils than there were monks extant. By the time they were almost halfway through the meal, the young priest had not touched a morsel of food, his hunger being all for Imperia. He edged up to her and pressed against her, never uttering a word, yet speaking that eloquent, charmed language which women grasp so clearly, despite its lack of periods, commas, accents, letters, figures, characters, notes and images. The fat Bishop, sensual and very attentive to the garment of ecclesiastical hide into which his late mother had sewn him, suffered Madame's dainty hands to ply him with hippocras; he had already reached his first belch when the clatter of a cavalcade resounded in the street. The number of horses and the cries of the pages made it plain enough that here was some prince, spoiling for love. In effect, shortly after, the Cardinal of Ragusa, to whom Imperia's people had not dared bar the way, entered the room. At this woeful spectacle, the poor courtesan and her lover looked as shamefaced and embarrassed as a pair of convalescent lepers. To seek to oust the Cardinal was to tempt the Devil, especially since at that time no one knew who would be elected pope, three candidates having stood down for the greater profit of Christianity.

The Cardinal was a crafty Italian with a huge beard and a talent for sophistry which made him the life and soul of the Council. With the merest exercise of his understanding, he sized up the long and short of the adventure. One infinitesimal consideration remained to weigh before he decided how to go about pledging his cockboat in bottomry, or, if you prefer, hypothecating his most precious vessel. He had arrived, driven by a truly monkish hunger: to satisfy it, he was not the sort of man to shy at stabbing both monks and selling his own bit of the true Cross, which would indeed have been an evil act.

"Come here, friend!" he cried, calling Philippe aside.

The scion of Tours rose to his feet, more dead than alive. Now, he felt, the Devil was about to take a hand in his affairs.

"At your service!" he said to the terrible Cardinal.

The latter taking him by the arm led him to the top of the staircase, looked him square in the eye and without more ado continued:

"God's belly, you're a pleasant enough little lad, and I'm not particularly anxious to have your master know the color of your guts! Such satisfaction might prove expensive and cost me more than one churchly living in my old age. No! You can make your choice: either you marry an abbey for the rest of your life or you marry Madame tonight—and die for it in the morning!"

"And your passion over, My Lord," the wretched priestlet asked in despair, "may I come back?"

The Cardinal found it difficult to be angry, but:

"Choose!" he repeated sternly. "The gallows or the mitre."

"Ah," the priest answered cannily, "give me a good fat abbey!"

At these words, the Cardinal went back into the room, took up a quill, an inkhorn and a piece of parchment, and scrawled a note to the envoy of France.

"My Lord," said the young priest as he spelled out the name of the abbey, "the Bishop of Coire will not take his leave of you as summarily as I; he possesses as many abbeys as soldiers have wine shops in the town. Besides he seems to have 'erred through wine.' To prove my gratitude to you for the splendid abbey you gave me, I think I owe you a good piece of advice. You know how malignant this cursed plague has been, how it ravaged Paris and how swiftly it has spread. Well then, tell him you have just come from the sickbed of your old friend the Archbishop of Bordeaux! 'Twill make him fly like a straw in the gale."

"Oh, ho!" cried the Cardinal, "you deserve better than an abbey. 'Sbelly and 'steeth! Here, my little friend, here are a hundred golden crowns for your journey to the Abbey of Turpenay. I won them at cards yesterday and I take pleasure in presenting them to you."

As she heard these words and saw Philippe de Mala disappear without giving her the chatoyant, quintessentially amative glance she had expected, the fair Imperia divined all the priest's cowardice. She puffed like a dolphin. She was not yet a sufficiently good Catholic to forgive her lover for his reluctance to perish at her whim; Philippe's death sentence glittered in the viper's glance she flung after him. This made the lecherous Italian very happy for he realized he would soon recover his abbey. Meanwhile our priestlet, heedless of the gathering storm, made good his escape, slinking along, silent and with his ear to the wall, like a wet cur who is being thrown out of church. Madame heaved a sigh from the depths of her heart. A fine dressing she would have given it if ever she could have laid her hands on humankind, for the fire consuming her had risen to her head and tongues of flame licked the air about her. Surely she was fully justified; was this not the first time a *priest* had humbugged *her?* Meanwhile the Cardinal smiled, anticipating all the more advantage and pleasure for himself. A fellow of infinite cunning, was he not? To be sure, he had a red hat. . . .

"Yes, my good friend," he told the Bishop, "I congratulate myself on being in your company and on managing to oust Madame's worthless little footboy, especially since—" he turned to Imperia, "had you approached him, my beautiful, frisky doe, you would have perished miserably through contact with a simple priest. . . ."

"What? How's that?"

"He is secretary to the Archbishop of Bordeaux! This morning the good man was seized with the plague."

The Bishop opened his mouth wide enough to swallow a round cheese.

"Eh? How do you know it?"

"All too well!" The Cardinal grasped the good German's hand. "I have just been ministering to him and bearing him consolation. At this very moment the holy man finds a fair breeze to waft him to Paradise."

Forthwith, the Bishop of Coire gave a demonstration of how light on their feet fat men really are, for, by the grace of God, the large of paunch, in compensation for their works, possess internal tubes as elastic as balloons. My Lord Bishop leaped backward with one bound, sweating at the strain and snorting like a bull that finds feathers in his fodder. Then, grown suddenly pale, he tumbled down the steps, without so much as taking leave of Madame. As soon as the door had closed upon the Bishop and while he was running madly through the streets, My Lord Cardinal of Ragusa burst out laughing.

"Ah, my sweet, surely I deserve to be pope? And better than that, to be your lover this evening?"

But seeing Imperia thoughtful, he came towards her, seeking to take her snugly in his arms and to cuddle and cocker her after the fashion of cardinals, a class of men who wring their belles better than all others do, even soldiers, because they are leisurely and do not waste their essential properties.

"What!" she cried, stepping back, "you would be the death of me, you religious lunatic? All you care about is your own enjoyment, eh, you brutal ruffian? And my sweet tail can rot between my legs? I'm to let your pleasure kill me, then you'll canonize me, eh? . . . You've the plague and you desire me! Ha! Turn on your heels and go elsewhere, you witless monk! And don't so much as touch a hair of my head," she added as she saw him advancing, "or I'll rip you up with this dagger."

And from her poke, the artful hussy drew a delicate, small dagger which, if need were, she could wield with consummate effect.

"Ha, my angel of Paradise, my sweet chuck," the other

laughed, "don't you see through the trick? I had to oust that old bull of Coire!"

"Yes, yes, I know; but I can soon tell whether you really love me!" she shouted. "I insist that you leave at once. If the plague snaps you up, my death means nothing to you. I know you! I know what price you would be willing to pay for a second's joy in the hour of death, even. You would drown the earth, yes, you boasted of it once when you were in wine. As for me, I love myself, my treasures, my health, and that is all. Go; and if your guts aren't chilled by the pestilence, you can come back tomorrow. But today, I hate you, my good Cardinal," she added with a smile.

"Imperia," he cried, falling to his knees, "my holy Imperia, please do not make sport of me thus."

"No," she said, "I never make sport of holy and sacred things."

"Ha, you vile slut, I shall excommunicate you no later than tomorrow."

"God be praised, now you're taking leave of your cardinal senses."

"Imperia! cursed daughter of the Devil! oh! oh!—my beautiful—my sweet—"

"Where's your self-respect? Get up off your knees. For shame!"

"Do you want any particular dispensation *in articulo mortis?* Will you have my fortune, or, better still, a piece of the true, original Cross? . . . Do you want it?"

"This evening all the riches of Heaven and earth could not buy my heart," she answered, laughing. "I would be the vilest of sinners, I would be unworthy to receive the body and blood of Christ, if I had not my little whims."

"I shall burn your house down over your head. Witch, witch! You have put a spell on me. You shall perish at the stake. . . . Oh, but listen to me, my love, my blessed mistress, I promise you the most exalted seat in Heaven! . . . What? You refuse? Death to you then, you shall die the death of a witch!"

"Be careful, my Lord Cardinal, or I shall kill you!"

At which the Cardinal foamed at the mouth with virile rage.

"You are going mad," she cried, "go away, you are wearing yourself out."

"I shall be Pope and you shall pay for this."

"You will have to obey me all the same."

"What must I do to please you this evening?"

"You must get out!" she cried, hopping as lightly as a wagtail into her room to bolt herself in while the Cardinal was left fuming and raging until finally he had to decamp.

But when the fair Imperia found herself sitting alone by the fire without her priestlet, she broke her little golden chains in her fury.

"By the double triple horn of the Devil, if that small boy has made me raise this row with the Cardinal and run the risk of being poisoned tomorrow, unless I pay him out in full, I will not die before I see him flayed alive under my very eyes."

Then:

"Ah," she said, weeping real tears now, "mine is a sorry existence, and for what little pleasure I can glean here and there I must lead a dog's life, not to mention forfeiting my salvation."

But, just as she had spoken herself out and was bawling like a calf that is being slaughtered, she looked into her Venetian mirror. And there she saw the flushed face of her priestlet—who had slyly hidden himself—peeping at her from behind.

"Ah," she said, "you are the most perfect monk, the loveliest little monking, monkeying monk that ever monkified in this blessed and amorous town of Constance! Ah, ah, come, my gentle cavalier, my angel boy, my little tabor, my paradise of delights. I'll drink your eyes and eat you up with kisses, I'll kill you with love! Oh, my flowery, verdant, sempiternal god! Come to me; out of the little priestling you are, I shall make a king, an emperor, a pope and a happier man than the lot of them. Ay, you may put everything to fire and sword; I am yours! and you shall see, for soon you shall be a cardinal, even if, to redden your biretta, I have to shed all my heart's blood."

Mad with happiness, her hands trembling, she poured the Grecian wine into one of the golden goblets the Bishop of Coire had brought and presented it to her lover. And she, whose slipper princes found more to their taste than that of the Pope, gladly fell upon her knees to serve him.

But he gazed at her in silence, out of eyes so avid for love that:

"Come!" she said, quivering with pleasure. "Quiet, little one! Let us have supper first."

The Venial Sin

I

How Goodman Bruyn Took Unto Himself a Wife

ESSIRE BRUYN—the same who completed the castle of La Roche Corbon, near Vouvray, on the banks of the Loire—was a boisterous sort of fellow in his youth. While still a little shaver, he was continually ravishing virgins and turning the house upside down; in brief he was headed straight for the devil. After his father, the Baron of La Roche Corbon, died and was duly put to bed with a shovel, Bruyn became his own master. He could give free rein to the wildest debauchery every day; he applied himself body and soul to the grateful task of indulging his own pleasure. In time, by dint of making ducks and drakes of his money, catching his enjoyment on the fly, bleeding his hogsheads, carousing with trollops and turning the world into a sewer, he found himself excommunicated from the society of decent people and left with only robbers and moneylenders for friends. Soon even the usurers turned as bitter and harsh as chestnut husks, when Bruyn could offer as sole security only the feudal rights to La Roche Corbon, for Rupes Carbonis itself he held in fee from Our Lord the King. This put Bruyn in just the humor to cry havoc, striking here and smiting there, breaking men's collar bones everywhere and picking quarrels with everybody over the merest trifles.

Seeing this, his neighbor, the Abbot of Marmoutier, a very outspoken man, assured Bruyn that his behavior was a manifest sign of lordly perfection, that he was following in the right road but that he would be doing better still to go to the Holy Land, which the Mohammedans were befouling, and to disembowel them for the greater glory of God. The Abbot promised Bruyn that he would come back without fail, laden with riches and indulgences, either to Touraine or to Paradise, where all barons formerly came from.

Bruyn was lost in admiration before the prelate's lofty wisdom; then, having been equipped by the monastery and blessed by the Abbot, he quitted the country to the great delight of his neighbors and friends. In the years that followed, he delivered

up countless towns in Asia and in Africa to sack, fell upon the miscreants without warning, ripped up Saracens, Greeks, Englishmen and sundry other nationals, heedless of whether they were allies and whence they came. Among his sterling merits was a lack of curiosity: he never questioned his victims until after he had slain them.

In this pursuit, which proved agreeable to God, to the King and to Bruyn, he won fame as a good Christian and a loyal knight. He also enjoyed himself thoroughly in these foreign parts, since he proved always more prone to give crowns to the wenches than coppers to the poor, even though he met finer exemplars of poverty than of pulchritude. But like the worthy scion of Touraine that he was, he took the wenches as they came. Ultimately, when Bruyn grew satiated with Turks, relics and other benefits of the Holy Land, he returned from the Crusades (much to the astonishment of the people of Vouvray) laden with crowns and precious stones, rather the reverse of some who set forth rich and came home heavy with leprosy but light of purse.

On his return from Tunis, King Philippe made Bruyn a count and appointed him Seneschal in our land and in Poitou. There people admired him unfeignedly and loved him much, not only because of his excellent qualities, but also because he founded the church of Les Carmes Deschaulx—the seat of the barefooted Carmelites in the parish of l'Égrignolles—as a sort of peace offering to Heaven for the wild follies of his youth. By this act, he was cardinally committed to the good graces of Church and God. He had been wicked in his youth, infamous in his prime; now, as his hair began to thin, he grew wise, orderly and discreet in his lechery. Seldom was he angry and then only when someone blasphemed God in his presence. This he would not stand for, having himself done enough cursing for every one in his wild youth. He never quarrelled nowadays, either, because, as he was Seneschal, people gave in to him at the outset. To be sure, he saw all his desires come true, which is enough to make even a minion of Hell calm and sedate from his horns to his heels. Besides he possessed a castle sitting on a hillock from the vantage of which it gazed at its own reflection in the Loire. Outside, it was jagged at every seam and slashed like a Spanish doublet; within were regal tapestries, furniture and trappings, Saracen pomps and riches which drew exclamations of wonder, not only from the good people of Tours but even from the Archbishop and the clerks of St. Martin, to whom he presented a banner fringed with fine gold. Wealthy domains abounded on all sides of the castle, with humming windmills and dense forests that yielded a harvest of rents of every kind and made Bruyn one of the strongest bannerets in the province, well able to muster a thousand men in time of war for the service of Our Lord the King. In his old days, if his bailiff, a diligent hangman, happened to bring in some poor peasant suspected of wrongdoing:

"Let this one go, Breddiff," he would say with a smile. "He will count against those I slaughtered so inconsiderately overseas. . . ."

Often, on the other hand, he would suffer rogues to hang bravely from an oak tree or to swing on his gallows. But this was solely in order to do justice and to prevent the custom from dying out in his domain. His people were consequently as meek and orderly as nuns who have but newly taken the veil; they lived in peace and quiet, too, for Bruyn protected them from robbers and highwaymen, whom he never spared, knowing by experience what havoc these cursed beasts of prey wrought. Devout, moreover, and conscientious, he finished off everything, from saying his prayers to bibbing wine, with dispatch; he conducted his trials after the Turkish fashion, sweeping away the cobwebs of procedure, cracking jokes to entertain the losers and dining with them to console them. Those whom he hanged were laid in holy ground; he considered them as men who, punished severely enough by forfeiting their lives, now belonged to God. Finally, he pursued the Jews only in proper season, when they were gorged with usury and riches, after he had allowed them to store up their plunder as bees do honey. They were, Bruyn said, the most reliable tax-collectors. Nor did he ever despoil them save for the profit and use of churchmen, the King, the province or himself.

These debonair ways won him the affection and esteem of all, great and small. If he came back from the Bench smiling, the Abbot of Marmoutier, an oldster like himself, would say:

"Ha, ha, Messire, there must have been some hanging or you would never be laughing so heartily."

And when, on the way from La Roche Corbon to Tours, he rode through the outskirts, by St. Symphorien:

"Ah!" the little wenches would cry: "Today is Justice Day, here comes Goodman Bruyn!"

And their gaze, quite unafraid, followed the progress of the figure astride the big white hack he had brought back from the Levant. On the bridge, the little boys would stop playing ball, and:

"Good day, Master Seneschal!" they cried.

To which the goodman answered jokingly:

"Play away, children, you'll be whipped soon enough!" and:
"Ay, Master Seneschal," they would reply.

What is more, Bruyn kept the country so content and so thoroughly purged of thieves that, the year of the great Loire flood, only twenty-two malefactors were hanged all winter, not counting one Jew burned in the commune of Châteauneuf for stealing a consecrated wafer, or possibly, as some said, for purchasing it, since the man was rich.

One day in the following year, about the time of the Feast of St. John's Haying (or St. John Mower, as we say in Touraine), a band of Egyptians, Bohemians or other thieving nomads stole some holy objects from the church of St. Martin. By way of insulting and mocking our own true faith, in place of the Holy Virgin and in the very spot where She had stood, they left a naked girl—a shameless fair wench, about the age of an old dog, and, like themselves, a mummer and a blackamoor. For this crime, both the royal and ecclesiastical authorities decided that the Mooress should be made to pay for the whole band. She should be burned and roasted alive in the square of St. Mark by the fountain near the Herb Market.

Thereupon Bruyn, opposing the others, established skilfully and beyond a shadow of doubt that to win over this African soul to the true faith would be a thing both profitable and pleasing in God's sight and that, if the Devil inhabiting this female shape proved stubborn, then the faggots cited in her sentence would assuredly avail to burn him. All of which the Archbishop found to be wisely reasoned, highly canonical, and congruous with Christian charity and gospel. The ladies of the town and other persons of authority loudly protested that they were being cheated of a fine ceremony, since the Mooress, who was crying her eyes out in jail and bleating like a bound goat, would surely be converted to God and live as long as a crow, if allowed to. To this the Seneschal replied that, if the alien would commit herself utterly to the Christian religion, there would be another ceremony, brave, too, but with a difference, and that he would personally undertake to make it royally magnificent. He would, he said, be her sponsor at the baptismal font and a virgin would partner him in this office, which would please God all the more. For Bruyn was technically what is known in Touraine as a *cocquebin*, the name serving to qualify young virgin men, unmarried or supposedly so; but name or no, the wenches, for their part, never fail to spot them, because such lads are more cheerful and blithesome than those seasoned in wedlock.

The Mooress did not hesitate a moment between the fiery faggots and the waters of baptism. She had liefer be a live Christian than a grilled Egyptian; so, in order to save her body from baking a few seconds, her heart must burn all her days, since, for the greater surety of her religion, she was sent to a nunnery near Le Chardonneret and there took the vow of sanctity.

The ceremony was concluded at the Archbishop's palace where, to celebrate the occasion and do honor to the Savior of men, the lords and ladies of Touraine danced and tripped to tuneful measures, for, in this land, there is more dancing and music, feasting, flirting, merriment and revelry than anywhere on the face of the earth.

Our good old Seneschal chose for co-sponsor the daughter of the lord of Azay-le-Ridel, which later became Azay-le-Brûlé. This nobleman had gone to the Crusades and had been captured before Acre, a far distant city, by the Saracens, who demanded a royal ransom since he was a lord of high position. In order to make up the required sum, the lady of Azay had pledged his estate as security to the Lombards and extortioners. She was left without a penny in the world, to await her lord's return in a mean lodging in the town; she lacked even a carpet to sit upon, but was proud as the Queen of Sheba and steadfast as a mastiff guarding his master's property. Aware of her great distress and eager to earn the right to assist her, the Seneschal with great delicacy requested her daughter to be the godmother of the Egyptians. Now Bruyn had kept a heavy chain of gold, ravished at the fall of Cyprus; this he determined to clasp around the lovely damsel's neck; but, at the same time, he also hung his estate there, his snowy locks, his money, his horses, in brief all he possessed. One glance at Blanche d'Azay dancing a pavane with the ladies of Tours was too much for him. Though the Moorish girl, bent on making the most of her last day, amazed the assembly by her various dances—*turdion, volte, passe* and *élévations*—Blanche carried the day, as everybody agreed, so virginally and gracefully did she move.

Admiring this winsome maiden, whose ankles seemed to fear the boards and who amused herself so ingenuously for her seventeen years (why, she was like a cicada, trying her sweetest note!), Bruyn was seized with an old man's desire, an apoplectic and vigorous desire born of his weakness and warming him from his heels to his neck only, for there was too much hoar upon his head for love to find lodging there. All at once the good man realized that what he lacked in his manor was a wife and suddenly it appeared much lonelier to him that it was. For what indeed was a manor without a mistress! As well say a clapper without its bell. In fine, a wife was his only unrealized desire: hence he wished to have a wife promptly, for if the lady of Azay kept him waiting he might easily pass from this world to the next in the meantime.

During the baptismal entertainment, he gave scant thought to the grievous wounds he had received in the Holy Land and less still to the fourscore years that had bared his brow. His sight certainly seemed unimpaired. How clearly he saw his young partner, who, obeying her mother's orders and anticipating no danger from this oldster, regaled him with her every glance and gesture! Thus Blanche, naïve and ingenuous as she was (quite the contrary of the wenches of Touraine, who are as brisk as spring morning), allowed the good man to kiss her: the hand, first; then, what is more, the neck—and rather low, too, according to the Archbishop, who married them the following week, at a splendid wedding with an even more splendid bride!

Ay, Blanche was slender and graceful as never another girl, and, still better than that, she was a virgin as virgin never was, virgin to the point of knowing nothing about love, not even how or why it was made; virgin to the point of being surprised that certain ladies liked to linger late abed; virgin to the point of believing that babies were found in cabbage-patches. Her worthy mother had brought her up in total innocence, without allowing her to stop to consider how she sucked in her soup between her teeth. Thus she was a flower, blossoming intact, joyous and innocent, an angel lacking but wings to fly away to Paradise.

When she left her mean lodgings and her weeping mother and went to consummate her betrothal at the Cathedral of St. Gatien and St. Maurice, the country folk flocked to town to feast their eyes upon the bride and upon the carpets that had been laid out along the Rue de la Scellerie; and to a man they vowed that never had daintier foot touched the ground of Touraine or prettier blue eyes gazed heavenward or braver festival strewn flowers and carpets on the streets. The young girls of the town, those from St. Martin and from the borough of Châteauneuf, all envied the long, tawny tresses with which Blanche must have fished up her count; but they hankered even more after the gold embroidered dress, the precious stones from overseas, the white diamonds and the chains with which she was toying and by which she was forever bound to My Lord Seneschal. So happy was the old soldier at her side that his joy burst, radiant, through his every wrinkle, his every gesture, his every glance. Though naturally about as straight as a bill-hook, he held himself so erect as he walked beside Blanche that he looked for all the world like a guardsman parading past the reviewing-stand. And he laid his hand upon his diaphragm like a man whose pleasure stifles and hurts him. Thrilled by the silvery bells, the procession, the golden pomps and resplendent state of the marriage (which had been the chief topic of conversation ever since the Archbishop's entertainment), the girls prayed for a shower of Moorish wenches, a rain of old seneschals and a deluge of Egyptian baptisms. But their prayers have remained unanswered. There was destined to be only one such in Touraine, a land which is far away from Egypt and Bohemia.

After the ceremony, the lady of Azay received a large sum of money; it enabled her to speed post-haste to Acre to fetch her husband. For escort, the Count of La Roche Corbon gave her his lieutenant and soldiers, whom he equipped with every necessity. She set out on the wedding day, having placed her daughter in the hands of the Seneschal and enjoined him to care for her well. Much later, she was to return with her lord, who was leprous; at the risk of being contaminated, she looked after him herself and cured him, her devotion winning the admiration of all.

The wedding over and at an end (it lasted three whole days to the great delight of the people) Messire Bruyn led the maid to his castle amid rare pomp, and, following the bridal custom, laid her solemnly to rest upon his bed, which was blessed by the Abbot of Marmoutier. Then he came and lay beside her, in the vast feudal chamber of La Roche Corbon, which had been hung with green brocade and gold lacing.

When old Bruyn, perfumed from head to foot, found himself lying flesh to flesh with his adorable wife, he kissed her first upon the brow, then upon the little round, white breast, on the same spot where she had allowed him to clasp the fastening of the chain. But that was all. The old stager had been over-confident when he believed he was up to scotching the rest; so, despite the jocund nuptial songs, despite the epithalamia and jokes rehearsed in the rooms below where the company was still dancing, he was forced to refrain from amour. He refreshed himself with a drink of the marriage beverage which had been blessed, according to usage, and placed beside them in a golden bowl; the spices fired his stomach well enough, but not the heart of his dead cod. Blanche, for her part, was not at all astonished at her husband's felony; she was a virgin in mind; in marriage she saw only what appears to the eyes of young girls: dresses, banquets, horses, her position as lady and mistress, her rank as a count's wife, the amusements she would have and the pleasure of giving orders. So, child that she was, she toyed with the trimmings and gold tassels on the bed, marvelling at the richness of the plot where the flower of her innocence was to be buried. Bruyn began somewhat tardily to realize the extent of his guilt. But he put his trust in the future—a future which was destined to impair systematically day by day, ever a little more, the force upon which he had relied for the delight of his wife. So the Seneschal determined to substitute the word for the deed. He proceeded to entertain his wife in sundry incorporeal ways, promising her the keys to his closets, attics and chests, conferring the perfect and uncontrolled government of his houses and domains, and, to use a saying popular in Touraine, hanging half the loaf about her neck. Blanche was happy as a young charger, full of hay; she found her goodman the most gallant knight in the world; and, sitting up, she began to smile and to consider with even greater satisfaction the noble bed of green brocade upon which she could henceforth sleep every night lawfully and without sin. The cunning lord had met very few virgins in his life; but he had frequented strumpets and he knew, from wide experience, what monkeys women are between the four posts of a bed. Observing that Blanche was getting playful, Bruyn feared the hand-to-hand tricks, the sportive kisses and the minor antics of love which, in the past, he had never failed to enjoy but which at present would have found him cold as the *obit* of a pope. Accordingly, he edged back towards his side of the bed, trembling for his happiness, and said to his entrancing wife:

"Well, my love, now you're a seneschal's lady, and very properly seneschalled at that."

"Oh, no!" she protested.

"What do you mean: no?" he said, panic-stricken. "Are you not a lady?"

"No!" she repeated. Then: "I shall not be a lady until I have a child."

"Did you see the meadows as we came here?" the old fellow resumed.

"Ay!"

"Well, they are yours. . . ."

"Oh, how lovely!" she cried, laughing. "What fun I shall have chasing butterflies there!"

"There's a good child!" her lord said. "And the woods?"

"Oh, I could never go there alone; you will have to take me. But," she added, "give me a little of that liquor which La Ponneuse took so much trouble to mix for us."

"Why do you want it, love? It would only set your body on fire."

"But that's what I want!" she replied, gnawing her lips with vexation. "I want to give you a child as soon as ever I can. I am sure that liquor is good for the purpose."

"Whew, my love!" said the Seneschal, sighing with relief as he knew by her words that Blanche was virgin from head to foot. "In the first place, the will of God is required for that business; then women must be in a state of harvest."

"And when shall I be in that blessed state?" she asked with a smile.

"When Nature so wills it," he answered, laughing up his sleeve.

"What must be done to bring this about?" she persisted.

"Bah! a cabalistic and alchemical operation, which is fraught with danger!"

"Ah," she said with a dreamy expression, "that must be why my mother wept at the change I must undergo. But Berthe de

Preuilly was ever so grateful when she became a wife; she told me it was the easiest thing in the world."

"It is a question of age!" the old Seneschal explained. "But tell me—do you remember that fine white mare you saw in the stables? . . . the hackney? . . . the one they all speak of so much in Touraine?"

"Oh yes! She's a good, gentle beast!"

"Very well, you shall have her: you may ride her whenever and as often as the fancy takes you!"

"Oh, how kind you are! They were not lying when they told me you were the best and dearest—"

"At La Roche Corbon," Bruyn interrupted, "everything is yours, my love: the steward, the chaplain, the treasurer, the equerry, the cook, the bailiff, even the Sire de Montsoreau, the young varlet whose name is Gauthier and who bears my banner! and the men-at-arms, too, the captains, followers and beasts— all these are yours to do your bidding instantly, under pain of being chafed by a collar of hemp!"

"But tell me—" Blanche put in quickly. "This operation of alchemy—can't it be performed immediately?"

"Oh no," the Seneschal answered. "To do that, it is absolutely essential that both the one and the other of us should be in a perfect state of grace before God. Otherwise we would have a wicked sinful child—which is forbidden by the canons of the Holy Church. That is why there are so many hopeless scapegraces in the world: their parents were unwilling to wait dutifully until their souls were pure, so they gave wicked souls to their children. But the noble and virtuous children are born of immaculate fathers. . . . That is why we husbands cause our beds to be blessed, why the Abbot of Marmoutier blessed this bed. . . . Have you not transgressed the ordinances of the Church?"

"Oh no!" she said quickly. "Before Mass, I received absolution from all my faults. And I have not committed the tiniest sin since."

"Ay, you are perfect!" the cunning lord cried. "And I am delighted to have you for a wife. As for myself, I swore like a heathen!"

"You did? And why?"

"Because the dancing kept on and on . . . and I could not have you to myself and bring you here and kiss you."

With great gallantry, he seized her hands and covered them with kisses, whispering endearments, blandishments and little, superficial words of dalliance that made her quite happy and contented.

Then, worn out by the dancing and all the ceremonies, just before she composed herself for sleep:

"Tomorrow I shall take care that you do not sin!" she warned him.

And she left her old husband deeply infatuated with her white beauty and enamored of her delicate nature, but also as embarrassed to know how to maintain her in her innocence as how to explain why oxen chew their fodder twice over. Although he foresaw scant personal advantage to himself from them, he was so consumed with ardor as he saw the exquisite perfections of Blanche, lost in an innocent and gentle sleep, that he resolved to preserve and defend this matchless jewel of love. . . . With tears in his eyes, he kissed her fair golden tresses, her beautiful eyelids, her ripe red lips; and he did it very softly, too, for fear of awaking her.

Such, then, was his whole fruition; such the mute pleasures which still fired his heart, without affecting Blanche in the least. The poor old man deplored the snowy wastes of his barren senility, as he realized that God had found amusement in giving him nuts when his teeth were gone.

II

How the Seneschal Struggled with His Wife's Maidenhead

*D*URING the early days of his marriage, the Seneschal grossly abused his wife's admirable innocence, inventing the most extraordinary fables for her benefit. In the beginning, the exercise of his judicial functions offered him plenty of valid excuses for leaving her alone occasionally. Then he kept her occupied with country pursuits, taking her to his vineyards of Vouvray, for instance, during the vintage season. In a word, he lulled her to sleep with a thousand cock-and-bull stories.

Sometimes he would point out that noblemen did not behave like common people and that the children of counts were planted only under certain celestial conjunctions which were reckoned by learned astrologers; sometimes that people should abstain from begetting children on feast days because it entailed great work—and Bruyn observed church feasts with the regularity and will of a man who wished to enter into Paradise without contest. At other times, he pretended that, if the parents happened not to be in a state of grace, children begun on St. Claire's Day were born blind, on St. Genou's Day gouty, on St. Aignan's Day scurvy-headed, on St. Roch's Day plague-stricken, and that those hatched in February were chilly, in March, too turbulent, in April quite useless, while all the fine lads of this world were conceived in May. Bruyn wished his child to be perfect; it must have hair of two colors; for this, a combination of all the required conditions was imperative. Again, he would tell Blanche that it was a husband's right to present his wife with a child according to his sole and lone will; that if she set store by wifely virtue, she must conform to the wishes of her husband: finally that they must wait the return of the lady of Azay, so that she

34

might be present at the confinement. From all his, Blanche concluded that her prayers vexed the Seneschal and that he was perhaps right. After all, was he not an old man and fraught with experience? She therefore gave way to him and thought no more of this much-desired child, except to herself—in other words she never ceased thinking of it, as a woman will do when she has a bee in her bonnet. And she never for a moment suspected that she was behaving like a trull or a strumpet running after a tasty bit.

One evening, Bruyn chanced to be holding forth about children. It was a subject he usually avoided as a cat avoids water, but he had sentenced a lad that morning for grave misdeeds and he was complaining of him to Blanche. "Surely," he said, "the culprit was begotten by people laden with mortal sins?"

"Alas!" Blanche sighed. "If you will give me one, even though you have not received absolution yet, I shall correct him so well that you will be pleased with him. . . ."

Immediately the Count realized that his wife had a fierce maggot in her brain and that it was time to wage war upon her maidenhead in order to make himself master of it and exterminate it, to mule it and harness it, or to appease and extinguish it.

"What, my love, you wish to be a mother?" he said. "But you don't know a wife's business yet, you have not learned your rôle as mistress of the house."

"Oh, ho!" she said. "Then to be a perfect countess and lodge a little count in my flanks I must play the great lady, eh? Very well then, play the great lady I shall, and with a vengeance."

So in order to obtain issue, Blanche began to hunt stags and hinds, leaping ditches, galloping her mare over hill and dale, through wood and field; she took great delight in watching her falcons fly and in unhooding them; and very prettily she bore them on her graceful wrist. In short, she was forever hunting, which was exactly what the Seneschal had desired. But at this pursuit, Blanche acquired a nun's and prelate's appetite—that is to say, she wished to procreate, developed her powers and could scarcely control her hunger, when, on her return, she gave play to her teeth. Thus by dint of reading such legends as were plainly written by the roadside and by dint of inflicting upon birds and other wild beasts a death which cut the knot of their half-consummated amours, Blanche compounded a mystery of natural alchemy, while her cheeks gained a new color and her nutritive organs worked at high pressure. This failed to pacify her warlike nature, but, by the same token, it vigorously prickled her desire, which laughed, entreated and frisked about all the more merrily. The Seneschal thought to disarm his wife's rebellious virtue by turning her out to scour the country. But his fraud proved ill-fated, for the unknown ardor coursing through Blanche's veins only emerged from these assaults the more powerful, suing for jousts and tourneys as passionately as a page newly knighted.

The good Seneschal then realized that he had erred grossly and that there are no cool spots on a grill. Now he was at a loss to know what outlet to provide for a virtue so lusty: the more he fatigued it, the bolder the front it put up. From this combat one party must emerge beaten and bruised—and the longer he thought of it, the more earnestly Bruyn wished, by God's help, to go to the grave with a brow unmarred by a diabolical contusion. Poor Seneschal! He had enough trouble managing to follow his lady to the chase without being unhorsed; he toiled and sweated under the weight of his trappings, exhausting his life in the pursuits which brought his wife new vigor and high pleasure.

In the evening, frequently she wished to dance. And the good man, swathed in his heavy clothing, found himself worn to a frazzle by the exercises in which he was compelled to participate. He had either to give her his hand while she performed the acrobatics of the Moorish girl or to hold a lighted torch for her while she was pleased to dance the candle-step; in spite of his sciatica, abscesses and rheumatism, he was forced to put on a smile and to reward the evolutions, mummeries and comic pantomimes she indulged in for her pleasure by polite and gallant praise, for he loved her so madly that, had she asked for the moon, he would have straightway set out to fetch it.

Nevertheless one fine day he recognized that his system was far too feeble to cope with the spirited nature of his wife; so, laying down his arms humbly before the Amazon Virginity, he determined to let things take their course, relying somewhat on

Blanche's modesty, religion and bashfulness. But always he slept with one eye open, for he rather suspected that God had created maidenheads to be taken like partridges, pierced by a spit and roasted.

One wet morning—it was the sort of weather in which snails cut their paths, a season melancholy and suitable for daydreaming—Blanche was sitting at home in her chair. She was dreaming —for no force produces more lively concoctions of substantive essences, and no recipe, specific or philtre proves more penetrant, transpiercing, super-pricking and titillating than the subtle warmth that simmers during certain weather between the nap of a chair and the virgin's bestriding it. So, without knowing it, the Countess was incommoded by her maidenhood which was combustotorrifying her brain and gnawing her all over. To see her languishing grieved Bruyn sorely; and, wishing to banish thoughts which he considered principles of extra-conjugal love:

"What makes you so sad, my sweet?" he asked her.

"I am ashamed!"

"Ashamed! What makes you ashamed?"

"I am ashamed because I am not a proper woman, for I have no child and you no lineage. How, without offspring, can one be a lady? No, no; just look about us: all our neighbors have off-spring, and I married to have it just as you did to give it me. The noblemen of Touraine are all amply supplied with children; their wives produce them thick as flies; you alone have none. People will laugh at us, yes, they will! And what is to become of your name, and your fiefs and your seigniories? As for us women, a child is our natural company; our dearest joy is to bundle it up, to fondle it, to swaddle it, to dress and undress it, to pamper and pet it, to pick it up from its crib and to put it to bed again, to rock it in our arms, to sing it lullabies and to feed it! For my part, I know that if I had but a fraction of a child, I would kiss it and wash it, do it up in blankets and undo it again; I would have it jump about and laugh all day long, just as ladies do."

"But for the fact that women die in hatching children and that you are still too frail and too close in the bud, you would already be a mother!" the Seneschal answered, dizzy at the torrent of her words. "Why don't you buy one ready-born? It will cost you neither labor nor pain."

"But," she objected, "I want the labor and the pain; otherwise the child would not be our own. I know very well that it must be the fruit of my body because at church they say that Jesus was the fruit of the Virgin's womb."

"Very well then, let us pray to God it may be so," cried the Seneschal, "and let us intercede with the Virgin of l'Égrignolles. Many a lady has conceived after a novena; you must not fail to do one."

So Blanche set out for Notre Dame de l'Égrignolles that same day, riding her noble mare and decked out like a queen in her little high-heeled shoes, her tall hood studded with precious stones, in her robe of green velvet, laced down with a fine, gold lace and open at the breast, with sleeves of scarlet, and a golden girdle that showed off her slight waist, slim as a pole. Her dress, she intended for the Lady Virgin; indeed, Blanche had promised it to Her for the day of her churching. . . . The Sire de Montsoreau galloped on ahead, his glance, bright as a hawk's, keeping the people back, while he and his knights insured a safe journey. Near Marmoutier, the Seneschal, drowsy with the heat (it was the month of August) jogged along on his steed, swinging like a diadem on a cow's head. Seeing so comely and frolicsome a lady beside such an old fossil, a peasant wench, who was squatting near a tree, drinking water out of her jug, asked a toothless old hag, who picked up a few coppers by gleaning, whether this princess was not going out to bury her dead.

"Eh but no, no such thing!" the hag answered. "It is our lady of La Roche Corbon, wife of the Seneschal of Poitou and Touraine, in quest of a child."

"Ha, ha, ha!" the wench laughed like a split pea. Then, pointing to the dapper knight who led the cavalcade: "Let him that's ahead put it to her and she can spare herself vow and candles and all. . . ."

"Ay, my girl," the old baggage said, "it's queer to me that she's going to Notre Dame de l'Égrignolles where the priests aren't handsome a whit. She'd do better to stay a spell in the shadow of Marmoutier belfry, she'll be fruitful aplenty with those good, lively fathers!"

"A plague on your priests!" cried a weaving-woman as she woke up. "Look ye, the Sire de Montsoreau is fiery and handsome enough to open My Lady's heart, the more since it's ready to pop. . . ."

And the crowd guffawed, at which the Sire de Montsoreau was all for going and hanging them on a lime tree by the road as a punishment for their evil tongues. But:

"Oh, Messire, do not hang them yet!" Blanche cried out quickly. "They have not spoken the last word; we shall see on our return."

Observing her blush, the Sire de Montsoreau riveted his eyes upon her, as though to riddle her with all the mystic comprehensions of love. But the words of the peasant women had begun to bear fruit in her understanding and the devirginomanumission of her intelligence was already at work. Her maidenhead was like tinder; only a word was needed to inflame it.

In effect, Blanche now saw certain appreciable physical differences between her aged husband's qualities and the perfections of Gauthier, a gentleman who wore his three-and-twenty years very lightly, who sat up in his saddle as straight as a tenpin, who, in contrast to the slumbering Seneschal, was as brisk as the chimes of Matin bells and who displayed dexterity and courage where his master failed lamentably. He was one of those dapper young fellows whom the hoydens would sooner hug to them at night than a nightcap; there are no flies on such lads and the wenches need have no fear—for which certain other women vituperate them, though none should be blamed and each should sleep as he likes.

So much did the Seneschal's lady meditate, and so imperially well, that, by the time they reached the Bridge of Tours, she loved Gauthier inwardly and surreptitiously, as a virgin loves, without suspecting what love is. In consequence, she became a proper woman, that is one who wishes another's property, a goodly woman desiring the good of others and the best that men have. She fell into a fit of love-sickness, reaching the depths of its miseries at the first leap, for, between the earliest coveting and the last desire, all things are flame. She had never known what she was now learning: that a subtle essence can flow into the eyes causing such powerful corrosions in all the veins of the body, in the recesses of the heart, and the nerves of the members; in the roots of the hair, the perspiration of the substance, the limbo of the brain; in the orifices of the flesh, the windings of the pluck, the tubes of the hypochondrium and in sundry other parts, which suddenly dilated within her, grew warm, tickled, envenomed, clawed, stood prickly and on end as though a thousand basketsful of needles were drilling her body. It was a virgin's desire, a well-conditioned desire which so troubled her vision that she lost sight of her old husband, and was all eyes for young Gauthier, in whom Nature was as richly cushioned as an abbot's chin.

When the good man entered Tours, the exclamations of the crowd awakened him; he and his retinue progressed with great pomp to the church of Notre Dame de l'Égrignolles, formerly called La Greigneur, as who might say the most excellent. Blanche went into the particular chapel where prayers for children are offered up to God and to the Virgin; she was unaccompanied, as was customary, though remaining in the presence of the Seneschal, his varlets and such loiterers as gathered outside the grill. When she met the priest who had charge of prayers said for children and who received the supplicants' vows, Blanche asked him whether barren women were numerous; to which the prelate replied that he had no cause for complaint, and that the children brought the church a good revenue.

"And do you often see young women with husbands as old as My Lord?" Blanche asked.

"Seldom," he told her.

"But have they obtained lineage?"

"Invariably!" the priest said with a smile.

"But the others—those whose husbands are younger?"

"Sometimes. . . ."

"Ah!" she cried, "then it is more certain with a man like the Seneschal?"

"Quite so!" said the priest.

"Why?"

"Because, Madame," the priest answered gravely, "before that age, God alone takes a hand in the affair: afterwards, men do!"

At this period, it was still true that all wisdom was to be found among the clergy. Blanche made her vow, which was a very considerable one; her finery was worth at least two thousand gold crowns.

"You are very joyful!" the Seneschal observed as on their return homeward she made her horse prance, frisk and jump.

"Yes, I am," she said. "I shall have a child—there's no doubt about it! The priest told me that any man can help me do it. I shall choose Gauthier!"

The Seneschal longed to slay the monk; but he decided the crime would prove too expensive and resolved to wreak vengeance subtly with the Archbishop's help. Then, before the housetops of La Roche Corbon came into sight, he ordered the Sire de Montsoreau to go back to his country and hide his light under a bushel, which young Gauthier did, for he knew his lord's ways. In his stead, the Seneschal appointed René, son of the Sire de Jallanges, whose fief was held from La Roche Corbon. He was a youngster, not quite fourteen years of age; Bruyn made him page until such time as he would be old enough to dub knight. The command of his soldiers he entrusted to an old cripple with whom he had ranged about in Palestine and elsewhere.

And the good man fondly believed he could avoid donning the horned harness of cuckolddom; he imagined he would be able still to girth, bridle and curb his wife's factious maidenhead which was even now struggling like a mule caught in a rope.

III

What Constitutes No More Than a Venial Sin

*T*HE SUNDAY following René's arrival at La Roche Corbon, Blanche went out hunting without her goodman; and in the forest, close to Les Carneaux, she saw a monk who appeared to be pushing a wench about more than was necessary. Spurring her horse on, she called to her servants:

"Ho, there! Stop him! He's killing her."

But once she was close to them, she turned her back on them quickly; and the sight of what this monk had in hand prevented her from hunting that day. She came back pensive; then, the dark lantern of her intelligence opened and a great light rose within, illuminating a thousand things that she had never really seen—church pictures, for instance, and prints, lays and fables of troubadours and the antics of birds. Of a sudden she discovered the sweet mystery of love written in all languages, even in that of the fish. How foolish it is to keep such knowledge from maidens! It was early indeed when Blanche went to bed and she lost no time beating about the bush.

"Bruyn," she said, "you have deceived me. You ought to set to work as that monk of Les Carneaux did with the girl."

Old Bruyn suspected the adventure; he realized that his evil hour was at hand. As he gazed at Blanche, there was too much fire in his glance to allow of any ardor elsewhere.

"Alas! my love," he said gently, "when I took you for my wife, I had more love than strength. I have abused of your gentleness and virtue. The great sorrow of my life is that I feel all my capabilities centred in my heart only. This sorrow is hastening my death little by little, so you will soon be free! . . . Ah, wait for my departure from this world! Such is the only boon asked of you by one who is your master and could command, but who wishes to be no more than your prime minister and slave. Do not put my white hairs to dishonor! For such betrayal, lords have been known to slay their wives. . . ."

"Alas! and shall you slay me, then?"

"No," the old man answered, "I love you too much, my sweet. Oh, but you are the flower of my old age, the joy of my soul; you are my child, my well-beloved daughter; the sight of you refreshes my eyes and I could endure anything from you, were it sorrow or joy. Blanche, I give you full license to do whatever you will, so that you do not heap too many curses upon Bruyn, who made a great lady of you, a rich and much-respected lady. Are you not destined to be a lovely widow? Ah, your happiness will soothe the pangs of my death. . . ."

And from his dry eyes he was still able to conjure up a tear which trickled warmly down his cheek, rugous and brown as a pine-cone, to fall upon Blanche's hand. Moved to compassion as she recognized how deep the love of a husband who was dying in order to please her:

"There, there!" she said with a laugh. "Don't weep! I shall wait!"

Thereupon the Seneschal kissed her hands and regaled her with little endearments, as he said in a voice trembling with emotion:

"Ah, Blanche, my darling, if you knew how, while you are asleep, I devour you with caresses, kissing you now here, now there. . . ."

And the old ape fondled her with a pair of hands that were all bones.

"And," he went on, "I dared not rouse the puss which would have strangled my honor since in this act of love I set only my heart on fire."

"Ah," Blanche answered, "you may fondle me thus even when my eyes are open, it makes no difference to me."

At these words, the unhappy Seneschal seized a small dagger which lay on a table by the bed and, placing it in her hand, cried with passion:

"Kill me, my angel, ay—or else let me believe that you love me a little."

"Yes, yes!" she said, thoroughly frightened, "I will try to love you a lot."

Thus this young maidenhood conquered and subdued the old man, for, in the name of that sweet Cytherean plot that lay fallow, Blanche, with the inherent artfulness of women, made her old Bruyn come and go like a miller's mule.

It was forever, "My good Bruyn, I want this!" "Bruyn, I want that!" "Now, Bruyn!" "Come along, Bruyn!" "Bruyn!" right and "Bruyn!" left, so much so that the Seneschal was more oppressed by his wife's magnanimity than he would have been by her outright enmity. She wrung the wretched man's brain, insisting that everything in the house should be in crimson, forcing him to turn the whole place topsy-turvy at the merest flicker of her eyebrow. And, when she happened to be sad, the Seneschal, driven to distraction, would answer every question that rose to his judicial bench, with a curt:

"Hang him!"

Any other man would have perished like a fly in this vestal battle; but Bruyn had too robust a nature to be easily downed. One evening that Blanche had made a babel of the house, foundered man and beast and would, through her insufferable temper, have driven the Eternal Father to despair (for all His treasures of patience, since He endures us) she said to the Seneschal as she got into bed:

"My dear Bruyn, it is low down that I feel fancies itching and pricking; thence they rise straight to my heart, they burn my brain and there they incite me to evil deeds; and at night, I dream of the monk of Les Carneaux. . . ."

"My love," the Seneschal answered, "these are deviltries and temptations against which the monks and nuns know how to defend themselves. Therefore, if you would gain salvation, go and confess to the good Abbot of Marmoutier, our neighbor. He will give you sound advice and direct you in all holiness along the proper way."

"I shall go no later than tomorrow!" she said.

At daybreak she trotted off helter-skelter to the monastery, where the holy monks, marvelling at the sight of so winsome a lady in their house, were fated to commit more than one sin that evening. For the present, however, they led her with great joy to their Reverend Father.

Blanche found the Abbot in a private garden at the foot of a high rock under a cool arcade and, though she was accustomed to set small store by white hairs, the holy man's countenance inspired her with a profound respect.

"God preserve you, Madame!" he said. "You, who are so young —what is it brings you so close to death?"

"Your precious counsel, Father!" she said, curtseying before him. "And if it please you to lead an unruly sheep, I shall be well content to have so wise a confessor."

"My daughter," answered the monk, with whom old Bruyn had arranged both this hypocrisy and the parts to be played, "had I not the chill of fivescore winters upon this ravaged head, I could not possibly listen to your sins. But speak on; if you enter Paradise, it will have been my doing."

At once the Seneschal's wife hastened to retail her routine sins; and, when she was purged of her minor iniquities, she broached her postscript:

"Ah, Father," she sighed, "I must confess to you that not a day goes by but I am harrowed by the desire to have a child. Is that evil?"

"No," said the Abbot.

"But," she resumed, "my husband is condemned by nature to forgo piercing the veil of misery, as the old women by the roadside call it."

"Very well then," the priest answered, "you must live virtuously; you must banish all such thoughts."

"But I have heard it professed (Madame de Jallanges, it was) that there is no sin where neither profit nor pleasure was to be had."

"There is always pleasure in it," the Abbot said, "but then surely you are reckoning the unhappy child as profit? Ah, my daughter, I conjure you to let this be graven upon your mind: it will always be a mortal sin in God's sight and a crime in the eyes of mankind for a woman to bring forth a child as a result of having lain with a man to whom she is not married by bell, book and candle. Therefore such women as transgress the sacred laws of wedlock suffer proportionally grievous penalties in the next world: they are given over to horrific monsters with sharp, trenchant claws who thrust them into sundry burning, fiery furnaces, in remembrance of the fact that here below they warmed their hearts a trifle more than was lawful."

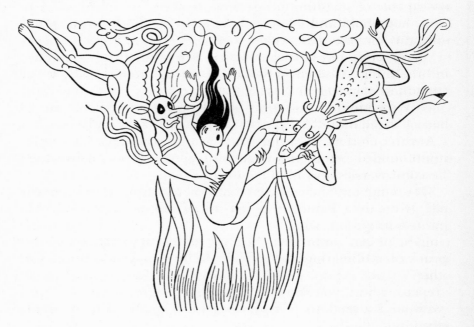

Thereupon Blanche scratched her ear; and, having meditated a little:

"How then did the Virgin Mary do it?" she asked.

"Ho!" answered the Abbot, "that was a miracle."

"And what is a miracle?"

"A thing which cannot be explained, which must be believed without question."

"Eh, but could I not perform a miracle, then?"

"This particular miracle happened but once," the Abbot explained, "because it was the Son of God."

"Alas, Father, is it God's will that I die then? Or that through dutiful observance, I go mad? Of this I vow there is great danger. For when things stir and burn within me, I lose my senses, nothing matters to me at all; to find a man I would leap over the walls and scour the countryside shamelessly; and just to see what excited that monk of Les Carneaux so much, I would strike at the root of everything. While these furious passions prick my body and ravage my soul, neither God, nor Devil, nor husband exists. I stamp up and down, I run about like a mad-woman, I am capable of smashing up garden, crockery, barnyard, ostrich-farm, household and everything else. I could not begin to tell you how horrible it is. And I dare not confess all my misdeeds to you, because just to speak of them brings water to my mouth, and the thing (God curse me for it!) itches monstrously. What if madness grips me and prickles me and slays my virtue? Will God, Who kindled this great love in my body, deliver me to eternal damnation?"

At this question, it was the priest who scratched his ear, utterly dumbfounded before the lamentations, the depths of wisdom, the controversies and intelligence this maidenhood secreted.

"My daughter," he said, "God has distinguished us from beasts and given us a Paradise to win to. That we may do so, He granted us reason, which is as a rudder to govern us amid the tempest of our ambitions and desires. Furthermore there is a means of sublimating the body by fasting, excessive labors and other virtues. Again, instead of fussing and fretting like an ob-streperous brat, you should pray to the Virgin, sleep on a hard board and attend to your household duties instead of living idly."

"But Father, when I sit in my pew at church, I see neither priest nor altar but only the child Jesu, Who sets me to wanting the thing more than ever. But to finish—supposing my head were turned, my mind wandered and I were caught in the toils of love . . . ?"

"If you were," the Abbot said rashly, "you would be in the position of St. Lidoire. One day (it was very hot and she was lightly clad) while the saint lay sound asleep, one leg thrown here, the other there, she was approached by a young man with a load of mischief, who slyly lodged a child within her. Now the saint was utterly ignorant of this dastardly trick and vastly sur-prised when she was brought to bed, for she had believed that her unusual size connoted a serious malady. So she did penance for it as for a venial sin, since she had received no pleasure from the wicked act, according to the statement of the criminal who declared, on the scaffold where he was executed, that the saint had in no wise stirred. . . ."

"Ah, Father, you may be sure I should not stir any more than she did."

With these words, the winsome Blanche tripped away, the picture of charm and gaiety, smiling prettily and wondering how she could commit a venial sin.

On her return from the great monastery, as she crossed the court of the castle, she caught sight of young Jallanges, riding under the direction of the aged groom. The lad was turning and wheeling about on his fine horse, bending with the movements of the animal, dismounting and mounting again with leaps and vaults, his thigh taut, his body lissome, graceful as could be, and skilful, handsome, alert beyond description; in a word he would have kindled desire in Queen Lucretia, even, who killed herself for having been contaminated against her will.

"Ha!" Blanche said to herself. "Were that little page but fifteen years old, I would gladly fall asleep with him in the offing."

Indeed, despite the extreme youth of her charming servitor, Blanche stared a great deal during the collation and supper, at René's black hair, his white skin, his grace of manners and especially at his eyes, abundantly filled with a limpid warmth and a great fire of life, which, lad as he was, he dared not dart out.

Now, in the evening, as the Seneschal's lady sat dreaming in her chair, by the chimney-corner, old Bruyn asked her what was the matter.

"I am thinking," she said, "that you must have been up in arms in love's battle very early in life, to be thus completely ruined!"

"Ay," he answered smiling, like all old men questioned on their memories of amour, "at the age of thirteen and a half, I had already put my mother's chamberwoman in the family way. . . ."

Blanche wished to hear no more of it. But she believed that the page René must be quite as well furnished; at this, she grew very joyful, teased the old man playfully and wallowed in her silent desire like a cake in a flour-pan.

IV

How and by Whom the Child Was Contrived

HE SENESCHAL'S wife did not waste time in planning how best to awaken the page's love quickly; she had made short shrift of setting the natural trap in which the wariest are invariably caught. This is how the thing happened. When the sun was at its hottest, our good Bruyn took his siesta, Saracen-fashion; it was a habit he had never failed in since his return from the Holy Land. During this time, Blanche sat alone in the garden or worked at the lesser tasks of women, such as stitching and embroidery; more often, however, she stayed indoors, supervising the washing, arranging her linen, or running about as she pleased.

But now she devoted this lost hour to completing the page's education, to hearing him read or recite his prayers.

The following day, on the stroke of noon, the Seneschal retired to sleep, having duly succumbed to the sun which darts its brightest and fiercest rays on the hillside of La Roche Corbon; slumber is irresistible there unless the senses are fanned, bellowed and kept effervescent by a diabolic maidenhead. Blanche perched herself gracefully in her goodman's great, seigniorial chair, which did not prove too high, in view of the hazard of perspective upon which she counted. The artful minx settled down as snugly as a swallow in its nest; she leaned her head maliciously upon her arm, like a child curled up in sleep. But as she made these preparations, she cocked an avid eye, smiling and rejoicing in anticipation of the little secret thrills, fits, starts, squints and trances her page would indulge in as he lay at her feet, about as far from her as the jump of an old flea. In fact, she moved forward so far, and so expediently close to the velvet cushion on which the lad with whose life and soul she trifled was due to sit, that, had he been a saint of stone, his glance could not have avoided following the flexuosities of her dress in order to admire the perfections and beauties of the nervous, thin leg moulding her white stocking. Obviously, then, a weak varlet was bound to fall in the trap into which the doughtiest of knights would gladly have plunged.

When Blanche had writhed and twisted, placing her body here, then turning to displace it there until she had found the ground where the toils would best be spread, she called softly:

"René! Oh!"

René, who she knew was in the guardroom, did not fail to answer the summons: suddenly his dark head appeared between the curtains:

"What is My Lady's pleasure?" the page asked. Very respectfully he held his small red drugget cap in his hand—less red, by far, than his fresh, dimpled cheeks.

"Come here, lad!" she said, under her breath, for the attraction he exercised upon her cut her respiration.

And, truly, never jewels darted flames such as those in René's eyes, never vellum gleamed more snowy-white than his flesh, never woman lived so shapely of form. Then, being herself upon the verge of desire, she found him still more beautifully modelled; besides, as you may well imagine, the brave fire of love rose from all this youth, from the warm sunlight, the silence and all the rest.

"Read me the litanies of Our Lady the Virgin," she told René, as she pushed an open book on her prie-dieu toward him. "I wish to know whether your master is teaching you properly."

"Do you not think the Virgin beautiful?" she asked with a smile, as the silver and gold of the illuminated tome winked up at her.

"It is a painting," he answered timidly as he ventured to glance at his infinitely gracious mistress.

"Read, read...."

So René began reciting the sweet, mystical litanies; but, as you have guessed, Blanche's antiphonal *Ora pro nobis* kept coming ever more faintly, like the echoes of a horn dying out in the far woodland. When the page ardently intoned *O Rose of Mystery!* the lady, who assuredly did not fail to hear, countered with a gentle sigh. Suspecting that his mistress had fallen asleep, René covered her with his glance, poring over her at leisure, desiring to sing never an anthem but that of love. His rapture brought his heart leaping and quivering to his throat; thus, as was but natural, these twin maiden fires vied with each other in burning. Nor would anyone seeing them have dreamed of leaving them together. René feasted his gaze, plotting a thousand fruitions that brought water to his mouth as he considered this lush fruit of love. In his ecstasy, he let the book fall from his hands, which made him as shamefaced as a monk caught at child's play. But it also proved that Blanche was sound asleep: the pawky girl did not stir, nor, indeed, would she have opened her eyes before the gravest dangers, for she reckoned on something else falling besides the prayer-book.

Is there craving worse than that of a woman who longs to bear children? Now the page noticed his lady's foot, daintily shod in a graceful blue buskin. She had set it quaintly upon a stool, for she sat too high for comfort in the Seneschal's chair. This foot was of narrow proportions, delicately curved, small at the end, two fingers broad and no longer than a house-sparrow, tail included. It was a truly delightful foot, a virginal foot that merited a kiss as a robber merits the gallows; a roguish foot, a foot wanton enough to damn an archangel; it was an augural foot, a devilish enticing foot. A foot to inspire whoever beheld it with a will to make a pair of new ones just like it in order to perpetuate in this workaday world the noble handicraft of God. The page was tempted to slip the shoe off this persuasive foot. With this in mind, his eyes, aglow with all the fire of his age, swung, quick as the clapper of a bell, from the delectable foot to the face of his slumbering lady. He listened to her sleep, drinking in her very breath. Once again, he could not decide whether it would be sweeter to plant a kiss upon the fresh red lips or upon this eloquent foot. In fine, through respect or fear or possibly through great love, René chose the foot, and kissed it hurriedly, like a maid who dares not. Immediately he took up the book again, his blush turning to an even deeper red, and, exercised by his desire, he cried like a blind man:

"*Janua cœlis, O Gate of Heaven!*"

Blanche did not awaken, confident that the page would progress from the foot to the knee and thence to heaven itself. But to her great chagrin, the litanies ended without further mischief and René, believing he had savored too much happiness for one day, beat a swift retreat from the room, made mercurial, and richer by his bold kiss than a thief who has robbed a poor-box.

The Seneschal's lady, left alone, mused that the page would be long indeed at the task, if he amused himself singing the *Magnificat* at Matins. Accordingly she determined on the morrow to raise her foot ever so slightly and thus bring to light the neb of that hidden beauty they call perfect in Touraine because it never took hurt in the air and is forever fresh. You may imagine how impatiently the page, seething with desire and consumed by imagination, awaited the hour when he was to read in this breviary of gallantry; how he duly called; how the intoning of the litany began again, and how Blanche did not fail to fall asleep. This time young René ran his hand over the pretty leg and even ventured so far as to verify whether the polished knee and something else were satin. At this sight, the luckless child, steeled by abject terror against his desire, dared only offer brief devotion and insignificant caresses; and although he kissed this fair surface very gently, he still remained timid. Feeling this through the senses of her heart and the intelligence of her body, Blanche who was straining every muscle to keep from moving cried:

"Ho, René, come, I am asleep!"

Hearing what he interpreted as a severe reproach, the page was terrified and he fled, abandoning book, task and everything else. Thereupon the Seneschal's lady added this prayer to the litany: "Holy Virgin, how difficult children are to make!"

At dinner, as he came to serve his lord and lady, a cold sweat trickled down the page's back. But he was amazed to see Blanche bestow upon him the most lascivious glance woman ever favored man with; and very pleasurable and powerful it proved, too, since it changed this child into a man of courage.

That very evening, Bruyn having remained in his seigniory a little longer than usual, the page sought out Blanche and found her sleeping. Whereupon he made her dream a beautiful dream. He relieved her of what had weighed so heavily upon her; she made so lavish an expenditure of love's favors that the surplus would have sufficed to bless two others with the power of maternity. Suddenly My Lady seized her page by the head and hugging him to her:

"Oh, René!" she cried. "You have awakened me."

Truth to tell, there was no known sleep that could have resisted; they discovered, indeed, that saints must sleep like tops!

As a result, without further mystery and by virtue of a benevolent property which is the assisting principle of husbands, that sweet, graceful plumage particular to cuckolds rose from the good Seneschal's pate without his experiencing the least tremor or shock.

After this ambrosial collation, his lady was more than partial to taking her siesta French-fashion while Bruyn took his according to the Saracen. But, thanks to these siestas, she learned that contact with the page's fresh youth was tastier than with the aged Seneschal; and by night, she buried herself under the sheets far from her husband, whom she found devilishly rancid and malodorous. At length, what with falling asleep and awakening by day, what with indulging in siestas and rehearsing litanies, My Lady Seneschal felt flourishing within her that fulfilment after which she had so often and so passionately hankered. But by now she found the means far more agreeable than the end.

You may be sure that René knew how to read, not only in books, but also in the eyes of his beautiful lady; for her sake he would cheerfully have flung himself upon a flaming pyre, had she but wished it. When at last they had plied their task amply and to good purpose at least a hundred times, the little lady began to worry about the soul and future of her friend the page. One rainy morning, while they were playing at tag, like two children, innocent from head to foot, Blanche, who was always being captured, cried:

"Come here, René. Tell me. . . . Do you know that while I have committed no more than venial sins, because I was asleep, you have committed mortal ones?"

"Ah, Madame," René sighed, "if that be a sin, then where will God find room to lodge the damned?"

Blanche burst out laughing, and kissed him on the brow:

"Be quiet, you little wretch! It is a question of Paradise and we must live there in company if you wish to stay with me forever."

"Oh, I make my paradise here!"

"Leave off!" she said. "You are a wretch and a scapegrace not to think of what I love most—meaning yourself! You know that I am with child; soon I shall be no more able to hide it than the nose on my face. Well, then, what will the Abbot say? What will

My Lord Seneschal say? He may kill you if he loses his temper. In my opinion, child, you should go to the Abbot of Marmoutier, confess your sins to him and ask him to see what had better be done with regard to my Seneschal."

"Alas!" the wily page sighed. "If I betray the secret of our joys, he will place his interdict upon our love."

"Yes, I daresay he will," she agreed. "But your happiness in the next world is to me a very vital matter!"

"Do you insist then, my darling?"

"Yes," she answered, rather weakly.

"Well then, go I shall. But sleep once again that I may bid it a long farewell!"

And the charming couple rehearsed their litanies of adieux, as though both had foreseen that their love must finish in its springtime. Then, on the morrow, more to save his beloved lady than for his own sake, and also to do her bidding, René de Jallanges set out for the great monastery.

V

How the Love-Sin Was Grievously Expiated
and Led to Great Mourning

"GOD'S truth!" the Abbott exclaimed when the page had run the gamut of his sweet sins. "You were the accomplice in a great felony and you have betrayed your lord! Do you know, you wicked page, that for this deed you shall burn for ever and ever throughout eternity? Do you know what it means to forfeit permanently all chance of Heaven above, for the sake of one fleeting, perishable moment of pleasure here below? Unhappy wretch! I see you plunged without end into the abyss of Hell unless you repay in this world the debt you owe God for such an offence."

Thereupon the good old Abbot, who was of such flesh as saints are made of and who enjoyed great authority in the land of Touraine, terrified the young man by piling up representations, Christian discourses, remembrances of churchly commands and as many myriad arguments as a devil can accumulate in six weeks to seduce a virgin. He called forth so many that René, in the loyal fervor of innocence, made full submission. Of this child, now in a fair way to become thoroughly evil, the Abbot wished to make a man holy and virtuous for all time. He therefore commanded René first to fall at his lord's feet and confess his transgressions, then, if he survived this confession, to make a Crusader's vows on the spot, to depart for the Holy Land forthwith and to remain there for an appointed term of fifteen years, battling against the Infidel.

"Alas, Reverend Father," René moaned breathlessly, "can fifteen years suffice to atone for so much pleasure? Ah, if you but knew, I have had joy enough for a thousand years."

"God will be merciful!" the Abbot said. "Go, my son, and sin no more. On this count, *ego te absolvo*...."

In great contrition, the luckless René returned at once to the castle of La Roche Corbon; and the first person he met was the Seneschal, who was polishing up his arms, helmets, gauntlets and so forth. Bruyn sat out of doors on a great marble bench; he enjoyed the sight of his brave trappings gleaming in the sunlight; it brought back to him all the merry pranks he had played in the Holy Land, the tricks, vagaries, trollops. When René fell on his knees before him, the good lord was greatly astonished:

"What now?" he asked.

"My Lord," René begged, "order these men here to withdraw."

When the servants were gone, the page confessed his sin, recounting how he had assailed his lady in her sleep and how he had undoubtedly invested her with child in imitation of the man with the saint. He had now come, he said, by order of his confessor, to place himself at the disposal of the offended party. Having spoken, René de Jallanges lowered his dazzling eyes, which had brought about all the mischief, and remained quite still, prone but fearless, his arms hanging by his side, his head bare, awaiting his evil hour and humbling himself before God. The Seneschal was not so white that he could not turn paler; on the contrary, he blanched like linen new-dried. For several seconds he stood speechless with fury. Then this oldster, who in his veins lacked the vital energy to procreate a child, mustered more vigor in this moment of frenzy than was necessary to undo a man. Seizing his heavy mace in his hairy right hand, he raised it, brandished it, and poised it like a bowl at a game of skittles, ready to bring it down upon René's pallid brow. The latter, knowing that he had grievously wronged his lord, remained serene; he bared his neck to the other's vengeance, believing he was about to expiate the whole sorry fault for his sweetheart in this world and in the other.

But if the gallant youth and all the natural seductions of this charming crime found grace before the tribunal of the old man's heart, Bruyn was nevertheless severe; and, hurling his mace viciously at a dog whom he smashed to a bleeding pulp:

"May a thousand million claws rend through all eternity all the joints and guts of the punk who spawned the man who sowed the oak that made the chair on which you hornified me! And

God grant the same to those who begot you, cursed page of misfortune! Go back to the devil whence you came! Get out of my sight, leave the castle, leave the country, and don't let me catch you lingering a second longer than necessary or I will surely arrange you a death by slow fire that will make you curse your wicked strumpet twenty times an hour. . . ."

As the Seneschal, rejuvenated by these oaths, began roaring, the page took to his heels, escaping the rest; and he did well. Bruyn, consumed by a fiery rage, reached the garden hotfoot, cursing everything upon his way, lashing out on every side and swearing at the top of his lungs; he even knocked over three large pots in which a servant was bringing the dogs their mess. The good man was so beside himself that he would have killed a mercer for selling a comb or a huntsman for blowing a horn. Directly he saw his no longer virginal wife—she was gazing down the road to the monastery, waiting for the page, unaware that she would never see him again:

"Ho, Madame," he roared, "by the triple red fork of the Devil, am I a child to swallow such cock-and-bull stories? Shall I believe that you are so sluiced as to suffer a page's passage without waking up? By the Death! By the Head! By the Blood!"

"Truly," she said, seeing that the mine was sprung, "I felt it, and pleasurably; but since you had not taught me the thing, I thought I was dreaming."

The Seneschal's great ire melted like snow in the sunlight, for the strongest wrath of God Himself would have vanished at a smile from Blanche.

"May a thousand devils carry off this alien child! I swear that. . . ."

"There, there, Bruyn! Come, don't swear!" she said. "If it is not yours, it is mine. Didn't you tell me the other evening that you loved anything that came from me?"

Thereupon she mustered so many arguments, flatteries, complaints, quarrels, tears and other paternosters of women—for example, first of all, the estate would not revert to the King; next, no child was ever more innocently poured into the mould; then this, then that, and a hundred and one other things—till finally the good cuckold grew calm. Then Blanche, seizing a propitious interruption, asked:

"Where is the page?"

"He has gone to the devil."

"What? You killed him?"

Suddenly she turned pale . . . tottered. . . . Bruyn seeing all the joy of his old age falling, grew desperate; to save Blanche, he would gladly have produced the page. He therefore ordered him to be summoned; but René, scarcely anxious to be carved up, had fled for dear life and set out for abroad to fulfil his vow of religion. From the Abbott, Blanche learned the penance imposed upon her lover; she fell into a state of profound melancholy.

"Where is he?" she would often sigh. "Where is that poor wretch who is facing the direst perils for my love's sake?"

And she would keep on asking like a child that will give its mother no rest until its prayer be granted. Hearing these lamentations, the Seneschal felt he was to blame; he would bustle about, doing any number of things (except one) to make Blanche happy. But nothing could replace the sweet attentions of the page. . . .

At length one day she bore the child she had so much desired. You may imagine what a treat it was for the old cuckold: the father's likeness was fully reproduced in the features of this sweet fruit of love. Blanche found in it a deep consolation; she recaptured a little of the hearty gaiety and flowery innocence that gladdened the Seneschal's old age. Growing used to watching the tiny lad scamper about and to hearing his laugh and Blanche's, in answer, eventually Bruyn came to love him. He would have flown into a great rage against anyone who might question the authenticity of his parentage.

Now as the adventure of Blanche and her page had not gone beyond the castle, it was said throughout all Touraine that Messire Bruyn had still found the wherewithal for offspring. Blanche's virtue remained intact; through the quintessential instructions she drew from the natural reservoir of women, she recognized how necessary it was to hush the venial sin that hung over her child. She became prudent, she behaved properly, she was cited as a virtuous person. Then, by experience, she grew to appreciate her goodman's kindness; and, without giving him license to touch more than her chin (she still considered herself as belonging to René) in return for the flowers of age that Bruyn offered her, Blanche coddled him, smiled on him, kept him in good spirits, fondled him and served up all the pretty little tricks and attentions a woman bestows on the husband she deceives. She played her part so well that her husband ceased to invoke death. Instead, he sat ensconced in his chair and the longer he lived, the greater his zest for life. But one evening he died, without knowing where he was going, for he called to Blanche:

"Ho, ho! My love! I cannot see you now! Is it night?"

It was the death of the just; and well he merited it as a reward for his labors in the Holy Land.

Blanche went into deep and heartfelt mourning, weeping him as one weeps a father. Her melancholy persisted; she refused to lend an ear to any music of a second wedding. For this she was praised by all decent people, who were quite unaware that she had a husband in her heart and that she lived in hope. But for the greater part of the time she was widow in fact and widow in heart, for, hearing no news of her lover at the Crusades, the poor woman believed him dead. At night, sometimes, as she dreamed of him lying mortally wounded in a distant land, she would wake up in tears.

Thus during fourteen years, she lived on in the memory of her ephemeral happiness. At last, one afternoon, when she was chatting with certain ladies of Touraine after dinner, her little lad appeared. He was now thirteen and a half; he resembled René more than it is lawful for a child to resemble its father, nor was there anything of the late Bruyn about him save his name. The child then, gay and pretty as Blanche, came in from the garden, running, perspiring, overheated, excited, tumbling over everything in his way, as children do, and making straight for his beloved mother. Jumping on her lap and interrupting the conversation:

"Oh mother, I must tell you something! I saw a pilgrim in the court. He took me in his arms and hugged me so tight!"

"What!" cried the Countess, turning to one of the servants who was detailed to follow the young Count and watch over his precious days. "I have forbidden you to leave my child in the hands of strangers, even of the holiest man in the world. You shall leave my service. . . ."

"Alas, Madame," the old equerry answered in despair, "that

man wished him no harm. He actually wept as he kissed him fondly. . . ."

"He wept, eh?" she said. "Ah, it's the father!"

So speaking, she bowed her head over the chair in which she sat, which, you may be sure, was the chair in which she had sinned.

Hearing these fantastic words, the ladies were too surprised at first to see that the poor Countess was dead. Nor did they ever learn whether her sudden death was caused by sorrow at the departure of her lover, who, faithful to his vow, had forgone seeing her; or by exultation at his return and hope of annulling the interdict the Abbot of Marmoutier had placed upon their love.

And great indeed was the mourning for the Sire de Jallanges lost his spirits when he saw his mistress laid under ground; and he became a monk at Marmoutier, which, at that time, some called Maimostier, as who might say *maius Monasterium,* the greatest monastery; and it was indeed the most noble convent in France.

His Majesty's Sweetheart

*I*N THOSE days there was a goldsmith living at the forges of the Pont au Change. This man had a daughter whose exceeding beauty and gentle charm were the talk of Paris. Consequently many pursued her in the conventional manner of lovers and some, even, would gladly have paid her father large sums of money to have her in lawful wedlock. All of which gratified him very much indeed.

One of his neighbors, a parliamentary advocate who, by boldly selling his pettifogging jargon, had acquired more estates than a dog has fleas, took it into his head to offer a house in return for the father's consent. The goldsmith played up to form. He bargained away his daughter, without considering that the juridical hyena had the face of an ape, few teeth in his jaws (and those shaky) ; nor did he trouble to smell him, though he was as rank and putrid as all attorneys who wallow in the offal of the courts of law, parchments, archives, cartularies and sundry obscure proceedings.

As soon as the pretty maid laid eyes on the prospective groom, she exclaimed:

"God help me, I will have none of him."

"That is not my business," said the father, who already fancied the house, "I give him to you for a husband. Tune your instruments to the same song. From now on, it is his affair; his duty is to please you."

"So that's the way of it?" she said. "Well, before I obey you, I shall tell him off properly!"

And the same evening, after supper, when the suitor began to plead his burning case, telling her how mad he was about her and promising her great luxury for the rest of her life, she cut him short:

"My father has sold you my body, but if you take it, you will be making a punk of me. I would rather give myself to men off the street than to you. Unlike the usual fiancée, I vow you a disloyalty which will end only in death, yours or mine."

Then she began to weep as all inexperienced maidens will; for later they never cry with their eyes. He mistook this strange behavior for the snares and artifices girls employ to whet a fiancé's ardor and turn his devotion into dower, inheritance and other matronly rights. So the old hypocrite paid no heed and laughed at the sweet maid's outburst.

"What day shall it be?" he asked.

"Tomorrow!" she replied. "The sooner it is, the sooner I shall be free to have lovers . . . to lead the glad life of women who love where they choose."

Thereupon the idiot, caught like a finch in a child's snare, went away to make the necessary preparations. He put in a word at the Court House, trotted over to the Ecclesiastical Tribunal, bought dispensations, and, dreaming only of the pretty girl, completed all these errands with far greater dispatch than any other legal business he had ever had.

Meanwhile the King had just returned from a journey. At Court, the goldsmith's daughter was the sole topic of discussion: how she had refused a thousand crowns from this one, how she had spurned that one, how, in fine, she would submit to none and how she had snubbed the finest youths in the city, lads who would have left God their seats in Paradise to possess this dragon of chastity for a single day. Now His Majesty, who was partial to such game, strolled through the town, made for the Pont au Change forges and went into the goldsmith's shop, intending not only to buy jewels for the lady of his heart but also to bargain for the most precious one in the collection. Either His Majesty did not like gems much or these particular gems did not suit him; at all events, the shopkeeper moved away and rummaged in a secret compartment for a large white diamond. Then:

"My love," His Majesty said to the daughter, while her father's nose was buried in the drawer, "you were not made to sell precious stones, but to receive them. If you gave me all the rings in the place to choose from, I know which one many men hereabouts dote on, which one most pleases me, which one I shall ever be subject or slave to, which one exceeds in value the entire riches of the land of France!"

"Ah, Sire," the belle replied, "I am to wed tomorrow! But if you lend me the dagger at your belt, I will defend the flower of my virtue and I will reserve it for you. In the words of the gospel: '*Render therefore unto Cæsar the things which are Cæsar's*'."

Forthwith, the King gave her the little dagger; and her brave reply so enamored him of her that he quite lost his appetite. Incontinently, he had an apartment prepared in one of his palaces in the Rue de l'Hirondelle for his new sweetheart.

And now, picture, if you will, the advocate, all agog to tie the knot and, amid the disgust of his rivals, leading his bride altar-ward to the brave peal of bells; picture the nuptial music, the banqueting, fit to bring on diarrhœa; picture the happy man that evening, the dancing over, coming into the hymeneal bower where his lovely bride was to repose. A lovely bride? It was a fac-tious witch, a wild she-devil he found, seated in an armchair, re-fusing to share her lord's bed, and crouching beside the fireplace, warming her ire and the bud of her beauty. The good husband, rather surprised, kneeled before her, inviting her to the first pas-sage of arms in the pretty battle of connubial love. She uttered never a word. Then, when he sought to raise her garments, only just to peep at the treasure that had cost him so dear, she dealt him a thwack that made his bones rattle. And still she remained speechless.

This sport did not displease our friend; he was confident the thing would end you may imagine how. So he played the game according to rule, cheerfully receiving the blows that fell to him. At length, by dint of scuffling, scrambling and grappling, he managed now to rip off a sleeve, now to slit a petticoat until he was able to slip his hand upon the dainty prize he coveted. At the enormity of his act, the lovely bride scowled, rose to her feet, and, drawing the King's dagger:

"What do you wish of me?" she asked him.

"Everything," he answered.

"Eh, but I would be a great harlot to give myself against my liking. If you fancied you would find my maidenhead unarmed, then you made a great mistake. Here is the King's dagger, with which I kill you, if you so much as take one step forward."

Without taking her eyes off the man-at-law, she picked up a cinder; then, drawing a line across the floor:

"This is the boundary of the King's domain," she added. "Do not enter it, for my aim is true!"

The lawyer had no intention of flirting with this dagger; he stood rooted to the spot as he heard this stern decree, the costs of which he had already paid. But, through the rents in her dress, he caught sight of such a lovely bit of plump, soft, white thigh and such dazzling patches of flesh that death seemed sweet if he might only taste of them a little. Springing into the King's domain, he cried:

"Little I care if I die!"

Before the fury of his onslaught, the siren tumbled back awkwardly upon the bed. But she kept her wits about her and put up a gallant resistance: for all his pains, he came no nearer to his prey than the fur, at the same time catching a blow which sliced a piece of lard off his back without injuring him very severely. Thus it had not proved too costly to trespass upon royal ground.

But, maddened with this slight advantage, he cried:

"I cannot live without possessing this beautiful body, those marvels of love! Kill me, then!"

And once again he fell upon the royal preserves. The girl, with her head full of her King, was not at all moved by such desperate love.

"If you threaten to pursue this ecstatic hunt, it is not you but myself I shall kill."

The wild glitter in her eye terrified the wretched man; he fell back in a chair deploring the evil hour in which he had wed her; and thus a night that proves so rapturous to lovers he spent in lamentations, prayers and frenzied ejaculations. And the promises he made! She would be served implicity; she could dissipate everything; she would eat off plates of gold; out of the simple girl she was, he would make a great lady; he would buy estates and their titles for her; finally, if she but suffered him to break one lance with her in the tilts of love, he would leave everything to her and die in whatever way she chose. But she, still adamant, told him in the morning that she gave him leave to die, but that was all the happiness she could allow him.

"I have not cheated you," she said. "In fact, I am keeping my promise. I am giving myself to the King; I am sparing you the pedlars, draymen and birds of passage with whom I threatened you."

When it was broad daylight, she donned her wedding finery and waited patiently for the wretched, superfluous husband to go off on his clients' business. Then she made a dash into the town in search of the King. But she got no further than a bowshot from her door, for His Majesty had detailed a servant to mount guard over the house. The man, going straight up to the padlocked matron, asked outright:

"Do you not seek the King?"

"Yes," she confessed.

"Well then, I am your best friend," the crafty, schooled courtier said. "I ask you your aid and protection, just as I now give you mine...."

He proceeded to tell her what sort of a man the King was; how he should be handled; how he stormed about one day and did not utter a word the next; how this went and that; how she would be magnificently lodged and sumptuously provided for,

but how she must keep the King well in hand. He chattered to
such purpose that he had made a thorough-going harlot of her
before ever she entered the Hotel de l'Hirondelle (where Madame d'Étampes lived later).

When he found that his good wife had vanished, her luckless
husband belled like a wild buck; subsequently, he became a profoundly melancholy man. His colleagues heaped as many humil-
iations and mockeries upon him as St. James enjoyed honors at
Compostella; but (poor cuckold!) he suffered and stewed so
grievously that at last they tried rather to assuage his grief. These
artful pundits of the law, by way of jurisprudential chicanery,
decreed that: whereas said wife had wilfully refused to participate in the initial jousting, said grieving goodman was not a
cuckold, and that if and supposing the horner had been anyone
but the King, they would have undertaken to annul and dissolve
said marriage. But the husband adored his strumpet to the point
of death; so he left her necessarily with the King but trusted that
he would some day have her for himself, convinced that a lifetime of shame was not too great a price to pay for a single night
with her. A man must love deeply to go to such lengths; many a
lusty friggler would sneer at this affection. Our cuckold could
not put her out of his mind; he even neglected his suits, clients,
larcenies and all the rest of his pettifogging. He would wander
through the Court House like a miser searching for a lost treasure, filled with care and so absent-minded that one day he piddled against the robe of a counsellor, believing he stood beside
the wall where the advocates void their causes.

Meanwhile the King was loving his beautiful sweetheart night
and day. He could not have his fill of her, for she practised a
charming and particular technique of love, equally skilful at
kindling or extinguishing a fire. Today, she would snub the
King, tomorrow pet him; she was never the same, being a child
of a thousand fancies; a very pleasant lady, withal, piping and
chirruping as none of her sisters, forever laughing and rich in
little tricks and coquetries of every sort.

A lord of Bridoré killed himself to spite her for ignoring his
pleas, though he had offered her his domain of Bridoré in Touraine. Alas! of these gallant erstwhile scions of Touraine, who
bartered an estate for one good tilt with love's lance, there are

none left! His death saddened the siren; and when her confessor blamed her for it, she vowed that, King's sweetheart or no, she would accept all domains in future and secretly bestow joy upon gallants to save their souls from perdition. Thus she began to build up the vast fortune which won her the consideration of the whole town. But by the same token, she prevented many a nobleman from perishing, playing her parts so skilfully, and in-

venting such splendid yarns, that the King never knew how she helped him make his subjects happy. How thoroughly she turned his head! She could have made him believe the floor was the ceiling—a delusion His Majesty was the likeliest of men to credit. Did he not spend the greater portion of his time at the Hotel de l'Hirondelle in a decumbent position? Might he not then permissibly find it hard to tell the difference? The King was forever probing as though bound to ascertain whether such noble material could possibly wear out. But it was himself he wore out, poor man! He was destined to perish of the wounds of love.

Though she was most careful to grant her favors to only very handsome men of supreme standing at Court and though these favors were rare as miracles, her rivals and enemies declared that for ten thousand crowns a simple gentleman might sample his sovereign's pleasure. This was the blackest of falsehoods for when she and the King eventually fell out, in answer to a reproach he made on this score:

"I abominate, I curse, I consign to thirty thousand fiery devils those who put this idea in your head!" she answered proudly. "I never yet have had a man who did not deposit more than thirty thousand crowns at the gate."

The King, for all his anger, could not help smiling; he kept her on for another month or so in order to silence scandal. In the end, the Demoiselle de Pisseleu could not consider herself lady or mistress unless her rival were ruined. A highly enviable ruin, in effect; she married a young nobleman and they were very happy together, for so much ardor and love was in her that she could have amply supplied such of her sisters as sin too early in life.

But to return to our story. One day the King's sweetheart was passing through the town in her litter; she had set out to buy spangles, braiding, high-heeled slippers, ruffs and other amative ammunition. She looked so lovely and was so charmingly attired that as he saw her, any man—but especially a priest!—might well have believed Heaven had opened before him. Her pretty foot was dangling gracefully out of the litter. Suddenly, near the Croix du Trahoir, she came face to face with her husband. At once she drew her head quickly in, as though she had seen an adder. For she was a good wife! I know not a few who would have passed by proudly to affront their husbands by showing their contempt for his conjugal authority.

"Eh, but whatever is the matter?" asked Monsieur de Lannoy, who was respectfully accompanying her.

"It is nothing!" she whispered. "That was my husband! Poor man, how he has changed! He used to look like an ape; today he is the living image of Job."

The hapless advocate stood agape, his heart breaking at the sight of that delicate, thin foot, of that wife he loved so dearly.

Whereupon the Sieur de Lannoy, like a true Court blood, said insolently:

"Just because you are her husband, that's no reason to stand in her way."

At this thrust, she burst out laughing, while the cuckold, instead of killing her bravely, wept craven tears. Her laughter rent his head, his heart, his soul, his entire being; he was so upset that he almost tumbled over an old townsman who was busy cockering himself up at the sight of the King's mistress. To behold this wondrous flower, his, once, in the bud, but now blown to a full fragrant beauty; to view her white flesh, her faëry figure, her voluptuous breast, was too much for him; his hunger and madness grew ever more grievous; it beggared description. A man must himself insanely adore an unrequiting mistress thoroughly to appreciate the agony our lawyer suffered. Even then, it is rare for a heart to be so utterly consumed. He swore that life, fortune, honor, all might go hang, if he could but once lie flesh to flesh with her, if he could but once give the reins to his desire, if he could but once make such a feast of love that reins (and chitterlings) might snap for all he cared. He passed the whole night long, crying: "Ho! Yes! ah, I shall have her!" and "God's will, I'm her husband, am I not?" and "Devil take me!", striking his forehead and tossing on his bed.

There are chances and coincidences which combine so opportunely in this world that little-minded men refuse them credence, declaring them supernatural. But men of high intellect hold them for true, because they could not possibly be invented. Just such a chance befell our wretched lawyer no later than the day after the terrible vigil he had kept, chewing the cud of his fond erotic hope. A client of his, a man of eminent rank and a familiar of His Majesty's, called on him one morning. He would require, he told him, a large sum of money immediately—about twelve thousand crowns, say. To which the canny lawyer replied that twelve thousand crowns were not to be found on the street-corner as easily as what usually lies there, that besides the bonds and guarantees of interest, a man with twelve thousand crowns resting idle at home must be discovered; and that even in a great city like Paris there were few such men. He proffered all the clap-trap usually employed by men of chicanery:

"Is it true that you have an avid and relentless creditor, My Lord?"

"Ay, all too true!" the other sighed. "It is none other than the

King's sweetheart. Do not breathe a word of it; but this evening, in consideration of twenty thousand crowns and my domain of Brie, I shall take her measure."

The advocate turned deathly pale; the courtier perceived he had blundered. Being but newly returned from the wars, he was unaware that His Majesty's inamorata possessed a husband.

"How pale you are!" he exclaimed.

"It's my fevers," the old humbug answered. "But," he went on, "is it to her you give contracts and money?"

"Ay, certainly!"

"Who manages the transaction? She, too?"

"No," the nobleman explained, "the minor arrangements of these weighty trifles are conducted by her servant, the trickiest chamberwoman that ever existed. She is sharp as a needle; these nights stolen from the King have lined her purse handsomely."

"I know a Lombard banker who can accommodate you," the lawyer went on, "but we shall drop the matter and you shall not touch a copper of the twelve thousand crowns unless this maid comes here to collect the price of that object so perfectly alchemical, that, by Heaven, it turns blood into gold!"

"Ha! It will be playing them a good trick to make her sign a receipt," the nobleman said with a laugh.

The maid did not fail to keep the appointment. Naturally there on the table lay our friends the ducats, bright and beautiful, lined up in a row like nuns going to Vespers. So lovely, so radiant were the fair, lordly piles, that even a donkey would have smiled at the sight, though blows and kicks were raining down upon him. But it was no ass our good advocate had prepared this spectacle for; indeed, the little servant smacked her lips with relish as she offered up a thousand monkeyish paternosters to the ducats. Seeing which, the husband whispered four golden words in her ear:

"These are for you!"

"Ah!" she exclaimed. "I have never been paid so much."

"And you shall have them, my sweet," the dear man continued, "without having to bother about me."

Then, drawing her a little to one side:

"Your client has not told you my name, eh? No? Well, I am the lawful husband of the lady His Majesty debauched . . . the lady you serve. . . . Take her those crowns over there, then come back; I shall give you yours on terms which will be to your taste."

The servant, afraid at first, now regained her composure. Being very curious to find out how she could earn twelve thousand crowns without touching the advocate, she hastened back.

"Here, my child: look!" he said. "Here are twelve thousand crowns. With that sum I could buy estates, men, women and the conscience of at least three priests. Therefore if I give you these twelve thousand crowns, I believe I can have you body, soul, innards and all. I shall place an advocate's faith in you, measure for measure. I want you to go at once to the nobleman who expects to spend the night with my wife; you must trick him, telling him that the King intends to sup with her and that tonight he will have to seek his amusement elsewhere. Then, when that's done, I shall step into this brave lad's shoes—and into the King's, too."

"But how?" the maid inquired.

"Oh," he answered, "I have bought you, tricks and all; you won't have to look at those crowns twice before you find some way by which I can enjoy my wife. Nor, by bringing about this conjunction, will you be committing a sin. It is a work of piety to further the holy union of a husband and wife, whose hands alone have come together—and that in front of a priest."

"By my faith, come along!" she cried. "After supper, the lights will be out; you can slake your thirst of my lady, so long as you don't utter a word. Luckily on such joyous occasions, she cries more than she speaks and she asks questions by gesture only, for she is very modest indeed and does not relish low jests, like the ladies of the Court. . . ."

"Good!" said the advocate. "Here, take the twelve thousand crowns; and I promise you twice as much again, if by fraud I obtain possession of what belongs to me by right."

They arranged about the hour, the door, the signal, and all the rest of it. Then the maid left, bearing away, under escort and on muleback, the rich spoil our trickster had wrung, crown by crown, from widows, orphans and others, and which were all going the way of that small crucible where everything melts, even our lives (which come from it). Then our advocate proceeded to shave; he perfumed himself and donned his finest linen; he did without onions at dinner so his breath might be

sweet; he rested, bathed, curled his hair elaborately and practised
every trick a clown of the law courts can imagine to affect the
appearance of a gallant knight. He put on the airs of a young
blood, strove to be lithe and graceful, sought to disguise his obscene face; but it was all in vain, he still smelled of the lawyer.
He was not so clever as the pretty laundress of Portillon who,
wishing to appear at her best one Sunday for one of her lovers,
washed out her fissure and, slipping the penultimate finger in no
uncertain place, sniffed:

"Ha, my darling!" she cried. "So you're determined to smell.
There, there, I'll rinse you with blue water."

No sooner said than done; she plunged her rustic *crypsimen*
back into the ford, which prevented dilation.

Our intriguer fancied himself the handsomest lad in the world,
yet above all his drugs and salves, himself was most malodorous.
Lightly clad, though the cold chafed like a hempen collar, he sal-
lied forth and reached the Rue de l'Hirondelle in short order.
Here he had to wait for some time. At last, just as it grew dark
and as he was beginning to think he had been fooled, the maid
opened the door and the good husband slipped gleefully into the
King's house. Then the maid locked him carefully in a closet
close to his wife's bed. Gazing through the chinks, he saw her in
all her beauty, as she disrobed in front of the fire, and then put
on a thin skirmish-gown through which her charms were wholly
visible. Believing herself alone with her servant, she was making
the jests women will as they undress.

"Am I not worth twenty thousand crowns this evening? And
this—surely a Château de Brie is not too great a price for it?"

As she spoke, she gently raised two white outposts, firm as ram-
parts and well able to sustain many assaults, for, though they
had been furiously attacked, they had never yet softened.

"My shoulders alone are worth a kingdom," she said. "I defy
the King to match them! But heavens! I am beginning to tire of
this existence! It is no pleasure to be forever working."

The little maid smiled; her loved mistress continued:

"Upon my word, I should like to see you in my place."

The maid laughed outright as:

"Sh, my lady!" she warned. "He is there!"

"Who?"

"Your husband."

"Which one?"

"The real one."

"Hush!" said her mistress.

And the maid told her the whole story, intending to keep her favor and the twelve thousand crowns as well.

"Oh, la! I'll give him his money's worth," the advocate's wife said. "I'll give him time to cool down. If he has a taste of me,

may I lose my beauty, may I turn as ugly as a beggar monk's brat! You get into bed in my place; you will thus be earning your twelve thousand crowns. Tell him to decamp early in the morning, so that I may not learn the trick you played on me. Just before daybreak, I will come in and lie beside him."

The luckless husband was shivering with cold; his teeth chattered like castanets. As the maid came to the closet, pretending to fetch some linen, she whispered:

"Don't let your desire cool. Madame is making grand preparations tonight; you will be well served. Do your worst, but remember: not a sound, or I am ruined."

At last, when the good husband was chilled to the bone, the lights were extinguished. The servant called softly through the curtains to His Majesty's sweetheart that her nobleman was there.

Then she jumped into the bed, while her beautiful mistress went out, as though she were the maid. The lawyer emerged from his icy retreat and plunging deep under the warm covers:

"Ah," he said to himself. "How good this is!"

Good it was. The maid gave him more than his money's worth; he experienced the difference between the full profusions of royal households and the niggardly output of townsmen's wives. The maid, dying with laughter, played her part marvelously well, regaling the trickster with most attractive cries, writhing, twisting, shivering, jerking spasmodically like a carp out of water, and heaving sighs of "Ah! ah!" which spared her from talking. So many and fervid were her requests and so amply were they requited by the lawyer that when he finally fell off to sleep he was like an empty pocket. But just before leaving off, the lover wished to possess a keepsake of his sweet night of love. Aided by a convulsion, he plucked out some of his partner's hair (where from, I do not know, for I was not there) and gripped in the hollow of his hand this precious token of the lovely creature's ardent virtue.

Towards morning, when the cock crew, the King's sweetheart slipped in beside her husband, and pretended to sleep. Then the chambermaid tapped the happy man lightly on the brow and whispered:

"It is time to go. Put on your breeches and hop it! It's daylight."

The good man, deeply grieved to lose his treasure, wished to see the source of his vanished happiness.

"Oh, oh!" he said, proceeding to collate the evidence, "I have blond, here, and there it's dark!"

"What have you done?" the maid exclaimed. "Madame will discover the theft!"

"Ay, but look!"

"Ah!" she answered with a contemptuous air. "You, who know everything: don't you realize that what is uprooted perishes and loses its color?"

With which she burst into fits of laughter and threw him out of the house.

The story leaked out and became common property. The luckless advocate (his name was Féron) died of mortification since he and he alone had not had his wife, while she, who was accordingly called La Belle Féronnière, married a young nobleman, the Count of Buzançois, after she left the King.

And in her old age, she would tell the story of this excellent trick, and laugh as she did so, explaining that she had never been able to stand the rascal's smell.

Which teaches us not to attach ourselves more than we must to wives who refuse to wear our yoke.

The Devil's Heir

HERE was once a good old canon of Notre Dame, in Paris, who lived in a fine house of his own, close to St. Pierre aux Bœufs in the Parvis. He had come to Paris a simple priest, poor as a church mouse, naked as a dagger unsheathed. But he happened to be handsome, abundantly equipped by nature with everything: a man, if you will, of powerful parts, so robustly constituted that he could without the slightest strain perform the work of several men, if necessary. He therefore devoted himself very thoroughly to the confessing of ladies, giving a kindly absolution to the melancholy, a drachm of his balm to the sickly, and some sort of tidbit to all his charges. So renowned were his discretion, his benevolence and other ecclesiastical qualities that he had customers even at Court.

Now in order to lull the jealousy of the church authorities, of husbands and of sundry others and to cast a cloak of sanctity over his pleasurable and gainful practises, the Maréchale Desquerdes gave him a bone of St. Victor's—a remarkable member which carried all the Canon's miracles to completion. To the curious, it was said: "He has a bone which will cure everything." Nor could any one offer the slightest objection; was it not most unseemly to regard a holy relic with suspicion? Beneath the shade of his cassock, our worthy priest enjoyed the best of reputations, that of a man valiant in arms. The fellow lived like a king; he struck coin with his sprinkler and turned holy water into good wine. Moreover his name lay snugly bedded among all the *et ceteras* of the notaries in the wills or in caudicils (which certain people erroneously spell codicils, for the word is derived from *cauda*, a tail, as if to say the tail of the legacy). Doubtless he could have become an archbishop, had he said jokingly: "I would like to put on a mitre, 'twould keep my head warmer!" But out of all the benefices offered him, he chose a mere canonry; hanging on to the profits of the confessional.

There came a day, however, when the lusty Canon grew weak in the loins; he was all of sixty-eight years of age and had worn down many a confessional. Then, calling all his good works to mind, he decided that he might at last abandon his apostolic labors, especially as he possessed about one hundred thousand crowns, earned at the sweat of his body. From that day forward, he confessed only ladies of lofty lineage, and very well he did it too. Court people said that, despite the efforts of the best young clerics, there was still none like the Canon of St. Pierre aux Bœufs to give the soul of a lady of condition a proper whitewashing. In course of time, by force of nature, the Canon became a noble nonagenarian, very snowy about the head, with trembling hands but still square as a tower. Having spat so much without hawking, now he hawked without being able to spit. He who had so often risen for humanity no longer rose from his chair. He drank dry, though, ate his fill and spoke never a word, thus preserving the appearance of a canon of Notre Dame.

Everyone witnessed the immobility of our Canon, everyone heard the stories of his evil life which, for some time, had circulated among the always ignorant common people, everyone observed his mute seclusion, his flourishing health, his young old age and other things too lengthy to cite. Consequently, certain people, seeking to cry miracle and to harm our holy religion, went about saying that the true Canon had died long since and that for over fifty years the Devil had inhabited the old priest's body. For their part, his fair customers of other days were inclined to agree. Surely none but the Devil could, by his great heat, have supplied the hermetic distillations they recalled obtaining from him on demand? Besides, he had a bit of the devil in his eye, and elsewhere, too: "Le diable au corps" they phrased it. But then, since they had undoubtedly burned and eradicated this devil, since he would not have stirred for a queen of twenty, the well-disposed, those not wanting in sense and those who argued everything out (they would have found lice in a bald head!) reasoned otherwise. Why, they demanded, should the Devil

choose to assume a Canon's form? Why frequent the church of
Notre Dame at canonical hours? Why venture so far as to sniff
incense, to lap up holy water, to do a thousand and one other
things?

To these heretical pronouncements, some replied that doubtless the Devil sought conversion; others that he dwelled in the
shape of a canon to mock at his three nephews and heirs by making them wait for their inheritance until themselves died. It was
an ample succession; nor did the nephews fail to visit him daily
to make sure if the good man's eyes were still open. Invariably
they found his gaze clear, bright and beady as a basilisk's—which
pleased them greatly for they loved their uncle very much (in
words!).

In this connection, one old woman related a story which proved
beyond doubt that Canon and Devil were one. Two nephews, the
Proctor and the Captain, were accompanying him home from
supper at the Penitentiar's. In the dark—they had neither torch
nor lantern—they caused him by accident to tumble over a pile
of stones heaped up to raise a statue to St. Christopher. At first,
in falling, the old man had struck sparks; then, amid the shouts
of his loving nephews and by the light of the torches they brought
from the old woman's house, he was found standing up as straight
as a tenpin, gay as a stone-falcon and lively as a shuttle. It was
the Penitentiar's mellow wine, he explained, that gave him the
courage to sustain this shock. His bones, he added, were exceedingly hard and had, in the past, withstood ruder assaults. The
nephews, believing him dead, were vastly astonished. They realized that Time would not easily succeed in dispatching their
uncle, if stones proved useless at that job. When they called him
their good uncle they were not wrong, for he was indeed of good
stuff.

Other evil tongues whispered that the Canon had found so
many stones in his path that he stayed at home in order not to be
ill of the stone and that the fear of still worse was the cause of his
seclusion. From amid all these sayings and rumors, the fact remains that the old Canon, Devil or not, kept to his house, refused
to die and had three heirs with whom he lived as he lived with
his sciatica, lumbagos and other concomitants of human life.

There were, as we have said, three heirs. One was the most

maleficent soldier ever born of the womb of woman; and a great wrenching he must have given his mother in breaking his egg, for he emerged with teeth and whiskers. He ate twofold, for the present and for the future, keeping wenches whose bonnets he paid for, inheriting from his uncle the continuance, power and good use of what so often proves serviceable. In the fiercest battles, he sought to deal blows without receiving them, which is and always will be the sole problem in warfare; but he never spared himself when it came to fighting. Bravery was his sole virtue. As Captain of a company of Lancers, he was highly esteemed by the Duke of Burgundy, who never troubled very much about what his soldiers did off the field. This nephew of the Devil was called Captain Cochegrue. Creditors, bores, townsmen and others whose pockets he slit, called him Maucinge—Ape of Evil—because he was both mischievous and strong. To crown his charming qualities, his back was somewhat marred by the blemish of a hump. Nor was it prudent to consider it as a vantage point to view the horizon from. He would have summarily gutted the prospective climber.

The second nephew had studied the law; through his uncle's influence he had become a worthy proctor. He pleaded at the law courts, attending to the business of the ladies whom the Canon had been eminently successful in confessing. This nephew was called Pille-Grue—Filch-Grue—a jest upon his surname Cochegrue. Pille-Grue was spare of body; he seemed to effuse a very chill water; he was pale; his physiognomy recalled the muzzle of a polecat. Still, he was undoubtedly worth a copper more than his brother the Captain: he did bear his uncle a mite of affection. But for the last two years or so, his heart had cracked a little; drop by drop, his gratitude had oozed out. Occasionally, in damp weather, he liked to put himself in his uncle's shoes and to anticipate the pressing of the Canon's juicy vintage.

Pille-Grue and his soldier brother considered their own share of the inheritance extremely modest. Rightfully, in law, fact, justice, nature and reality, they had to cede as much as one-third of the entire legacy to a needy cousin, the son of the Canon's other sister. This third nephew, who was certainly not in his uncle's good books, remained in the country, near Nanterre where he was a shepherd.

At his cousins' advice this herder of beasts, a typical peasant, came to town. If he stayed with the uncle, his clumsiness, boorishness and lack of understanding, his ignorance and his asinine tricks, they hoped, would disgust the legator and have him kicked out of his will. Poor Chiquon (as the shepherd was named) had been living in town almost a month; he had found it both pleasanter and more profitable to mind an abbé than to look after sheep. He made himself the Canon's dog, his slave, the staff of his old age. "God keep you!" he would exclaim dutifully when the cleric broke wind, and "God bless you!" when he sneezed, and "God guard you!" when he belched. If he was not off to see if it rained or where the cat was, he was beside his uncle, listening to him in silence, or, when opportune, speaking and suffering the old man to cough in his face and admiring him as the noblest canon there ever was in the world. All of this he did heartily and in the best of faith, unaware that he was licking him as bitches do their puppies; while the uncle, who required no lessons to know which side his bread was buttered on, snubbed poor Chiquon unmercifully. He had the lad spinning about like a die; he was forever calling him and telling the two cousins how this wretched numbskull of a Chiquon would be the death of him. Hearing this, Chiquon would strive to do better, racking his brains in order to serve him. But since he had a backside shaped like a brace of pumpkins, shoulders as broad as a barn, and limbs like a bear, and withal was about as spry as an elephant, he was rather more like Old Silenus than like a gentle Zephyr. Obviously the poor shepherd, utterly simple as he was, could not shape himself anew; he necessarily remained awkward and fat, waiting for his inheritance to reduce his flesh.

One evening the Canon, discoursing upon the Devil, expatiated upon the awful agonies, tortures and tribulations, which God prepares for the damned. His audience, our good Chiquon, eyes agape like an open oven, would not credit a word of it.

"What?" the Canon exclaimed. "Are you not a Christian?"

"Oh, ay!" Chiquon answered. "Certainly I am."

"Well then, there is a Paradise for the good. Must there not be a Hell for the evil?"

"Certainly, Master Canon; but the Devil's no use. If you had

a rascal turnin' all downside-up hereabouts, you'd throw him
out, would you not?"

"Yes, Chiquon. . . ."

"Well then, my dear nuncle, God would be right foolish makin'
this world so curious and all, and leavin' a hellion in it whose
special job it is to destroy the whole works! Lawks! If God there

be, I'll acknowledge no Devil, you may take my word for it. I'd
dearly like to see the Devil, too. Ha! it's not *I* am afraid of his
claws."

"Alas! had I your faith, I would not worry about my youthful
days, when I heard confession a good ten times between cock-
crow and cockshut!"

"Heh, but keep on confessin', Master Canon, I warrant your
confessions will be accounted a precious service on high."

"Dear, dear! Is that true?"

"Ay, Master Canon."

"You do not tremble, Chiquon, to deny the Devil?"

"I mind him no more than I mind a sheaf of corn!"

"You will come to grief if you persist in that doctrine!"

"No fear, Master Canon. God will protect me from the Devil for I think Him wiser and cleverer than the doctors make Him out."

Just then, Chiquon's cousins came in. From the Canon's tones, they realized that his abuse of the shepherd was simply a trick to disguise the affection he bore him. They stared at each other wide-eyed. Then seeing their uncle laugh:

"If you should happen to make a will," they asked, "whom would you leave the house to?"

"Chiquon!"

"And the Rue St. Denis quit-rent?"

"Chiquon!"

"And the fief of Ville-Parisis?"

"Chiquon!"

"But uncle," the Captain boomed, "shall everything fall to Chiquon?"

"No," the Canon answered with a smile, "because no matter how strictly I draw up my will, my inheritance will fall to the cleverest of you three. I am so near to the future that I see your destinies clearly."

As he spoke, the wily Canon darted as expressive a glance at Chiquon as a trollop darts at a love-bird to attract him into her burrow. The gleam in this fiery glance was sufficient to enlighten the shepherd. From that moment, the shadows rose from his benighted understanding; he began to listen with both ears, his brain opened out like a virgin the day after her marriage. The Proctor and the Captain, taking the Canon's words as gospel truth, bowed themselves out and left, thoroughly perplexed at the absurd designs of their uncle.

"What do you think of Chiquon?" said Pille-Grue to Maucinge.

"I'm thinking . . . I'm thinking," the soldier growled, "that I'm thinking I shall lie in wait in the Rue de Jérusalem and send his head rolling at his feet. He can stick it on again, if he likes.''

"Steady!" said the Proctor. "You have a way of wounding that is yours alone. People would recognize it and say: 'Cochegrue did it!' For my part, I was thinking of asking him to dinner. Afterwards, we could play the sack game—you know, putting our heads in a sack, as they do at Court, to see who can walk best. Well, we would sew him up, drop him into the Seine and invite him to swim. . . ."

"We must let the plan ripen!" the soldier put in.

"Oh, it's ripe enough!" the advocate replied. "Our cousin gone to the devil, the legacy is ours!"

"I'm quite willing," the bully said, "but we must go cheek by jowl and move together like a man's two legs. For if you are fine as silk, I am strong as steel, and a dagger's every bit as good as a skein—you hear that, my good brother. . . ."

"Ay," said the advocate, "the cause is heard. Now which shall it be: thread or iron?"

"God's belly, is it a king we have to do away with? Must we bandy so many words for a mere lout of a shepherd? Come! twenty thousand francs of the legacy to the first man who cuts him off! I'll cheerfully tell him: 'Pick your head up, my lad!' "

"And I: 'Swim, friend,' " the advocate cried, his face slit in laughter like a doublet.

Then they went off to supper, the Captain to his wench, the Proctor to a goldsmith's whose wife was his mistress.

Who was astonished? Chiquon! Although his cousins had walked in the Parvis and spoken to each other as people speak when they pray to God in church, the luckless shepherd heard them plotting his death. This set him wondering whether words have a way of rising or whether his ears had reached down.

"Do you hear, Master Canon?"

"Ay," answered the other. "I hear the logs crackling in the fireplace."

"Ho, ho!" Chiquon declared. "I may not believe in the Devil but I do believe in St. Michael, my guardian angel. I'm off, for he's callin' me!"

"Go, my child," said the Canon, "and take care you do not

get wet or have your head chopped off—for I seem to hear rain
and the beggars in the street are not always the most dangerous
beggars. . . ."

At these words, Chiquon, amazed, stared up: the Canon wore
a gay air, his eyes were twinkling, and his feet well crooked. But
as Chiquon had to forestall the death which menaced him, he
reflected that he would always find time to admire the Canon or
to pare his nails. So he trotted quickly down the streets, like a
woman pattering off to her pleasure.

His cousins, who had no presumption of the divinatory science which takes shepherds by storm, held him of no account.
They had often discussed their secret goings-on before him.

One evening, to amuse the Canon, Pille-Grue had told him
about his mistress, the goldsmith's wife, and described how she
tricked the husband upon whom he, Pille-Grue, had adjusted
certain horns, as handsomely carved, burnished, scrolled and
historiated as a king's salt-cellars. To hear the fellow, the good
lady had a whole arsenal of pleasantries: she was dynamite on
the uptake; she dispatched an embrace while her husband, blissfully unconscious, was climbing the stairs; she devoured the
commodity as she might down a strawberry; she dreamed only
of wantoning; she was invariably sportive and skittish. Gay, too,
as an honest woman who wants for nothing; contenting her good
husband, who adored her as passionately as he did his gullet;
subtle as a perfume; such a paragon, in fine, that she had managed to conduct her household and love affairs simultaneously
for five years without impairing her reputation as a virtuous
woman. She enjoyed her husband's confidence, the keys of his
house, his purse and all that was his.

"And when, then, do you play upon love's sweet flute?"
asked the Canon.

"Every evening. Very often I stay all night."

"How is that?" the Canon asked in surprise.

"This is how I manage. In the room next door there is a
clothes-chest; I climb into it. When her good husband comes
home from his crony's—the draper's—my mistress pleads a slight
illness, leaves him lying in bed alone, and comes to the room
with the chest. Here she obtains a radical cure for her ailment.
Next morning, when my goldsmith is at his forge, I decamp. As

the house has one exit on to the bridge and another into the street, I use the door where the husband isn't. There is always the excuse of his lawsuits, which I keep alive and happy, for where would I be if they ended? An income-bearing cuckoldry it is, too; the petty expenses and straight fees of litigation cost

him more than the horses in his stable. He likes me very much, as any good husbandman cuckold should love the lad who helps him dibble and dabble, plant, cultivate and harrow the natural garden of Venus. He will do nothing without me."

As Chiquon recalled these goings-on, a great light, issuing

from his sense of danger, burst over him. He acted upon such counsel as self-preservation inspires in all animals to a degree sufficient to allow them to reach the end of their life-span. He hotfoot for the Rue de la Calandre, where he supposed the goldsmith to be supping with his crony's wife. He knocked, was challenged through the little grill in the door, answered that he was the bearer of state secrets and was admitted into the draper's house. Coming straight to the point, he asked the happy goldsmith to get up from table, drew him into a corner, and said:

"If one of your neighbors planted a copse of horns on your forehead and someone delivered him to you, bound hand and foot, would you toss him into the river?"

"Gladly!" said the goldsmith. "But if you're playing the fool with me, I'll give you a sound thrashing."

"Come, come!" Chiquon went on. "I'm a friend of yours; I've come to tell you that for every time you've been entertainin' the draper's wife in your way, your own wife has been entertainin' Lawyer Pille-Grue, in hers. If you care to return to your forge, you'll find it red-hot. When you get there, the gentleman who's so kindly sweepin' and policin' you know what, will hide in the big clothes-chest. Now you make believe that I want to buy that chest from you; I shall be on the bridge with a cart, awaitin' your orders."

The goldsmith picked up his cloak and his hood, quitted his crony without so much as a word, and dashed for his hole like a poisoned rat. He arrived, knocked; the door was opened, he entered, clambered up the stairs at top speed, found two covers laid, heard the lid of the chest bang shut, saw his wife emerging from the love-chamber, and:

"My dear," he said, "there are two covers laid here!"

"Well, sweet, are we not two?"

"No," he insisted, "there are three of us."

"Is your crony coming?" she asked looking straight at the stairs with perfect innocence.

"No, I mean the crony in the chest."

"What chest?" she demanded. "Are you in your right mind? Where do you see a chest? Do people put cronies in chests? Am I the sort of woman to keep chests full of cronies? Since when have cronies stayed in chests? Are you come home mad to be mixing your chests with your cronies? The only crony I know is Master Corneille, the draper; the only chest, the one we keep our clothes in."

"Hm, my good wife!" the goldsmith said, "there's a low, evil young fellow who came specially to inform me not only that you allowed our lawyer to bestride you but that he was hidden in your chest."

"I?" she exclaimed. "Why, I simply can't stomach these pettifoggers! Everything they do is wrong."

"There, there! Never mind, my love," the goldsmith went on. "I know you for the good woman you are; I wouldn't fall out with you over a wretched chest. The man who warned me is a boxmaker; I shall sell him the cursed thing. Heaven knows, I never wish to set eyes upon it again. As for him, he shall sell me two instead—two fine, small ones, with no room for even a child. That is how we shall nip these jealous harpies' gossip in the bud!"

"I am very glad!" she answered. "I don't care very much for that chest and there happens to be nothing inside. You can easily have it carted away tomorrow morning, the sooner the better. Devil take the chest, anyhow! Shall we sup?"

"No, no," he said, "I shall sup more heartily when I get rid of that chest."

"It's quite clear that it will be easier to get the chest out of that room than out of your head."

"Ho, there, hallo!" the husband cried, summoning his smiths and apprentices. "Come down here!"

His men appeared in the twinkling of an eye. The master gave brief orders as to its handling, and, a moment later, the amatory article of furniture was conveyed across the room. As it passed, the advocate suddenly found his feet high in the air—an unwonted position which made him tumble over a little.

"Go ahead, go ahead," urged the goldsmith's wife. "It's the lid banging."

"No, my love, it's the feet!"

Without further opposition, the chest rolled gently down the stairs.

"Ho there, carter!" cried the goldsmith. Chiquon drove up, whistling his mules; the good apprentices lifted the litigious chest on to the cart.

"Hi! hi!" cried the advocate.

"Master, the chest is talking!" said an apprentice.

"In what language?" asked the goldsmith, as he dealt him a swift kick between two agreeable appendages which by good fortune are not fashioned of glass. The apprentice fell back on a stair and pursued his research into the linguistics of chests no further. Shepherd and goldsmith conveyed the whole burden to the water's edge, without paying the slightest attention to the high eloquence emerging from the spouting wood. Then, having tied some stones to it, the goldsmith threw it into the Seine.

"Swim, friend!" cried the shepherd in a voice derisive enough to suit the occasion as the chest plopped into the water like a duck.

This accomplished, Chiquon pursued his way along the quay, as far as the Rue St. Landry, hard by the cloisters of Notre Dame. There he stopped before a house, identified it by its door and knocked loudly:

"Open!" he cried. "Open in the King's name."

At this challenge, an old man (none other than the famous Lombard Versoris) ran to the door.

"What is the matter?" he called.

"The Provost sent me to warn you!" Chiquon explained. "Be sure to keep a good watch tonight. For his own part, he will have his archers at hand. The hunchback who robbed you has come back. Keep under arms; the fellow is as likely to lift what's left, as not!"

Having given this warning, Chiquon took to his heels, racing off to the Rue des Marmousets, where Captain Cochegrue was banqueting with La Pâquerette, the prettiest wanton of the day and by far the most fetching in perversity, as all the filles de joie agreed. Her glance was keen and sharp as a dagger, her appearance so titillating to the sight that she would have set all Paradise arutting. To cap these qualities, she was as bold as a woman with no other virtue left save her insolence.

Poor Chiquon was in a quandary as he made for the Marmousets quarter. Would he manage to discover Pâquerette's lodgings? And, if he did, would he not find the love-birds abed? Fortunately, a good angel arranged matters to his complete satisfaction. As he turned down the Rue des Marmousets, he noticed lights at all the windows, then heads in nightcaps protruding, while the good trollops and trulls, the housewives, husbands and damsels of the quarter, all of them just risen from their beds, looked at one another as though a robber were being led by torchlight to the gallows.

"What on earth is goin' on?" Chiquon asked a townsman who had rushed to his door, halbert in hand.

"Oh, nothing much!" the worthy man answered. "We thought it was the Armagnacs descending upon the town. But it's only Maucinge beating Pâquerette."

"Where?" asked the shepherd.

"Yonder, you see? That handsome house there . . . with the pillars, and the mouths of flying frogs so prettily engraved over them. . . . Don't you hear the varlets and maids?"

Indeed the air was filled with cries of "Murder!" "Help!" "This way!" "Quick!" and from within, the echo of a rain of blows, then the gruff voice of Maucinge:

"Death to the strumpet! Ha, you're singing now, eh, slut? You want money, eh? Golden crowns? I'll crown you! Take that!"

And Pâquerette moaning:

"Ow! Ow! I'm dying! Ouch! Help! Help! Help! O-o-o-oh!"

Next came the great thwack of a swordblow, then a heavy thud as the comely wench's slight body fell to the floor. A great silence followed. After all the lights were extinguished, servants, maids, guests and others went indoors again, with our shepherd, arriving in the nick of time, among them. But at the sight of the broken glassware littering the room, the tapestries slashed, the tablecloth and all the dishes on the floor, everybody stood back.

Chiquon, with the high courage of a man who has but one end in view, threw open the door to Pâquerette's handsome bed-chamber. He found her all undone, her hair dishevelled, her neck twisted, lying lifeless on a bloody rug. Beside her stood Maucinge, dazed, murmuring in a tone considerably lower and perplexed as to what note to pitch the rest of his anthem on.

"Come, my little Pâquerette, don't play dead! Come along; let me patch you up. Ah, my sly fox, dead or alive, you look so pretty lying there in your blood that I've got to hug you!"

The cunning soldier picked her up and tossed her on the bed, where she fell in a lump, stiff as a varlet fresh-hung. At once, he realized it was time he took himself and his hump out of it; but, crafty as ever, before decamping:

"Poor Pâquerette!" he said. "How could I murder such a good girl, a girl I loved so dearly! Alas! I have killed her; the thing is crystal clear, for were she alive, her sweet pap would never droop down like that! Ah, Lord, 'tis like a coin at the bottom of a wallet."

At which Pâquerette cocked her eye and turned her head slightly to examine her flesh. It was white and firm. Then she celebrated her return to life by a resounding smack as she boxed the Captain's ears.

"This will teach you to malign the dead!" she said with a smile.

"But why was he killin' you, cousin!" the shepherd asked.

"Why? Tomorrow the bailiffs are coming to seize everything here! He has no more money than decency; he reproached me because I wished to gratify a handsome lord who can save me from the arm of the law."

"Pâquerette, I'll break every bone in your body!"

"Come, come!" Chiquon said soothingly, as Maucinge recognized him. "Is that what all the trouble's about? Well, my good friend, I'm bringin' you all the money you want."

"You?" asked the Captain, stunned. "Where from?"

"Come here; let me whisper in your ear. Tell me: if thirty thousand crowns were lyin' about at night under a pear tree, you'd stoop to pick them up, eh? You wouldn't let them go to waste, eh?"

"Chiquon, you die like a dog if you are making mock of me or I kiss you wherever you like if you bring me face to face with thirty thousand crowns. And I don't care if I have to kill three townsmen on the quay corner."

"You won't kill even a fly! Here is how things stand. I have a sweetheart—oh, in all virtue! She's the servant of that Lombard who lives in the Cité, near our good nuncle's. I've just heard on certain authority that the dear man left for the country this mornin'. And he buried a whole bushel of gold under a pear tree in his garden. He thought only the angels saw him, but not so! The wench happened to have a bad toothache; so she was takin' the air at her garret window. She spied the old curmudgeon un-intentionally and coyly told me all about it. If you swear to give me a good share, I will lend you my shoulders: you can climb to the top of the wall and skin down the pear tree hard by it. Well, how's that, eh? Now will you say I'm a lout and a beast?"

"Faith, no, you are a right loyal cousin and an honest man. If ever you want some enemy put out of circulation, call on me—I would kill even a friend of mine for your sake. I, your cousin now? No, not your cousin, your brother! Ho there, my love," Maucinge called to Pâquerette, "draw up the tables. And wipe your blood away—it is mine, I pay for it and I shall requite you a hundredfold in my own. Have them fetch some of the best wine in the cellar; calm our frightened birds again; pull down your skirts; and laugh—I insist! Look to the food, too, and let us resume our evening prayers where we left off; tomorrow I shall make you braver than a queen. This is my cousin whom I wish to regale even if I have to turn the whole house out of the windows to do so; we will find everything in the cellar again tomorrow. Up and at 'em! Fall to on the hams!"

Thus in less time than it takes a priest to say his *Dominus vobiscum,* the whole rookery passed from tears to laughter as it had previously passed from laughter to tears. It is only in such strumpets' houses that love goes cheek by jowl with dagger thrusts and that tempests of joy rage between four walls. But these are things which the prim ladies with high-necked dresses cannot understand.

Captain Cochegrue was as gay as a hundred schoolboys when class lets out; he kept urging his good cousin to drink plentifully; while Chiquon, wolfing everything down country-fashion, pretended to be drunk and spluttered out a host of inanities —how he would buy the whole of Paris on the morrow, how he would lend the King one hundred thousand crowns, how he would wallow in gold. He talked such nonsense that the Captain, believing him quite witless and fearing an untoward avowal, led him outside. Cochegrue had not the slightest intention of dividing the spoils; instead, when the time came, he meant to rip Chiquon up and find out if there was not a sponge secreted in his stomach for the shepherd had just downed a full quart of good Surennes wine.

They walked toward the Cité, discussing a myriad theological topics, which got very much muddled. Presently they crept stealthily along the garden wall, with only it between them and the Lombard's crowns. Captain Cochegrue, using Chiquon's

broad shoulders as a springboard, leaped at the pear tree like a veteran of many sieges; but Versoris, who lay in wait, struck at his neck and drew back his sword so smartly that, with the third blow, Cochegrue's head fell to the ground. But not before he had heard the shepherd's voice, calling:

"Pick your head up, my lad!"

Thereupon the generous Chiquon, in whose person virtue was duly rewarded, believed it wise to return home to the good Canon, the distribution of whose inheritance was, by the grace of God, methodically simplified. He sped hotfoot to the Rue St. Pierre aux Bœufs. Very soon he was sleeping as soundly as a newborn babe, without the slightest idea about what first cousin —or second, for that matter—meant.

On the morrow, he rose, as shepherds do, with the sun, and went to his uncle's room to ascertain whether he were spitting white, whether he coughed—and had he slept well? But the old chamberwoman informed him that, hearing the Matins bells ring—it was the day of St. Maurice, first patron of Notre Dame —the Canon had gone in reverence to the Cathedral, where all the Chapter were to breakfast with the Bishop of Paris.

"Is Master Canon out of his mind to be goin' out like that," Chiquon exclaimed, "gettin' his feet wet and catchin' cold? I shall light a fine, warm fire to thaw him out when he comes back."

So he went to his uncle's study, where to his astonishment, he saw the Canon sitting in his armchair.

"Ho, ho! What on earth did that witless Buyrette mean? I knew you were too well advised to be sittin' up in your stall at this hour of the day!"

But the Canon answered never a word. The shepherd—like all observers, a man of hidden sense—was not unaware that old men occasionally have curious crotchets, that they hold converse with the essence of occult things and mumble to themselves quite irrelevantly. Out of deep respect for the Canon's abstruse meditations, he moved off to sit down in silence some distance away, waiting until these reveries came to an end. Glancing at him, Chiquon noticed the Canon's toenails; they looked long enough to pierce through the soft leather of his slippers. Then, as he considered his dear uncle's feet more attentively, he was amazed to see the flesh of his legs so crimson that it reddened his hose, under which he was apparently ablaze.

"So he is dead then?" Chiquon mused.

At the same moment, the door opened. Chiquon looked up. There stood the Canon, returned from Mass, his nose frozen.

"Ho, ho!" Chiquon cried. "Are you out of your senses, nuncle?

Kindly take notice that you should not be standin' at the door—for not three seconds ago you were sittin' in your armchair by the fire. And there cannot possibly be two canons like you in the world?"

"Ah, Chiquon, time was when I would gladly have been in two places at once. But that does not lie in man's power: he would be too happy. Are you seeing double? I am alone here."

Then Chiquon turned his head toward the armchair and saw that it was empty. Dumbfounded, as you may imagine, he walked up to it. On the floor was a tiny heap of cinders, which emitted an odor of sulphur.

"Ah!" he exclaimed breathlessly. "I perceive that the Devil treated me like a gentleman. I shall pray God for him."

Naïvely, then, he told the Canon how the Devil had amused himself by playing at Providence and had helped him to get decently rid of his wicked cousins. This the good Canon admired much and conceived easily for he still enjoyed a fund of sound sense and he had often observed things which were distinctly to the Devil's advantage. So the worthy old cleric remarked that invariably as much good lay in evil as evil in good and that consequently a man should not worry too much about the next world—a grave heresy which many a council has put right.

Thus it was the Chiquons grew rich and thus nowadays, through their grandfather's fortune, the present family was able to help in the building of the Pont St. Michel, a bridge where, under the angel, the Devil cuts a fine figure, in memory of this adventure, now consigned to the chronicles of true history.

The Merry Jests of King Louis the Eleventh

KING LOUIS THE ELEVENTH was a jovial fellow, much given to joking. Save where the cares of kingship or the concerns of religion interfered, he was fond of living high. He was a hunter, too, stalking bird of a very human Paradise as often as rabbits and other royal game. The sorry scribblers who have made him out a hypocrite simply prove that they never knew him. As a loyal friend, an accomplished fowler and a merry blade, our monarch had not his match.

He it was who, when in rare form one day, averred that four things in life are excellent and opportune: to void hot, to drink cool, to rise hard and to swallow soft. Certain persons have vituperated against him for consorting with filthy sluts. This is utter nonsense: his sweethearts, one of whom was legitimatized, all came from great houses and all presided over sizy establishments. Louis did not believe in extravagance and waste; he closed his fist over the solid. So because certain ogres of the common wealth found no crumbs to pick up from his floor, they have slandered him. But the genuine fanciers of truth know that he was a very good sort in private life, and more, a thoroughly attractive person. If he had his friends decapitated or otherwise punished (which he did with no sparing hand) it was only after they had grossly deceived him. His vengeance was invariably justice. Only in the writings of our friend Verville have I seen an instance where this worthy sovereign erred. Obviously, once does not make a habit, and even here greater blame attaches to his crony Tristan than to the King. This is the story as Verville relates it; personally I suspect our chronicler of jesting. I reproduce his account because certain readers do not know my noble countryman's exquisite work. But I abridge, and I offer it in its substance only. As scholars know, the details are ampler by far.

Louis XI had given the Abbey of Turpenay (mentioned in the tale of *The Fair Imperia*) to a gentleman who, since he enjoyed its revenue, also adopted its name and had people call him Monsieur de Turpenay. It happened that once when the King was at Plessis-lez-Tours, the real Abbot of Turpenay, a monk, presented himself before His Majesty, armed with a petition. He remonstrated that, canonically and monastically speaking, he was rightfully entitled to the abbey; that the usurping gentleman wronged him of his right; and that he, the Abbot, consequently called upon His Majesty to do him justice. Nodding his peruke, the King promised to give him satisfaction.

Now our monk, importunate as all hooded animals, used often to wait upon the King after the royal meal. Louis, bored with the holy water of the convent, called for his crony Tristan.

"Friend," he said, "there is a Turpenay here who offends me. Rid the world of him for me."

Tristan, taking a frock for a monk and a monk for a frock, went to the gentleman whom all the Court knew as Monsieur de Turpenay. Having accosted him, he managed to draw him aside; then, buttonholing him, gave him to understand that the King desired he should die. The wretched man sought to resist by pleading and to plead by resistance; but he could not gain the slightest hearing. He was delicately strangled between the head and the shoulders in such wise that he died. Three hours later, Tristan informed the King that he was distilled. Five days after—the space in which souls return to earth—the monk happened to come into the room where the King sat. Louis, seeing him, was much astonished. Calling Tristan, he whispered into his ear:

"You failed to do as I told you."

"Saving your Majesty, I did what you said: Turpenay is dead."

"Eh, but I meant this monk!"

"I understood the gentleman!"

"What? It is done, then?"

"Ay, Sire!"

"Very well then"—turning towards the monk—"Come here, monk!"

The monk approached.

"Kneel down," the King said.

The luckless monk was terrified. But the King went on:

"You may thank God, Who did not will that you die as I ordered. The man who took your estates has been killed instead. God has done you justice. Go, pray God for me, and do not stir from your convent."

Surely this proves the loving-kindness of King Louis the Eleventh? He might very well have had this monk—the cause of the error—hanged. As for the other gentleman, did he not die in the King's service?

So much for Verville's narrative. . . .

Another story tells of the early days of his sojourn at Plessis-lez-Tours. Out of respect for Her Majesty, King Louis was unwilling to conduct his drinking-bouts and give the inner man free play in his château—a royally delicate attention which his successors have neglected to show. He had fallen in love with a lady named Nicole Beaupertuys, who was, truth to tell, the wife of a townsman. So he dispatched her husband to the province of Ponent and placed Nicole in a house near Le Chardonneret —on the site of the Rue Quincangrogne—because it was a lonely spot, far from other habitations. Thus husband and wife were both in his service and Louis had, by La Beaupertuys, a daughter who died a nun.

This Nicole had a tongue sharper than a popinjay's; she was of noble, stately proportions, furnished with two large, full, ample cushions of nature, firm to the touch and white as an angel's wings. She was known, moreover, to be fertile in peripatetic manœuvres. With her, the same thing was never twice encountered in love, so profoundly had she investigated the lofty solutions of the science, the ways of accommodating the olives of Poissy, the network of the nerves and the occult doctrines of the breviary. All of which pleased His Majesty mightily. She was happy as a lark, forever laughing and singing; she never caused anyone the slightest sorrow. This is characteristic of women with an open free nature. They never lack an occupation, equivocal or not!

Often the King and a few merry cronies foregathered at her house; but, to avoid detection, he always arrived by night and without his suite. Being distrustful and in constant fear of ambush, he gave Nicole the most vicious dogs in his kennels—mastiffs apt to tear up a man without so much as crying 'ware. These royal dogs knew only Nicole and the King. When His Majesty came, Nicole let them loose in the garden; the door of the house being safely barred and shut tight, the King kept the keys in his pocket. Accordingly he and his friends could in perfect safety devote themselves to all manner of sport without fear of betrayal; they could roister to their hearts' content, play gustful tricks and improvise the lustiest pastimes. On such occasions, friend Tristan watched over the neighborhood. Often wenches were summoned for his cronies or odd people, suggested by Nicole's fancy or that of his guests, for his own personal amusement. Anyone else venturing to stroll along the Mail du Chardonneret was straightway challenged to produce a pass from the King, failing which he found himself swiftly strung up high enough overhead to bless passersby with a laying-on of feet! People from Tours were there to gratify the King's little fancies; he suavely recommended silence; the folk at large knew nothing of these entertainments until after his death. It was this monarch, they say, who invented the game of *Baisez mon cul,* elsewhere called K. M. R. A. Though it is not, strictly speaking, the subject of this tale, I set it down because it brings out the King's council and facetious nature.

There were three notorious misers at Tours. The first was Master Cornelius, who is sufficiently well-known; the second, Peccard by name, sold ecclesiastic giltwork, trappings and jewels; the third, who was called Marchandeau, was a very wealthy vintner. Despite their sordid avarice, the two last, natives of Touraine, sired a line of worthy people.

One evening when the King was with La Beaupertuys—he was in high good humor having drunk of the best, joked heartily and worshipped at Madame's shrine long before Vespers—he said to his crony Le Daim, to La Balue, the Cardinal, and to old Dunois, who was still as randy as a stallion:

"Come, let us have a good laugh, friends. . . . What a joke it would be to see a miser standing within reach of gold yet unable to touch it. Ho, there!" he summoned a varlet. "Go to My Lord Treasurer and bid him bring me six thousand golden crowns —at once! Next, you will go and apprehend bodily my friends Cornelius, the gilder Peccard in the Rue des Cygnes, and old Marchandeau. And you will bring them here, by order of the King!"

Then they settled down again to their drinking and to a judicious wrangle concerning the relative merits of a woman with a gamy odor and one who gloried in soap, a thin and a stout one. As the company comprised the flower of wisdom, they ruled that the best of possible women was the one a man had all to himself, like a dish of steaming mussels, at the precise moment when God sent him a good notion to impart to her. My Lord Cardinal asked which was the more precious to a lady: the first kiss or the last? To which La Beaupertuys answered that it was the last, for then she knew what she stood to gain. These sayings and

others, which have most unfortunately been lost, were interrupted by the arrival of the six thousand golden crowns—a sum
worth fully three hundred thousand francs today, so sadly has
everything decreased in value.

The King had the crowns set on a table close to the light;
they shone like the guests' eyes, which unconsciously lit up. At
which they laughed in spite of themselves. . . . They had not
long to wait for the misers: the varlet brought them in pale and
panting, except for Cornelius, who knew the King's strange
quirks.

"Look, friends," cried Louis, "look at these crowns on the
table."

Three pairs of eyes nibbled away at the golden piles; La
Beaupertuys' rarest diamond sparkled less than their thin, fishy
glances.

"This is yours," the King added.

Thereupon they not only ogled the crowns but also surveyed
each other from top to toe. Watching them, the company recognized that old baboons are more expert at pulling faces than any
other beasts. The faces of the trio turned very curious indeed,
like those of cats drinking milk or girls itching for marriage.

"There," said the King, "all this belongs to the man who puts
his hand into the gold and says '*Baisez mon cul*' to the others
three times. But if he does not look as solemn as a fly raping its
mate, if he cracks so much as a smile while he repeats the jest,
then he must pay Madame ten crowns. Still, he may try three
times."

" 'Twill be soon won," said Cornelius, whose mouth (he was
a Dutchman) was as often compressed and solemn as Madame's
orifice was open and laughing. Bravely, he thrust his hand
among the crowns to see if they were genuine; gravely, he
picked them up. But just as he looked at the others to say civilly,
"*Baisez mon cul!*" the two misers, fearing his Dutch gravity, said
"God bless you!" as if he had sneezed. Which made everyone,
including Cornelius, laugh.

When the vintner tried to take the crowns, he felt such a tickling in his cheeks that laughter oozed through every pore in his
old scummer face like smoke escaping through the cracks of a
chimney. He could not utter a word.

Next came the gilder's turn. He was a little bit of a bantering fellow, his lips squeezed as tightly as the neck of a man hanged. He seized a handful of the crowns, looked at the others, and said with a jeering air:

"*Baisez mon cul!*"

"Is it dirty?" asked the vintner.

"You may look and see," the gilder answered gravely.

Now the King began to tremble for his crowns, as Peccard repeated the phrase without laughing; he was about to speak the sacramental words for the third time when La Beaupertuys made an affirmative gesture. This put him out of countenance; his mouth burst into fragments like a genuine maidenhead.

"How did you manage," Dunois asked, "to keep a straight face before six thousand crowns?"

"Ah, My Lord, I thought first of one of my law-suits, which is to be tried tomorrow; then of my wife, who is a sorry plague."

The desire to win this tidy sum made them try again; His Majesty was amused for almost an hour at their facial contortions, their manœuvres, preparations, grimaces and all the monkeyshines they practised. As well try to wash a blackamoor white. For men who preferred raking in to shelling out, it was indeed a bitter pill for each to have to pay Madame one hundred crowns—the fruit of ten vain efforts.

When they were gone, Nicole said resolutely to His Majesty:

"Sire, would you have me try?"

"Lord Almighty, no!" Louis shuddered. "I can kiss you for less!"

Spoken like the thrifty man His Majesty always was. . . .

One evening, fat Cardinal La Balue was pursuing La Beaupertuys with his gallantries, proffering words and gestures somewhat beyond the measure allowed by the canons of the Church. Luckily for her, La Beaupertuys was a sly baggage, not one to be questioned with impunity on the state of her mother's chemise.

"Truly, My Lord Cardinal," she protested, "the thing our King loves is not meant to receive the holy oils."

Then came Olivier Le Daim, but she would not listen to him either; to his nonsense she replied with a threat. Should she ask the King whether he wished her to be shaved?

As the King's barber did not entreat her to keep his courting secret, she suspected that these plots were ruses practised by His Majesty. No doubt his friends had aroused his suspicions. To wreak vengeance upon the monarch was impossible. But she determined to pay out these lords, at least. She would trick them, make fools of them and amuse Louis into the bargain.

Once when they came to supper, Nicole was entertaining a lady of the city who had a favor to ask of the King. She was a person of authority; the favor sought was the royal pardon for her husband. She obtained it as a result of this adventure.

Nicole first drew King Louis aside for a moment into an antechamber and begged him to urge their guests to fall to, tooth and nail; they must drink deep and eat ravenously. She besought him to make merry and to crack jokes with them, then, when the table was cleared, to pick trifling quarrels with them, to tear all their words to pieces and to pitch into them. She would, she guaranteed, amuse him vastly by turning them inside out. Finally she adjured him, above all else, to be attentive to the lady who must, in all good faith, appear to be basking in the fragrance of his favor, for she had very sportingly taken a hand in this good joke.

"Well, gentles," said the King, as he came out again, "let us to the table! We have had a good day's hunting!"

The barber, the Cardinal, a fat bishop, the Captain of the Scots Guards and a parliamentary envoy—a judge beloved of the King—followed the two ladies into the room where you scrape the rust off your jawbones.

There they padded the mould of their doubtlets. What does the phrase mean? It means to pave the stomach, to practise the chemistry of nature, to register the various dishes, to regale your tripe, to dig your grave with your teeth, to ply the sword of Cain, to inter sauces, to nurture a cuckold; more philosophically still, it means to prepare chyme with your tusks. Now do you follow? How many words are needed to pierce the crust of your understanding?

The King did not fail to make his companions absorb this vast, noble meal. He stuffed them with peas, returned to the hotchpot, praised the prunes, extolled the fish, asking one: "Why do you not eat?", encouraging: "Let us drink Madame's health!", urging one and all:

"Gentlemen, let us taste these crayfish! Come, let us kill this bottle? You do not know how delicious this forcemeat is! And that lamprey? What? Will you let it lie on the platter? There, praise God, there is the prettiest barbel ever swam in the Loire. Come, finish up this potted liver! Game of my own hunting, that is: whoever refuses does me a personal affront."

And again:

"Drink, the King is looking the other way. Try conclusions with those preserves, they are Madame's own. Pluck off some of those grapes, they are from my private vines. Oh, do let us eat some medlars."

While inducing them to swell their principal organ, the good monarch laughed with them. They joked, disputed, spat, blew their noses and raised as merry a riot as if the King were absent. So many victuals were tucked in, so many flagons drained and stews ravaged that the guests' faces turned red as the robes of a cardinal, their doublets seemed in a fair way to burst, and from their funnels to the lining of their paunches they were as crammed with meat as Troyes sausages.

Going into the sitting-room again, they broke into a profuse sweat, began to puff and pant, inwardly cursing their gluttony. His Majesty affected a silence. They were the readier to keep quiet because all their powers were straining to decoct intestinally the huge platefuls commingled in their stomach, which wobbled and rumbled very violently. One said to himself: "I was stupid to eat of that sauce!" Another scolded himself for having absorbed a dish of eels cooked with capers. A third lamented inwardly: "Oh, oh! that forcemeat is disagreeing with me!" My Lord Cardinal, the biggest-bellied man of the lot, snorted through his nostrils like a frightened horse. He was the first of them compelled to give vent to a resounding belch; and he wished himself in Germany, where this calls for a compliment. But here, the King, hearing this gastric exclamation, glared at the Cardinal with knitted brows.

"What does this mean?" he demanded. "Am I a simple clerk?"

This filled them all with consternation, because His Majesty usually made much of a belch roundly-heaved. The rest of the guests determined to find another outlet for the vapors which already roiled in their pancreatic retorts. First, they strove to retain them, for a while, in the folds of the mesenteries, and they swelled up like revenue-collectors. Seeing this, La Beaupertuys took the monarch aside.

"It may amuse you to know," she said, "that I had Peccard the gilder make two large dolls exactly like this lady and me. We shall pretend to withdraw to the presidial throne. When these fellows are griped by the drugs I put in their goblets, they will seek to repair there, too. But they will find the place always occupied. And I wager their writhings will amuse you."

La Beaupertuys and her friend disappeared to go and turn the wheel, according to a womanly custom whose origin I shall tell elsewhere. After an honest lapse of water, La Beaupertuys came back alone, giving them to believe that she had left the lady in the laboratory of natural alchemy. Then His Majesty, singling out the Cardinal, made him rise and, holding him by the tassel of his amice, began a serious discussion of his personal affairs. To whatever the King said, La Balue replied affirmatively in order to be delivered from this favor and permitted to escape quickly, for his cellar was under water and he was on the point of losing the key to his postern. His fellow-guests were at a loss to know how to arrest the progress of the fæces, to which nature has given, even more than to water, the virtue of finding a certain level. These substances of theirs were evolving, undergoing modifications, pressing forward and straining like so many insects spoiling to issue from their cocoons and raging, tormenting, defying the higher powers, since nothing equals the ignorance and insolence of these cursed objects, importunate as all things prisoned to which we owe our liberty. They slipped at every turn like eels out of a net; no guest but required vast efforts and skill to keep from befouling himself in the King's presence. Louis took great pleasure in questioning his guests; he was delighted by the vicissitudes of their physiognomies, which reflected the sordid grimaces of their writhings.

The justiciary said to Olivier:

"I would give my very office to be out on the heath for about three-and-one-half seconds."

"Oh there is no joy on earth like a good clearage!" the other answered wistfully. "From today on, I find nothing to astonish me in the sempiternal droppings of a fly."

The Cardinal, believing the lady had obtained her receipt

from the depository, left the tassels of his badge in the King's hand, gave as violent a start as if he had forgotten to say his prayers, and made for the door.

"What ails you, My Lord Cardinal?" the King inquired.

"Please God, what ails me? It would seem that everything is on a huge scale in your house, Sire."

The Cardinal made good his escape, leaving his fellow-victims

amazed at his subtlety. Very proudly he stalked toward the ady-
tum, loosing ever so little, the while, the strings of his purse. But,
when he opened the blessed little door, he found the lady at her
functions upon the throne, like a pope undergoing consecration.
Then, reining in the plunging column, he went downstairs to
the garden. But the echo of his feet on the last steps roused the
dogs; they barked furiously and he was in great terror of having
one of his precious hemispheres bitten. Not knowing where to
deliver himself of his chemical produce, he went back to the
room shivering like a man who has been standing out of doors.

Seeing their Cardinal return, the others believed that he had
drained his natural reservoirs and cleaned out his ecclesiastical
guts. He was happy, they thought. Accordingly the barber rose
quickly, pretending to make an inventory of the tapestries and
count the rafters. He managed to reach the door before his rivals.
Relaxing his sphincter in advance, he hummed a gay tune as he
made for the retreat.

Arriving there, he was forced, like La Balue, to murmur an
apology to the eternal performer and to close the door as promptly
as he had opened it. Back he came with his placenta of collected
molecules obstructing his private channels. And one by one, the
guests withdrew in regular succession without being able to get
rid of the bulk of their sauces. Soon they were all in the King's
presence again, in as deep distress as they had been before. With
what understanding they exchanged glances! How much better
they agreed dorsally than ever they had orally! Indeed, there is
never an equivoke in the transactions of the natural parts; all is
rational there and easy to grasp; it is a science we learn at our
birth.

"Upon my word," said the Cardinal to the barber, "I believe
that lady will go on voiding till tomorrow. What does La Beaupertuys mean by inviting such a diarrhœtic here?"

"She's been working for an hour at what I could get done in a
jiffy, plague take her!" groaned Olivier Le Daim.

All the courtiers, seized with colic, were stamping up and
down to hold their importunate matters in check, when the lady
in question returned to the room. How beauteous and gracious she appeared in their eyes may be imagined; they would
willingly have kissed her in the quarter where they themselves

itched so grievously. Never had they hailed day with greater favor than they hailed this lady, the liberator of their cœliac agonies. La Balue rose; the others yielded precedence to the clergy out of honor, esteem and churchly reverence. Biding their time, they continued to pull faces at which the King laughed inwardly with Nicole, who abetted him in taking the wind out of these loose-bowelled gentlemen. The good Scots Captain, who had, more than all the others, eaten of a dish in which the cook placed laxative powders, beshitted his trousers under the impression that he was merely letting a gentle zephyr. He skulked shamefacedly in a corner, praying that the body of the case might not constitute an act of *lèse-majesté* and offend the royal nostrils. Just then My Lord Cardinal returned horrendously distraught, for he had found La Beaupertuys ensconced upon the episcopal throne. In his torment, not knowing that she was in the room, he uttered a blood-curdling gasp as he saw her sitting beside her master.

"What's this, what's this?" the King asked, staring at the Cardinal in a way to give him the fever.

"Sire," said La Balue insolently, "the affairs of purgatory are in my ministry: I needs must tell you that there is witchcraft afoot in this house."

"Ha, priestlet! You would make sport of me?" the King sneered.

At these words, the company no longer knew their breeches from the lining; in abject terror, they exploded.

"So, you dare fail in respect!" the King stormed. They grew pale. "Ho, there, Tristan my friend!" Louis raised the window suddenly. "Come up, here."

Almost at once, the Grand Provost of the Royal Household appeared. Now at bottom all these lords were mere nobodies, exalted by the favor of the King; in a colicky moment, he could crush them at will. Thus, save for My Lord Cardinal, who relied upon his cassock, Tristan found them all breathless . . . petrified. . . .

"Lead these gentlemen to the Prætorium, on the Mail, friend. After grossly overeating, they have polluted their clothing."

"What do you think of me as a jokester?" Nicole asked.

"The joke is good," the King opined, laughing, "but devilishly ordurous."

The royal answer reassured the courtiers: obviously this time His Majesty had no intention of playing with their heads.

For which they blessed Heaven. . . .

This monarch was very partial to such dirty jokes. But he was not at all a bad sort, the guests agreed, as they made free against the Mall edge with Tristan who, like a good Frenchman, kept them company and escorted them home. That is why, traditionally, ever since, the worthy citizenry of Tours has never failed to turdefy the Mail du Chardonneret. Did not the gentlemen of the Court set the fashion?

I will not abandon this great monarch without committing to paper the comical farce he perpetrated with La Godegrand. She was an old maid, sorely grieved at never having found a lid for her saucepan in the forty long years of her placid existence. So she stewed in her own juice, her yellow skin crackling at her enforced, mulish virginity. Her lodgings stood adjacent to La Beaupertuys' house, on the corner of the Rue de Jérusalem. Thus from the vantage-point of a balcony that ran parallel to the wall, anyone could easily see whatever was going on or hear whatever was being said downstairs at the spinster's. Many a time His Majesty had amused himself at the old girl's expense, while she, of course, never knew how utterly she lay exposed to his culverin.

One market day, His Majesty happened to have a young townsman of Tours hanged. The lad had violated a somewhat aged noblewoman, under the impression that she was a young maiden. To be sure, there was small harm in this: indeed, to be taken for a virgin would have redounded greatly to this lady's credit. Unfortunately, on realizing his error, the lad had not only heaped a million abominable insults upon her. Worse, he had suspected her of trickery and taken it into his head to rob her of a rare goblet of vermilion silver, in payment of his outlay on her behalf. A handsome specimen, the lad was, like a fine thoroughbred with flowing mane and tail; and the townspeople, moved by a feeling of curiosity and regret, turned out to see him swing. As may be supposed, the bonnets present at this hanging far outnumbered the hats. Very well the lad swung, too; after the fashion and custom of those hanged in that age, he died gallantly, with his lance erect, which gave rise to much talk in town. On this head, many a lady remarked that it was sheer murder not to preserve so lusty a cockerel.

"What would you say to putting this handsome corpse in La Godegrand's bed?" La Beaupertuys asked His Majesty.

"It will frighten her to death!" Louis answered.

"Oh, no, Sire, never! You know how desperately she hankers after a live man: you may be sure she would jump at a dead one! Yesterday I saw her playing the fool with a young man's cap! She put it on top of a chair and curtseyed and spoke to it—la! how you would have laughed at her mincing and mummeries."

While the quadragenarian virgin was at Vespers, His Majesty ordered his men to unhang the lad who had just finished the last scene of his tragic farce. They dressed him in a white shirt; then two officers scaled the wall of La Godegrand's little garden, laid him on the inside of her bed, and left him there. Meanwhile His Majesty stayed in the room with the balcony, playing with La Beaupertuys, while awaiting the old maid's bedtime.

The church of St. Martin was not far, since the Rue de Jérusalem touches the walls of the cloisters; nor was it long before they saw La Godegrand mincing home, all aflutter. Once there, she laid down her alms-bag, her chaplet, her rosary and other ammunition old maids carry. Presently she poked the fire, blew it, warmed herself in front of it, settled back in her chair and stroked her cat for want of a worthier object of affection. Next, she went to her larder and sighing, supped, and supping, sighed, alone at her eating, gazing mournfully at her tapestries. Finally, having downed her drink, she gave vent to a resounding blast that His Majesty heard plainly.

"What if the corpse said '*God bless you!*' "

The pair laughed heartily up their sleeves at La Beaupertuys' jest. With all due attention the very Christian monarch watched the old maid undressing. One by one the clothes came off while she gazed at herself admiringly, plucking a hair here or scratching a pimple which had maliciously risen upon her nose, picking her teeth and accomplishing a thousand odd duties which all women, alas! virgin or no, must accomplish, much to their sorrow. After all, were it not for such slight flaws of nature, they would be too proud, and men could no longer have joy of them.

Having finished her musico-aquatic discourse, the old maid slipped in between the sheets. Then, suddenly she uttered a fine, curious, full, lusty cry as she saw, as she felt the cool body, sweetly redolent of youth. Immediately, she sprang away, out of co-quetry, but, unaware that he was truly dead, she soon edged back close to him, for she thought he was mocking her and counter-feiting death.

"Go away, you bad young man!" she cried, though, as may be imagined, the tone of her voice was most humble and gracious. Then, seeing that he did not stir, she surveyed him at closer quarters. Imagine her amazement at the wonders of human nature when she recognized the young townsman and her delight as she essayed a few purely scientific experiments in the interest of the hanged!

"What the deuce is she up to?" La Beaupertuys asked the King.

"She is trying to revive him; it is a work of Christian humanity."

The old girl was rubbing, cockering and limbering up this splendid young man, imploring St. Mary the Egyptian to aid her to resuscitate this husband, fallen from Heaven all amorous into her ken. Suddenly, as she looked at the corpse she was so charitably warming, she thought she detected a slight flicker of the lids. Laying her hand on his heart, she felt a very feeble beating. At last, what with the warmth of her bed, the ardor of her affection and the temperature of old maids (certainly the most torrid of all blasts blown from the African desert) she knew the infinite delight of restoring life in this fine, stalwart male who, as luck would have it, had been very poorly hanged.

"That is how my hangmen serve me!" Louis laughed.

"Ha!" said La Beaupertuys, "you cannot hang him again; he is too handsome."

"The decree does not say that he shall hang twice; but he shall certainly marry the old creature. . . ."

The good lady rushed off to fetch a master surgeon, an accomplished leech who lived in the Abbey, and brought him home at top speed. He plied his lancet on the spot, trying to bleed the young man; but as no blood came:

"Ah," he said, "it is too late! The blood has all flowed to the lungs!"

But suddenly the fine young blood seeped out, ever so slightly, trickled a whit more freely, then flowed in profusion; the hempen apoplexy, which had but begun, was arrested in its course. The young man moved . . . he showed signs of life . . . then he fell back, by the will of nature, into a state of utter weakness, of profound attrition, a prostration of flesh and a general flabbiness. The spinster, all eyes, followed the various mighty changes as they took place in the person of this ill-hanged man. Plucking the surgeon by the sleeve, pointing out the patient's piteous organic condition:

"And will he always sag like this?" she asked, with a curious glance in her eye.

"Eh, but very often," answered the honest surgeon.

"Oh, he was far nicer hanging."

At this, the King burst out laughing. Seeing him through the window, the old maid and the surgeon were grievously frightened: that laugh seemed to spell a second death sentence for their poor invalid.

But Louis kept his word, and married the pair. That full justice be done, he gave the husband the name of Sieur de Mortsauf in lieu and place of the name he had lost upon the scaffold. A judicious choice, too; it symbolized the adventure. As La Godegrand had pots of money, they founded a fine family in Touraine; it is still extant and much respected, for Monsieur de Mortsauf served his King very faithfully on diverse occasions. But he never relished seeing either gallows or old women; and he never again made an amorous assignation at night.

This teaches us to examine women with the utmost care, to recognize them and to distinguish such local differences as exist between old and young, for, if we are not hanged for our errors of love, nevertheless we are incessantly running great risks.

The Lord High Constable's Lady

*A*MBITIOUS of high fortune, My Lord Constable of Armagnac married the Countess Bonne, who was already considerably enamored of young Savoisy, son of the Chamberlain to His Majesty King Charles the Sixth.

The Constable was a rough warrior, miserable in appearance, tough in hide, exceedingly hirsute, always uttering curses,

always busy hanging people, always in the sweat of battles or musing on other stratagems than those of love. Scarcely exercised, therefore, about savoring the stew of marriage, this good soldier treated his wife as a man will who nourishes higher projects—a course which ladies hold in just horror. Why should they like the joists of their beds to be the sole judges of their cockering dalliance and their brisk amour?

Accordingly, no sooner constabled, the fair Countess only

clung the more passionately to her love for Savoisy. It filled her heart—which the lucky youth was not slow to notice.

Both wished to study the same music. They soon keyed their instruments to the same pitch and read the score together. Queen Isabella had cause to perceive Savoisy's horses were far more often stabled at the house of d'Armagnac, her cousin, than in the Hôtel St. Pol, where the Chamberlain had lived since the destruction of his house, ordered by the University, as every one knows.

This pawky, wise princess foresaw with dread a grievous misadventure in store for Bonne, especially as My Lord Constable was about as reluctant to wield his sword as a priest is to bestow a benediction. Being sharp as a needle and fine as a diamond, as she met her cousin coming out from Vespers one day and taking holy water with Savoisy:

"My dear!" she said. "Don't you see blood in that water?"

"Bah!" Savoisy answered the Queen. "Love liketh blood, Madame. . . ."

A saying Her Majesty found so apt that she put it into writing and subsequently into action, when her royal lord slew one of her lovers, whose favor, as you will see, dates from the incident supplying this narrative.

You are aware, through constant experience, that during the springtime of love each of two lovers is afraid of betraying the mysteries of his heart. As much through the flower of discretion as through the pleasures of gallantry's sweet deceptions, they vie with each other as to who can best conceal his thoughts. But a single day of forgetfulness is enough to bury all the prudence of the past. The luckless woman is snared in her joy as in a net; her lover makes known his presence—and sometimes his farewell—by some article of clothing, a scarf or one spur left behind by fatal misfortune. Then a dagger thrust cuts the web so gallantly woven by their golden delights. But when life is lived to the full, no man should shy at death; and a husband's sword spells a brave death for a gallant, if brave deaths there be. So, indeed, were the fair loves of the Countess destined to finish.

One morning, Monsieur d'Armagnac was afforded a breathing spell by the Duke of Burgundy's flight from Lagny. He therefore took it into his head to pay his lady a surprise visit. He meant to awaken her too gently for her to be angry; but the Countess, deep in her morning slumbers, replied to his gesture without opening her eyes:

"Leave me alone, Charles!"

"Ho, ho!" growled the Constable, hearing the name of a saint he did not number among his patrons, "I've a growth of Charles on my head!"

Without touching his wife, he leaped out of the bed and rushed upstairs, his face blazing, his sword drawn. Suspecting the Countess's maid of having had a finger in the pie, he made straight for her room.

"Ah, ah, you slattern of hell!" he cried, as he began to vent his fury. "Say your prayers now! I am going to kill you forthwith because of the tricks of that Charles who comes here."

"Oh, My Lord," the woman answered, "who told you that?"

"You may be certain I shall not fail to rip you open unless you confess the most trifling assignations and the manner of their granting. If your tongue should get tangled, if you bat an eyelash, I shall nail you down with my dagger. Speak."

"Crucify me!" the maid answered. "You shall know nothing."

The Constable taking this excellent reply amiss, ran her clean through, then and there, so furious he was. After which, he proceeded to his wife's chamber, but on his way downstairs he met his groom, whom the girl's shrieks had awakened:

"Go upstairs," he told him, "I have had to correct La Billette somewhat severely."

Before reappearing in Bonne's presence, he fetched his son, who was sleeping a child's sleep, and dragged him roughly to her room. At the mite's cries, the mother opened her eyes—and pretty widely, as you may imagine. A great terror swept over her as she perceived the lad in her husband's arms, the Constable's right hand red with blood, the fiery glance he darted upon her, and the infant.

"What is the matter?" she asked.

"Madame," the man of dispatch demanded, "is this fruit of my loins or of Savoisy's, your lover?"

At this question, Bonne turned deathly pale. Springing upon her son like a frightened frog leaping into the water:

"Ay, he is indeed ours," she assured him.

"Unless you care to see his head roll at your feet, confess yourself to me! And the whole truth, mind you! You have taken some lance-corporal and made him Acting-Constable!"

"Yes, I have!"

"Who is it?"

"It is not Savoisy. I shall never tell the name of a man I do not know."

The Constable rose, seized his wife by the arm and was about to cut her speech short with a swordblow, when she cast an imperious glance at him, crying:

"Very well, kill me; but take your hands off me!"

"You shall live," the husband countered, "because I have a chastisement in store for you ampler than death."

Fearing the arguments, wiles, pitfalls and artifices familiar to women in these fortuitous cases—they study the appropriate variations night and day, by themselves or in concert—he departed upon this harsh, bitter speech. He went straightway to question his servants, turning upon them, too, a countenance divinely terrible. None but answered as to God the Father on the Day of Judgment, when all of us shall be called to account.

None knew what serious mischief lay behind his summary questions and his crafty interlocutions. But from what they said, the Constable concluded that no male in his household was involved in the business except the watchdog in his garden, whom he found dumb. Taking the hound in his hands, he strangled him ragefully. The dog's slackness brought him by induction to suppose that the Vice-Constable came into his house by way of the garden, whose sole entrance was a postern opening out on the waterside.

For such as are not familiar with it, the locality of the Hôtel d'Armagnac must be explained. It stood near the royal houses of St. Pol on a noble site now occupied by the Hôtel de Longueville. In those days, the Hôtel d'Armagnac had a fine stone portico on the Rue St. Antoine; it was fortified on all sides; the high walls by the riverside, facing the Ile aux Vaches, where the Port de la Grève stands today, were topped by small towers. For a long time, the design of the house was to be seen at the house of My Lord Cardinal Duprat, Chancellor to the King.

Our Constable racked his brains, plumbed his deepest stratagems and, at bottom, picked out the best, adapting it so neatly to the present circumstances that the gallant must inevitably fall like a hare caught in a trap.

"God's death!" he cried. "My planter of horns is caught. Now I have plenty of time to decide how I shall deal with him."

This doughty captain, who waged such relentless wars against Duke Jean Sans Peur, commanded the following order of battle for the assault of his enemy. First, he selected a goodly number of his most loyal and highly-skilled archers. These he posted in the towers over the quay. They were ordered under the sternest penalties to draw on any member of his household who sought to leave the garden, without distinction of persons, save for his wife. On the other hand, they were to admit the favored gallant at any time of the day or night. The same thing was done on the portico side, in the Rue St. Antoine.

Next, all his retainers, including even the chaplain, were forbidden to leave the house under pain of death. Finally, the guard on either side of the house was committed to soldiers of his own private troop; their duties were to keep a sharp look out on the side streets. Inevitably the unknown lover to whom My Lord Constable owed his horns must be caught red-handed when, suspecting nothing, he arrived, at the usual hour, to plant his standard insolently in the very heart of My Lord's legitimate appurtenances.

Into such a trap the wariest of men must fall, short of being as seriously protected by God as good St. Peter was by the Savior, when He prevented him from going to the bottom of the sea the day they were inspired to find out whether the waters were as solid as dry land.

Having a bone to pick with the men of Poissy, My Lord Constable was obliged to be in the saddle after dinner. The Countess Bonne had known this. As early as a day ago, she had summoned her youthful servitor to that delightful duel in which she proved always the stronger.

While the Constable was posting his watchmen, setting a girdle of death about his house, and ambushing his pikemen near the postern, his lady was not wasting time threading peas or looking for black cows in the embers of the hearth.

To begin with, the impaled chamberwoman disimpaled herself, dragged herself to her mistress and informed her that My Lord Cuckold knew nothing. Before giving up the ghost, she comforted her beloved lady, assuring her that she could have perfect confidence in her sister, the laundress of the house. This sister, the dying woman vowed, was perfectly willing to be made mincemeat of, if it pleased Madame. She was the sliest and suavest hussy in the quarter. Among the common people, from Les

Tournelles to the Croix du Trahoir, she was famed for her fertile inventions in desperate plights of love.

Next, while weeping over the decease of her good chamberwoman, the Countess sent for the laundress, bade her leave her suds and joined her in rummaging the bag of good tricks in an effort to save Savoisy, even at the price of all future happiness.

From the outset, the two females planned to give him wind of My Lord Constable's suspicion and to engage him to lie low.

The washerwoman, like a mule with a tub on her back, attempted to go out of the house. At the portico, a man-at-arms barred the way. To all her arguments, he turned a deaf ear. Then, with signal devotion, she determined to take the soldier on his weak side and proceeded to tickle him with such tittuppy fondling that he frisked very thoroughly with her, though he was armed to the teeth. But, the sport done, he still refused to let her go into the street; and though she tried to get herself a passport sealed by some of the handsomest, whom she believed more gallant, no archer, pikeman or man-at-arms dared open the smallest outlet for her.

"You are wicked, ungrateful devils!" she said, "not to return the compliment and give *me* an opening."

One advantage, however, she gained at this business: she learned what was afoot. She scurried back to tell her mistress of the Constable's strange machinations.

Again, the two women took counsel. They discussed these warlike preparations, these watching posts and defences, these equivocal, treacherous, diabolical orders and dispositions. In less time than it takes to sing two *Alleluias,* they recognized, by that sixth sense with which all females are equipped, the special peril that menaced the luckless lover.

Madame, having soon ascertained that she alone was allowed to leave the house, ventured straightway to make the most of her privilege. But she did not go the length of a bowshot by herself, for My Lord Constable had ordered four pages to be always on duty to accompany her and two ensigns of his own troop never to leave her.

Whereupon the poor lady returned to her room, weeping as copiously as all the Magdalenes one sees in church pictures.

"Alas!" she moaned, "they are going to slay my lover, then,

and I shall never see him again . . . so soft-spoken, he was, so gracious in our sport . . . that splendid head, which has so often rested on my knees, shall be hacked and disfigured! What! Can I not throw my husband an empty, worthless head in place of that adorable, precious one . . . a foul head for a fragrant one . . . a hated head for a head of love?"

"Ha, Madame," cried the laundress, "why not dress the cook's son in a nobleman's clothes? He is madly in love with me, he bores me to death! Why not dress him up, then push him out through the postern."

The two women exchanged the glances of devilish assassins.

"The moment this bungler is killed," she went on, "all the soldiers would fly off like snipe!"

"Yes, but will not My Lord recognize the wretch?"

The Countess struck her breast:

"No, no, my friend," she cried, shaking her head, "it is noble blood we must spill here, and without stint!"

She reflected for a moment; then, jumping with joy, suddenly she kissed the laundress.

"Because I have saved my lover through your counsel," she told her, "I shall pay you for his life to your dying day!"

Whereupon she dried her tears, put on the face of a bride, took up her alms-bag and prayer-book, and rushed to the Church of St. Pol.

She could hear the bells ringing; it must be just about time for the last Mass, a sweet devotion in which the Countess never failed, for she was idle, like all Court ladies. This particular service was known as the Bedizened Mass, being attended wholly by fops, fashionables, handsome young gentlemen and bejewelled, richly perfumed ladies. No dress there but bore rare armorial broideries, no spur but was gilt.

The Countess Bonne went off to the parish church in great state, escorted by her pages, two ensigns and sundry men-at-arms, leaving a much-puzzled laundress at home with instructions to keep her weather eye open.

Among the band of brave gallants who frisked about the ladies in church, not a few, rejoicing in the beauty of the Countess, had gladly given their hearts to her, after the way youths will.

setting down many upon their tablets, with the sole object of conquering at least one in the vast score.

Of these birds of fine prey, who, with open beaks, scanned benches and paternosters more often than altar and priests, there was one upon whom the Countess sometimes bestowed the favor of a glance. He seemed less frivolous, more deeply smitten than the rest.

He always stood motionless, as though glued to the same pillar; the mere sight of his chosen lady filled him with rare delight. His pale face wore a look of gentle melancholy; it testified to a stout heart, one of those which nourish ardent passions and plunge delightedly into the despairs of unrequited love. There are few such, because generally people like a very definite something better than the felicities that lie flourishing in the inmost depths of the soul.

Though his clothes were well-tailored, clean and neat, displaying even a certain amount of taste in their arrangement, this gentleman, the Countess thought, was a poor knight seeking fortune, come from afar, with cape, sword and title for all portion. Bonne wished him the favor of women and fortune, partly because she suspected his secret poverty, partly because he loved her deeply, a little, too, because he had a pleasing countenance, fine long black hair and a trim figure and because he remained humble and submissive. Unwilling to let a gallant stand idle, and moved by a sound housewifely instinct, she fanned the flame of his adoration at will by means of minor favors and little glances that coiled towards him like biting adders. She trifled with the sum of this young life's happiness like a princess accustomed to playing with objects more precious than a simple chevalier. Did not her husband the Constable risk the whole kingdom as you would a tester at piquet?

Only three days since, as they filed out of church, Bonne had laughingly pointed out this devotee of love to the Queen.

"There's a man of quality!"

The phrase passed into the fashionable idiom; later it became an epithet for people of the Court. From the wife of My Lord Constable of Armagnac, and no other source, the French language derives this graceful turn of expression.

As luck would have it, Bonne's guess about the gentleman had been correct. He was a bannerless knight named Julien de Boys-Bourredon. Not having inherited enough woodland on his estate to cut himself a toothpick, knowing no opulence other than the rich nature with which his late mother had most opportunely furnished him, he conceived the idea of deriving a profitable income from it at Court. He was not unaware how avid the ladies are of such fine revenues and how highly and dearly they prize them when they can invariably be realized between two suns. Many, like him, have taken the narrow road of women to make their way; but far from measuring out his love in little doses, when Boys-Bourredon came to the Bedizened Mass, when he saw the triumphant beauty of the Countess Bonne, he spent funds and all. He fell deeply, sincerely in love, which proved very useful so far as his money went, for he lost both thirst and appetite. This kind of passion is of the direst; it encourages a love of diet, during the diet of love, twin maladies either of which is enough to snuff a man out.

Such, then, was the youth of whom the Countess was suddenly minded and toward whom she was even now speeding with an invitation to die for her.

Entering the church, she caught sight of the poor chevalier. Faithful to his pleasure, he stood there, with his back to the pillar, awaiting her advent as longingly as an invalid awaits sunlight, springtime, dawn. Moved to pity, she glanced away and sought to go to the Queen to request her assistance in this desperate extremity. But one of the ensigns stepped up, and, with a great show of respect:

"Madame," he said, "we have orders not to permit you to speak to man or woman, even to the Queen herself or to your confessor. Remember that the lives of us all are at stake."

"It is your business to die, is it not?" she demanded.

"And to obey, too," the soldier countered.

The Countess kneeled down in her usual place. Looking up again at her slave, she noted that his face had grown thinner and more hollow.

"Bah!" she said to herself. "I shall have that much less remorse for his death; he is half-dead now!"

At this thought, she favored Boys-Bourredon with one of those ardent ogles that are permitted only to princesses and harlots. The false love shining in her beautiful eyes brought a delicious pang to the gallant leaning against the pillar. What man but welcomes the warm assault of life as it flows thus around the heart and swells every vein in his body? Though the chevalier spoke never a word, his reaction afforded Bonne the pleasure, forever new in woman's heart, of witnessing the triumph of her magnificent glance. The blush which rose to his cheeks spoke volumes more than the bravest words of orators, whether Latin or Greek. Better still, it was understood.

At this grateful sight, Bonne determined to make sure it was no freak of nature; she took pleasure in experimenting how far the power of her eyes carried. After warming the cockles of her slave's heart thirty times or more, she was confirmed in her belief that he would die bravely for her sake. This idea moved her deeply. On no less than three successive occasions, between prayers, she was tickled with the desire to heap up all the joys man can savor and to shower them upon him in a single offering of love. By so doing, she mused, she would have no cause, later on, to reproach herself with having dissipated not only his life but also his happiness.

When the officiating priest turned round to sing this fine gilded flock the *Off you go,* Bonne went out past the pillar where her courtier stood. As she swept by, she tried to suggest, in an eloquent glance, that she wished him to follow. Then, to strengthen the intelligence and significance of this gentle appeal, the artful jade turned round and again flashed her request for his company. At first, she saw, he had moved a little from his place, but, all too modest, had not dared advance. Her last glance assuring him he was not being overconfident, he mixed with the throng, coming forward with the slight, noiseless step of an innocent stripling who fears to venture into one of those good places people call bad ones. Whether he walked before her or behind, to her right or to her left, the Countess kept dangling her brilliant glance before him to entice and attract him to her more surely, like a fisherman who jerks his line gently to judge of his gudgeon's weight. So perfectly did she practise the tactics of daughters of joy when they work to draw holy water under their mills that you would have sworn nothing resembles a harlot so much as a lady of high degree. As she reached her mansion, she hesitated a few seconds. Then she looked around again at the luckless chevalier, inviting him with so diabolical a glance that he rushed to the queen of his heart as though in answer to a call. At once she offered him her hand; the pair, boiling and shuddering for contrary reasons, found themselves in the house.

In this evil hour, Madame d'Armagnac was ashamed of having employed all these harlotries to the profit of death. She was ashamed, too, of betraying Savoisy in order the better to save him. But the slighter remorse was as lame as the greater; and it came tardily. Seeing everything under way, she leaned heavily upon her squire's arm and:

"Come to my room quickly," she told him. "There is something I must tell you!"

Boys-Bourredon, unaware that his life was at stake, could summon no words in answer, so utterly did the hope of approaching happiness choke him.

When the laundress saw this handsome gentleman, so quickly hooked:

"Eh, but it takes a Court lady," she exclaimed, "for a job like this!"

Then she greeted the courtier with a profound salutation not unmixed with the ironical respect due those who have the great courage to die for so little a thing.

"Picarde," the Countess said, drawing the laundress by the skirt, "I have not the heart to tell him how I intend to reward his silent love and his touching belief in the loyalty of women. . . ."

"Bah, Madame, why tell him? Let him go away through the postern, happy. So many men die at the wars for nothing, let this man die for something! I'll supply another like him if that will console you."

"No," said the Countess, "I will tell him everything. It shall be the punishment for my sin. . . ."

Believing his lady was plotting with her maid to forestall any interruption to the promised interview, the unknown lover stood discreetly aloof, gazing away into space. He was musing, meanwhile, that she was a very bold woman. Yet he found a thousand reasons for justifying her—a humpback would have done so!—and he considered himself quite worthy to inspire such recklessness. He was lost in these pleasant thoughts when the Countess opened the door of her chamber and invited him to follow her in. There this puissant lady cast aside all the apparel of her lofty fortune and, falling at his feet, became a simple woman.

"Alas, gentle sir," she said, "I have behaved shamefully with you. Listen: as you leave this house, you will meet your death. ... My mad love for another man dazzled me; and though you may not take his place here, you will have to take it before his murderers. Such, then, is the joy to which I have summoned you."

"Ah," answered Boys-Bourredon, as a black despair gripped his heart. "I am grateful to you for making use of me as of a thing belonging to you. . . . Ay, so much do I love you that, daily, I dreamed of offering you, as ladies do, a thing which may be given but once. Here is my life, then; take it!"

His glance as he spoke held all the joy with which he would have gazed upon her throughout the long days. And as she heard the brave, passionate words, Bonne rose suddenly.

"Ah, but for Savoisy, how I would love you!" she cried.

"Alas!" Boys-Bourredon answered. "My fate is accomplished! For my horoscope predicted that I should perish through the love of a great lady. Ah God!" he sighed, seizing his good sword, "I shall sell my life dearly; but I shall die content, knowing that my life assures the happiness of the woman I love! And in her memory I shall live better, far, than I could have in reality."

This hero's gesture, this shining countenance wrung Bonne's heart. But a moment later, she was wounded to the quick as she realized his apparent willingness to leave her without having asked the slightest favor.

"Wait, let me arm you," she said, making as if to kiss him.

"Ha, Madame!" he answered—and a gentle tear dimmed the fire in his eyes. "Would you make death impossible for me by setting too high a price upon my life?"

"Come!" she cried, overwhelmed by this ardent love. "How all this shall end, I do not know. But come! After, we can all go and perish together at the postern. . . ."

The same flame blazed in their hearts, the same harmony struck for them both. They embraced each other in the best of all ways and, amid the ecstatic rapture of that mad fever which (I hope) you know well, they sank into a profound oblivion of

Savoisy's dangers, of their own, of the Constable, of life, of death, in brief of everything.

Meanwhile, the sentinels on the portico had run to apprise My Lord Constable of the gallant's arrival and to tell how during Mass and on the road homeward he had ignored the Countess's warning glances. They met their master hurrying toward the postern, for, on their side, the archers stationed on the quay had signalled from afar that the Sire de Savoisy was entering.

Savoisy had arrived at the hour assigned. Like all lovers, thinking only of his lady, he failed to notice the Constable's spies and slipped in at the postern. Owing to this conflict in gallants, as his men ran up from the Rue St. Antoine, the Constable would not listen to them. Stopping them short with an imperious gesture which they thought unwise to disregard:

"I know," he said, "the beast is caught!"

With which they all rushed through the postern amid loud cries of: "Death to him! Death to him!" Men-at-arms, bowmen, My Lord Constable, captains, fell pêle-mêle upon Charles Savoisy, godson to the King, attacking him directly under the Countess's window. By a strange coincidence, the ill-starred youth's groans, tragically exhaled, mingled with the howls of the soldiers, just as the two lovers were uttering passionate sighs and cries. They hastened, in great fear.

"Ah," said the Countess, white with terror, "Savoisy is dying for my sake."

"I will live for your sake," Boys-Bourredon made answer, "and I shall always be happy to pay the same price for my bliss as he has done."

"Hide in that chest!" the Countess whispered. "I hear the Constable's step."

Monsieur d'Armagnac burst in, bearing a head which he laid, all bloody, on the mantel.

"Here, Madame," he cried, "is a picture which will enlighten you upon the duties a wife owes her husband."

Proudly, Bonne faced the Constable.

"You have killed an innocent man," she answered without changing color. "Savoisy was not my lover."

Such dissimulation and feminine audacity masked her expression that her husband stood there looking as foolish as a girl who has allowed a certain nether note to escape her before a numerous company. Already he suspected he had committed a desperate blunder.

"Whom were you thinking of this morning, then?" he demanded.

"I was dreaming of the King!"

"Why didn't you say so?"

"Would you have believed me, swayed, as you were, by such brutish fury?"

The Constable scratched his ear.

"How did Savoisy have a key to our postern?" he asked.

"I do not know," she said curtly, "if you will do me the favor of believing what I have told you!"

The Countess turned lightly on her heel like a weathercock spinning in the wind, and pretended to busy herself with household affairs. As you may suppose, Monsieur d'Armagnac was much embarrassed with poor Savoisy's head, and Boys-Bourredon, for his part, felt no desire to cough as he heard the Constable growling furiously to himself. At last the Constable struck two heavy blows on the table, and roared:

"I shall go and fall upon those of Poissy!"

With which he departed, and, at nightfall, Boys-Bourredon escaped from the mansion in some disguise or other.

Poor Savoisy was bitterly lamented by his lady, who had done all a woman could do to save her lover. Later, he was more than lamented, he was sorely missed, for the Countess told Queen Isabella of this adventure and Her Majesty, touched by the chevalier's grandeur and courage, seduced Boys-Bourredon from her cousin's service to put him to her own.

Boys-Bourredon was a man whom Death had warmly recommended to the ladies. Amid the exalted fortune to which the Queen had raised him, he behaved so haughtily that he vexed King Charles one day when the poor monarch was in his right senses. The courtiers, jealous of favor, informed the King of his cuckolddom. In a trice, Boys-Bourredon was sewn up in a sack and pitched into the Seine, near the Charenton ferry, as everyone knows. Naturally, ever after the day My Lord Constable was minded to ply his daggers so inconsiderately, his good wife turned the two deaths he had caused to splendid profit. She threw them up so often in his face, that she made him soft as putty and started him down the road a husband should walk. Himself proclaimed her a modest, virtuous Constable's lady, which indeed she was.

As this book should, according to the maxims of antiquity's great authors, join certain useful points to the hearty laughs you will find in it; as it should contain precepts of high taste, I beg to suggest that the quintessence of this tale lies in the following truths. Women need never lose their heads in even the most desperate cases, because the god of love will not abandon them, especially when they are beautiful, young and of good family; and gallants should never go to their amorous assignations like giddy young goslings but rather with discretion, keeping a sharp lookout near the burrow in order to avoid falling into certain snares and thus preserve themselves; for, after a good woman, the most precious thing on earth is undoubtedly a pretty gentleman.

The Virgin of Thilhouse

*T*HE LORD of Valennes—a pleasant spot, the manor of which is not far from the borough of Thilhouse—had taken unto him a sorry wife, who, through taste or distaste, pleasure or displeasure, illness or health, allowed him to forego the delights and sweets stipulated in every marriage contract. In all fairness, it must be stated that this lord was a very filthy, disgusting creature, forever chasing wild beasts and no more entertaining than a roomful of smoke. What is more our Nimrod was easily over sixty, but he kept very mum about it. Does the widow of a man hanged care to discourse upon rope?

Nature, like a tapestry weaver, knows not what she is about. The crooked, the bandy-legged, the blind, and the ugly she flings here below by the basketful, with as much respect as for the handsome. To one and all, she gives the same mouth for the porridge. Thus, never a beast but obtains stabling, peradventure; thus, too, the proverb "Never a pot so ugly but some day finds its cover." Accordingly, My Lord of Valennes was always on the search for pretty pots to cover. Often, he hunted not only the wild, but also the domestic beast, though sport of this feather was very scarce in the land and to pluck a maidenhead proved an expensive business. At last, after much ferreting about and much exhaustive inquiry, he learned of a weaver's widow in Thilhouse, who had a real treasure in the person of a little maid of sixteen. Never had the mother suffered her child to stray from her apron-strings. With admirable maternal solicitude, she accompanied her on the priviest of errands, after which herself put her to bed on her own pallet. She watched over her, would suffer no lingering abed of mornings, and set her to such work that the pair

131

earned eightpence a day between them. On feast days, she held her in leash at church, begrudging her the merest exchange of glad words with the lads of the village. Even then, she kept an eagle eye on the maiden lest a stray hand venture too freely afield.

The times just then were so hard that mother and daughter found barely enough bread to keep from dying of hunger. As they lodged with poverty-stricken relatives, in winter they often lacked wood, in summer, clothes. They owed enough rent to frighten a bailiff—a class of men not easily perturbed by the debts of others. In fine, if the daughter grew more beautiful, the mother grew poorer; the latter kept incurring debts on the head of the former's virginity, much like an alchemist and the crucible on which he pits all hope.

Having established and perfected his plans, My Lord of Valennes happened to stop at the spinner's hovel one rainy day. To dry out, he sent his men to fetch faggots from Plessis, hard by. While waiting, he sat on a stool between the two poor women. Under cover of the gray shadows, in the dim light of the cabin, he pored over the sweet face of the virgin of Thilhouse, her red, firm, healthy arms, her forepeaks, hard as bastions and beautifully calculated to shelter her heart from the chill, her waist, round as a young oak—the whole fresh and sheer and dainty and graceful as the first frost of the year, verdant and tender as an April bud, redolent of all the beauty in the world. Her eyes were of a modest, virtuous blue, their glance more coy than the Virgin's; she was less advanced, never having borne a child.

If anyone had asked her: "Will you make love?" she would have cried: "Gladly! What do you make it with?" so innocent was she and so little open to the comprehension of the thing. The old nobleman twisted about on his stool, scenting the girl and craning his neck like a monkey trying to catch nuts. The mother noticed this, but dared not speak; she was afraid of the lord who owned the whole country. When a faggot was set in the grate and began to flare up, the hunter said to the old woman:

"Ha! there's a flame almost as warm as that in your daughter's eyes!"

"Alas, My Lord," she sighed, "we can cook nothing on that fire!"

"Yes you can!"

"How?"

"Ah, my good woman, lend your girl to my wife, who needs a maid, and we will be glad to give you two faggots a day."

"Ha, My Lord, and what shall I cook on this fine fire!"

"Well," urged the old profligate, "why not good porridge? I will allow you a measure of corn per season."

"But where shall I put it?" asked the old woman.

"In your crib," said the purchaser of maidenheads.

"But I've neither crib nor bin nor anything else?"

"Very well then, I will give you cribs and bins and saucepans and furniture and a good bed with hangings, and everything."

"Mercy on us!" said the widow. "The rain will spoil them for I've no house."

"Look!" said the nobleman. "Do you see that house there? It's La Tourbellière, where my poor huntsman Pillegrain lived, the one who was ripped up by a boar?"

"Ay."

"Well, you may settle down in it for the rest of your days."

"Upon my faith," cried the mother, dropping her distaff, "do you mean what you say?"

"Certainly."

"Well then, what pay will you give my daughter?"

"Whatever she cares to earn in my service," he replied.

"Oh, My Lord, you are having your joke of me."

"Not at all!" he told her.

"Oh, but you are!" she insisted.

"By St. Gatien, by St. Eleutherius, by the thousand million saints that throng Heaven, I swear. . . ."

"Well then, if you are not jesting, I would like these faggots to pass through the hands of the notary, say!"

"By Christ's Blood and the sweeter blood of your daughter, am I not a gentleman? Does not my word suffice!"

"Oh, ay; and I'm not one to say no, My Lord; but true as I'm a poor sinner, I love my child too dearly to leave her. She is too young and too weak, still; she would break down in service. Only yesterday the curé was telling in his sermon how we shall have God to answer to for our children."

"There, there!" cried the lord. "Go send for the notary."

An old woodcutter ran to fetch the scrivener; the latter appeared and, then and there, drew up a perfectly sound contract to which My Lord of Valennes affixed his cross, for he did not know how to write. When everything was properly sealed and signed:

"Well, old woman," he said, "have you ceased to be answerable to God for your daughter's maidenhead?"

"Ah, My Lord, the curé said 'Until the age of reason.' My daughter is quite reasonable."

Then, turning toward the maid:

"Marie Ficquet," she continued, "your most precious possession is your honor. Where you are going, everybody, not to mention My Lord, will be trying to rob you of it. But you see how much it is worth! By that token, do not get rid of it save wittingly and in a proper manner. In order not to contaminate your virtue before God and men (except for a legitimate motive) be sure beforehand that your business is flavored with a bit of marriage. Otherwise, you will go to the bad."

"Yes, mother dear!" the virgin replied.

So she left her wretched lodging and went to the Château de Valennes, there to serve My Lady, who found her both pretty and to her taste.

When those at Valennes, Saché, Villaines and nearby boroughs learned what a high price the virgin of Thilhouse fetched, the housewives realized that nothing was more profitable than virtue. They all endeavored to raise and maintain their daughters virgins; but the job proved as parlous as that of rearing silk worms (so infinitely fragile!), for maidenheads are like medlars —they ripen quickly on the straw. To be sure there were some girls in Touraine noted for their innocence; they passed for virgins in all the convents of the religious. But I would not care to vouch for these, for I was never afforded the opportunity of investigating them according to Verville's method for the recognition of perfect virtue. In any case, Marie Ficquet followed the wise advice of her mother. She turned a deaf ear to her master's sweetest pleas, to his golden words and to his monkeyshines unless he would give them a slight flavor of marriage.

If the old lord made as though to fondle her, she put up her back like a cat at the approach of a dog, and:

"I will tell Madame!" she threatened.

At the end of six months, My Lord had not recovered the price of a single faggot. What with her various duties, the girl Ficquet waxed ever harder and more firm. One day, in answer to her lord's gentle request:

"Once you have taken it off me," she asked, "will you give it me back again?"

At other times, she would say:

"If I were as full of holes as a sieve, not one would you have, so ugly I think you!"

Taking these village taunts for flowers of innocence My Lord never ceased making various little signs, lengthy harangues and a hundred thousand vows. He was constantly observing the maid's fine, lusty breastworks, her resilient hips, moulded in powerful relief under her skirts as she made certain movements; he never wearied of admiring other features fit to damn the understanding of a saint. At length the dear good fellow became enamored of her with all the passion of an old man, which, in contrast to a youth's, increases in geometric progression. The oldster loves with his weakness, which grows daily greater and the lad with his strength, continuously on the wane.

In order to leave this fiendish girl no loophole for refusal, the nobleman approached one of his stewards, a man well over seventy, and gave him to understand he should marry to warm his old bones. Marie Ficquet, he suggested, would fit him to a tittle. The aged steward, who through sundry household services had acquired an income of three hundred pounds in Touraine currency, desired but one thing: to live peacefully without ever opening a front door again. But his master, as a personal favor, begged him to have a go at marriage. As for his wife, My Lord assured him, he would have nothing to worry about. So, out of sheer obliging, the aged steward strayed into matrimony.

On the day of their betrothal, Marie, with all her arguments exploded and never an objection to offer her pursuer, set a fat dowry and a sizy settlement as the price of her deflowering. Then she gave the old friggler leave to sleep with her as often as he could, promising him a tilt for every grain of corn he had bestowed on her mother. But, at his age, a bushel was ample. . . .

The wedding ceremony over, his lady no sooner abed, My Lord did not fail to scurry off to the well-glazed, handsomely carpeted, nobly tapestried chamber where he had lodged his wench, his cash, his faggots, his house, his corn and his steward. You may take it for granted that he found the virgin of Thilhouse the most beautiful girl in the world; that she made the prettiest picture in the soft light of a fire crackling in the chimney; that, under the sheets, she kept brangling and seeking the bone of contention, that she was sweet to the smell, as a maiden should be. At the outset then, My Lord had no reason to regret the price of this jewel. But, unable to refrain from dispatching the first mouthfuls of this luscious royal morsel, he proceeded like a past master to trifle with this youthful formulary. So the happy man, by excess of gluttony, frittered and slipped and blundered and, finally, forgot all he knew about the charming dalliance of love. Observing this, after a moment the good wench asked her aged squire innocently:

"My Lord, if you are there, as I think you are, kindly give a little more swing to your bells."

This remark, which somehow or other became common property, made Marie Ficquet famous. In our part of the country, people still say "She is a maid of Thilhouse" when they wish to mock a bride and denote a "fricquenelle."

"Fricquenelle" is applied to the sort of girl I hope you will not find in your bed on your wedding night, unless you have been brought up on the philosophy of Zeno, in which case the sorriest mischief will not faze you. Not a few people, in fact, are forced to be stoics in this queer situation, which is fairly often met with, for Nature turns but changes not, and there will always be good maids of Thilhouse, both in Touraine and elsewhere. Now if you ask me what the moral of this tale consists in and where it appears, I am quite justified in telling the ladies that the *Droll Stories* were written rather to point the moral of pleasure than to provide the pleasure of pointing a moral.

But if it were a broken-down old sucker who questioned me, I would say, with all the gracious consideration due his yellow or gray wig, that God wished to punish the Lord of Valennes for seeking to purchase a commodity intended to be given.

*I*N *THE* beginning of King Henry's reign—the second of the name, who loved the beautiful Diane so madly—there still existed a ceremony whose usage began to dwindle, then disappeared altogether, like an infinite number of the good things of yore. According to this proud and noble custom every knight chose a brother-in-arms.

Having recognized each other as brave, loyal men, the knightly pair were wedded for the rest of their lives. They became brothers bound to defend each other against the onslaught of the foe in battle and the slander of friends at Court. So sure were they

of each other's honor that if, in the absence of one knight, somebody accused his brother of disloyalty, wickedness or dark felony:
"You lie in your throat!" the knight was expected to say, and so
go into the field forthwith. Needless to add, they seconded each
other in all affairs, good or evil, and they shared all happy or
adverse fortune. They were better than such brothers as are only
bound by the hazard of nature, since they were united in brotherhood by the bonds of a special, involuntary and mutual senti-
ment. Inevitably, then, this fraternity in arms produced exploits
of a fortitude as splendid as those of the ancient Greeks, Romans,
or any others. . . . But that is not my subject; the chronicle of
these deeds has been penned by the historians of our land, as
everyone knows.

In these olden times, two young gentlemen of Touraine, the
Cadet de Maillé and the Sieur de Lavallière, became brothers-
in-arms the day they won their spurs. They were leaving the
household of Monsieur de Montmorency, where they had been
imbued with the lofty doctrines of this great captain. They had
proved how contagious valor was in such choice company; at the
Battle of Ravenna they had earned the praise of the doughtiest
knights. In the thick of this fierce fight Lavallière saved Maillé,
who, forgetting their past wrangles, appreciated the full nobility
of the other's soul. As both had had their doublets slashed, they
baptized their fraternity with their blood and were nursed together, in the same bed, under the tent of Monsieur de Montmorency, their master.

An exception to the family tradition of charm, the Cadet de
Maillé was not pleasant to look upon. He had no more than the
devil's beauty in his favor. But he was lithe as a greyhound,
broad shouldered and built massively, like King Pepin, that fearsome adversary. So handsome, on the contrary, was the Sire de
Château Lavallière, that rich laces, swagger breeches and openwork shoes seemed to have been invented for his own personal
adornment. His long, ash-blond locks were pretty as a lady's; for
that matter, he was the kind of child with whom any lady would
gladly have played. The Dauphine, niece to His Holiness the
Pope, observed laughingly one day to the Queen of Navarre, who
was partial to such witticisms, that this page was a plaster to cure
every ache. Which made the winsome little lad from Touraine

blush, for, being only sixteen, he took this gallantry as a reproach.

On his return from Italy, the Cadet de Maillé found the step-ping-stone of a good marriage waiting for him, duly provided by his mother in the person of Mademoiselle d'Annebault. A gracious maiden she was, well-favored in appearance and amply supplied with the world's goods; she owned a fine mansion in the Rue Barbette, filled with rich Italian furniture and paintings, and she would fall heir to many considerable estates.

A few days after the death of King Francis—a tragedy which sowed terror in every breast, for His Majesty died of the Neapolitan malady and henceforth what security was there with even the highest born princesses?—our friend Maillé was forced to leave Court and go to Piedmont on business of grave import. Naturally he was most reluctant to leave so youthful, so sprightly and so alluring a wife exposed to the perils, pursuits, snares and pitfalls of this gallant assemblage with its innumerable bloods, all as bold as eagles, all proud of mien, and all coveting women as amorously as people eye hams at Easter-time. Intensely jealous as he was, the whole business grieved him thoroughly; but after prolonged scheming, it occurred to him to shield his wife in the following manner.

He summoned his good brother-in-arms to come at daybreak on the morning of his departure. As soon as he heard the Chevalier de Lavallière riding into his courtyard, he leaped from his bed, leaving his wife, very white, very beautiful in the warm, gentle, dozing sleep so dear to all who treasure indolence. Lavallière came to him. The two brothers, hiding in the embrasure of the window, greeted each other with a loyal clasp of the hand. Then, without more ado, Lavallière told Maillé:

"I would have come last night in answer to your summons, but I had an appointment with my lady and a love-suit to discharge. I could in no wise fail her; but I left her as soon as it was day. . . . Do you wish me to go with you to Piedmont? I told her of your departure; she promised me to do without a lover; we made a solemn agreement. And if she deceives me, a friend is always better than a mistress! . . ."

"Ah, my good brother," cried Maillé, deeply moved by these words, "I have to ask a loftier proof of your nobility. . . . Will you take care of my wife, protect her against all comers, be her guide, hold her in check and vouch for the integrity of my crown? During my absence, you can stay here in the green room; you shall play cavalier to my wife."

Lavallière frowned.

"It is not you or your wife or myself I fear for," he replied,

"but the slanderers who will use all this to tangle us up like skeins of silk."

"You may have faith in me," Maillé interrupted, as he pressed Lavallière to his heart. "Were it God's holy will that I suffer the sorrows of cuckolddom, I would grieve less sorely if it proved to your advantage. But I swear I would die of chagrin, for I am head over heels in love with my sweet, fresh, virtuous bride. . . ."

He looked away to hide the tears that rose to his eyes; but the handsome courtier perceived the moisture in his glance, and taking Maillé's hand:

"My dear brother," he said, "I swear to you on my honor as a man that ere anyone lifts a finger against your wife, he shall feel my dagger in the pit of his bowels. Unless I die, you shall find her intact in body, if not in heart, for thought is beyond the power of a gentleman. . . ."

"Ah, it is written in Heaven," cried Maillé, "that I must forever be your servant and debtor!"

Then he left immediately, afraid of breaking down before the interjections, tears and other stews ladies are wont to serve up when saying good-bye. Lavallière escorted him to the city gates, returned to the mansion, waited for Marie d'Annebault to arise, told her of her husband's departure and placed himself at her disposal. He behaved with such consummate grace that the most virtuous of women could not have downed a desire to keep the chevalier to herself. But there was no need of these fine paternosters to indoctrinate My Lady. She had overheard the brothers' conversation and was deeply offended at her husband's doubt. Alas, God alone is manifestly perfect! All the ideas of men have their bad side; to grasp everything, even a staff, by the right end is a splendid science in life, but it is an impossible one. What makes it so vastly difficult to please the ladies is this: they lodge within them a thing more womanish than themselves. (Were it not for the respect due them, I would use another word.) Nor should we ever awaken the fancies of this malevolent thing. But the perfect government of women is a task fit to break a man's heart. We must remain in complete submission to them; that, I believe, is the best way to solve the agonizing enigma of marriage.

Marie was delighted with Lavallière's gracious offer and his courtly elegance. But a malicious idea hovered in her smile. To put it in a nutshell, she intended to set her youthful bodyguard between honor and pleasure. She would requite him so lavishly with love, shower so many little attentions upon him and pursue him with such burning glances that he must prove faithless to friendship to the profit of gallantry.

Everything was in splendid shape for the execution of her design, considering what familiarity she and Lavallière were expected to maintain in her house. And, as nothing on earth can stop a woman from carrying out her plans, at every turn the subtle huntress spread a net to fowl him.

At times, she would keep him seated close to her by the fireside at midnight. She would sing softly for him, making a great show of her shapely shoulders, of the white temptations that filled her corselet; she would cast a myriad burning glances at him, without betraying by her expression the thoughts behind her brow. At times, she would stroll with him of a morning through the gardens of her mansion, leaning very heavily upon his arm, pressing it, sighing, making him tie the laces of her shoes, which were forever coming undone at a given moment. Then it would be the catalogue of soft words and favors that ladies possess so thoroughly: slight attentions paid to a guest, such as coming to see if he is comfortable, if his bed is properly made, if his room is clean and neither close nor chilly nor too draughty at night nor too sunny in the daytime. She would entreat him to reveal the least of his tastes, the merest of his fancies.

"Are you used to taking anything in bed in the morning? Hydromel, say, or milk or spice? . . . Does our meal time suit you? I will do anything to please you. . . . Tell me! . . . Oh, you are afraid to ask me . . . come along, now."

She accompanied this warm, pleasant coddling with a hundred affectations. For example, when she entered the room, she would invariably protest:

"I'm bothering you, send me away! . . . I know: you want to be alone. Well, I'm off!"

Lavallière never failed to beg her graciously to remain.

Nor did she—the slyboots!—ever fail to come lightly clad, disclosing samples of her beauty calculated to set the veriest patriarch neighing, even one as broken-down as Methuselah's father at the age of one hundred and sixty.

But Lavallière was too clever by half; he let the lady perform all her tricks, happy that she was busied with him. It was that much gained, anyhow. Loyal brother that he was, he continually recalled the absent husband to the lady's mind.

One evening—it had been a very hot day—Lavallière, fearing My Lady's stratagems, launched out into a tirade: how dearly

Maillé loved her, what an honorable man he was, what an ardent gentleman and how ticklish as to his escutcheon—and crown. . . .

"If he is so ticklish about it," she demanded, "why has he placed you here?"

"Was it not the height of wisdom?" he replied. "He had to charge someone to defend your virtue—not that it needs defending so much as protection against wicked rascals."

"So you are my keeper!"

"Ay, and I am proud of it."

"Truly," she observed, "he made a sorry choice."

She punctuated the phrase with an ogle so downright lascivious that, by way of reproach, the good brother-in-arms stared coldly at her. Then he left her alone to nurse her pique at his refusal to prime and load for the battle of love.

She remained lost in profound meditation. Where, she wondered, was the real obstacle that lay between her and success? Obviously it was quite impossible for any lady to dream of any gentleman disdaining that bagatelle upon which men set so high a price and so great a value. Her thoughts dovetailed so well, each leading on to the next, that out of little pieces she made up a whole. When she came to examine this whole, she discovered herself wallowing in the depths of love—a lesson for ladies never to play with man's weapons. No one can handle birdlime without getting his fingers sticky.

Thus Marie concluded where she should have begun, namely by reasoning that if Lavallière avoided her toils, it was because he had been caught in those of a rival. As she surveyed the field carefully, looking for some sheathe to her guest's liking, she settled upon the beautiful Limeuil, one of Queen Catherine's daughters, Madame de Nevers, Madame d'Estrées and Madame de Giac. These were Lavallière's declared friends, he must love at least one of them to distraction.

With this conclusion, she added jealousy to the other reasons inciting her to seduce this Argus, not in order to cut off his head, but to perfume and kiss it, without harming a bone in his body.

She was certainly younger, more beautiful, more enticing and more charming than her rivals; such, leastways, was the melodious decree of her own thought. So, moved by the chords and springs of conscience and by the various physical stimuli which

set women in motion, she returned to the charge for a fresh assault on his heart. Women like to storm a well-fortified place.

She began to play the kitten: she nestled up so close to him,
wheedled him so gently, handled him so deftly, and cozened him
so saucily that, one evening when she was in a melancholy mood
(though gay enough at bottom) she heard her guardian-brother
asking her:

"What is the matter with you?"

To which, dreamily, she answered, while he listened as to the
sweetest of music, that she had married Maillé against her heart's
wishes and was therefore unhappy; that she had tasted none of
the sweets of love; that her husband did not in the least know how
to manage the thing and that her life would forever be fraught
with tears. She made herself out virgin in heart, and in everything else, too, as she confessed to him that she had experienced
only the unpleasant features of amour. Further, she opined that
the actual performance must surely abound in sweetmeats and
dainties of every kind. Did not the ladies of the Court all run
after the commodity? How they coveted it, and how jealous they
were of such as sold them samples, for to some of them it came
pretty high! She told him how curious she was about it and how,
for one good day or night of love, she would give her whole life,
to stand forever subject to her lover without a murmur. But, she
added, the person with whom she would most enjoy it was unwilling to listen to her, though their dalliance could be kept
eternally secret because of her husband's faith in him. Finally,
she wound up, if he went on refusing, she would die of it.

Every one of the paraphrases of the little canticle all women
know at birth poured out in a thousand chopped phrases, punctuated by heavy sighs, wrenched from the very heart, spiced with
tremors and writhings, appeals to Heaven, eyes rolling skyward,
faint sudden blushings and clutches at her hair. . . . Every seed
and herb and flower of temptation was pressed into the stew, and
since, deep under these words, surged a twinging desire that
would have made even a monster beautiful, Lavallière fell at the
lady's feet, seized them, and, bursting into tears, covered them
with kisses. How delighted Marie was to leave them to him to
kiss may be readily imagined. More, without looking too closely
at what he intended to do with them, she abandoned her dress to

him, fully aware that it must be taken by the bottom to be lifted. But it was decreed that, for that evening, she should be good. Handsome Lavallière cried in despair:

"Ah, Madame, I am a luckless man, and a wretch!"

"No, no, that is not true. Come now. . . ."

"Alas, the bliss of loving you is denied me!"

"How?" she demanded.

"I dare not confess my condition to you."

"Is it so very evil?"

"Ah, you would be ashamed of me!"

"Tell me!" she urged, "I will hide my face in my hands."

The insidious siren covered her eyes—but managed to look at him between her fingers.

"Alas!" he lamented, "the other evening, when you spoke to me so graciously, I was consumed with treacherous passion. Never dreaming my happiness to be so near and not daring to confess my love, I ran to a certain brothel where all the gentlemen go. There, for love of you, and to save the honor of my brother whose escutcheon I would blush to befoul, I was so properly caught that I am in great danger of dying of the Italian sickness."

The terrified lady screamed like a woman in labor, and, deeply moved, pushed him back with a slight, gentle gesture. Poor Lavallière, finding himself in too piteous a position, sought to flee from the room. But he had not reached the tapestries at the door, when Marie looked up again and murmured:

"Ah, what a pity!"

Then she fell back into a fit of profound melancholy, grieving for the wretched gentleman and growing the more enamored of him because he was thrice-forbidden fruit.

"Were it not for Maillé," she told him one evening that he looked more handsome than ever, "I would willingly take your disease. We would suffer the same terrors together."

"I love you too dearly," vowed the brother, "not to be good."

And he left her, to go to his beautiful Limeuil.

As Lavallière could not ignore Marie's ardent ogling, you may imagine what a blaze consumed the pair at mealtime and in the evening. Yet she was compelled to live without touching her beloved otherwise than with her glance. Thus occupied, she found herself fortified at every point against the gallants of the Court;

for there are no bounds so impassable and no safer bodyguard than love. It is like the Devil: whom it holds in its clutches, it girds about with flames.

One evening Lavallière, having escorted his brother's lady to a ball given by Queen Catherine, was dancing with his beautiful Limeuil, of whom he was madly enamored. In those days, knights bravely conducted their amours in pairs or even in troops. Now all the ladies were jealous of La Limeuil, who was resolving at that very moment to yield to Lavallière. Before they took their places in the quadrille, she had made the most blessed of engagements for the morrow, during the hunting. Our great Queen Catherine, for political motives, used to foment these amours and stir them up, as a pastrycook blazes his ovens by poking. Her Majesty, then, glancing over the pretty couples enlaced in the Ladies' Quadrille, was saying to her husband:

"Whilst they are battling here, how can they possibly plot against you?"

"Yes, but the Huguenots?"

"Bah, we shall catch them at this game too!" she said, laughing. "Look at Lavallière, there . . . he is suspected of being a Protestant . . . he has been converted to my dear Limeuil. And very nicely she does, too, for a maid of sixteen summers! It won't be long before they're grafted together. . . ."

"Ah, Madame, do not believe it!" said Marie. "He is ruined by that same illness of Naples which made you Queen."

At this guileless outburst, Queen Catherine, the fair Diane and His Majesty, who were all sitting together, burst into peals of laughter and the news soon sped from mouth to mouth. It brought down endless shame and mockery upon Lavallière. La Limeuil, whom his rivals had not hesitated to warn, turned a stony face upon him; ere long, the wretched gentleman, stared and pointed at by everyone, was wishing somebody else in his shoes. For the rapidity with which this loathsome disease spread had struck every heart with abject terror. He found himself shunned like a leper. The King made an offensive remark, at which Lavallière left the ballroom, followed by poor Marie in despair at the speech. She had irreparably ruined the man she loved; she had destroyed his honor and blighted his life. Alas! the physicians and master surgeons had incontrovertibly proven not only that persons Italianized by this love-disease inevitably lost their most appreciable attractions and their generative powers, but also that their bones turned black.

No woman would think of contracting a legitimate marriage with the handsomest gentleman in the kingdom, if he were remotely suspected of belonging to the folk whom Master François Rabelais calls "his very precious crusties. . . ."

On their way home from the Hôtel d'Hercule, where the fête had been held, Lavallière was very silent and melancholy.

"My dear Lord," his companion sighed, "I have done you a grievous hurt. . . ."

"Ah, Madame," Lavallière answered, "my hurt is reparable; but into what a plight are you fallen? You should never have suspected what danger attends my love."

"No," she said. "Now you are certainly mine, since, in return for the shame I brought you, I must forever be your mistress, your hostess, your lady, even more: your servant. Yes, I mean to devote myself to you, to wipe out the traces of this shame, to watch over you, to nurse you until I have cured you. And if those competent in such matters declare the malady relentless, if you must die like our late King, then I still crave your company to perish nobly of your ills. Even then," she said weeping, "no torture imaginable can atone for the evil I have done you!"

A torrent of sobs came hard upon these words; her virtuous heart turned faint and she fell into a swoon. Lavallière, beyond himself with fear, put his arm about her, laying one hand upon her heart to cup a breast of matchless beauty. The warmth of the contact restored the lady to consciousness; it fired her with such delights that she was on the point of swooning again.

"Alas," she lamented, "for the future, that sly, superficial caress will symbolize the joys of our love. Yet they stand a hundred notches above the satisfactions my poor Maillé believed he was giving me! Ah, leave your hand there," she continued, "it is against my soul it rests, it is my very soul it fondles."

At these words, Lavallière looked extremely sheepish. Ingenuously he confessed that the terrible felicity he experienced at the mere touch was increasing the pains of his malady. Death, he cried, was preferable to this martyrdom.

"Let us die then," she exclaimed.

But their litter was passing through the courtyard of the mansion and as no means of death seemed to present itself, each proceeded virtuously to slumber, far from the other and heavy-laden with love. Lavallière had lost his beautiful Limeuil; Marie had experienced peerless pleasures.

Owing to this untoward scandal, Lavallière found himself under the ban of love and marriage; daring no longer show his face anywhere, he realized how costly the patrolling of a lady's *fosse* can be. But the more honor and virtue he expended, the more pleasure he derived from his exalted brotherly sacrifice. The following facts go to show how arduous, thorny and well-nigh intolerable his sense of duty proved during the last days of his guardianship.

The confession of a love she believed requited, the harm she had done her champion and the experience of an unknown pleasure emboldened the lovely Marie. She fell into a platonic love, ever so slightly tempered by trifling indulgences quite without danger. It was this circumstance gave rise to the infernal pleasures of the game called Goose, invented by ladies who, since King Francis' death, feared contamination yet wished to gratify their lovers. To these cruel tactile delights, Lavallière, playing his part to the end, must needs lend himself. Every evening, our mournful lady attached her guest to her petticoats, fondled his hands, kissed him with her glances and pressed her cheek softly against his own. In this virtuous embrace, the chevalier was caught like the Devil in a church font, while she expatiated upon her love, ardent and obviously boundless since it stretched across the infinite reaches of unsatisfied desire. All the fire a woman puts into a substantial passion, when night knows no other lights than her eyes, she transferred into the mystical motions of her head, the exultations of her soul and the ecstasies of her heart. Then, naturally, with the serene rapture of two angels united by the mind alone, they intoned in concert such sweet litanies as the lovers of their day offered up in honor of love. These anthems the Abbot of Thélème has paragraphically rescued from oblivion, by engraving them on the walls of his abbey, situated, according to Master Alcofribas, in our land of Chinon. There I have seen them in Latin; I now translate them for the benefit of Christians.

"Alas," Marie sighed, "you are my life and strength, my happiness, my treasure!"

"And you," he countered, "you are a pearl, an angel!"

"You, my seraph!"

"You, my soul!"

"You, my divinity!"

"You, my lodestar, by morning and eve, my honor, my beauty, my universe!"

"You, my great, my divine master!"

"You, my glory, my faith, my creed."

"You, my gentle, my beauteous, my valorous; my noble, my beloved, my knight, my defender, my king, my love!"

"You, my fay, my flower by day, my dream by night!"

"You, my every thought, daylong, nightlong!"

"You, the delight of my eyes!"

"You, the voice of my soul!"

"You, the light of my days!"

"You, the gleam through my nights!"

"You, best beloved among women!"

"You, best adored among men!"

"You, my blood, a better self than myself!"

"You, my heart, my very life!"

"You, my saint, my only joy!"

"To you I yield Love's palm. Great though my own be, your love is greater still, for you are my lord."

"No, yours the palm, my goddess, my Holy Virgin!"

"No, I am your servant, your handmaiden, a nothing that you can crush to dust!"

"No, no; I, I am your slave, your faithful page whom you can use as the air of Heaven, whom you must tread as you would a carpet! My heart is your throne!"

"No, love, for your voice transfigures me!"

"Your glance consumes me."

"I see all things through you."

"I feel all things through you."

"Oh, lay your hand upon my heart—your hand only—and you shall see me pale as my blood aspires the heat of yours."

Amid these contests, their eyes, already ardent, flamed still more brightly, and Lavallière became somewhat the accomplice of Marie's joy at feeling his hand on her heart. As he strained all his muscles in this superficial contact, as his desires tensed and his ideas of the thing went to all lengths, it happened that his passion evolved no uncertain consummation. Their eyes wept blistering tears; they set one another hotly, furiously ablaze as houses catching afire; but that was all! Lavallière had promised to return the

body safe and sound to his friend; that he would do. But not the heart. . . .

It was high time when Maillé announced his return. No virtue could avoid dissolving at this grilling job; the less license the lovers had in their acts, the more pleasure they found in their fantasies.

Leaving Marie, the good companion went beyond Bondy to

meet his brother and see him safely through the forest. Reaching the borough of Bondy, the two friends, according to the ancient custom, slept together.

There, in their bed, they exchanged news, one recounting the adventures of his journey, the other the latest Court gossip, tales of gallantry and so on. But Maillé's first request was concerning Marie, who, Lavallière swore, was intact in the precious spot which lodges the honor of husbands. This pleased the tender Maillé mightily.

On the morrow, they were all three reunited to Marie's intense vexation. With the high jurisprudence of the female, she made a great to-do over her husband. But she pointed the while to her heart with the most charming of gestures for Lavallière's benefit, as though to say: "This is your own possession!"

At supper, Lavallière announced his departure for the wars. Maillé, dejected at this stern resolve, wished to follow his brother; but Lavallière refused point blank.

"Madame," he told Marie, "I love you more than life, but not more than honor."

He turned very pale as he spoke, and Marie, too, as she heard him, for never had there been so much true love in their games of Goose as there was in these words.

Maillé insisted on escorting him as far as Meaux. On his return, he and Marie happened to be discussing the unknown and mysterious causes of Lavallière's departure. Suddenly Marie, who suspected poor Lavallière's grief, said:

"I know why. He is ashamed to stay here because everybody knows that he has the Neapolitan disease."

"Lavallière?" Maillé cried in amazement. "But I saw him when he went to bed at Bondy the other evening, and yesterday at Meaux. There's not a word of truth in it; the man is as sound as a bell!"

The lady burst into tears, admiring his supreme loyalty, the sublime resignation in his farewell, and his nobility as he suffered in silence. She, too, kept her love in the depths of her heart; and when Lavallière fell before Metz, she too died, as has been related elsewhere by Messire Bourdeilles de Brantôme in his small-talk.

The Curé of Azay-le-Rideau

*I*N THOSE days priests were no longer permitted to take women unto themselves in lawful wedlock. But, in compensation, they had decent enough concubines, and pretty ones, if they could manage it.

Of course, as every one knows, this was strictly forbidden by the Church Councils. It was not pleasant to think of people's private confessions being repeated to a wench who would laugh at them—not to mention such other secret doctrines, ecclesiastical dispositions and speculations as abound in the politics of the Church of Rome. The last priest in our country to maintain a woman theologically in his vicarage and to regale her with his scholastic love, was a certain curé of Azay-le-Ridel, a most agreeable spot later called Azay-le-Brulé and today Azay-le-Rideau. Its château is one of the wonders of Touraine.

Now this era when women were not averse to the odor of priesthood is less remote than some may think. Monsieur d'Orgemont, son of the preceding Bishop, still held the See of Paris, nor was the bitter strife of the Armagnacs by any means at an end. Truth to tell, this curé did well to have his living in such an age, for he was nobly formed, tall, strong, of a fine corpulence and high in color. He ate and drank like a convalescent. Why not? He was always recovering from a gentle malady that attacked him at certain times so that, had he lived at a later period, he would have had to be his own headsman to observe canonical continence properly. He was a son of Touraine, that is a dark man with enough fire in his eye to light and enough water to quench all the domestic ovens that needed lighting or quenching. Never, indeed, has Azay seen such a curé since!

A handsome priest he was, square-shouldered, flush, forever

blessing, forever whinnying, preferring weddings and christenings to funerals, a merry joker, pious in church and everywhere a man. Of course there have been plenty of curés who drank hard and played a good knife and fork. There have been others who blessed freely and some who whinnied without stint. But all of them rolled into one could hardly have matched the sterling worth of our curé; single-handed, he ably filled his living with benedictions, kept it in joy and consoled the afflicted. He did it so well that none saw him emerge from his house but wished to be in his heart, so dearly did they love him. He it was who first said in a sermon that the Devil was not so black as he was painted, and who, to please Madame de Condé, transformed partridges into fish, averring that the perch of the Indre were fluvial partridges, and, on the other hand, partridges were aërial perch. He never played a sly trick under cover of morality. Often he said jestingly that he would rather lie in a soft bed than in the clauses of a good will, and that God, being well-supplied with everything, needed naught. As for the poor and the afflicted, none ever came to his vicarage for wool and went away shorn. His hand was constantly in his pocket; he actually softened (he, who was otherwise so firm!) at the sight of all this misery and wretchedness, as he braced himself to stop up all these wounds. How many good stories have been told about this king among clerics!

It is he who caused such laughter at the wedding of My Lord of Valennes, near Saché. There was enough food served to feed a small town at least, though it is only fair to add that people had come all the way from Montbazon, Tours, Chinon, Langeais and everywhere around. They stayed a week, too. The Dowager Lady of Valennes, the bridegroom's mother, bustled about, superintending the preparation and service of the various victuals, roasts and other delicacies. As our good curé came back to the room where the guests were enjoying themselves, he ran into a little scullion. The latter was looking for Madame to tell her that the elementary substances, the fatty rudiments, the juices and sauces were prepared for a pudding of high quality, over the secret compilation, mixing and manipulation of which she wished herself to preside. It was to be a special treat for her daughter-in-law's relatives. Our curé gave the spoilsauce a fillip on the ear, told him he was too greasy and dirty to appear before people of high condition, and undertook to deliver the message personally. Then the jokester pushed the door ajar, brought the fingers of his left hand together in the form of a sheathe, and working the middle finger of his right hand very gently in and out of this cavity, he looked slyly at Madame de Valennes and said:

"Come, all is ready!"

Those who did not know what was afoot burst out laughing when they saw Madame rise and go to the curé. She, of course, knew that the curé was referring to her pudding and not to what the others believed.

But a true story tells of how this worthy pastor lost his mistress, to whom the Suffragan would brook no successor. Not that our curé went in lack of household utensils on that score. In the parish, all the women considered it an honor to lend him theirs, the more since he was not the sort to spoil anything and always took care to scour them out thoroughly, the dear man!

Here are the facts. One evening he came home to supper with a melancholy face for he had just put a farmer underground. The deceased met his death in a strange manner; those of Azay still speak of it often. As the curé was only nibbling away at his food and showing no stomach for a fine dish of tripe, cooked exactly to his liking, the woman asked:

"Have you visited the Lombard? (She referred to Master Cornelius, *passim*.) Or have you met two black crows? Or did you see the dead man move in his grave, that you should be so upset?"

"Ho! ho!"

"Have you had a disappointment?"

"Ha! . . . ha! . . ."

"Come, tell me?"

"My sweet, I am still overwhelmed by poor Cochegrue's death. At the present moment, within a radius of twenty leagues, not a good housewife's tongue or a virtuous cuckold's trap but is agog over it."

"What was the matter?"

"Listen! Good old Cochegrue was coming home from market; he had sold his wheat and two fat pigs. He was riding his pretty mare, which, since Azay, had begun to grow amorous, though he had no wind of this, as he pranced and trotted along, reckoning his profits. Suddenly, at the bend of the old road by Charlemagne's Moor, they came upon a masterly stallion whom Monsieur de la Carte had put out to graze in an enclosure hard by. His owner expected this steed to sire a noble pedigree. A superb trotter, handsome as only an abbot can be, and so large, so powerful that My Lord Admiral, who came to look him over, declared him in every sense a crack beast. . . .

"Well, when this fiend in horseflesh first scents the riggish mare, he lies low without neighing or risking the slightest equine exclamation. But the moment the mare takes to the road, the stallion clears forty rows of vines and gallops in pursuit, his hoofs ringing over the stones. From his arsenal, he lets fly all the ammunition of a lover long deprived of venery and he sets up a series of cries that would have drawn their vinegar from stalwarts of the stoutest kidney. He stirred such a hullabaloo that the people of Champy heard him and were terrified.

"Cochegrue, suspecting the trouble, spurs his rampant mare on, making for the moor and relying on her speed. The good nag understands, minds him and flies like a bird; but the great lecher comes following after, his feet thundering like a blacksmith beating iron, straining every nerve, his mane flying in the wind, replying to the mare's even gallop with a terrific, clattering din. The farmer, feeling death approach in the shape of the erotic beast, digs his spurs into his mare's flanks and she rushes on. At last Cochegrue, pale and half-dead with fright, reaches the outer yard of his farm; but, finding the door to his stables closed, he yells: 'Help! Help! Wife!'

"Then he proceeded to ride round and round his pond, believing he could avoid the cursed pursuer. Meanwhile the latter, aflame with thoughts of amour, was growing wilder and more ardent to the great peril of the mare. Cochegrue's people, panic-stricken, dared not open the stable door for fear of the weird embraces and furious kicks of the roughshod lover. So Cochegrue tried to do it himself. But just as the poor mare was halfway through the door, the cursed stallion fell upon her, hugged her, gave her his savage greeting, gripped her with both his legs, squeezed her, pinked her and drove home a ninety horse-power engine of pleasure. In the process, he kneaded and mangled

Cochegrue so severely that only a fragment was found of him, crushed like a mash of nuts after the oil has been drawn from them. It was shocking to see him squashed alive, to hear his cries mingling with the amorous loud sighs of the horse!"

"Oh that mare, that mare!" the curé's good wench exclaimed.

"What?" he cried in amazement.

"Of course! You menfolk couldn't crack so much as a plum for us!"

"By all that's holy, you wrong me!" he roared. With which the dear man threw her angrily on the bed and proceeded to stamp her so violently with his puncheon that she burst on the spot, splitting into bits. And she died, without either physicians or surgeons being able to determine in what manner the solutions of continuity were completed, so violently were her hinges and mesial partitions wrenched. Manifestly, there was a proud man and a splendid curé, as has been pointed out above.

The good people of the countryside, even the women, agreed that far from being blameworthy, he was thoroughly justified. Perhaps the proverb: *"Que l'aze le saille!"* so popular in that age, owes its origin to this circumstance. At all events, it is so coarse in its actual wording that I forbear from repeating it out of regard for the ladies.

But it was not on this head alone that our great and noble curé displayed his strength long before his bereavement. He also carried off such a feat that no thieves dared ever again ask what angels he bore in his bag, even had they been twenty or more to fall upon him. One evening, after supper—his consort was still with him and he had enjoyed goose, wench, wine and all the rest of it —he was buried in his armchair discussing the location of the new barn he must build for the tithes. Suddenly a message came for him from My Lord of Saché, who was about to give up the ghost and who therefore wished to be reconciled with God, to receive Him and go through the usual lachrymation.

"He is a good and loyal lord," declared the curé. "I shall go."

He went straightway to his church, took the silver box in which the holy wafers were kept, rang the little bell himself so as not to awaken his clerk, and set out down the road with light foot and glad heart. Near the Gué Droit, which is a ford that crosses the moors and runs into the Indre, he caught sight of a picaroon. And what is a picaroon? It is a clerk of St. Nicholas. What, pray, may that mean? That means a man who can see clearly on the darkest night, who instructs himself by examining and apprehending purses, and who takes his degrees on the highway. Do you follow? Well then, this picaroon lay in wait for the box which he knew to be very valuable.

"Oh, oh!" cried the priest, putting down the sacred vessel on the parapet of the bridge. "Stop, you! And don't move!"

He walked up to the robber, tripped him up, confiscated his loaded stick and, as the rascal rose to grapple with him, he gutted him with a blow beautifully directed at the pit of his belly.

Then he picked up the Eucharist and said bravely to it:

"Eh, but if I had relied upon your providence, we'd have been in a pretty pickle!"

Now to utter such blasphemy on the road to Saché, was to milk the ram, for he was addressing the Archbishop of Tours, not God. The prelate had severely rebuked him, threatened him with suspension and admonished him before the Chapter because, from the eminence of his pulpit, he had told certain lazy people that good crops came not through the grace of God but from sound tillage and hard work. Obviously this truth reeked of the faggot. As a matter of fact, he was wrong; the fruits of earth require both divine and human dispensations. In any case, he died in this heresy, steadfastly refusing to understand how crops could flourish if God so willed it without man's tools—a doctrine which the learned doctors have since proved true by establishing that, time out of mind, wheat grew without the aid of man.

I cannot leave this paragon of pastors without recording an act in his life which proves how favorably he imitated the saints, sharing goods and mantle with paupers and passers-by. One day he was riding his mule home to Azay from Tours, where he had paid his respects to the Official. On the way, a mere step from Ballan, he met a pretty girl on foot. Now it grieved him to see a woman travelling like a dog, especially this particular woman: she was plainly fatigued and scarce able to bring one foot up before the other. The good priest, who knew enough not to frighten game, especially the hooded variety, invited her so politely and graciously to ride behind him on his mule that the wench hopped on. But not without the protestations and monkeyshines those of her sex invariably make when invited to eat or to take what they really want. The sheep paired off with the shepherd, the mule jogged along at a mule's gait, while the maid slipped up and down, first one way then the other, shaking about so uncomfortably that, as they left Ballan, the curé pointed out the advisability of her holding on to him. At once the fair creature linked her plump arms around her cavalier's waist, though making out she dared not.

"There! Are you still slipping about now?" asked the curé. "Are you comfortable?"

"Yes, I am, very comfortable. What about you?"

"I?" the priest exclaimed. "I am better than that."

Comfortable he was indeed; before long he basked happily in the warmth of a back against which two projections kept rubbing pleasurably; at length they seemed to be trying to imprint themselves on his shoulder blades, which would have been a pity: that was no place for such fair white merchandise. Gradually the jog of the mule brought into conjunction the inward heat of these two good riders and made their blood course more swiftly through them, for there was not only the throb in their veins but the jog of the mule to consider. Thus the good maid and the curé ended by knowing each other's thoughts but not those of the mule. Eventually, when both were acclimatized, mitred and dovetailed, they felt a jactitation which resolved itself into secret desires.

"Heh," said the curé turning round to look at his companion, "there's a fine copse of trees that has grown very thick. . . ."

"It is too near the road," the wench answered. "Bad lads will cut the branches or the cows will eat away the young leaves."

"Are you not married?" asked the curé, trotting the mule again.

"No," she said.

"Not at all?"

"My faith, no!"

"What a shame, at your age. . . ."

"Ay, you are right, sir; but you see a poor girl who has had a child is a sorry beast!"

The curé took pity on such ignorance. He remembered that among other things the canons urged pastors to indoctrinate their flock and show them the duties and responsibilities of this life. So he considered he was discharging the functions of his office properly by exposing the burden she would one day have to bear. Begging her gently not to be afraid, he assured her that were she willing to trust in his loyalty, nobody need ever know of the marital experiment he proposed then and there to perform with her. As, ever since Ballan, so the girl thought, her desire had been carefully sustained and increased by the warm movements of the beast, she answered the curé roughly:

"If you speak thus, I shall get down."

But the curé persisted in his gentle plea to such purpose that, as they reached the wood of Azay, the girl wished to get down. In fact, the priest took her down, for a different sort of riding was required to settle this discussion. Then the virtuous maiden ran into the thickest part of the wood to escape from the curé, crying:

"Now, you wicked man, you will never find me!"

The mule strayed into a glade where the grass was tasty; the girl stumbled over a root. She blushed. The curé came to her. There, as he had rung his bells for Mass, he went through the service for her and both drew on account a large advance against the joys of Paradise. The priest had it at heart to instruct her thoroughly: he found his pupil docility itself, as gentle of soul as she was soft of flesh, a perfect jewel. He was therefore deeply grieved at having so greatly abridged the lesson by giving it so near Azay, where he could not very well begin again, like all teachers, who to drive it home thoroughly repeat the same thing over and over for their pupils.

"Ah, blessed child," he cried, "why did you make such a fuss that we only came to an understanding near Azay?"

"You see," she explained, "*I* live at Ballan."

In conclusion, I must tell you that when this worthy man died in his rectory, a vast number of people, children and others, came there in grief and affliction, weeping sorrowfully. All exclaimed:

"Ah, we have lost our father!"

And the wenches, the widows, the wives, the little girls all exchanged disconsolate glances and regretted more than a friend in him, saying:

"He was far more than a priest, he was a man!"

Of these vicars, the seed is cast to the winds and will never again flourish, in spite of the seminaries.

Even the poor, to whom he left his savings, found themselves still the losers. An old cripple whom he had helped, went bellowing through the courtyard: "I'll not die, no, I'll not die!" meaning to say "Why did not death take me in his stead?"

This made some people laugh; at which the shade of the good curé must not have been displeased.

The Wife's Appeal

HE FAIR laundress of Portillon-lez-Tours, one of whose droll sayings has already been recorded in this tome, was a wench endowed with the cunning of at least six priests and three women. In consequence, she never lacked suitors; on the contrary, they swarmed about her thick as flies about their hive of an evening.

Now late one afternoon an old silk dyer was returning home from his country place at La Grenadière, on the pretty hillock of St. Cyr, to his scandalously sumptuous house in the Rue Mont. fumier. He rode through Portillon toward the Bridge of Tours. It was very hot indeed. Seeing the fair laundress sitting on her doorstep, he was suddenly seized with a wild desire. For a long time, he had been dreaming of the lovely maid; now he determined to make her his wife. Soon she was transformed from a village laundress into a dyer's spouse, a substantial townswoman, with laces, fine linen, and furniture to burn. She was happy, too, in spite of the dyer, whom she handled to perfection.

The dyer had a great crony, a manufacturer of silk-machinery, a short man, deformed, and compact of wickedness. On the wedding day, he told the dyer: "You have done well to marry, friend, *we* shall have a pretty wife!" A remark he capped with the thousand other sly jests people usually make at the bridegroom's expense. The pair wed, the humpback proceeded forthwith to court the bride, who shrank instinctively from ill-fashioned people, laughed at his pleas and poked ready fun at the various springs, engines and spools that littered his shop. But nothing served to rebuff our humpback's great love, which soon became so irksome to her that she resolved to cure it by playing a thousand practical jokes.

Once, after an evening of his sempiternal pestering, she told her pursuer to come to the back door. Towards midnight, she promised, she would open everything for him. It was, mark you, a fine winter's night and the Rue Montfumier runs to the Loire; even in summer, a wind, sharp as a thousand needles, blows through this pocket of the city. Our good humpback, muffled up in a great coat, did not fail to turn up and, while waiting for the appointed hour, strolled back and forth to keep warm. Towards midnight, he was half-frozen, storming about like thirty-two devils caught in a stole, and on the point of foregoing his happiness, when a feeble light shone through the cracks of the windows. His eyes followed it as it moved toward the little door.

"Ah, it is she!" he gasped.

His hope warmed him again. He pressed close to the door and heard a faint voice:

"Are you there?" the dyer's wife said.

"Ay."

"Cough, so I may know it is you."

The humpback began coughing.

"No—it is not you."

Then the humpback said in a loud voice:

"How do you mean: it is not I? Can't you recognize my voice? Open the door."

"Who is there?" cried the dyer, opening the window.

"Oh, you've awakened my husband! Alas, he came back from Ambroise unexpectedly this evening. . . ."

The dyer, seeing the figure of a man standing in the moonlight at his door, tossed a great potful of cold water over him and yelled "Thieves! Thieves!" so loudly that our humpback was forced to take to his heels. But, in his terror, he failed to clear the chain stretched across the bottom of the road and fell headlong into the common sewer, which the alderman had not yet replaced by a sluice draining into the Loire. Struggling in this bath, expecting to die at any moment, he heaped curses on the fair Tâcherette, as the townsmen called her because her husband was Tâchereau.

Carandas—to give the humpback his proper name—was not sufficiently infatuated to credit Tâcherette's innocence. Thenceforth he swore her a devil's hate. Nevertheless a few days after, when he had recovered from his dip in the dyer's drain, he came to sup at his crony's. The latter's wife argued so convincingly, flavored a few words with such honeyed sweetness and wheedled him with so many fair promises that his suspicions evaporated.

He begged for a new tryst; the fair Tâcherette, with the expression of a woman dreaming of just such things, whispered:

"Come tomorrow evening. My husband is spending three days at Chenonceaux: the Queen wants to have some old material dyed and to discuss the colors with him. It will take a long time. . . ."

Carandas, tricked out in his smartest clothes, did not fail to appear punctually. He found a brave supper waiting. A lamprey and a bottle of Vouvray wine stood on immaculate white linen— an ex-laundress married to a dyer is not a person to remonstrate with on the color of her napery—the whole most daintily prepared. How ineffably pleasurable to see the polished pewterware, to inhale the fragrance of the food, to gaze across the room at the thousand nameless joys that were La Tâcherette, rosy, fresh and luscious as an apple on a day of great heat! Carandas, parched by these ardent perspectives, was about to assail her on the spot. Suddenly Master Tâchereau knocked loudly on the street door.

"Oh!" cried his wife. "What on earth has happened? Get into that closet . . . quick! . . . I've been taken to task because of you before; if my husband found you here, he would kill you! He has such a violent temper!"

She pushed the humpback hastily into the closet, locked it, pocketed the key and went to let her husband in. (She had expected him back from Chenonceaux for supper.)

The dyer was greeted with a shower of warm kisses on both eyes and both ears; he in turn drew his wife to him, sought her cheeks with his lips, and gave her a series of great, smacking wet-nurse kisses, which echoed through the house. Then the couple sat down to supper, chatted away merrily and, in due time, retired to bed. Meanwhile Carandas, forced to stand in a cramped position, and unable either to cough or to make the slightest move, heard everything. He was in among the linen, squeezed in as tight as a sardine in a box, with about as much air as a barbel has sun at the bottom of a river; but he had, to divert him, the music of love, the sighs of the dyer and the sportive pranks of Tâcherette. When at last he supposed Tâchereau asleep, the humpback tried to work open the lock.

"Who is there?" called the dyer.

"What is the matter, my love?" his wife said, her nose peeping over the counterpane.

"I heard a scratching," said the good man.

"It's the cat," his wife explained. "We shall have rain tomorrow."

The husband laid his head down again on the pillow, not, however, without a little petting from his wife.

"La, my lad, what a light sleeper you are! It would go ill with a wife who took it into her head to plant a growth on yours! There, now, behave yourself. Oh, oh, daddy, your nightcap is on crooked! Come, put it on right, my little corker; you must look handsome even when you're asleep. There! Are you all right?"

"Ay!"

"Are you asleep?" she asked, kissing him.

"Ay!"

In the morning, the pretty matron tiptoed to the closet and opened the door for the prisoner. He emerged pale as death.

"Air! . . . Air! . . . Give me air!" he gasped.

And he fled, cured of his love, bearing away as much hatred in his heart as a sack filled with buckwheat. Subsequently he removed from Tours and went to the city of Bruges, where certain merchants had sent for him to arrange machinery for making coat-of-mail.

Now Carandas had Moorish blood in his veins; he was descended from an ancient Saracen, left half-dead after the great battle between the Moors and the French in the commune of Ballan (a place mentioned in the preceding tale). The adjacent moors, incidentally, are named after Charlemagne. Nothing will grow on this soil because of the cursed, miscreant heathens buried there; the grass is noxious even to the cows.

Carandas, then, living abroad, never lay down on his bed or rose up from it without planning to slake his thirst for vengeance. It was forever the subject of his dreams; nothing short of

Tâcherette's death would satisfy him. Many a time he vowed:

"I would gladly devour her flesh. Ay, I would have one of her paps cooked and chew it up without sauce!"

His was a fine, deep-dyed, crimson hatred; a cardinal hatred; the hatred of a wasp or of an old maid; more, it was all known forms of hatred fused into a single fury, boiling over, seething and resolving itself into a new concoction, a very elixir of gall, evil and deviltry, simmering over the flames of the most fiery coals of Hell. In a word, here was a master hatred.

One fine day, Carandas returned to Touraine with much riches brought from the land of Flanders, where he had sold his mechanical secrets. He bought a fine house in the Rue Mont-fumier—a landmark which today astonishes the passer-by with its queer humped embossments cut on the stones of the wall. Carandas found many notable changes at the house of his friend the dyer. Tâchereau now had two lovely children who, curiously enough, resembled neither father nor mother. But children must necessarily bear some sort of resemblance to somebody. So there are always canny folk to resuscitate the features of their ancestors, if handsome—the flatterers! By this process, the dyer discovered that his two sons favored an uncle of his, once a priest at Notre Dame de l'Égrignolles. Certain wags, however, insisted that these two brats were the spitten image of a handsome shave-pate who officiated in the church of Notre Dame la Riche, a celebrated parish between Tours and Le Plessis.

Now believe one thing, inculcate it upon your minds and consider yourselves lucky indeed if, from this book, you glean, gather, extract and formulate this single principle of all truth, to wit: a man can never dispense with his nose, therefore he will forever be snotty. In other words, he will always remain a man. By that token, he will continue throughout all future time to laugh, to drink, to find himself under his shirt without being better or worse for it, to indulge in the same occupations. These prefatory ideas are set down solely in order to imbed more firmly in your consciousness one fact: our biped soul will always accept as true what flatters his passions, caresses his hatred and serves his amours. Hence, the science of Logic.

Appropriately, then, the first day Carandas saw his friend's children and the handsome priest and the dyer's pretty wife and

Tâchereau all seated together at table; the moment he perceived to his disadvantage, the choicest piece of lamprey going from Tâcherette (in the wake of no uncertain look) to her friend the priest, he thought:

"My crony is a cuckold; his wife is sleeping with the little confessor; the children were begotten with fine holy water. Well, I'll show them that humpbacks have something more than other men!"

This was, of course, true—as true as that Tours was always and always will be dipping its feet in the Loire, like a young girl playing while she bathes in the water, splashing about flick-flack as she beats the waves with her white hands. Ay, this town is merrier, happier, fresher, more amorous and flowery and fragrant than all the other towns in the world, not one of which is worthy to comb her hair or to buckle her girdle. Should you go there, you may be certain that down the middle of it you will find a neat line drawn by a delightful street where everyone strolls, where there is always a breeze, shade, sunlight, rain and love. Ha! ha! laugh away, but go there and see! It is a street always new, always royal, always imperial; a patriotic street; a street with two sidewalks; a street open at both ends; a well-planned street; a street so broad that no one has ever cried "Make room, there!" . . . A street which never wears out, a street which leads to the Abbey of Grant-Mont and to a trench connecting beautifully with the bridge; a street at the end of which lies a fine fair-ground. . . . A well-paved, well-built, well-washed street, clean as a looking-glass, populous, silent at certain times, a coquette after dark, under its nightcap of pretty blue roofs. . . . In brief, it is the street where I was born; it is the queen of streets, forever between earth and sky, a street with a fountain, a street which lacks nothing to be celebrated among streets. It is the real street, the only street in Tours! If there be others, they are dark, tortuous, narrow, dank and all of them come respectfully to salute this noble street, which lords it over them. Where was I? For, once in this street, no man wishes to leave it, so pleasant it is. Anyhow, I owed this filial homage, this descriptive hymn sung from the heart, to my native street, whose corners lack only the brave figures of my good Master Rabelais and of Master Descartes, both unknown to the natives.

Well, when Carandas came back from Flanders, he was enter-
tained by Tâchereau and by all those who liked him for his
jokes, drollery and facetious sallies. He seemed to be cured of his
old love; he behaved graciously towards Tâcherette and her
priest, he embraced the children. When he was alone with the
dyer's wife, he recalled the night in the closet and the night of
the sewer.

"Ha, ha! What a fool you made of me, eh?" he said.

"You deserved it," she answered laughing. "If, in your great
love, you had allowed yourself to be tricked, ridiculed and baited
a little longer, you might perhaps have gimcracked me, like the
others."

At which Carandas burst into peals of laughter, though inwardly fuming. As his eyes fell on the closet which had almost
been the death of him, his anger grew more violent because she
was more beautiful than ever, like all those perennially fresh for
bathing in that fount of youth whose waters are the very sources
of love.

With revenge in view, he studied the particular angles of the
cuckoldry at the dyer's, for there are as many technical varieties
of procedure as there are households. To be sure, all loves are
alike just as all men are alike. But proof is furnished to the ab-
stractors of true things that, for the greater happiness of women,
each love has its special feature, and that, if nothing is so like one
man as another man, conversely nothing is so different. That is
what confuses all things or what explains the myriad fancies of
women who seek the best of men with a thousand pains and a
thousand pleasures—and rather more of one than of the other.
But how can we blame them for their experiments, their vicissitudes and their contradictory aims? Why, Nature is forever
frisking and squirming and wriggling about and you expect a
woman to stand still in one place? Do you know if ice is really
cold? No! Well then, nor do you know if cuckoldry is not a
happy hazard, the generator of brains well-furnished and better
fashioned than all others. Try seeking something more substantial than ventosity under the sky. This will doubtless help
to spread the philosophical reputation of this centrivulvopetal
tome. Yes, yes, go on; the man who cries "Here is rat poison!" is
further advanced than those who are busy trying to raise Na-

ture's skirts, for she is a proud, highly capricious slut and allows herself to be seen only at certain times. Do you understand? Hence in all languages, she belongs to the feminine gender, being a thing essentially fickle, rich and alert in tricks.

It was not long before Carandas recognized that, among cuckoldries, the best regulated and most discreet is ecclesiastical cuckoldry. This is how Tâcherette laid her plans. Invariably she made for her cottage at La Grenadière on the eve of the Sabbath, leaving her husband to finish his work, to balance and check his books and to pay the workmen's wages. Sunday morning Tâchereau came out to join her and invariably found a good breakfast and a gay wife waiting for him. Always he brought the priest along. The fact of the matter is that this damnable priest had crossed the Loire in a small boat late on Saturday to go and keep Tâcherette warm, calm her fancies and enable her to sleep well during the night—a job that young men feel very much at home in. But this fine curber of fancies returned to his house on Sunday morning just in time for Tâchereau to come and invite him to La Grenadière. The cuckold always found the priest in bed. The boatman being well paid, nobody knew anything about these goings-on, for the priest crossed over after nightfall and returned at daybreak.

As soon as Carandas was certain of the arrangement and constant practise of these gallant diversions, he determined to wait for a day when the lovers would meet again, hungry for one another after some fortuitously imposed fasting. This meeting occurred soon after. The prying humpback saw the boatman waiting at the end of the beach by the Canal St. Anne; he saw the priest who, like the gallant and craven hero of love celebrated by Master Ariosto, was young, blond, slender and shapely. Straightway, Carandas hastened off in search of Tâchereau, who still loved his wife and believed himself the only man with a finger in her pretty pie.

"Hey, good evening, old friend!" said Carandas to Tâchereau. Tâchereau tipped his cap.

Carandas proceeded to tell him all about the secret love-parties, slobbering out arguments of every kind and goading the dyer in every quarter. Presently, seeing him ready to kill his wife and the priest:

"My good neighbor," Carandas said, "I brought back a poisoned sword from Flanders. A mere scratch with the point of it means death instanter. Tickle your slut and her paramour with it and they perish!"

"Let us go fetch it," said the dyer.

The two merchants rushed to the humpback's house, picked up the sword and sped away to the country.

"But shall we find them in bed?" Tâchereau asked.

"You can wait!" the humpback sneered.

Tâchereau was spared the grievous torment of waiting to witness the joy of the lovers. His fair wife and her sweetheart were busily spreading the pretty net you doubtless know to catch that charming bird which is forever escaping. And they kept laughing and trying again and laughing.

"Ah, darling," Tâcherette gasped, pressing him to her as though to engrave his outline on her white body, "I love you so much that I would like to eat you up. . . . No, better still, to have you in my flesh, so you could never leave me."

"I would like it too," the priest answered, "but you cannot have all of me there. You will have to be content with having me in detail, by inches!"

It was on this lyrical passage that the husband entered, brandishing his naked sword. One glance at her lord's face told Tâcherette that it was all up with her lover, the priest. But, suddenly, she sprang at her husband with outstretched arms, halfnaked, her hair dishevelled, beautiful in shame, but more beautiful still in her love:

"Stay, unhappy man!" she cried. "You are about to kill the father of your children!"

Thereupon the good dyer, overwhelmed by the paternal majesty of Cuckolddom, and perhaps, too, by the fire in his wife's eyes, let the sword fall on the foot of the humpback, who had followed him. Thus perished Carandas.

Which teaches us not to be spiteful.

Epilogue

*H*ERE endeth the first series of these tales, a roguish sample of the works of that merry Muse born of old in our blessed land of Touraine. A good wench she is, too, that Muse, knowing by rote the fine axiom her friend Verville penned in his *Way to Success:* "It is only necessary to be brazen in order to obtain favors."

Alas, mad little maid, get you to bed again, sleep; you are panting from your journey; mayhap you have outrun the present. Dry your fair, naked feet, then; stop up your ears and get you back to Love.

If, to conclude these comical inventions, you dream other poesy woven of laughter, heed not the foolish clamor and insults of such as hear the song of a joyous Gallic lark, only to cry: "Faugh! Nasty bird!"

Prologue to Second Ten Stories

*C*ERTAIN people have censured the Author for knowing no more about the language of oldentimes than a fish knows about higher mathematics. Formerly such cavillers would have been pointedly denounced as cannibals, boors and sycophants; their origin would, by insinuation, have been ascribed to the good town of Gomorrah. The Author forbears from presenting them with this delicate bouquet of mediæval criticism. Enough for him to thank Heaven he is not in their skin. In any such plight, he would eye himself with shame and disgust, he would consider himself the vilest of cacographers thus to slander a luckless book so far removed from the track beaten by the spoil-sheets of our day. Ah, wretched race, you waste a precious gall you could discharge to better purpose among yourselves. For his failure to please one and all, the Author finds consolation as he recalls another scion of Touraine, an old author of eternal memory. He, too, had to endure exactly that sort of contumely from birds of the same feather, who strained his patience to such a point that in one of his prologues he declared he was determined never again to take his pen in hand. Another age, but the selfsame manners. Nothing suffers change, neither God above, nor men below. So, with a laugh, the Author sets his shoulder to the wheel again, relying upon the future to reward his arduous labor.

Arduous labor it is indeed, to excogitate *One Hundred Droll Stories* under the fire of broadsides directed at him not by jealous ruffians alone, but by his kind friends into the bargain. For the latter did not fail to come to him tragically in that dark hour, and:

"Are you mad?" they cried. "What on earth are you thinking

of? What man ever held a round five-score such tales in the baggage of his imagination? Give up the hyperbolic label on your budget, my good fellow! You will never reach the end!"

Now these folk are neither misanthropes nor cannibals. Whether ruffianly or not, I do not know. But undoubtedly they are very good friends—the kind of friends who are brave enough to heap a thousand cruelties upon you your whole life long, who are rough and sharp as currycombs because, they allege, they are yours hand and foot, purse and faith, in all the grievous mishaps of this life, and, in the hour of extreme unction, their full worth is discovered.

It would be bearable if these people stopped at such lugubrious kindnesses. But no, they will not. Their terrors proved groundless:

"Ha, ha! I knew it!" they exclaim triumphantly. "Did I not foretell it?"

In order not to discourage fine sentiments (intolerable though they are) the Author bequeaths his old openwork slippers to these friends, and he assures them, for their greater peace of mind, that within the recesses of that reservoir of nature, his brain, he holds threescore and ten fine stories, his own personal property and exempt from seizure or attachment. God's truth, these are splendid yarns, decked out in the bravest of phrases and very carefully supplied with incidents, amply clothed with the most original comicality—a comicality drawn from the diurnal, nocturnal, untrammelled woof which humankind weaves every minute, hour, week, month and year of the great ecclesiastical computation, begun in the dark ages when the sun could not see to shine and the moon was still waiting to be shown her way. These seventy subjects you may, without *lèse-majesté*, call traitorous subjects; they are full of tricks and stratagems, they are brazenfaced, lecherous vagabonds; they are scoffers, fly-by-nights, pickpockets; but, by the Prophet's belly, when you add them to the others here produced, they represent a slight instalment of the fivescore promised.

Save for the evil times which, fallen lately upon bibliopoles, bibliomaniacs, bibliographers and bibliotheca, now prey upon all bibliolatry, the Author would have tossed them all off in a single bumper, not drop by drop, like a man suffering from dysury of the brain. His fly is as active as any. *Per Braguettam,* there is no danger of such infirmity in him; on the contrary, he gives good measure, putting several tales into one, as is clearly proved by quite a few in this series. For the *finale,* you may be certain he has chosen the best and most ribald of the lot, thus forestalling those who would accuse him of a senile discourse. Therefore temper your hatred with a mite of friendship, lighten your friendship with a whit less hatred.

Others, equally friendly, have forgotten Nature's niggardly allowance in the matter of writers (there are no more than seven perfect in the boundless ocean of human creation). They hold that, in an age when every man goes about dressed in black, as if in mourning for something, it is necessary to concoct works boresomely earnest or earnestly boresome. According to them, no litterateur can live henceforth unless he enshrines his conceptions in some colossal edifice: whoever cannot reconstruct a castle or cathedral, of which never a stone, never a bit of mortar, even, may move, must die unknown, like the Pope's slippers. These friends were requested to state which they preferred: a pint of good wine or a tun of small beer; the tale of Hans Carvel's ring as related by Rabelais or a modern story piteously expectorated by a schoolboy? Dumbfounded and nonplussed, they were then told quite dispassionately:

"You have heard, my good people, have you not? Well then, be off and mind your own business."

For the benefit of all others, the following must be added.

That good man to whom we owe sempiternally authoritative fables and tales, put his tool to them; no more. His material he had taken from others. Yet the workmanship lavished on these small figures has vested the highest value in them; and though, like Master Louis Ariosto, he was vituperated for dwelling upon frivolities and trifles, a certain small insect, graven by him, was destined to become a monument more surely perennial than the most solidly fashioned works. In the particular jurisprudence of Wit and Wisdom, it is the custom to prize one little leaf wrested from the tablets of Nature and Truth more dearly than the ruck of tepid volumes from which, for all their beauty, nor laugh nor tear can be extracted. The Author has full license to speak advisedly. He does not mean to set himself up on tiptoe in order to attain supernatural height; the whole question concerns the majesty of art, not his own stature. For what is he but a poor clerk whose sole merit it is to have ink in his horn, to listen to the gentlemen at the bar and to set down in careful script the testimony of each deponent? He is responsible for the workmanship, Nature for the rest. It is not true that, from the Venus of My Lord Phidias, the Athenian, down to Godenot, a little old man (known as the Sieur Breloque and curiously elaborated by one of the celebrated authors of our age), everything is studied from the eternal mould of human imitations, which is the common property of us all? In this honest profession, happy the thieves; far from being hanged they are esteemed and cherished. But the man who gives himself airs, who struts about and who swells up with pride at an advantage due to a mere constitutional hazard, proves himself a triple fool, a jackass with ten horns on his head. Glory lies only in the cultivation of the faculties, plus a certain amount of patience and daring.

As for the soft, fluty voices rising delicately in sweet-lipped whispers to the Author's ear, complaining that their owners dishevelled their hair and spoiled their petticoats at certain places, his answer is:

"Why did you come?"

To these observations, he is forced by the arrant slanders of certain folk to add a notice for the well-disposed. Let them use it to put an end to the calumnies directed at him by all sorry quill-drivers.

These *Droll Stories* are written, according to all authorities, in the age when Queen Catherine, of the house of Medici, was up and stirring—a good long reign, since she was always meddling with public affairs to the advantage of our holy religion. An age, too, which laid many a man low, from our defunct master, Francis, first of the name, to the States General at Blois, where fell Monsieur de Guise.

Now even schoolboys who play at marbles know that in that era of rebellions, pacifications and disorders, the language of France was also somewhat disturbed. For one thing, each poet made up a French language for his own private use, just as they do nowadays: then there were all manner of weird Greek, Latin, Italian, German and Swiss words, alien phrases, and Spanish jargons, imported by foreigners. Thus a poor writer has plenty of elbow-room in the babel of this language, which has since been attended to by Messieurs de Balzac, Blaise Pascal, Furetière, Ménage, Saint Évremond, de Malherbe and others. They, it was, first swept French clean, gave foreign words their walking papers and conferred the rights of citizenship upon legitimate words, which everybody used and knew but which Messire Ronsard was ashamed of.

Having had his say, the Author returns to his *inamorata*. To such as prize him, he wishes a thousand happy moments; to the others, bad luck according to their deserts. When the swallows fly off again, he will come back this way, not without the third and fourth series. These he hereby promises to Pantagruelians, to lusty wags and to good cockerels of all standing, who abominate the doldrums, elucubration and gloom of literary mopes.

The Three Clerks of St. Nicholas

*I*N *THE* days of old the rendezvous of gourmets in Tours was the *Inn of the Three Barbels*. The landlord was reputed to be the king of cooks; he would cater for wedding feasts as far afield as Châtellerault, Loches, Vendôme and Blois. This man, an old hand who had his game at his fingers' ends, never lit a lamp by day, knew how to save on an egg, charged for hair, hide and feathers, kept his weather eye cocked for everything and had never been bilked in his life. For a penny short of his bill, he would have called a prince of the blood to book.

Otherwise, he was a decent enough jokester, ready to laugh and drink with the best of tosspots, forever cap in hand before anyone provided with plenary indulgences in regard to *Sit nomen Domini benedictum*. He would urge such people to spend freely and prove to them, by conclusive arguments, that wines were dear, that, think what they willed, nothing was given away in Touraine, therefore everything must be bought, and, accordingly, paid for in full. Had it been possible, without incurring disgrace, he would have charged so much for fresh air and so much for a view of the landscape. Thus, with other people's money, he maintained a fine household, grew round as a butt and larded with fat. The townspeople sirred him.

At the time of the last Fair, three youths came to Tours. They were apprentices in knavery, with more of the stuff of rogues than of saints in them; they already knew by experience how far they could go without getting their necks caught in a noose. They had arrived intent upon living well and amusing themselves at the expense of a few hucksters and tradesmen. Having given the slip to the lawyers under whom they were studying

scripts and charters, these disciples of Satan proceeded straightway to the *Inn of the Three Barbels,* where they demanded the
best suite of rooms. They volunteered the information that they
were very important merchants who travelled only with their
persons, for they were above dragging their wares about with

them. They had the place topsy-turvy in no time; nothing was
good enough for them; they commandeered all the lampreys in
market. The landlord bustled about, turned his spits, drew his
choicest wines and set to work preparing a millionaire's banquet
for three deadbeats who raised one hundred crowns' worth of
trouble and would not have produced under the direst pressure
so much as the odd twelve Touraine *sous* one of them was jin-

gling in his pocket. But, if they were short of cash, they were long on tricks; the trio played their appointed parts like sharpers at a fair. Theirs was a farce based upon feasting and drinking; for five whole days they fell upon provisions of all sorts so eagerly and so effectually that a troop of German mercenaries would have ravaged less than they devoured.

After breakfast, their whistles well wetted, their bellies gorged to bursting point, the three strolled over the Fair Grounds. Here they rode roughshod over greenhorns and others, thieving, filching, gambling, losing, taking down signboards and pointers, changing them about so that the toymaker's hung outside the jeweller's stand and the jeweller's over the cobbler's; making a bear garden out of the shops, egging the dogs on to fight, cutting the ropes of tethered horses, throwing cats into the crowds, shouting "Stop thief!" and saying to everybody: "Are you by any chance Master Tweenbuttox?" or "You look like Monsieur d'Entrefesse of Angers?" They jostled everyone about, cut holes in sacks of flour, searched for their handkerchiefs in ladies' bags, and looking tearfully for a lost jewel, raised the ladies' skirts, saying:

"It must be in some hole, Madame!"

They misdirected small children, barged into the bellies of sky-gazers, prowled around, fleecing, flaying and orduring everybody about. In brief, the Devil himself would have seemed mannerly beside these cursed students, who had liefer be hanged than honest. As well expect honesty of them as mercy of two angry litigants.

Not weary, but tired of misbehaving, they would leave the Fair and go back to the inn, dining all afternoon and renewing their pranks by torchlight. After the peddlers, they had a fling at the women of the town. Employing a thousand fishy dodges, they would give these frail sisters no more than they had received from them, according to the maxim of Justinian: *Cuique jus tribuere,* to each his own juice. Then, having shot their bolt, they would tell the poor trollops laughingly:

"We were in the right, you are in the wrong!"

Finally, at supper, having no one to persecute, they fell upon each other or else, to keep up the fun, they would complain to the landlord about the flies, protesting that elsewhere innkeepers had them tied up so that gentlemen of quality might not be annoyed by them.

By the fifth day—the critical day in fever-cases—the landlord had not yet seen the color of his money, let alone the royal face upon the coins, though he kept his eyes wide open. He knew that, if all that glitters were gold, things would be cheaper. So he began to draw in his horns and to go about the business of his high and mighty clients a shade more reluctantly. Fearing he had made a poor bargain with them, he attempted to sound the depth of their pockets. When they saw this, the three clerks, with the assurance of a provost hanging his man, bade the land-lord serve them a good supper—and quickly, too, for they must leave directly. Their blithe expression allayed the other's fears: rascals without money would certainly look grave. He therefore prepared a supper fit for a canon; he even hoped they would get drunk, for, if things came to the worst, he could clap them in jail without a struggle. The three companions could not imagine how to escape from the room, where they felt about as comfort-able as a fish out of water. They ate and drank in desperation, studied the disposition of the windows, watched for the proper moment to decamp, but could find neither light upon their prob-lem nor dark to leap into. Cursing up and down, one of them was for going outside to let down his breeches because of a colic; the second, meanwhile, could run for a doctor to attend to the third who had fainted. The thing was feasible. But the con-founded landlord was forever popping in and out from stove to table and back again; his eyes were glued on these doubtful char-acters; he would take one step forward to get his crowns back, and two steps back not to get his crown cracked for being too for-ward, if lords they really were. He plied to and fro like a wary innkeeper who loves tips and hates taps. Feigning the utmost dili-gence to look after them, he constantly kept one ear in the room, one foot in the court; he was continually thinking they had called him, appearing if they so much as laughed, thrusting his face forward like a swan (or innkeeper) his bill.

"Gentlemen, what is your pleasure?" he would ask, and their pleasure would have been to ram his spits ten inches down his gullet, for he seemed fully aware of their need in this predica-ment. Alas! to have twenty crowns sterling, each of the three would have sold one-third of his eternity. As you may imagine, they sat on their seats as on a gridiron, their feet itching and their rumps burning. Already the landlord had set pears, cheese and compote under their noses, but they sipped at their wine, toyed with their food and each looked at the other two to see if either had some good trick up his sleeve. All three began to amuse themselves somewhat wrily.

The sharpest of the three clerks, a Burgundian, smiled and, seeing the dread hour of settlement at hand:

"We must adjourn for a week, gentlemen," he said, as if he were trying a case in court.

At which the others, in spite of the danger, hastened to laugh.

"What do we owe?" asked the one who had twelve *sous* in his belt. And he jingled them about as though he hoped to make them breed others by this impassioned movement. This clerk was from Picardy, a very devil in anger, the sort of man to take offense at a trifle so as to be able in all security of conscience to fling the landlord out of the window. He therefore spoke arrogantly, as though he were rich as Crœsus.

"Six crowns, gentles," answered the host, holding out his hand.

"I cannot suffer myself to be treated by you alone, Viscount," said the third student, a man of Anjou, as leery as a woman in love.

"Nor I," put in the Burgundian.

"Gentlemen, gentlemen, you are jesting," the scion of Picardy answered. "Your servant, I!"

"By the Lord!" cried he of Anjou, "you shall not let us pay three times; our host would not permit it."

"Well then," the Burgundian decided, "whoever tells the worst story shall pay the landlord."

"Who will be judge?" the man of Picardy asked as he put back his twelve *sous* in his belt.

"Who else but Master Host? Anyone with his taste must be competent in the matter," cried he of Anjou. "Come, you prince of good cooks, sit down there and lend us both your ears. The meeting will come to order."

Thereupon the landlord sat down, not without pouring himself out a generous draught.

"My turn first," the speaker continued, "I begin."

"In our duchy of Anjou, the country folk are very faithful servants of our holy Catholic religion; not one would give up his share of Paradise for want of doing penance or slaying a heretic. Upon my word, if a dissenter minister passed that way, he would soon be pushing up daisies—and never know where that evil death came from, either!

"Well then, there was once a worthy man of Jarzé who had made his Vesper devotions at the *Sign of the Fir Cone* and left most of his understanding and memory at the bottom of the winejug. On his way home, under the impression that he was sinking back upon his own bed, he fell into a ditch full of water from his pond. A certain neighbor of his, Godenot by name, seeing him already caught fast in the ice (it was winter) asked him with a laugh:

" 'Hey, what are you waiting for there?'

" 'A thaw,' the good toper spluttered, as he realized he was unable to move.

"Like a noble Christian, Godenot released him from his icy prison and took him to his house, opening the toper's door for him, because wine is the lord of this land and the people hold it in due reverence. Well, our toper staggered off to bed all right—but plumb into the servant's bed! An attractive enough wench, she was, and quite young. The hardened old plowman, doubly potvaliant, plowed the warm furrow manfully—he thought he was with his wife—and scattered such remnants of maidenly properties as still clung to her. Hearing the turmoil, his wife began to shout like mad. Her horrified screams shocked the husbandman into the realization that he was not in the road to salvation. The sorrow he felt at this beggars all description.

" 'Ha,' he said, 'God punished me for not going to church for Vespers!'

"He proceeded to apologize as best he could, blaming the pot for his double intoxication. Returning to his own bed, he kept dinning into her ears that he would not wish to have this sin upon his conscience, no, not for his best cow, even!

" 'Never mind!' his wife comforted him. She had called the wench to account; the latter had protested that she was dreaming of her lover—which earned her a sound thrashing as a lesson not to relax while she slept. Yet the erring husband dwelled upon the enormity of his misapprehension, wailed over his pallet and shed winy, godfearing tears.

"'My love,' she said, 'you shall go to confession bright and early tomorrow morning. Now let us say no more about it.'

"So the sinner trots off to the confessional and, in all humility, explains his troubles to the curé of the parish. The cleric was a kindly old fellow, worthy to be God's slipper in Heaven.

"'An error is not a sin,' he declared. 'Fast tomorrow and I absolve you.'

"'Fast? Gladly!' the penitent exclaimed. 'Fasting has nothing to do with drink!'

"'Ho,' the priest replied, 'you shall drink *water*. And you shall eat only a quarter-loaf of bread and an apple.'

"The peasant had but small faith in his memory. So all the way home, he repeated the ordered penance: 'A quarter-loaf . . . an apple . . . an apple . . . a quarter-loaf . . . a quarter. . . .' By the time he reached home, he was saying 'a quarter of apples and a loaf of bread.'

"Then, to cleanse his soul, he buckled down to the fast. His wife took a loaf from the cupboard and unhooked some apples hanging from the ceiling. He began ruefully to feed the inner man. Having come to the last mouthful of bread, he fetched up a cavernous sigh. Where was he to put it? Was he not crammed up to the eyes? His wife remonstrated: God did not wish a sinner's death, nor, if he failed to put a hunk of bread less in his belly, would he be blamed for having taken the wrong sow by the ear.

"'Hush, wife,' he said. 'I must fast even if I burst!'"

"Now I have paid my score," he of Anjou wound up, winking slyly at his friend from Picardy. "Your turn, Viscount!"

"The jugs are empty," called the landlord. "Ho, there! Wine!"

"Let us drink," cried the northerner, "a wet whistle plays the sweetest tunes."

Thereupon he wolfed down his full glass without leaving a driblet of wine in it and, having cleared his throat lustily, like a preacher, he told the following story:

"No doubt you know that in Picardy, before setting up housekeeping, our wenches usually earn their trousseaux—dresses, dishes, chests and all matrimonial utensils—by good honest work. To do so, they go into service at Péronne, Abbeville, Amiens and elsewhere, acting as chambermaids, scullery-maids and maids of all work: they wash dishes, polish glasses, fold linen, handle dinner trays and anything else they can. As soon as they possess something besides what women naturally bring their husbands, they get married. And they are the best housewives in the world, because they are tried in this service and in everything else, too.

"A wench from Azonville, the country I am lord of by inheritance, had heard much talk of Paris. It was, rumor said, a city where people would not stoop to pick up a sixpence, where a person found sustenance for a day by simply passing in front of the pastrycooks' and drawing a deep breath, so rich was the emanation from stove and oven. She decided to go there, vowing to bring back as much money as there was in a church poor-box.

"She tramped up to town, at the cost of a good deal of shoe leather, and arrived, armed with her person and a pocket full of air. At the Porte St. Denis, she fell upon a company of soldiers stationed there on sentry duty—there was trouble afoot, as the Protestants appeared likely to rush to their sermonizing. Seeing this hooded baggage come pattering up, the Sergeant cocked his hat, smoothed the feather in it, twirled his mustachio, raised his voice, rolled his eyes, put a hand to his hip and stopped her. Was she properly pierced? (The ears, of course! . . .) Surely she knew that wenches might not enter Paris otherwise. Then, joking but with a serious look, he demanded what brought her here, pretending to believe she meant to take the keys of Paris by assault. The ingenuous wench replied that she was looking for a good position in service and would not mind any amount of work provided she earned something.

" 'I have just the thing for you, my girl,' said the wit, 'I am from Picardy too. I'll get you a job here; we shall treat you as a queen would often like to be treated, and you will be so much to the good.'

"He led her to the guardroom, told her to sweep the floor, to scour out the pot, to keep the fire going and to look after things generally. If their service pleased her, he added, she would receive thirty Parisian *sous* per head from the soldiers. As the squad was there for a month, she would earn a good ten crowns;

then, when they left, their successors would make a good arrangement with her. Thus, by dint of honest labor, she could go home to her province with plenty of money and many presents from Paris. The wench cleaned the room, a song on her lips; she set everything to rights, humming as she worked, and had such a good meal awaiting them that the soldiers, that day, found their hovel looking like a refectory of Benedictine monks. Thoroughly satisfied, each gave her a *sou*. When they were gorged, they laid her in their officer's bed (he was in town at his lady's) and proceeded to cosset and cockle her handsomely, showering caresses upon her that were both military and philosophical (i.e. loving good things). Soon she was comfortably settled between the sheets. To avoid any argument or quarrel, these tall rodsmen of joy drew lots for turns, then lined up in single file, wielding their pikes like picks on Picard ground, hot at work, uttering no word, but each having at least twenty-six *sous* Touraine worth of her.

"It was rather heavy service to one unaccustomed, but the poor girl did her best; she did not close an eye (or anything else) the whole night long. In the morning, seeing the soldiers sound asleep, she rose, happy at bearing no scars from so furious an onslaught. Though slightly fatigued, she managed to cross the fields and get into the open country with her thirty *sous*. On the road to Picardy our wench met one of her friends. Like herself, this girl wished to try service in Paris, and pressed forward all agog. The girl stopped her, began to question her on conditions in the capital.

" 'Ah, Perrine, don't go there,' she wailed. 'You would need a chine of iron—and even then, it would soon wear out!' "

"Your turn, now, you hogbellied Burgundian!" the narrator cried, thumping his neighbor's natural protuberance with the fist of a drill-sergeant. "Spit out your story or pay up!"

"By the Queen of Guts," the easterner answered, "by my faith, by the blessed death, by God and by the Devil, I know only stories of the Court of Burgundy, which are current but in the coin of our realm."

"Eh, 'Sbelly, are we not in the land of Beauffremont?" the other asked, pointing to the empty jugs.

"Well then, I'll tell you an adventure that is famous in Dijon.

It happened when I was in command there, and must certainly have been committed to writing since. There was a Constabulary Sergeant named Franc-Taupin, an old mine of evil, forever grumbling, forever fighting. He looked out at everything with jaundiced eye and as he led a man to the gallows, he never dreamed of cheering him up by cracking a joke. He was the sort to find lice on a bald pate and shortcomings in God Almighty Himself. This fellow Taupin, rebuffed by everybody, took unto himself a wife; as luck would have it, he drew a woman as sweet as onion-peel. Noting his unsatisfactory disposition, she went to more trouble to bring joy to his house than any other wife would have to mount a pair of horns on his scalp. Yet though she delighted in obeying him implicitly, though for the sake of peace she would have tried to void stools of gold, had God been willing, this sourbelly was perpetually finding fault and favoring his wife with blows as unsparingly as a debtor favors the bailiff's man with promises. In spite of the poor woman's angelic attentions and industry, this harsh treatment continued until she was forced to appeal to her parents, who decided to step in. When they arrived, the husband complained that his spouse was a fool, that she did nothing but annoy him, that she made his life almost unbearable. Now she would wake him up just as he fell off to sleep; now she would not answer the door and he was left cooling his heels in the mist or the snow. Nothing at home was ever in order. His clothes lacked buttons, his laces lacked tags, his linen was falling to bits, his wine turning sour, his wood damp, his bed always creaking at inopportune moments. Everything, he said, was at sixes and sevens. To this orgy of lying, the wife replied by showing clothes and everything else in a state of proper upkeep. Whereupon the Sergeant reaffirmed that he was badly treated. He never found his dinner ready, or if it was, then the broth was like dishwater or the soup cold as ice; wine was wanting on the table or glasses to drink out of; the meat was served bare, without sauce or parsley; the mustard had turned; he found hairs in the roast, or the napkins smelled musty and took away his appetite; in fine, nothing she ever gave him was to his taste. The wife, much astonished, contented herself with flatly denying the extraordinary grievances he taxed her with.

" 'Eh,' said he, 'you say no, you putrid hussy!'

"Then, turning to her parents: 'Come and dine with us this very day; you shall be witness to her misbehavior. If for once she can serve me as I wish, I will own I am wrong in everything I said, I will never raise my hand against her; more, I will leave her my halbert—and my breeches. She can wear those and give orders around here.'

" 'Bravo!' she cried gaily. 'From now on, I shall be lady and mistress.'

"Relying upon the natural imperfection of women, Taupin decided that dinner should be prepared and served under the trellis in the court. It would afford him a chance to shout at her, if she did not trot quickly enough from larder to table. The good housewife went to work heart and soul. The plates were clean enough to see one's face in, the mustard was fresh and perfectly flavored, the dinner was admirably cooked to a temperature fit to burn the gizzard and appetizing as stolen fruit, the glasses beautifully polished, the wine cool as can be, and everything about the meal was so neat, so dazzling, so immaculate that it would have done honor to a bishop's housekeeper. But just as she was smacking her lips over the table, casting the final super-fluous glance a born housewife likes to give to everything, her husband knocked at the door. At that very moment, a cursed hen, who had been inspired to climb on to the trellis and gorge her-self with grapes, let fly a great fæcal volley that landed plumb on the tablecloth. The wretched woman almost swooned, so com-plete was her despair. But, mastering herself, she used the only conceivable means at hand to remedy the hen's intemperance: she covered the unsavory blot with a plate, on which she placed some fruit she happened to have in her pocket. All effort to achieve symmetry on the table went by the board.

"Then, to divert attention from the thing, she brought in the soup at once, bade her guests sit down and urged them gaily to fall to.

"Seeing how beautifully ordered and well prepared the dishes were, the company burst into loud exclamations of praise, except, of course, her fiend of a husband. He sat back, gloomy and sullen, frowning, growling, studying everything in order to find a straw with which to fell his wife. The latter, overjoyed at an opportunity of annoying him with her people there to protect her, smiled sweetly on him:

" 'Here is your meal, dear,' she said. 'It's nice and hot . . . the table is properly laid . . . the linen fresh and spotless . . . the salt-cellars full . . . the plates clean, the wine fresh, the bread golden. . . . Is anything missing? What do you need? Do you want something? What will you have?'

" 'Sh-t!' he roared in a towering rage.

"Lifting the fruit plate quickly:

" 'Here you are, my love,' she answered.

"The Sergeant sat flabbergasted, certain that the Devil had changed over to his wife's side. Her parents heaped reproaches on him, pronounced him in the wrong, decried and insulted him, and brought down more taunts on his head in a few moments than a recorder writes words in a month. From that day forward, the Sergeant lived in perfect harmony with his wife, who, at the least symptom of bad temper, at the merest shadow of a frown, would ask him:

" 'Will you have some sh-t?' "

"Who told the worst?" cried the man from Anjou, clapping the landlord on the back as gently as a hangman.

"*He* did! *He* did!" cried the others. Then they started quarrelling among themselves like so many Fathers in a Church Council, seeking to belabor each other, to hurl jugs and glasses about, to get to their feet and, by a break in the battle, to make a dash for liberty.

"I'll settle the argument," cried the host, who realized that where he had had three clients disposed to pay, now none gave the bill a thought.

They stopped, terrified.

"I'll tell you the best story of the lot," he offered, "and you give me ten *sous* per head!"

"The landlord has the floor!" cried the man from Anjou.

"In our borough of Notre Dame la Riche, upon which church this hostelry is dependent, there was once a beautiful girl, blessed not only with natural advantages but also with a good round sum

of money. As soon as her years and strength permitted her to
bear the yoke of marriage, she had as many lovers as there are
sous in the money-box at St. Gatien's on Easter Sunday. This girl
chose a man who, saving your presence, could perform night and
day as well as a pair of monks. They were soon engaged and the
wedding-day planned. But the delights of the bridal night did
not draw near without arousing a certain amount of apprehension in the girl's breast. You see, she was, through an infirmity of
the subterranean conduits, subject to expelling vapors which had
a way of bursting like bombshells.

"She was very much afraid that, in the course of the wedding-
night, while she was thinking of something else, her husband
might get wind of her bizarre ailment. So she finally confessed
her plight to her mother and invoked the latter's assistance. This
faculty of engendering wind, the lady told her daughter, was
hereditary in the family; she herself had been sorely embarrassed
by it in her day. But, in later life, God had vouchsafed her the
mercy of compressing her crupper so that for the last seven years
she had emitted nothing save one last time when, by way of parting, she had saluted her late lamented husband with a heroic
salvo of farewell.

" 'But,' she added, 'I possess a sure remedy that brings these
uncalled for expletives to nothing and exhales them soundlessly.
My dear mother—God bless her—bequeathed it to me. Since
these currents are in no wise malodorous, by my method all scandal is avoided. You must proceed as follows. First, allow the ven-
tose substance to simmer, holding it back at the neb of the noz-
zle; then push hard; presently the air, having become rarefied,
escapes like an angel's breath. In our family we call this stran-
gling the zephyr.'

"The girl, delighted at knowing how to strangle zephyrs,
thanked her mother and danced merrily away, storing up her
flatulence like an organ-blower waiting for the first note of Mass.
Then, reaching the bridal chamber, she resolved to discharge as
she climbed into bed; but the fantastic element proved static.
Her husband appeared—and I leave you to imagine how they
fenced in that pretty bout where with two things you do a thousand, if you can. In the middle of the night, the wife rose, under
a certain pretext, and speedily returned; but as she climbed back

into her place, there was a kind of sneeze, then a report like a culverin's, so loud that you would have thought the curtains were rent, just as I did.

" 'Eh, but I misfired!' she said.

" ' 'Sdeath, my love,' I told her, 'spare me your gunpowder. With such artillery, you could earn a living in the Army.'

"This accomplished lady was my wife. . . ."

"Ho, ho, ho!" roared the three clerks, as they burst into laughter, holding their sides and showering praise upon the landlord.

"Have you ever heard a better story, Viscount?"

"Ha, what a tale!"

"The king of stories!"

"Ha, ha, it has every other tale ever I heard lashed to the mast! From now on, the only tales are innkeepers'."

"By my faith as a Christian, it is the best story I have heard in all my born days."

"Why, I can hear the explosion!"

"And I—I should like to kiss the orchestra!"

"Ho, Master Innkeeper," said the man from Anjou gravely, "we could not possibly leave without seeing the hostess; and if we do ask to kiss her instrument, it is through great respect for so excellent a storyteller."

Thereupon they all exalted the host, his oral gift (and his wife's) so earnestly that the old fellow believed in the sincerity of this naïve hilarity and these pompous eulogies. He called up to his wife. As she did not come, the clerks, not without ulterior motives, cried:

"Let us go up to her."

With which they all left the room together. The host took a candle and preceded them up the stairs to light the way for them; but, seeing the street door ajar, the scoundrels made themselves scarce, fleeing, light as shadows, and leaving him, in settlement of his account, the prospect of another windfall from his wife.

The Privations of King Francis the First

*E*VERYBODY knows through what adventure King Francis, first of the name, was caught like a foolish bird and led to the town of Madrid, in Spain. There the Emperor, Charles the Fifth, kept him very carefully locked up in one of his castles, like an article of great value. Our deceased master, of eternal memory, grieved very much, for he craved the open air and his creature comforts; he understood the art of staying shut in a cage about as well as a cat understands that of rolling up a ball of wool properly. He fell into strange fits of melancholy. When his letters were read out in full Council, his mother, Madame d'Angoulême, Madame Catherine, the Dauphine, Cardinal Duprat, Monsieur de Montmorency and those who ruled the affairs of France deliberated long about his case. All of them, of course, knew the great lechery of the King. After due reflection, they determined to send Queen Margaret of Navarre to him; he loved her dearly, she was gay and schooled in wisdom, so she would undoubtedly bring him balm for his suffering. But she objected that her soul was at stake: she could not possibly stay alone with the monarch in his cell without the direst danger. Accordingly, an astute secretary, the Sieur de Fizes, was sent off to the Court of Rome to beg the Pope for a brief of special indulgences and official absolutions for such petty sins (in the light of their consanguinity) as the Queen might commit with an eye to curing His Majesty.

At this time, the Dutchman, Adrian VI, still wore the tiara. He was a good fellow withal, and in spite of the scholastic ties binding him to the Emperor, he did not forget that the eldest son of the Catholic Church was involved. Obligingly enough, he sent an express legate to Spain, with full powers to undertake the

194

salvation of the Queen's soul and the King's body without too great injury to God. This most urgent affair tormented the gentlemen of the Court to death; it set up an itching between the ladies' feet, for, in their deep devotion to the crown, almost all of them would have volunteered to go to Madrid. But Charles the Fifth remained darkly mistrustful; nor would he grant the King leave to see any of his subjects or even his own kin. It was therefore essential to arrange the departure of the Queen of Navarre. From then on, no conversation but dwelled upon his deplorable privation in the matter of amative exercise and how disastrous it was for a prince who was such an inveterate practician. At length, between fellow-feeling and sympathy, the women ended by thinking more of the rod of kingship than of the King himself. The Queen was the first to say that she wished she had wings. To this My Lord Odet de Châtillon replied that she did not need wings to be an angel. One lady, Madame l'Amirale, blamed God for the impossibility of dispatching by messenger the thing the unhappy monarch needed so sorely. Would not every one of the ladies have lent hers in turn?

"God did well to fasten it down," the Dauphine said charmingly, "for, with it gone, our husbands would leave us very traitorously in want."

So much was said and so much thought about it that when she left, the Queen of all Marguerites was charged by these worthy Christians to embrace the captive fondly for all the ladies of the realm; and had it been possible to pack up pleasure like mustard, for instance, she would have been laden with enough to sell to the two Castiles.

While, despite the heavy snows, Madame Marguerite was crossing the mountains by relays of mules, speeding to His Majesty's consolation as to a house on fire, Francis found himself rising to a position of agony more pricking and burdensome than his life had been known or was destined to afford. Amid this extreme reverberation of nature, he opened his heart to the Emperor Charles, hoping to be furnished with a merciful specific and objecting that it would bring eternal shame upon one king to let another die for want of gallantry. The Castilian proved himself a generous man. Expecting his guest's ransom to provide reparations for such prejudice as might be done to his señoritas, he made clear to the guards, by hints and insinuations, that they might gratify the royal prisoner in this respect.

Now there was a certain Don Hiios de Lara y Lopez Bara di Pinto, a poor captain who, for all his high genealogy, was very low in funds. For a long while, he had actually been thinking of seeking fortune at the Court of France. It occurred to him that by procuring His Majesty a soft cataplasm of sweet flesh, he would be opening for himself the door to honest abundance. How right or how wrong he was, those who know Court and King can tell.

When the Captain came in his turn to the King's chamber, he begged respectful permission to put a question which intrigued him as much as papal indulgences. The monarch, dropping his hypochondriac expression and twisting round on his chair, nodded his consent. The Captain begged him not to take offense at the license of his language and confessed to him that he, King Francis, was reputed to be one of the greatest fornicators in France. Would His Majesty give the Spanish gentleman his personal opinion on the ladies of the French Court? Were they really so expert in the technique of love? The unhappy sovereign, recalling his past raptures, heaved a deep, hollow sigh. No women of any country, including those of the moon, he said, possessed the secrets of this alchemy more effectually than the ladies of France. Further, at the mere remembrance of the savory, graceful and vigorous cockerings of a single one, he felt himself the man, if she were then available, to bestride her furiously, on a rotten plank one hundred feet above a precipice. . . .

As he spoke, the good King, a ribald fellow, if ever there was one, darted so hot a glance from eyes blazing with life and passion that, though the Captain was a brave soldier, he felt a most intimate quaking in his chitterlings before the sacred majesty of royal love. But, recovering his courage, he began to defend the ladies of Spain. Only in Castile, he boasted, was the science of amour properly applied, for Castile was the most religious place in Christendom. Surely the more a woman feared to be damned for surrendering to her lover, the better she went to it, since she realized it must be all her pleasure throughout eternity? He added that if His Majesty condescended to wager one of the best and richest manors in his kingdom, he, Don Hiios de Lara y Lopez Bara di Pinto would offer him a night of Hispanic love in which, unless he took care, a random queen would pluck up his soul by the root.

"Done!" cried His Majesty, rising from his chair. "The sooner the better! . . . By God, I will give you the manor of Ville-aux-Dames, in my province of Touraine, with full privilege of chase and all jurisdiction, high and low."

The Captain knew the doña of the Cardinal Archbishop of Toledo. He besought her to break the butterfly King of France on the wheel of Spanish kindness and to make good the advantage of the Castilian imagination over the simple movement of the French. To which the Marquesa de Amaesguy assented, both for the honor of Spain and for the satisfaction of ascertaining what paste God made kings of. (This was, at that time, a closed book to her; she had got no further than princes of the Church.) So she came, rampant as a lion that has broken out of his cage; under her savage onslaught, amid a cracking of bones and marrow, any other man would have given up the ghost. But the monarch was so well furnished, so utterly ravenous and so grasping that he did not feel himself grasped; and from this horrendous duel, the Marquesa emerged the loser, mortified, and convinced it was the Devil she had wrestled with.

The Captain, sure of his game, appeared the next morning to wait upon his lord and pay homage for his new fief. What was his amazement when the King observed banteringly that Spanish women were of a passable temperature, that they put their whole soul into their work but that they became frenzied when gentleness was called for. Each trance, he specified, seemed more like a sneeze, a seizure or a rape, whereas the French method kept bringing back the drinker more thirsty than ever, without the slightest suspicion of fatigue. With the ladies of his Court, love was a gentle pastime without parallel, not the work of a master baker at his kneading trough.

The poor Captain was strangely piqued at this language. Despite the knightly honor His Majesty boasted, the Spaniard believed the other was attempting to swindle him, like a student welching a sliver of love in a Paris stew. At all events, having no means of knowing whether the Marquesa had not overspanished the King, he asked for a return engagement, promising that he would produce a veritable goddess to win him his fief. King Fran-

cis was too courteous and gallant a knight not to grant this request; he even proffered a right royal remark to the effect that
he hoped to lose.

Vespers done, the guard smuggled a lady into the King's chamber. She was warm, white, radiantly fair, delicately wanton and

tittuppy, with long tresses and hands soft as velvet; her dress
belled at her slightest gesture, for she was gracefully plump; her
lips were parted in a gay smile, her eyes already moist. She was
the sort of woman to make hell a holy of holies; the first word
she uttered held such a cordial power that His Majesty's buttons
burst under the strain.

On the morrow, after breakfast, the siren vanished. At once the good Captain entered, triumphantly happy. The moment the King saw him:

"Baron de la Ville-aux-Dames," he cried, "may God grant you joys comparable to mine! I adore my jail! By Our Lady, I will not judge of love in your land and mine. No—I prefer to pay the wager."

"I knew you would!" the Captain said beaming.

"How did you know?" His Majesty demanded.

"Sire," said the other, "the lady is my wife."

Such was the origin of Larray de la Ville-aux-Dames in our country; through corruption, the name of Lara y Lopez ended in Larray. The family proved a good one, serving the Kings of France loyally, and faring well.

Shortly after, the Queen of Navarre came opportunely to the King, who, surfeited with Spanish manners, longed to take pleasure in the French. But what followed is not the subject of this story. I myself reserve the right to tell elsewhere how the legate went about obliterating such sin as hung about the thing and to quote the delightful comment made by our Queen of Marguerites, who merits a saint's niche in this volume for having written such peerless tales. The morality of this one is not difficult to understand.

In the first place, kings should no more allow themselves to be taken in battle than their archetype did in the game of Palamedes. But from this, it is manifest that the captivity of its monarch visits horrible and calamitous ills upon a people. Had it been a queen, or even a princess, what worse fate! At the same time, even among cannibals, I do not believe the thing could happen. Is there ever reason to imprison the flower of a kingdom? I think too well of the deviltries of Ashtoreth, Lucifer and the rest to imagine that, under their régime, joy could be hidden from all folk and the beneficent light in which poor sufferers find warmth, bedimmed. It was necessary that the most evil of fiends, i.e. a wicked old heretic woman, should happen to sit upon a throne for the fair Mary of Scotland to be incarcerated to the shame of all the knights of Christendom, who should have gathered spontaneously at the foot of Fotheringay and left no stone to tell the tale.

The Airy Tattle of the Nuns of Poissy

THE ABBEY of Poissy has been celebrated by olden authors as an abode of pleasure, where the transgressions of young nuns originated and whence a host of gay stories sprang up to amuse laymen at the expense of our holy religion. Poissy became the subject of proverbs which none of our latter-day savants understand, though they struggle to sift and grind in order to digest them.

Were you to ask one of them what the *Olives of Poissy* are, he would reply gravely that here is a periphrastic reference to truffles and that the *way to serve them* (cited facetiously in connection with these virtuous virgins) was doubtless connected with some special sauce. That is how these quilldrivers hit upon the truth once in a thousand times.

To return to the good recluses, it was said—as a joke, of course —that they had rather find a harlot under their chemise than a good woman. Other wags reproached them with imitating the lives of the saints but after their own method; of St. Mary the Egyptian, for example, they admired only her fashion of paying boatmen. Whence the jest: *To honor saints after the fashion of Poissy.* Then there is the *Poissy Cross* which kept the stomach warm, and *Poissy Matins* which concluded with offerings from little choristers. A lusty trollop who knew the delights of love was called *A nun of Poissy.* A certain familiar thing man can but lend was the *Keys to the Abbey of Poissy.* What the *Gate* of this abbey was we all know bright and early. This gate, door, hatch, postern or dormer, forever ajar, is easier to open than to close, and it costs much in repairs. In brief, at that period no pleasant trick in love was invented that did not come from the good Convent at Poissy. You may be certain that these proverbs, quips and jokes were so many cock-and-bull stories, full of exaggeration and untruth. The nuns of Poissy were excellent young ladies, who now one way, now another, cheated God to the profit of the Devil, as many others do, because it is in our natures to be frail and because, though nuns, they had their little imperfections. The flesh is not everywhere resistant; within them there was necessarily a vulnerable spot; hence the evil. The fact of the matter is that all the mischief was done by one abbess, who had fourteen children, all of whom flourished. (Had they not been perfected at leisure?) The fantastic liaisons and eccentricities of this woman—she was of royal blood—made the Convent of Poissy a fashionable institution. Thereafter every diverting adventure enacted in all the abbeys of France was ascribed to the effervescence of these luckless girls, who would have been delighted to live a tenth part of them. After, the Abbey was reformed, as everyone knows, and these holy nuns were deprived of what little happiness and liberty they enjoyed.

In an old register of the Abbey of Turpenay, near Chinon (amid the troubles of our day it found refuge in the library of Azay, where the present owner welcomed it) I came upon a fragment entitled *The Hours of Poissy*. It had evidently been composed by some gay Abbot of Turpenay for the entertainment of his fair neighbors of Ussé, Azay, Montgauger, Saché and other convents in these parts. I reproduce it herewith under authority of the cassock, but altered to my own style, for I have had to translate it from Latin into French.

At Poissy, the nuns were accustomed, when Mademoiselle, the King's daughter, their Abbess, was in her bed. . . .

It was she who first gave the name of Goose to the practise of going no further in love than the preliminaries, prologues, preambles, prefaces, protocols, notices, forewords, prolegomena, summaries, prospectuses, arguments, notes, prodromes, epigraphs, titles, bastard titles, current titles, scholia, marginal remarks, frontispieces, observations, gilt edges, handsome markers, clasps, rules, devices, vignettes, tail pieces and engravings, without once opening the book itself to read, re-read, study, grasp and digest its merry contents. She gathered in a doctrinal body the various trifling extrajudiciary pleasures of this pretty language (labial, to be sure, but soundless) which she had at the tip of her tongue. She died a virgin, perfectly shaped, immaculate. . . . This gay science was afterwards much developed by the ladies of the Court, who took certain lovers for Goose, others for honor, and, sometimes, still others who enjoyed the right of jurisdiction, high and low, and were masters of everything—a condition many prefer.

But to proceed. . . .

When this virtuous princess lay naked and shameless between the sheets, those girls whose chins were unwrinkled and whose hearts were blithe, would steal noiselessly out of their cells and hide in that of one of their sisters, a very popular nun. There they would have merry little chats, intermixed with sweetmeats, comfits, cordials and girlish quarrels; they would torment their elders, imitating them mischievously, mocking them in all innocence, telling stories that made them weep for laughter, and playing a thousand pranks. Sometimes they would measure their feet to see who had the daintiest, compare the whiteness of their plump arms, discover who suffered from a red nose after supper, count their freckles, locate each others' moles, decide who had the prettiest complexion, the highest color, the daintiest figure. As may be imagined, these figures consecrated to God included all sorts—thin, round, flat, hollow-chested, plump, supple and slender. Sometimes they would dispute about who required the least material to make a girdle, and the one with the slightest span was happy without knowing why. Or they would relate their dreams and describe what apparitions they had seen. Often one or two and sometimes all of them had dreamed they were holding the *Keys to the Abbey* in a grasp of iron. At times, they would consult each other about their little ailments. One had scratched her finger, another had a whitlow, a third had arisen that morning with a bloodshot eye, a fourth had put her index finger out while telling her beads. None but had some little disturbance or other.

One nun accused her neighbor:

"Ha, you lied to our Mother; your nails are whitened!"

"You lingered very long at confession this morning, Sister," another exclaimed. "Did you have many sweet sins to confess?"

Then, since nothing is more like a pussy than a tomcat, they would swear friendship, wrangle, sulk, fall out, take sides, become reconciled again, show jealousy, exchange playful pinches, laugh hilariously and play tricks on the novices.

Often, they asked:

"If a constable were to come here some rainy day, where would we put him?"

"In Sister Ovide's. Hers is the biggest cell; he could get in, plume and all."

"What do you mean?" cried Sister Ovide. "Are not all our cells alike?"

Whereupon the girls would burst out laughing like so many ripe figs. . . .

One evening their meeting was augmented by a pretty seventeen-year-old novice, who appeared innocent as a new born babe and deserved God without need of confession. Her mouth had watered for these secret palavers, banquets and junketings with which the young nuns mitigated the hallowed captivity of their bodies; she had shed tears at being denied admittance.

"Well, my sweet darling," Sister Ovide asked her, "did you have a good night's sleep?"

"Oh, no," the other answered, "I was bitten by fleas!"

"So, you have fleas in your cell, eh? You must get rid of them at once. Do you know how the Rules of our Order enjoin us to drive them out so that no sister ever again sees so much as the tail of one throughout her conventual life?"

"No," replied the novice.

"Very well, I shall tell you. Do you see a flea here? Do you notice any vestige of a flea? Do you discern an odor of fleas? Is there any sign of fleas in my cell? Look."

"I can find none," said the little novice, who was Mademoiselle de Fiennes, "and I smell nothing beyond our natural odor."

"Do as I tell you and you will never be bitten again. The moment you feel yourself pricked, my girl, you must undress, lift your chemise and be careful to commit no sin as you examine your body all over. Your whole concern must be with the cursed flea, you must search for it in good faith, you must mind nothing else, straining every nerve and thought to bring about the flea's capture. This in itself is a task of considerable difficulty, for you

may easily go wrong on the small black spots on your skin, a natural inheritance. Have you any, darling?"

"Yes," she answered, "I have two dark freckles, one on my
shoulder, the other on my back, rather low down, but my but-
tocks hide it. . . ."

"How did you see it?" asked Sister Perpetua.

"I knew nothing about it. It was Monsieur de Montrésor who
discovered it."

"Ha, ha, ha!" roared the sisters. "And was that all he saw?"

"He saw everything," the novice confessed. "I was very young;
he was just nine years old. We were playing together. . . ."

The nuns felt they had been all too ready to laugh at her and
Sister Ovide resumed:

"Now the flea in question may leap about from your legs to
your eyes, it may seek to hide in the hollows, forests and ditches,
it may travel up-hill and down-dale, persisting in escaping you.
The Rules of the Order command you to pursue it courageously,
saying *Aves* the while. Usually, at the third *Ave,* the beast is
taken. . . ."

"The flea?" asked the novice.

"Exactly, the flea!" Sister Ovide went on. "To avoid the perils
of the chase, you must take care, in whatever spot you put your
finger on the beast, to disturb nothing else. Without heeding its
cries, plaints, groans, efforts and writhings (if it happens to resist,
which is frequent enough) you press it under your thumb or any
other finger of the hand you hold it in. Meanwhile with your
other hand you look for a veil with which to blindfold the flea
and prevent it from leaping, as the beast, unable to see clearly,
does not know where to go. However, as it can still bite you and
may well be in a furious rage, you part its lips gently and delicately insert a twig of the blessed brush in the little holy water
bowl by your bedside. This compels the flea to behave properly.

"But do not forget that the discipline of our Order forbids you
to retain property of anything on earth; this beast, then, could
not belong to you. You must consider that it is one of God's
creatures; this should make you strive to render it more agreeable in His sight. Therefore, before you do anything else, you
must determine three extremely serious conditions, viz.: Is the
flea a male? Is it a female? Or is it a virgin?

"Assuming it be a virgin—this is very rare indeed, because these beasts have no morals, they are all highly lascivious hussies who yield to the first comer—you seize her by the hind legs, draw them out from under her little caparison, bind them with one of your hairs and bring her to the Mother Superior, who settles her fate after due consultation with the Chapter. If it be a male . . ."

"How can you tell if a flea be a virgin?" the curious novice asked.

"To begin with," Sister Ovide explained, "she is sad and melancholy, she never laughs like the others, she does not bite so hard, her lips are less open and she blushes if you touch her you know where. . . ."

"In that case," said the novice, "I was bitten by males. . . ."

The sisters burst into such uncontrollable fits of laughter that one of them gave vent to a booming nether note pitched in A sharp, together with a little water, *affetuoso,* to drown it. Sister Ovide pointing to the floor, said:

"You see, there's never wind without rain!"

The novice herself laughed, believing these guffaws due to the apostrophe the sister had let slip.

"Well then," Sister Ovide persisted, "in the event of a male flea, you take your scissors or a dagger, if your lover happened to give you his as a keepsake before you came here. At any rate, you take a sharp instrument and, with the utmost precaution, you slit open the flank of the flea. Do not be surprised if he howls, coughs, spits and begs your pardon. He will wriggle about, sweat like an ox, cast sheep's eyes upon you; he will use every means at his disposal to avoid this operation. Don't let it faze you. Pluck up your courage; remind yourself that you are doing this to set a perverted creature on the road to salvation. With scrupulous dexterity, pick out his tripe, liver and lungs, his heart, his gizzard and his noble parts; dip them into holy water several times, to lave and purify them. While doing so, do not fail to implore the Holy Spirit to sanctify the beast's interior. Finally restore these intestinal appurtenances in the body of the flea, who, by this time, will have become impatient to recover them. Being, by this means, baptized, the soul of the creature is made Catholic. Go fetch a needle and thread; then sew up the belly again with the utmost care and precaution in that you owe these attentions to your brother in Christ. You must even pray for him; the genuflections and ogles he gives you will reward your trouble. He will give over crying, he will abandon his desire to bite you; certain of his kind actually die of pleasure at being thus converted to our holy religion.

"If you follow these principles on any flea you catch, the others, seeing it and marvelling at the convert, will decamp. You have no idea how perverse they are and how terrified at the prospect of likewise becoming Christians. . . ."

"Surely, they are very wrong," the novice commented. "What happiness greater than to rest in the bosom of the Church?"

"Certainly," Sister Ursula agreed. "Here we are sheltered from the perils of the world and from love, so fraught with dangers. . . ."

"Is there any danger save that of having a child out of season?" asked a youthful sister.

"During the present reign,"—Sister Ursula shook her head—"love has inherited leprosy, St. Anthony's fire, scurvy and red soldier; in its pretty mortar it has collected the fevers, agonies, germs and sufferings of them all to produce a horrible evil compound by the Devil. It has, however, redounded to the advantage of convents because a vast number of ladies are forced into practising virtue and taking the veil through fear of love."

They all huddled up close to one another, frightened at the words, but wishing to know more.

"Does the mere fact of loving suffice to bring on this suffering?" a sister asked.

"Ay, ay, alas, sweet Jesu!" Sister Ovide lamented.

"You have but to love a pretty gentleman once," Sister Ursula pursued, "and you run the risk of seeing your teeth drop out one by one, your hair fall apace, your cheeks turn blue and your eyebrows peel off amid excruciating pain. Then farewell to your sweetest charms, and a pretty price they cost you! There are poor women who get funguses like cock-lobsters on the end of their nose; others have a myriad-clawed beast forever squirming and gnawing away at their tenderest parts. The Pope has at last been obliged to excommunicate this sort of love."

"Oh, how lucky I am to have had nothing of that sort!" the novice exclaimed prettily.

Hearing this echo redolent of love, the sisters suspected our novice of having basked in the warmth of some *Poissy Cross* and of egging Sister Ovide on for sport. All were delighted to number such a gay baggage among them; at once they asked her to what adventure they owed the pleasure of her company.

"Alas!" she said, "I let myself be bitten by a big flea who was already baptized."

At this speech, she of the A sharp could not withhold another sigh.

"Ah," cried Sister Ovide, "two of a pair! You are bound to give us the third. If you spoke that language in the choir, Mother

Abbess would diet you like Sister Petronella. A sordet to your trump, Sister."

"You knew Sister Petronella," Sister Ursula addressed the speaker. "Is it true God granted her the gift of going but twice a year to the bank of deposit?"

"Ay," Sister Ovide replied. "Once she actually stayed squatting all night long, saying: 'I am here by the will of God!' But at the first verse of Matins, she was delivered, in order that she should not miss the office. The late Abbess, however, would not allow that this was a special favor vouchsafed from on high; she objected that God's glance did not sink so low. Here are the facts.

"Our late Sister—our Order is even now supporting her canonization at the Papal Court and would already have obtained it but for lack of funds to defray the brief—our Petronella, then, nursed ambitions. She wished to have her name writ upon the Calendar of Saints, which certainly could do our Order no harm. She therefore began to live in prayer alone, lost in ecstasies before the Virgin's altar, which is over by the field. Presently she heard the angels flying up to Paradise so distinctly, she averred, that she was able to catch the tunes they were chanting. As you all know, that is where she got the sweet music of the *Adoremus,* for what man could have originated a single note of it? For days at a time, her eyes stared out, fixed as a star; she would fast, putting no more nourishment in her body than I could get into my eye. She had made a vow never to taste meat, either cooked or raw; she ate only one crust of bread each day; on major Feast Days, she would eke out her diet with a bit of salted fish, but never a drop of sauce. At this regimen, she grew thin as a shadow, yellow as saffron and dry as a churchyard bone, for hers was an ardent nature and anybody with the good luck to knock up against her would have drawn fire as from a flint.

"But, scant though her fare, she could not escape an infirmity to which we are all more or less subject, unluckily or perhaps luckily, for otherwise we would be somewhat cramped. The function in question is the necessity of expelling after meals, commonly and like all animals, a substance varying in charm according to the individual. Now Sister Petronella differed from her fellows in this respect: she produced a substance as arid and

hard as an amorous hind's, which form of course the most tightly
cohesive concoctions a gizzard can turn out, as you doubtless
know if you ever put foot upon them in a forest path. Indeed,
from their firmness, they are called bullets in the language of
high venery. This faculty of Sister Petronella's was not unnat-
ural; her fasts maintained her temperament in permanent ebul-

lition. According to the old sisters, her nature was so combusti-
ble that when she bathed, she went *frist!* like a hot coal. Certain
sisters accused her of cooking eggs between her toes, secretly and
by night, in order to support her austerities. But these were
slanders invented to tarnish her great holiness, which had been
a source of bitter jealousy in other convents.

"Our sister was piloted along the road to salvation and divine
perfection by the Abbot of St. Germain des Prés, of Paris. The

cleric was a holy man; invariably he capped his counsel with the final injunction to offer to God our every care and to bow to His will, for nothing happened save at His expressed command. This doctrine, which has every appearance of wisdom, supplied matter for vast controversies and was finally condemned on the advice of the Cardinal of Châtillon, who pointed out that it did away with sin and consequently with a good part of the Church's revenues.

"Sister Petronella lived on, imbued with this doctrine and unaware of its danger. After Lent and the fasts of the great jubilee, for the first time in eight months she experienced a need to go to the throne-room, whither indeed, she repaired. There she lifted her skirts bravely and assumed the proper inclination and posture to do what we poor sinners do rather more often. But Sister Petronella could only manage to expectorate the merest beginning and she kept wheezing away while the remainder refused to proceed. Though she wrestled and writhed, twisting her lips, knitting her brow and pressing every spring of the human mechanism, her host preferred to remain in her blessed body; content to poke his head out of the window, natural as a frog taking the air, and without in the least feeling a vocation to plunge into the vale of misery, among the others. On the contrary, he alleged he would not be in an odor of sanctity there. In which, ordurous though he was, he showed a great deal of sense.

"The excellent saint, having employed every means of coercion at her disposal, having strained her buccinators to the limit and stretched the muscles of her thin face to bursting point, understood that no suffering on earth was so serious and that her agony was attaining the apogee of sphincterial torture.

" 'Oh, my God, my God,' she prayed urgently, 'unto Thee do I offer it.'

"At this orison, the petrified body broke off, neck to neck with the orifice, and fell clattering against the walls of the privy, with a *croc, crooc, crooook, paf!* Of course, my dear sisters, you understand that bumwad was quite unnecessary and that the rest of the business was held over until the following week."

"But did she see the angels?" a nun asked.

"Have angels bottoms?" put in another.

"Of course not!" Sister Ursula pooh-poohed. "Don't you know one day in Assembly, when God ordered them to sit down, they answered that they lacked the wherewithal."

Whereupon they sped off to bed, some of them alone, others approximately so. They were good girls and they harmed only themselves.

I cannot take leave of them without relating an adventure which occurred in their house while the reform, previously cited, was whitewashing it and sanctifying them.

At that period, the See of Paris was adorned by a veritable saint. He did not trumpet his works abroad, but devoted all his energies to the poor and the afflicted; these, it was, he lodged in his bishop's heart. Oblivious of himself, the grand old man ministered to the sorrowful, sought out misery in every form in order to patch it up with encouragement, assistance, money or support; he would intervene in the evil hour of rich or poor to comfort their souls and remind them of God; and, Heaven bless him! he would wear himself out watching over his flock, the dear shepherd! This good man went about blissfully unconscious of his cassocks, cloaks or breeches, so but the naked members of his church were covered. He was so charitable that he would have put himself in pawn to get even a heathen out of trouble. His servants were forced to look after him, yet what a scolding he gave them if they presumed to substitute new garments for his threadbare ones, which he used to have patched and darned until they fell to pieces!

This fine Archbishop knew that the late Sieur de Poissy had left his daughter without a rap, after having eaten, drunk and gambled her inheritance away. The maid lived in a hovel, without fire in winter or cherries in spring; working at various small tasks, unwilling to marry beneath her or to sell her virtue. Until he should find a young husband for her, the prelate took it into his head to send her the shell of a man to mend, in the person of his old trousers and breeches. In her complete poverty the poor girl was very glad of the job.

One day while the Archbishop was planning to go to the Convent of Poissy to look over the reformed nuns, he gave a servant

the oldest pair of breeches he possessed—they implored a patch
—and:

"Take this to the ladies of Poissy, Saintot," he told the man.

Naturally he thought he had said "to the lady of Poissy." As
he was engrossed in conventual affairs, he neglected to tell his
servant where the young lady lodged. (He had discreetly kept
her desperate condition a secret.)

Saintot took the breeches and set out for Poissy, merry as a
wagtail; he stopped with various friends he met on the road,
tipped the pot at taverns and showed the Archbishop's buttons
more than one thing they learned during this journey. Arriving
at the convent, he told the Abbess that his master had bidden
him give her the breeches. Then the varlet departed, leaving the
Reverend Mother with the garment, which, according to the
style of the day, modelled in relief the archiepiscopal proportions of his continent nature besides the image of the things
which the Eternal Father has denied to angels and which, in the
prelate, were more than ample. The Lady Abbess advised the
sisters of precious tidings from the Archbishop; they swarmed
about her, speeding curious and active as ants into whose republic a chestnut husk has fallen. As they undid the breeches,
which gaped horribly, they gave vent to loud exclamations and
veiled their eyes with one hand, trembling with fear lest they see
the Devil emerge at any moment. For the Abbess cried:

"Hide yourselves, my daughters. This is the abode of mortal
sin."

The Mother of the novices, hazarding a peep between her
fingers, revived the courage of the holy brood, swearing by an
Ave that no living beast was lodged within. Then they all
blushed at their ease as they gazed at this Habitavit. Doubtless,
they thought, their prelate's intention was to have them discover
therein some sage admonition or some evangelical parable. Although this sight caused certain ravages in the hearts of these
highly virtuous maidens, they ignored their cœliac flutterings;
sprinkling a little holy water in the bottom of the abyss, one
touched it, another passed her finger through a hole and all grew
bolder as they looked. It was actually rumored that when the
first stifling flurry was dissipated, the Abbess found herself saying in a calm voice:

"What is there at the bottom of this? With what deep purpose in mind did our Father send us an object that consummates the ruin of women?"

"It is fifteen years, Mother, since I have been allowed to gaze upon the devil's sack."

"Hush, my daughter, you prevent me from thinking calmly about what we had better do."

Whereupon the archiepiscopal breeches were pulled every which way, weighed and balanced in the hand, held up, sniffed, stretched out of shape and smoothed flat again, scrutinized, admired, and turned wrong side out. They gave rise to endless deliberation and discussion and thought and dreams, night and day. On the morrow, after Matins, in which the convent omitted one verse and two responses, a little nun said:

"Sisters, I have discovered the Archbishop's parable. He sent us his breeches to mend in order to mortify us. They are a holy warning to eschew idleness, the Mother Abbess of all vices."

At which they vied furiously with each other for the privilege of laying a hand on the Archbishop's breeches; but the Abbess, imposing her high authority, reserved to herself the organization of this patchwork. With the help of the Sub-Prioress, she toiled away at the breeches for ten days or more, threading them from knee to flypiece, lining them with silk and making the most beautifully sewn double hems in all humility. Then, at a meeting of the Chapter, it was decided that the convent should express in a pretty souvenir how grateful they were to My Lord Archbishop for having thought of his daughters in God. All of them, down to the youngest novice, must ply her needle over these symbolic breeches, in honor of the excellent man's virtue.

Meanwhile the prelate had so much on his hands that he forgot all about the garment. It came about in this way. He made the acquaintance of a lord at Court, who had lost his wife, a vicious fiend and sterile. This man informed the Archbishop that he had a great ambition: he wished for a virtuous woman, made in God's likeness, one who would oblige him by not hornifying him but rather present him with beautiful and healthy children. This lady, he said, he desired to receive from the Archbishop's hand, for in him he had confidence. The holy man replied with such a glowing account of Mademoiselle de Poissy, that the charming girl soon became Madame de Genoilhac. The wedding was celebrated in the archiepiscopal palace. A feast of high quality was spread at a table lined with ladies of lofty lineage and all the fashionable world of the Court. The bride stood out among them as the most beautiful of the lot, since she was indisputably a virgin. Did not My Lord Archbishop vouch for the flower of her maidenhood?

As the fruits, preserves and pastries were being set on the table with many decoration, Saintot said to the prelate:

"My Lord Archbishop, your well-beloved daughters of Poissy have sent you a wonderful dish for the centre-piece."

"Put it down," said the good man, admiring the high edifice of velvet and satin, embroidered with gold thread and trimmings, like an antique vase. As they did so, a gust of superfine odors rose from the lid.

The bride, opening it, found sweetmeats, sugarplums, comfits, almond paste and a thousand of those delicious confections which delight the ladies.

One of the latter, some curious and devout person, noticing a silk rosette, drew it toward her. To the great confusion of the prelate, she exposed to view the habitation of the human compass. Laughter burst from every throat and roared round the table like a discharge of artillery.

"It was most fitting to make this the centre dish," observed the groom. "These young ladies are wisely discerning. Therein lie the sweets of marriage."

Could there be a better moral than that expressed by Monsieur de Genoilhac? No other is needed, then. . . .

How the Château d'Azay Came to be Built

EAN—son of Simon Fournier, known as Simonin, a townsman of Tours but originally from the village of Moulinot, near Beaune—copied certain Farmers of the Revenue and assumed the title of his city of origin when he was appointed Lord High Treasurer to the late King Louis the Eleventh. One day he fell into great disgrace and was forced to flee into Languedoc with his wife, leaving his son Jacques penniless in Touraine.

The lad possessed nothing in the world save his person, his cape and his sword, though many an oldster of defunct manhood would have considered him wealthy at that. He was thoroughly determined to save his father and to establish his own fortune at the Court, which was held in Touraine at the time. Early morning saw him empty of gullet, completely hidden in his cloak (save for his nose, which he thrust out to windward) and ready for a stroll through town without the slightest suspicion of digestive troubles. He would enter churches, admire their beauties, scrutinize the chapels, flick flies off the paintings and count the aisles like an idler who wonders what to do with his time or his money. At times, he pretended to be reciting paternosters, but they were in reality mute prayers to the ladies. As they departed, he would offer them holy water, follow them from afar and, by these little services, endeavor to run into some adventure which, at the peril of his life, might supply a protector or a gracious mistress.

In his belt, he had two doubloons, which he nursed far more carefully than his skin, since the latter might always be replaced, the former never. Upon this hoard, he would levy a copper or two every day for the loaf of bread and the few mean apples on which he lived. For beverage, he drank at his pleasure and discretion of the waters of the Loire. A simple and prudent diet which not only proved wholesome for his doubloons, but also kept him alert and frisky as a greyhound, gave him a clear head and a warm heart. Is not the water of the Loire the most invigorating of all syrups, if only because it comes from afar and gathers warmth from the various strands it traverses before it reaches Tours? You may be certain the poor wretch dreamed of a thousand and one good fortunes and lucky meetings. The only trouble, of course, was that dreams they remained. Oh, the good times!

One evening Jacques de Beaune—he clung to the name though he was not My Lord of Beaune—was strolling along the embankment, cursing his fate as he perceived that his last doubloon was about to leave him without so much as by your leave. At the turn of a small street, he all but ran into a veiled lady who gratified his nostrils with a most heady gust of feminine, sweet fragrance.

The fair promenader was bravely mounted on dainty shoes and wore a costly dress of Italian velvet, with wide satin-lined sleeves. She must be very wealthy indeed, Jacques judged, as through her veil he caught sight of a sizy white diamond shining on her brow in the rays of the setting sun amid tresses so tastefully turned, rolled, heaped up and ordered that her women must have spent three hours at least to dress them. She walked like a lady accustomed always to recline in a litter; she was attended by an armed page. She must undoubtedly be either the cosset of some exalted nobleman or a lady of the Court, for she held her skirt rather high and arched her back charmingly like a woman who moves in high circles. Lady or wench, she pleased Jacques de Beaune mightily. Far from turning up his nose at her, he conceived the desperate design of attaching himself to her for the rest of his life. With an eye to this, he resolved to follow her wherever she led him, into Paradise or into the limbo of Hell, to the gallows or to a lovers' rendezvous. Through the depths of his misery, everything smiled up at him with the eyes of hope.

The lady sauntered along the bank of the Loire towards Plessis, breathing in the cool air of the waters as carps do, trotting forward, frisking and scurrying like a little mouse, intent upon examining and nibbling at everything. Presently the page realized that Jacques de Beaune was following her persistently, step by step, pausing when she paused, and, as she trifled, spying upon her as imperturbably as though he had a right to. Turning suddenly around on Jacques, he stared at him with the fierce threatening snarl of a mastiff. The lad of Tours knew what he was about. If a cat may look at a king with impunity, he a baptized Christian might certainly look at a pretty woman. So he went ahead, and, feigning to smile at the page, strutted now before, now behind My Lady. She for her part said nothing as she gazed up at the sky, which was putting on its nightcap, at the stars, and at everything she pleased to see. Things were going favorably. At length, when she reached opposite Portillon, she stopped. Then, in order to get a better view, she threw back her veil over her shoulder, and as she did so, darted a shrewd glance at our friend. It was the glance of a canny woman who wishes to ascertain if she is in danger of being robbed.

Now Jacques de Beaune could dispatch the work of three husbands rolled into one; he could have squired a princess and done her credit; he wore a brave, resolute air, very attractive to women. If he was a trifle brown from running about in the sun, his flesh would not look any the less white for it under the canopy of a bed. The glance she gave him was shining and slippery as an eel; it appeared livelier to him than that with which she would have scanned a prayer book. On it he built the hope of an amorous windfall. He would push the adventure to the very hem of the skirt, and, to progress further, he would risk not his life (he cared not a fig for it!) but his two ears and something even more precious.

He followed the lady into town; she returned along the Rue des Trois Pucelles, then led the gallant through a maze of little streets up to the square where the Hôtel de la Crouzille stands today. There she stopped at the door of an imposing mansion. The page knocked. A servant opened, the lady went in, closed the door behind her and left the Sieur de Beaune as open-mouthed, as distraught and as foolish as My Lord St. Denis before he was minded to pick up his head. He raised his nose in the air, hoping that some token of favor might be tossed down to him; all he discerned was a light moving up a stairway, passing through the apartments and, presently, stopping at a fine window, doubtless in the lady's room. The wretched lover stood where he was, plunged in profound melancholy, dreaming away and utterly at a loss to know what to do next. Of a sudden, the window, creaking, interrupted his reverie. Now, surely, his lady would call to him? Up went his nose again and, but for the buttress supporting the window, which acted as a sort of helmet, he would have received a shower of water and the vessel containing it, for the handle alone remained in the hand of the person sprinkling our gallant. Jacques de Beaune, delighted at this incident, straightway made the most of it. Throwing himself against the wall, he moaned: "I am killed!" in a very feeble tone. Then stretching out over the fragments of broken pottery, he lay as if dead, awaiting the outcome. The servants came rushing out, trembling with fear of the lady, to whom they had confessed their fault; they picked up the wounded man, who was hard put to it not to laugh as they carried him upstairs.

"He is cold," said the page.

"He has lost a lot of blood," said the butler, who was soiling his hands in the water as he felt for Jacques' pulse.

"If he recovers, I will pay for a Mass at St. Gatien," the culprit wailed.

"Madame takes after her late father," another said. "If she doesn't hang you, the least that can befall you is to be kicked out of her house and service. . . . Ay, he must be dead: he's so heavy!"

"Ha, I am in the house of a very great lady!" Jacques mused.

"Alas! Can he really be dead?" the cause of the catastrophe pleaded.

As they bore Jacques upstairs with the greatest difficulty, his doublet caught on the banister.

"Hey, my doublet!" the dead man gasped.

"He groaned," cried the culprit, heaving a sigh of relief.

The Regent's servants—this was indeed the house of the Regent, daughter to the late King Louis the Eleventh of virtuous

memory—brought Jacques de Beaune into the room and laid
him out stiff on a table, not believing for a moment that he
would recover.

"Go fetch a master surgeon," said Madame de Beaujeu. "Run
here, run there!"

In the time it takes to say a paternoster, the domestics sped

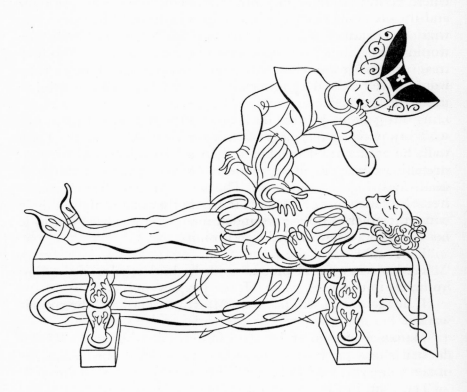

away. The Regent sent her women for unguents, bandages to
dress the wounds, healing-water and so many other remedies that
she was left unattended. As she gazed upon this handsome man,
lying in a swoon before her, as she admired his physique and his
features, courtly even in death:

"Ah," she sighed, "God wished to punish me. For one poor
little time in my life that a naughty thought awoke in the depths
of my nature to bedevil me, my patron saint grows angry and
robs me of the noblest gentleman I have ever seen. By Heaven,

by my father's soul, I will hang any man who had a hand in his death."

"Madame," said Jacques de Beaune, leaping from the table and falling at the feet of the Regent, "I live but to serve you and am so little bruised that this very night I promise you as many joys as there are months in the year, in imitation of Lord Hercules, a pagan baron. For the last twenty days," he went on craftily, believing that a few lies helped matters, "I have met you time and again. I fell madly in love with you yet dared not, through great respect of your person, make an advance. You may imagine how intoxicated with your royal beauty I must have been to invent the trick to which I owe the happiness of lying at your feet."

And very amorously he kissed the latter as he gazed up at her with an expression that would have ravished a saint. Time (which knows no respect for queens, even) had by then, as everyone knows, brought the lady to middle age. In this critical and inclement season, women hitherto virtuous and without lovers begin to desire, now here and now there, to enjoy a night of love unknown to all save God. It would be too hard on them to pass on to the next world with hands and heart and everything else unfilled for want of drinking at a spring so widely patronized. Madame de Beaujeu betrayed no surprise as she listened to the youth's promises, for royal personages must be used to having everything by the dozen. She kept this ambitious offer in the back of her mind or her register of love, which caught fire in anticipation. Then she raised Jacques to his feet. Amid his misery, he still found the courage to smile on his mistress, who had the majesty of a rose fullblown, ears like slippers and the complexion of a sick cat. But he reflected that she was richly attired, and had so pretty a figure, so royal a foot and so alert a crupper, that, in this evil fortune, he might yet find some unknown springs to aid him make good his boast.

"Who are you?" asked the Regent, assuming the stern air of the late King.

"I am your very loyal subject Jacques de Beaune, son of your Treasurer, who has fallen into disgrace despite his faithful services."

"Eh, well," the lady answered, "lie down on your table again.

I hear someone coming; it is not fitting my people should believe me your accomplice in this farce and mummery."

From her gentle tone, Jacques knew that the gracious lady pardoned the enormity of his love. Accordingly he lay down on the table, reflecting that certain lords had ridden to fortune at Court in an old stirrup. This reconciled him perfectly to his present felicity.

"Good," said the Regent to her handmaidens, "I need nothing: the gentleman is better. Thanks be to God and to the Holy Virgin, a murder will not have been committed in my house."

As she spoke, she ran her fingers through the hair of this lover who had fallen from Heaven at her very feet; then, dipping her hand in the water, she rubbed his temples. Then she undid his doublet, pretending to look out for his comfort; more scrupulous than a court expert examining a document, she proceeded to verify how soft and fresh was the skin of this youth who gave such stiff promises of bliss. All those who saw, men and women, marvelled that the Regent should act thus; but humanity is never unbefitting to royal hands. Jacques rose, made believe he was regaining consciousness, thanked the Regent very humbly and, insisting that he had recovered from the blow, sent away physician, master surgeon and the other black devils. Then he gave his name and bowing to Madame de Beaujeu, wished to withdraw as if afraid of her because of his father's disgrace, but doubtless terrified at his horrendous vow.

"I could not allow it," she said. "People who come to my house must not be treated as you were." She turned to her steward: "The Sieur de Beaune will sup here," she said. Then, to the others: "If the man who struck him so unwarrantedly makes himself known at once, he will be at the Sieur de Beaune's mercy. Otherwise, I shall find out who it was and he shall be hanged by the Provost."

At these words, a page advanced. It was the same who had accompanied the lady on her stroll.

"Madame," Jacques said, "I humbly beseech that he be granted both pardon and guerdon. For to him I owe the happiness of seeing you, the favor of supping in your company, perhaps that of having my father restored to the office in which your glorious father was pleased to place him."

"Well spoken," she said. "D'Estouville," she added, turning toward the page, "I give you a company of archers. But in future do not throw things out of windows."

Then the Regent, charmed with Jacques de Beaune, offered him her hand; and very gallantly he led her to her room, where they conversed to good purpose as they waited for supper. Jacques did not fail to parade his accomplishments, to vindicate his father, to win his way into high favor with the lady who, as everybody knows, ruled like her father and did everything on impulse. It would be very difficult, Jacques mused, for him to spend the night with the Regent. Such business was not transacted as simply as the nuptials of cats who never lack a gutter on the housetops where they may friggle to their hearts' content. A Regent, on the other hand, would be compelled to look to her reputation and find some means of getting her maids and servants out of the way. Jacques was therefore congratulating himself on knowing the lady without having to disburse the diabolical dozen. Nevertheless, her strategic talents stirred no uncertain qualms in his breast; at times he would grapple with himself and propound the harrowing questions: "Am I really up to it? Shall I rise repeatedly to the occasion? Can I fulfil the contracted arrangement?"

Under cover of the conversation, Madame was thinking of the very same thing. In the past she had solved many a problem quite as ticklish. She chatted on. . . . Retiring, for a moment, she summoned one of her secretaries, a past master in the diplomacy of governing a kingdom; he was ordered to deliver her a false message secretly during supper.

The repast followed. Madame did not touch a morsel, for her heart, swelling like a sponge, made her stomach shrink, and her mind dwelled fixedly upon this winsome, delectable man. She had no appetite save for him. Jacques, however, did not fail to make a hearty meal, for reasons of every kind. The messenger arrived, Madame la Régente frowned fiercely after the manner of the late King, her father, and stormed:

"Shall we never know peace in this state? God's truth, we cannot have one quiet evening at home!" She rose, paced the room. "Ho, there!" she cried, "my horse! Where is Monsieur de Vieille-ville, my squire? Not here? Ah yes, he is in Picardy. D'Estouville,

you will join me with my household at the Château d'Amboise."
Looking at her Jacques, she added: "You shall be my squire,
Monsieur de Beaune. You wish to serve your ruler? Here is a
good opportunity! By Heaven, come along! There are malcontents to settle; I have need of loyal servants."

In less time than a poor old beggar would have taken to say
fivescore *Aves,* her horses were bridled, saddled and ready. Madame, riding her hackney, with Jacques at her side and the men-
at-arms bringing up the rear, galloped away at top speed to the
Château d'Amboise. To be brief and to come to the head of the
matter without further commentary, the Sieur de Beaune was
lodged far from prying eyes, exactly twelve feet from Madame de
Beaujeu. The courtiers and people, all agog, wondered and spec-
ulated whence the rebels would arise; but the dozener, taken at
his word, needed no telling in what ambush the enemy lay. The
Regent's virtue, proverbial throughout the realm, saved her
from suspicion; she was reputed to be as impregnable as the
Château de Péronne. At cockshut, when everything, even eye and
ear, was closed, when the castle was wrapped in silence, Madame
de Beaujeu dismissed her maid and called for her squire. Who
came. . . .

Lady and adventurer sat side by side on a couch of soft velvet
in the shadow of a high mantelpiece. And the curious Regent
asked Jacques tenderly:

"Are you not bruised? It was naughty of me to make you ride
twelve miles . . . a gallant servitor, so freshly wounded by one
of my varlets! I was too anxious about it to go to bed without seeing you. Do you suffer?"

"I suffer with impatience," the dozener exclaimed, believing
it misplaced to hang fire on such an occasion. "And," he pursued,
"I am delighted to see that your servant has found favor in the
sight of his noble and beautiful mistress."

"There, there," she replied, "were you not lying then when
you told me . . ."

"What?"

"When you told me how you followed me a dozen times . . .
to church and to other places I frequented?"

"Absolutely!"

"Well, what surprises me," she said, "is that before today I never laid eyes on so intrepid a youth . . . on one whose valor stands out so prominently! I do not take back what you heard me say when I thought you wounded. I find you attractive; I would do you a good turn."

The hour of the infernal sacrifice had rung. Jacques fell at the Regent's knees, kissed her feet, her hands, and, rumor has it, everything else. Amid his osculation and preparations for action, he supplied many conclusive proofs to the ripe virtue of his sovereign that a lady who bore the burden of state was perfectly justified in amusing herself a little. In this conclusion, the Regent did not fully acquiesce; she wanted to be forced, so that the onus should fall upon her lover. For all that, you may be certain she had taken care to douse herself in perfume and to don her most fetching nocturnal déshabillé. Radiant, she was, in her desire for coalescence; it lent her a heightened color which greatly improved her complexion as she blushed. Despite her feeble resistance, she was carried by assault, like any girl, in her royal couch, where the good lady and the young duodenarian were very thoroughly consolidated. Presently, from jape to brangle, brangle to rumpus, rumpus to ribaldry and thread to needle, Madame la Régente declared that she believed more firmly in the virginity of Holy Mary than in the promised dozen. As good luck would have it, between the sheets Jacques de Beaune did not find this lady particularly subject to age. Everything experiences a metamorphosis under the glimmer of the night-light. Many a woman of fifty by day is but twenty at midnight; many a girl of twenty at noon is a centenarian after Vespers. Accordingly Jacques, happier at meeting this conjunction than at meeting a king on a hanging day, stoutly maintained that his wager stood. Madame, herself astonished, guaranteed zealous collaboration on her part. More, if she came off second best in this duel, she agreed not only to pardon his father but also to give her cavalier the seigniory of Azay-le-Brûlé, with ample rights of vavasory.

So the good lad murmured: "One for saving my father from punishment! Two for estate in tail female! Three and four for rent and release! This for the forest of Azay! Item for rights piscatory! Now for the isles in the Indre! Here goes for the meadowland! So, let me redeem our estate of La Carte from confiscation (at what cost my poor father bought it!). Now for a post at Court!"

As he achieved this instalment, he considered the dignity of his codpiece involved: the honor of the crown was at stake, too, for he held France under him. To cut a long tale short, in return for a vow made to St. Jacques, his patron, by which he undertook to build him a chapel at Azay, he paid the Regent liege-homage in eleven rigid, sharp, substantial, unerring periphrases. The epilogic upshot of this low-pitched speech Jacques was rash enough to reserve for the Regent's waking, as a rare treat, the salute of a lusty gentleman, the grateful thanks of My Lord of Azay to his sovereign. A most tactful plan, to be sure. But when Nature is abused, she founders like a spirited horse; she lies down and would sooner die under the whip than move before she is pleased to rise restored. In the morning, although the falconet of the stronghold of Azay was cocked to salute the daughter of the King Louis the Eleventh, the discharge was necessarily that of sovereign to sovereign, with blank shot. The Regent rose and breakfasted with Jacques, who now considered himself the legitimate Lord of Azay. But he was reckoning without his host. The latter, making the most of his insufficiency, contradicted her squire. He had not won the wager, hence he had not earned the seigniory.

"By the belly of St. Paterne, I came near enough!" Jacques exclaimed. "But, my dear lady and noble sovereign, it is not meet either for me or for you to judge our cause. This is an allodial case. It must be carried before your Council, because the fief of Azay is a Crown holding."

"By God's halidom," the Regent replied with a laugh—a rare thing for her, "you shall be appointed to the post of the Sieur de Vieilleville in my household, your father shall not be prosecuted, I will present you with Azay and give you a royal post, if you can expose the case in full Council without hurt to my honor. But if one word escapes your lips to besmirch my reputation as a virtuous woman, I . . ."

"May I be hanged!" said the duodenial, turning the thing into a joke, as he saw a shadow of anger on the Regent's face.

In point of fact, the daughter of Louis the Eleventh thought more of her royalty than of a roguish dozen, of which she had made small bones. She believed she had had her night's entertainment without loosening her purse-strings. She preferred the parlous recital of the affair to another dozen that Jacques blithely offered.

"Very well, My Lady," he smiled, "I shall undoubtedly be your squire."

The captains, secretaries and other officials of the Regency, surprised at the abrupt flight of Madame de Beaujeu, had learned its cause and hastened to Amboise to find out where the trouble lay. They were ready to sit as soon as the Regent appeared. To scatter any suspicions they might have that she had tricked them, she called them at once and gave them some nonsense or other to discuss, which they proceeded to do with profundity and wisdom. The session over, her new equerry came to wait upon Madame la Régente. Seeing the councillors rising, he boldly called upon them to settle a case of law in which he and the property of the Crown were involved.

"Give him a hearing," said the Regent. "He has spoken the truth."

Without allowing the majesty of the august court to faze him, Jacques de Beaune addressed the councillors approximately as follows:

"My noble Lords, though I am about to speak to you of nutshells, I entreat you to hearken to this case and forgive the triviality of my language. A peer was walking with another in an orchard; they saw a fine nut tree, a work of God's, firmly planted, well-grown, fair to the sight and pleasant to tend, if a mite hollow. A nut tree forever fresh, forever sweet-smelling; a nut tree you would never grow tired of, had you but clapped your eyes on it; a nut tree—oh, but it seemed the tree of good and of evil, forbidden by the Almighty and for whose sake our mother Eve and her liegeman husband were banished! Now, My Lords, this nut tree raised a bone of contention between the two peers; it had its origin in one of those gay wagers occasionally laid between friends. The younger happened to have a staff in his hand, just as we all do who engage in husbandry and walk in orchards. Well, he ventured the opinion that he would dart his staff through the leafy nut tree twelve times and bring down a nut at each shot. . . ."

Then, turning towards the Regent:

"This is the knotty point of the case, I daresay—"

"Ay, gentlemen," she replied, aghast at her squire's impudence.

"The second peer betted to the contrary," the pleader resumed. "So my fine gambler propelled his staff with such accuracy and consideration, so beautifully and so well, that both derived pleasure from it. Then, by the joyous protection of the saints, who doubtless looked on with amusement, at each shot, a nut fell. There were, in effect, twelve. But, by pure chance, the last nut struck off happened to be hollow; it lacked the nutritive pulp to reproduce another nut tree had the owner of the orchard cared to plant it. Now here is the question: did the man with the staff win? I have said my say. Be ye the judges."

"The thing is crystal clear," said Messire Adam Fumée, of Touraine, then Keeper of the Seals. "There is only one thing the other can do."

"And what is that?" the Regent asked.

"He must pay up, Madame."

"That lad is rather too clever," she said, giving her squire a fillip on the cheek. "He will end on the scaffold!"

She spoke in jest. Yet her words proved to be the true forecast of his fate. My Lord Treasurer climbed the rungs of royal favor to the gallows of Montfaucon, a victim to another elderly lady's vengeance and to the arrant perfidy of his secretary. The latter, a man of Ballan, whose fortune Jacques had made, was called Prévost and not Le Gentil, as some have most erroneously dubbed him. This disloyal servant and arch-traitor is said to have handed Madame d'Angoulême the receipt for the money given him by Jacques de Beaune. By that time, Jacques had become Baron de Semblançay, suzerain of La Carte and of Azay, and a bigwig in the state. One of his sons became Archbishop of Tours, the other Chancellor of the Exchequer and Governor of Touraine. But this is not the subject of the present writing. . . .

To return to this excellent man's youthful adventure. Madame de Beaujeu, who had taken a hand in love's fair game rather late in life, was delighted to encounter such wisdom and such talent for public affairs in her chance lover. She made him Lord of the Privy Purse. He acquitted himself ably of this office, increasing the royal fortune in dozens of ways; eventually, his great renown won him the handling of the realm's wealth. As Lord High Treasurer, he performed his duties splendidly, not without considerable profit to himself, which was but fair.

The Regent paid her wager: her squire received the seigniory of Azay-le-Brûlé, of which the château had been long before razed to the ground by the first bombardiers who came into Touraine, as everyone knows. For this powdery miracle, had not the King intervened, these engineers would have been condemned as sinners and demoniac heretics by the Ecclesiastical Tribunal of the Chapter.

In Semblançay's heyday, Messire Bohier, Chancellor of the Exchequer, was setting up the Château of Chenonceaux; to make a wonder of it and a model of grace, he had it built astride the river Cher.

The Baron de Semblançay, wishing to oppose Bohier, took special pride in setting the foundations of his château at the bottom of the Indre; and there it stands today, as solid as ever on its piles, the gem of this fair green valley. It cost Jacques thirty thousand crowns, not counting the labor of his own serfs. As may be supposed, this château is one of the noblest, most graceful, exquisite and elaborate in our sweet land of Touraine; it bathes forever in the Indre like a princely lady, gaily decked with pavilions, with lacy casements, with handsome soldiers on its vanes, who, like all soldiers, are always turning every way the wind blows. Unfortunately Semblançay was hanged before finishing it; and nobody has since been found with sufficient funds to complete it. Yet his master, King Francis, first of the name, was once his guest there; the royal chamber may still be seen. The monarch was devoted to Semblançay; he used to call him "father" in honor of his white hairs.

One evening, as Francis was retiring, he turned to the oldster, and:

"Midnight, father! Twelve good, clear strokes of the clapper!"

"Eh, Sire," Semblançay answered, "to twelve strokes of a clapper at this same hour (an old tool now but strong in those days!) I owe my domain, the money spent on it and the honor of serving you. . . ."

His Majesty asked his servitor what he meant by these strange words, and, while the sovereign was getting into bed, Jacques de Beaune related the tale of the dozen. Francis was very keen on these ribald anecdotes, considered this one droll and took particular pleasure in it because at the very time his mother, the Duchesse d'Angoulême, though in the decline of life, was running after My Lord Constable of Bourbon for just such dozens. The wicked love of a wicked woman, it was, for out of it grew the kingdom's peril, His Majesty's capture, and poor Semblançay's death, as has been stated before.

I have sought here to relate how the Château d'Azay came to be built, because Semblançay undeniably owed his high fortune to such a beginning. He did much, too, for his birthplace, which he adorned; he spent vast sums to complete the towers of the cathedral.

This joyous adventure was handed down from father to son and lord to lord at Azay-le-Rideau; the story still frisks there under the king's curtains, which have been curiously respected down to our own day. To attribute this dozen of Touraine to a German knight, who, by the deed, would have brought the domains of Austria to the House of Hapsburg is the falsest of fabrications. The modern author who brought this story to light was a great scholar but he allowed himself to be deceived by certain chroniclers: the archives of the Holy Roman Empire make no mention of acquisition by any such means. I am vexed at him for believing that a codpiece nourished on beer could have risen to such alchemy, the honor of the cods of Chinon, so highly prized by Rabelais. For the profit of the country, the glory of Azay, the conscience of its château and the renown of the House of Beaune (whence sprang the Sauves and the Noirmoutiers) I have reëstablished the facts in their true, historical and admirable amenity. Should any ladies visit the château they can still find a few dozens in the neighborhood. But these come only retail. . . .

The Unauthentic Courtesan

HE TRUTH concerning the demise of the Duc d'Orléans, brother of King Charles the Sixth, is not generally
known; it came about through a number of causes, one
of which will be the subject of this tale.

This prince was assuredly the crudest and most
libidinous scion of the kingly race founded by My Lord St.
Louis (who was in his lifetime King of France) without excepting the greatest lechers in the whole family. And what a
family it was! It matched the peculiarities and vices of our brave,
pleasure-loving nation so aptly that Hell might be better pictured
without Master Satan than France without its valorous, glorious,
hard-friggling kings. Which gives us as hearty a laugh at the phi-
losophy-merchants who go about saying "Our fathers were better!" as at the kind, philanthropical pantaloons who prate that
men are on the road to perfection. Blind folk, all; they will not
observe the plumage of oysters or the shells of birds, which change
no more than our ways do. Heigh ho! Amuse yourselves while
young! Keep your whistle wet and your eyes dry for a hundred-
weight of melancholy is not worth an ounce of revelry.

The wild behavior of the Duc d'Orléans, who was Queen
Isabella's lover root and branch, gave rise to many jocund adventures, for he was a prime wag, endowed with the nature of an
Alcibiades, and a chip of the old French block. He, it was, first
conceived the idea of having relays of women, so that when he
travelled from Paris to Bordeaux, wherever he put up to unsad-
dle, he found a good meal and a bed decked with a pretty bit of
fluff. Happy prince, who died riding, as he had always done, even
in bed! Of his comical pranks, our excellent sovereign Louis the
Eleventh has handed us down a capital sample in the *Cent Nou-*

velles Nouvelles. This book was written under his direction during his exile at the Court of Burgundy where of an evening he and his cousin Charolais would divert themselves by telling the gay jokes of the age. When the true stories gave out, all their courtiers vied with each other in making up better ones. In the tale in question, My Lord Dauphin described the part played in the adventure by My Lady of Cany as having fallen to a townsman. Anyone may find it under the title of the *Reverse of the Medal;* it is one of the most delicately mounted jewels of the collection and leads off the five-score stories. But now for my own.

Among the followers of the Duc d'Orléans was a lord from the province of Picardy named Raoul d'Hocquetonville, who, to the future damage of the prince, had married a young lady kin to the House of Burgundy and rich in lands. In contradistinction to most heiresses, she was of such dazzling beauty that her mere presence sufficed to throw all the ladies of the Court, even the Queen and Madame Valentine, into the shade. Yet her Burgundian blood, her inheritances, her pulchritude and her delicate nature were completely dimmed by the holy lustre of her utter innocence, her sweet modesty and her chaste upbringing. Nor had the Duke breathed in the fragrance of this heaven-sent flower very long before the fever of passion laid him low. He fell into a state of profound melancholy, completely forsaking the simplest brothel; at most, occasionally and with regret, he took a bite at that succulent royal German morsel Isabella. All the fury of love possessed him; he swore to have joy of the graceful lady through witchcraft, force, or treachery if not with her consent. The remembered sight of her body drove him to seek the most pitiful gratification as he, once a rakehell, now lay alone through the long, empty nights. First, he pursued her ardently with soft, golden words; but almost immediately her carefree air told him that she was determined to remain virtuous. Without showing surprise at his proposal or flying into a huff, she said quite simply:

"I will be frank with you, My Lord: I do not care to accept another's love. Not that I despise such joys as it may provide, for these must be paramount when so many women fling their persons, houses, reputation, future and all they possess into its fiery maw. No, that is not why I decline. It is rather for the sake of my

children, whom I love to distraction. I refuse to have cause to
blush, when I intend to bring up my daughters with this principle of preservation: for a woman, virtue is the sum of human
happiness. Ah, My Lord, if the days of our old age are more
numerous than those of our youth, surely the former must be the
burden of our thought? From those who reared me, I learned to
appreciate life at its true value; I know that everything is transitory save the security of natural affection. Thus I would be respected by everybody, but especially by my husband, who is all
the world to me. Accordingly, I earnestly desire to stand honest
in his sight. I have had my say. I implore you to leave me to attend peaceably to my household duties. Otherwise I shall positively tell my lord and master; and he would quit your service on
the spot."

This brave reply served but to aggravate the Duke's infatuation. He planned all the more sedulously to seize this noble woman in his toils and possess her, dead or alive. Nor did he doubt
that he would soon have her in his clutches; he placed un-
bounded confidence in his proficiency as a sportsman. Was he not
a past master at this frantic hunt, the most joyous of all because
it employs the tactics of every species of venery against a sweet
game that is taken by pursuit, by means of mirrors, by torchlight,
at night or in the daytime, in town or in the country, in the bush,
by the water's edge, in nets, by falcons, with lance, horn and shot,
by a decoy bird, with net, springe and bird call, in the lie or on
the fly, with cornet, lime, bait and twig, in fine by every pitfall
invented since Adam was cast out of Paradise. It gets killed then
in a variety of ways, too, but almost always astraddle.

Our cunning fowler spoke no more of his passion but had
Madame d'Hocquetonville appointed to a post in Her Majesty's
household. One day that Isabella had gone to Vincennes to visit
the ailing King, leaving the Duke master of the Hôtel St. Paul,
he ordered the most delicious of royal suppers to be served in the
Queen's apartments and sent one of his own pages to summon
the stubborn lady by express command. The Comtesse d'Hocquetonville, believing she was wanted by the Queen on some
official matter, hastened to appear. The treacherous lover had arranged that no one should inform the lady of Her Majesty's departure. She therefore made directly for the splendid salon ad-

joining the Queen's bedroom. Here she found my Lord Duke —alone! Suspecting some perfidious ambush, she passed on into the further room, to find no sign of the Queen. Instead, she was treated to a loud burst of laughter from the Duke.

"I am lost!" she gasped. Then she attempted to escape.

But the good fowler of females had posted loyal servants at strategic points. Without knowing what was afoot, they shut up the mansion and barricaded the doors. Left in an apartment large enough to hold one-fourth of Paris, Madame d'Hocquetonville might as well have been abandoned in the midst of the desert with God and her patron saint for only aid. Suspecting the truth, the poor lady trembled in all her bones and fell back into a chair, as her suitor proceeded with much hearty laughter to unfold the working of this artfully contrived snare. The Duke made as if to approach; she rose, and first wielding her tongue as a weapon:

"You will have your joy of me—but dead!" she snarled. A thousand maledictions gleamed in her glance. "Ha, My Lord, do not force me to a struggle which must needs become known. I have yet time to withdraw without having Monsieur d'Hocquetonville suspect what unforgettable sorrow you have visited upon me. You look too often into the faces of my sex, My Lord Duke, to study men's. You do not dream what sort of servant you have in Raoul d'Hocquetonville. He would suffer himself to be hacked to pieces on your behalf, not only because he is bound fast to you by the ties of gratitude but also because he holds you dear. Yet as he loves, so does he hate! I believe him the man to bring his mace down upon your head without a murmur in vengeance of a single cry you might constrain me to utter. Do you wish my death and your own, wretch? You may be certain that the nature of a virtuous woman can neither hide nor hush her good or evil fortune. Now, will you let me go?"

The blackguard merely whistled. Madame d'Hocquetonville, hearing it, ran into the Queen's room and seized a dagger which she knew was concealed there. As the Duke followed her in to learn what this flight betokened:

"When you pass this line," she cried, pointing to the floor, "I shall kill myself."

The Duke, cool as a cucumber, picked up a chair, set it down and planted himself on the very edge of the board she had indicated. Like an auctioneer, he began heaping up arguments, painting roseate verbal pictures of a certain consummation in the hope of exciting this dogged woman, of whipping her brain, heart, senses and the rest to such a state of fervor that she must yield blindly to him. With the delicacy of manner princes are wont to practise, he explained many things to her. To begin with, he said, dutiful wives paid a pretty shot for their virtue because in order to earn the doubtful rewards of the future, they forfeited the most exquisite pleasures of the present. For reasons of conjugal policy, husbands were forced to avoid showing their wives all the jewels in the sweet reliquary of love. These treasures shed such a radiance upon the heart, they fired a woman to such ecstasies of delight and such poignant thrills of voluptuous fulfilment that, having savored them, she would not hear of tarrying longer amid the chill frugalities of domestic existence. Was not this husbandly selfishness a felony and an abomination? In gratitude for his wife's virtuous life and her dear-bought merits, the least a man could do was to strain every nerve, go all lengths and move very Heaven to provide her with all the blessed amenities, the lavish give and the grateful take, the light sparring and cockling, the pleasantries, the nectar and ambrosia, the most lickerish confectionery of love. My Lord Duke added that if she ventured but to sip at the seraphic delights of these honied pastimes she knew naught of, everything else in the world would pale into insignificance. If such were her desire, she might be certain he would entomb it in a silence deeper than death. What scandal, then, could come to smirch her virtue?

The insidious lecher noticed that the lady had made no effort to stop up her ears. So he set about depicting (after the fashion of arabesque paintings then all the rage) the most lascivious inventions of a debauched mind. Tongues of flame shot from his eyes; coals of fire blazed in his words; his voice rose, mellow and full, as he thrilled to the pleasure of retailing the diverse technics of his sweethearts. One by one, he named them for Madame d'Hocquetonville, disclosing even the sapphistries, cockerings and gentle relaxations of Queen Isabella herself. When he made use of a locution at once graceful and fiercely ardent, he believed he could detect the lady's grip on the redoubtable sharp dagger relaxing a mite. He made to approach. Ashamed at being caught in a dream, she gazed proudly at the diabolical leviathan who tempted her.

"Fair lord," she said, "I thank you. You make me love my noble husband all the more because, from what you say, I realize the extent of his esteem for me. He respects me too highly to dishonor his couch with the vices of harlots and trulls. I would consider myself forever disgraced and contaminated through all eternity were I to put my feet in the sloughs where these strumpets wallow. A man's wife is one thing, his mistress another."

"Nevertheless," the Duke smiled, "I wager that in future you will clasp Monsieur d'Hocquetonville a little harder in your sport."

At which the good woman shuddered, and cried:

"You are a monster! I despise and abominate you! So, unable to rob me of my honor, you would befoul my soul? Ha, my lord, you shall rue this evil moment. You recall:

> *'And though you have my pardon for it,*
> *God will remember and abhor it.'*

You composed these verses, did you not?"

"Madame," said the Duke, turning pale with anger, "I can have you bound—"

"No, no, I can free myself!" she replied, brandishing her dagger.

The rascal began laughing.

"Never fear," he said, "I shall manage to plunge you into the strumpets' sloughs that you affect to despise."

"Never, while I live."

"You shall go in with your two feet and your two hands, your two breasts of ivory and your two other snow-white mounds, and your teeth and hair and the rest of you. You will go in of your own free will, wild and rampant, spoiling to crush your rider as a mare in heat cracking her crupper, stamping, jumping and snorting through every orifice. By St. Castud, I swear it!"

Immediately he whistled a page and secretly ordered him to find the Sire d'Hocquetonville, Savoisy, Tanneguy, Cypierre and other ruffians of his crew and to invite them to sup in the

Queen's apartments. At the same time he sent for a few lusty, fair wenches to make up the party. Then he returned to his chair, ten paces away from the lady on whom he had kept his eye all the time he was whispering to the page.

"Raoul is jealous," he remarked. "So I owe you a good piece of advice. In this place," he added, pointing to a secret door, "the Queen keeps her rarest oils and perfumes. In this other little room, she performs her ablutions and sundry womanly functions. By long experience I know that none of you pretty pussies but has her own special distinctive scent. Now if, as you say, Raoul's is a horn-mad jealousy—the worst species of passion—you will use these strumpets' scents. (A strumpets' slough it was, you said, didn't you?)"

"Ah, My Lord, what do you intend?"

"You shall know when you need to. As for me, I wish you no harm; indeed, I pledge you my word as a loyal knight that I will respect you thoroughly and keep eternally silent about my discomfiture. You shall learn that the Duc d'Orléans has a good heart and revenges himself nobly on unrequiting ladies by placing the key to Paradise in their hands. You have but to lend an ear to the merry talk bandied about in the next room. Above all, do not cough—that is, if you love your children."

As the royal bedroom had no exit and the bars over the window left barely enough room for a head to pass, the profligate was certain of his captive as he closed the door. But, as a parting shot, he enjoined her to keep very still. A few minutes later the roisterers came rushing up to the Queen's apartments. A rich, tasteful supper smiled up at them out of the vermilion dishes on the table; a board, beautifully appointed, gleamed under the delicate lighting, with cups of silver and jugs brimful of royal wine.

"Up and at 'em!" their master cried. "To your seats, my hearties, and lay on. I was about to get very bored; then I thought of you. So I decided to enjoy a happy banquet with you after the manner of the ancient Greeks and Romans who said their prayers to Master Priapus and to the horned god yclept Bacchus in all lands. A bumper feast it shall be, too; for dessert, we shall have the company of some pretty crows—the triple-beaked variety! Upon my word, I have sampled them all and I would be hard put to it to decide which is the sweetest to peck at."

The company, recognizing their master at every turn, was delighted at this splendid speech. All, except Raoul d'Hocquetonville, who stepped forward:

"My Lord," he told the Duke, "I am prepared to help aplenty in any battle save that of the petticoats, to tilt in single combat but not the wine-cup. None of my good friends here has a wife at home; anything is permitted them. But not me. For I have a wife I love; to her I owe my company and an account of my every act and deed."

"I am a married man," the Duke cried. "Am I to blame?"

"How, my dear master, you are a prince of the blood, you can do as you please."

As may be supposed, these proud words brought chills and fever to the prisoner's heart.

"Ah, Raoul," she whispered to herself, "you are a noble soul!"

"You are a man I hold dear," the Duke replied, "I consider you the most loyal and meritorious of my followers. As for the rest of us," he looked at the three others, "we are low fellows. Come, Raoul," he pursued. "Sit down. When our high-flying linnets come, you can go home to your housewife. 'Sdeath, I had thought to treat you as a virtuous man who knows naught of how extra-conjugal joys should be treated. In the room next door, there, I had the queen of the odalisques waiting—a fiend of a woman, a compact of all female manœuvres. You have never had a palate for the flesh-pots of love; you dream only of warfare. Well, for once I wished you to savor the recondite marvels of sportive gallantry. What a shame for a man in my following to serve a fair lady ill."

To please his liege as far as permissible, Raoul sat down. Soon the company was laughing, exchanging ribald quips and conversationally ravaging the ladies. As men will do, they retailed their amatory adventures and good fortunes, mercilessly betraying the erotic idiosyncracies of all the sex with the possible exception of their current sweethearts. From this they passed on to horrible little confidences which increased in treachery and lechery fast as the wine in their cups diminished. The Duke, happy as an exclusive legatee, drew his guests out, telling falsehoods himself to elicit truths from them; his guests dispatched their food at a trot, downed their wine at a canter and let their tongues run away at full gallop. As he listened with flushed cheeks, Monsieur d'Hocquetonville gradually rid himself of his scruples. Virtuous though he was, the conversation aroused certain desires in him; soon he found himself indulging them and wallowing in iniquity like a saint polluted as he prays. The Duke did not fail to perceive it. Bent on satisfying his ire and bile, he addressed Raoul jestingly:

"By St. Castud, Raoul, we are as one man sitting at this table and a discreet one away from it. Go ahead: we will not breathe a word of it to Madame. By the rood, I want you to experience the joys of Paradise. In there," he explained as he knocked on the door behind which Madame d'Hocquetonville trembled, "in there is a lady of the Court. She is a friend of the Queen's, but the greatest priestess of Venus that ever was. There's not a concubine or Jezebel, a courtesan or a contortionist, a strumpet or trollop or trull can hold a candle to her. . . . She was conceived in a moment when Paradise was delirious with pleasure, when Nature was fructifying herself, when the plants were practising sweet hymeneal union, when the beasts were whinnying and belling for joy and all creation was a-riot with love. Though the woman make a bed of an altar, she is nevertheless too mighty a lady to risk showing herself and too illustrious to allow aught but cries of love to escape her lips. Light, you will not need: her eyes dart flames. Speech is unnecessary: she expresses herself with movements and writhings more rapid than the spasms of deer surprised in the brush. But take care, my dear Raoul. Your mount is vicious; hold on tight to the beast's mane, give her the spurs and keep a light seat for with one plunge she would nail you to the ceiling if you weighed down on her chine. She was instrumental in bringing about the death of our poor young friend the Sire de Giac; she drained away his marrow in one brief Spring. God's truth, what man would not forfeit one-third of his joys to come so but he might know the feast for which she rings the bells and sets the spark. And he who has known her once would, for a second night, cheerfully forfeit all eternity."

"But," Raoul objected, "can there be such extraordinary contrasts in things so naturally uniform?"

"Ha, ha, ha!"

The company burst into roars of laughter. Their tongues loosened by wine, their wits urged by a wink from their master, one after another began to narrate a thousand elaborate artifices and celestial variations amid a general shouting, gesticulating and licking of chops. Unaware that an innocent schoolgirl was listening, the lechers, who had drowned all self-respect in their goblets, fell to enumerating things fit to make the figures carved on mantelpiece, walls and ceiling blush with shame. My Lord Duke put the seal to the discussion by saying that the lady waiting abed next door for a gallant was indubitably the empress of these volcanic imaginations because she created new and fiendishly inflammable ones every night. They drained their cups. Raoul, as one possessed, willingly suffered the Duke to push him into the room. Thus the Duke was in a position to force the lady to choose by what poniard she would die—or live! At midnight, the Sire de Hocquetonville reappeared, at once happy and remorseful. The Duke arranged for Madame d'Hocquetonville to escape through a postern in the garden and arrive home before her husband.

"This work," she whispered into his ear as she slipped out, "will cost us all dear."

One year later, in the Rue Vieille du Temple, Raoul de Hocquetonville, who had left the Duke's service for that of John of
Burgundy, struck the king's brother on the head with a blow of
his mace and killed him, as everyone knows. His wife had died
some time before; she wilted like a flower deprived of air or
gnawed by a worm. In a cloister at Péronne, on her marble tomb,
her husband caused the following inscription to be engraved:

HERE LIES

BERTHE DE BOURGOGNE

The fair and noble wife

to

RAOUL, SIRE DE HOCQUETONVILLE

Alas! Pray not for her Soul

SHE

Blossomed again in Heaven

The eleventh day of January

In the year of Our Lord M CCCC VIII

In the twenty-second year of her age

Leaving two sons and her Lord

Brokenhearted

This epitaph was written proudly in Latin, but, for the con-
venience of all, it was necessary to translate it, though the word
fair is a feeble rendering of *formosa,* which signifies *beautiful in
shape.*

To My Lord Duke of Burgundy, dubbed The Fearless, the
Sire de Hocquetonville, before dying, divulged the sorrow
branded on his soul. In spite of this prince's natural callousness
in such matters, he used to remark that this epitaph moved him
to melancholy for a month. He would add that among his cousin's abominations there was one for which he would slay him
over again, were it possible, because this godless man had basely
sown the seed of vice in the most divine virtue of the world and
caused two noble hearts to prostitute each other. When he spoke
thus, he was thinking of Madame d'Hocquetonville and of his
own lady, whose portrait had been unwarrantedly placed in the
cabinet where the Duc d'Orléans hanged the pictures of his paramours.

This adventure was so utterly terrible that when the Comte de Charolais told it to the Dauphin—later Louis the Eleventh—his listener, out of regard for his great-uncle, the Duc d'Orléans, and for Dunois, his old comrade, the latter's son, refused to allow his scribes to include it in the anthology.

But the figure of Madame d'Hocquetonville is so immaculate in its virtue and so sublime in its melancholy that the present narrative may be forgiven. Her memory will mitigate the fiendish inspiration and vengeance of My Lord of Orléans.

Nevertheless, the well-merited death of this scoundrel caused much bitter warfare which finally Louis the Eleventh, out of patience, crushed at the point of the sword.

This proves that a woman is at the bottom of everything, whether in France or elsewhere. It also proves that sooner or later we must pay for our follies.

The Dangers of Excessive Innocence

Y LORD OF MONCONTOUR was a valiant soldier of Touraine. Near the field of Vouvray, he built the château of that name in honor of the victory won by the Duc d'Anjou, later our all-glorious king. Because he had borne himself heroically in the fray and slain the greatest number of heretics, he was authorized to assume the title of his domain. This gallant captain had two sons, the eldest of whom was in high favor at Court.

After the peace preceding the treachery of St. Bartholomew's day, as the good man returned to his manor (it was not ornamented then as it is today) he received the sad news of his son's death. The lad had been killed in a duel by the Sieur de Villequier. The unhappy father was the more prostrated because he had arranged a splendid marriage for his son with a young lady of the male branch of Amboise. This piteously untoward death seemed to banish all fortune and power from a house he had wished to render noble and puissant.

With this end in view, My Lord of Moncontour had placed his second son in a monastery under the guidance and government of a man renowned for his sanctity. The prelate brought him up according to the highest Christian principles, since his father's ambition was to have him become a lofty cardinal. Our abbot kept the youth virtually in prison, made him sleep beside him in his cell, suffered no evil weed to grow in his mind and reared him in purity of soul and true contrition, as all priests should be reared. On his nineteenth birthday, the lad knew no love other than the love of God; he had heard of no nature other than that of the angels—who in the interests of utter chastity have not our carnal appurtenances or they would make excellent use of such. This alternative, the King on High feared; He wished His pages immaculate. Very well He did, too; since the virtuous little folk are unable to tipple in taverns or friggle in stews as we do, He is divinely served. But then it must be remembered He is lord of all.

In his grievous misfortune, My Lord of Moncontour resolved to withdraw his younger son from the cloister and deck him in military and courtly purple in place of ecclesiastical. The lad, furthermore, should marry his deceased brother's fiancée, a very wise decision because a monklet, swaddled in continence and crammed with virtues, was calculated to serve the bride better and more satisfactorily than a soldier who had already been laid low, put to sack and branded by the ladies at Court. The frockite unfrocked, and extremely sheepish in his ways, followed his sire's sacred wishes and agreed to the marriage, without knowing what a wife was nor, what is even more ticklish, a girl. As luck would have it, the confusion attendant upon the demobilization of the armies had delayed his journey. This blessed innocent—more innocent than it is lawful for a man to be—reached the Château de Moncontour only the day before the wedding, which was solemnized with dispensations bought from the Archbishopric of Tours.

It is here necessary to describe the bride. Her mother, widowed many years ago, now lived in the house of Monsieur de Braguelogne, Civil Lieutenant of the Châtelet in Paris; while Madame de Braguelogne, to the great scandal of the period, lived with the Sieur de Lignières. But everyone had too many beams in his eye just then to justify a look at the rafters decorating his neighbors'. No family but had members who followed the road to perdition unfazed by their fellows; some ambled along, others broke into a smart trot, many galloped ahead and the minority proceeded at walking pace, for the road is abrupt indeed. Thus, in these times, the Devil did a rushing business in orgies. Was not misconduct fashionable? Alas, poor old Dame Virtue, trembling from head to foot, had sought refuge none knew where; here and there she managed to lead a wretched existence among honest women.

In the illustrious dynasty of Amboise, the Dowager Lady of Chaumont, an aged woman of scatheless virtue, still lived on; all the piety and nobility of the house seemed to have retired in her person. When the little virgin whom this tale concerns was but ten years old, this excellent lady had taken her to her bosom. Madame d'Amboise was therefore spared all anxiety; she was left the freer in her goings-on and since that time had visited her daughter once a year when Court passed that way. Despite such high maternal reserve, Madame d'Amboise was invited to her daughter's wedding; so, too, was the Sieur de Braguelogne. (Our old soldier knew his people!) But the dear dowager did not come; she was kept at home by her deplorable sciatica, her catarrh and the state of her legs, which had lost all power to gambol. Over this sorry state of affairs, she shed bitter tears. How loathe she was to loose this gentle, superlatively pulchritudinous virgin among the dangers of Court and of life! Yet the dove must be given her wings to fly! Not, however, without the promise of Masses and orisons every evening for her happiness. The good lady gathered a certain amount of comfort from the thought that the staff of her old age was to pass into the hands of one who was practically a saint and who had been brought up in the ways of righteousness by her friend the abbot. This latter circumstance had much to do with the prompt exchange of spouses. At length, kissing her tearfully, the dutiful dowager made the parting recommendations ladies usually offer brides: she must show respect to her mother, she must obey her husband implicitly in everything. . . .

Amid a great tumult, the virgin arrived, escorted by so many maids, duennas, servants, equerries and gentlemen of the house of Chaumont that her retinue might have belonged to a Cardinal Legate. Her betrothed arrived soon after: they met on the eve of their wedding. The feasting done, they were married with great pomp on the Lord's Day at a Mass celebrated in the château by My Lord Bishop of Blois, an old friend of the groom's father. The general banqueting, dancing and entertainment of all kinds lasted until morning; though on the stroke of midnight the bridesmaids put the bride to bed, according to the custom in Touraine. Meanwhile a thousand tricks were played on the innocent husband to keep him from going to his innocent wife. His arrant ignorance made him a ready butt, until My Lord of Moncontour put a stop to the wags' antics: it was high time for his son to go and prove himself. Our seraph departed to the chamber of his bride, whom he found more beautiful than the Virgin Marys of Italian, Flemish or any other paintings at whose feet he had said his prayers. He was naturally much embarrassed at becoming a husband so soon, because he understood nothing about the job. There was a certain function to perform, that much he knew; but through excessive reserve, he had not dared question even his father.

"You know what you have to do," the latter had said curtly. "Fall to, manfully!"

He looked at the exquisite creature that had been given him; she lay snug under the covers, burning with curiosity, her head lowered but not too much so to prevent a glance sharp as a halberd.

"I must obey him," she told herself, and, blissfully ignorant, awaited the pleasure of the somewhat ecclesiastical gentleman to whom, in point of fact, she belonged. The Chevalier de Moncontour perceived this. He drew up to the bed, scratched his ear, and kneeled, a thing at which he was expert.

"Have you said your prayers?" he asked in a very, very gentle voice.

"No," she returned, "I forgot. Do you wish us to say them?"

So the young couple inaugurated their wedded life by invoking God, which was not in the least unseasonable. But the Devil chanced to hear and straightway answered their prayer for, at the moment, God was busily occupied with the abominable new reformed church.

"What were you told to do?" the husband asked.

"To love you," she said in all simplicity.

"I was not told that. But I do love you, I am ashamed to say, better than I love God."

This speech did not shock the bride too severely.

"I would be very happy," went on the groom, "to rest in your bed, if it will not bother you too much."

"I will make room for you willingly; must I not submit myself to you?"

"Very well then," he said, "do not look at me. I shall undress and join you."

At this virtuous speech, the damsel turned her face to the wall in great expectation; certainly here was the first time she would find herself separated from a man by merely the confines of a shirt. The innocent tiptoed up and slipped into the bed; they were now united in fact but leagues away from a conjunction with which you are perfectly familiar.

Have you ever seen a monkey newly arrived from his home overseas and given a nut to crack? Knowing by high simian intelligence what delicious food lies hidden under the shell, the beast sniffs and twists about with all manner of apish larks, muttering Heaven knows what between his grinning jaws. Ah, with what affection he studies it, with what study he examines it, with what deep examination he holds it up, tosses it to the ground, rolls it about, pounces upon it in a frenzy of passion and, if he is a monkey of low extraction and intelligence, leaves the nut! This is exactly what the poor innocent did. Towards daylight, defeated, he was forced to confess to his beloved wife that, knowing neither how to perform his office, nor indeed what this office was, nor yet where to find it, he would have to make inquiries and obtain aid.

"Ay, you will," she sighed, "for unfortunately I cannot teach you!"

In spite of their investigations, improvisations and experiments of all sorts, in spite of the myriad inventions of innocents which experts in love would never suspect, the bridal pair fell asleep, disconsolate at being unable to crack the nut of marriage. But they prudently agreed to report that each had fared admirably. When the bride rose, still virgin, intact in the bud, she sang cock-a-hoop of her night's work, vowing hers was the king of husbands, chattering away nineteen to the dozen and giving as good as she got with all the freedom of the completely ignorant. The company found our bride too sharp by half when a lady of La Roche Corbon, with malice aforethought, put a wide-eyed young virgin of La Bourdaisière up to asking the bride:

"How many loaves did your husband lay in the oven?"

"Twenty-four," she replied.

As the groom moved to and fro listlessly and his wife followed him with her glance, hoping to see this state of innocence come to an end, most of the ladies believed that his joys of the night had proved expensive and that his wife was already repentant at having completely ruined him. At breakfast all the bad jokes—considered excellent at the time—set the table in a roar. Somebody declared the bride had an open look; another that some good strokes of business were done in the château that night; another that the oven had been burned; still another that both families that night lost something which they would never retrieve. A thousand like japes, cock-and-bull stories and farcicalities rained down upon the alas! uncomprehending husband. Because of the great affluence of relatives, neighbors and guests, nobody had gone to bed; they had danced, romped and frolicked all night, as is customary at weddings of the nobility.

The Sieur de Braguelogne seemed very happy at this until he noticed the lady of Amboise flushing at the thought of the bliss her daughter was savoring. His mistress kept darting a hawk's glance upon him, her beady eye eloquent with summons to a gallant assignation. The luckless Lieutenant Civil was well schooled in the ways of bum bailiffs and sergeants (was it not he who nobbed all the pickpockets and sharpers of Paris?). But he feigned not to see his great good fortune, though his elderly mistress was clamoring. For her love weighed heavily upon him; he had clung to her only in a spirit of justice, because it was not seemly for a Lieutenant Judiciary to change mistresses like a courtier. After all, he was in charge of the morals, police and religion of the city.

Nevertheless, his mutiny was destined to end. The day after the wedding, a large number of guests departed and Madame d'Amboise, Monsieur de Braguelogne and the immediate family could go to bed in peace. It was just before supper: My Lord Lieutenant was on the point of being half-verbally subpœnaed, nor, according to constitutional and magisterial procedure, could he have opposed any excuse for postponement. All afternoon Madame d'Amboise had been trying dodge after dodge in the hope of drawing Braguelogne from the room where he sat with the bride. Meanwhile in the virgin soul of the groom's mind, an expedient had sprung up like a mushroom. Why not question this excellent lady, whom he knew to be discreet? He recalled the godly precepts of the monk who had brought him up; one of the most important was to seek information concerning all things from older people experienced in the ways of life. Very well; he would lay his case before Madame d'Amboise.

In the beginning, he walked up and down with her several times, shy and speechless; he could conjure up no terms in which to express his predicament. The lady, for her part, kept quiet too, raging inwardly at the Sieur de Braguelogne for his deafness, blindness, and deliberate paralysis. As she walked beside this delicious morsel of innocence her mind was far away. How could she dream that a cat so well-supplied with fresh bacon could be anxious for old? No—her thoughts were very different.

"That old Ho Ho," she said to herself, "that old Ho Ho with a beard of flies' legs, a withered, senile, grizzled, seedy, moss-grown, decrepit beard . . . a beard lacking all comprehension, shame and respect for the gentle sex . . . a beard that pretends to hear, see and feel nothing . . . a broken-down, fly-blown, half-plucked beard . . . a beard out of order . . . a gutted beard, a beard without backbone! May the Italian evil deliver me from this low friggler with his withered, burned-out nose . . . a putrid, frozen, irreligious nose . . . a nose dry as a lute table . . . a pale, soulless nose, a mere shadow, a sightless thing . . . a nose shrivelled up like a vine-leaf, a nose I abominate . . . a decayed flatulent nose . . . a dead nose! Where were my eyes when I attached myself to this truffle-nose, to this rusty bolt that has forgotten its shot? Let the Devil have my share of this dishonorable nose, this unsavory old beard, this old gray head, this monkey face, these old rags and tatters of a man, this—words fail me! By Heaven, I shall get hold of a young husband to espouse me in earnest . . . and often . . . and every day! . . . a young husband to take me and—"

She was engrossed in these sage thoughts when the innocent ventured to launch into his anthem. His initial phrase, sweeping over her already excited senses, struck fire in her mind, like a piece of old flint on a soldier's musket. Convinced of the wisdom of trying her son-in-law:

"Ah, youthful beard!" she murmured to herself. "Sweet-smelling down! . . . Ah, lovely, brand-new nose . . . fresh beard . . . virgin nose . . . immaculate beard . . . nose fraught with joy, beard fraught with spring, dear master key of love!"

She found plenty to say all the way round the garden, which was a long one. She arranged with the innocent that he was to slip out of his room that night and come to hers. There, she vowed, she would teach him more than ever his father had learned. The youth was delighted; he thanked Madame d'Amboise profusely and begged her to breathe no word of their compact.

During all this time, Monsieur de Braguelogne had been thundering away to himself.

"You old Ha Ha, you old Homph Homph, may the chine cough choke you, may a canker devour you . . . you toothless old currycomb . . . you old slipper unfit for the foot . . . you old harquebus. . . . You're a ten-year-old codfish, an old spider that can only spin about at night, a corpse with its eyes open! . . . Old Devil's cradle . . . old lantern of an old cakeseller . . . you old death's eye. . . . You're the old mustache of an old apothecary, ay, a harridan fit to draw tears from the dead . . . you old organ pedal . . . you old thousand-sheathed knifecase. You're an old church porch, worn out by knees, and an old poor-box into which everyone has dropped. . . . I would forfeit eternity to be rid of you."

While he was concluding these gentle thoughts, the pretty bride was thinking of the great sorrow haunting a husband unable to follow the matrimonial path and ignorant of its very essence. She resolved to save him much trouble, humiliation and labor by finding out herself. How astonished and how delighted he would be that night when, as she taught him his duty, she would whisper:

"There is all the thing amounts to, my love!"

Having been reared by her beloved dowager to hold older people in profound respect, she determined to approach this kind old gentleman in her sweetest manner and beg him to reveal to her the blessed mystery of sex. The Sieur de Braguelogne, ashamed at being so deeply engrossed in the melancholy thoughts of his evening task that he had said nothing to his tittuppy companion, asked her summarily whether she was not a happy young bride with such a fine good young man.

"Ay, he is very good," she said.

"Too good, perhaps?" the Lieutenant smiled.

In short, things went so harmoniously that very soon Monsieur de Braguelogne was singing quite another canticle to a tune sparkling with pleasure. As she made her request, he undertook to go all lengths in order to enlarge her understanding. She promised to come and study the lesson in his room.

After supper Madame d'Amboise treated Monsieur de Braguelogne to a terrible high-pitched music with variations upon the theme of his ingratitude for the benefits she had brought him: position, finances, her fidelity and so forth. She spoke for fully a half-hour without exhausting one-quarter of her ire. From this, a thousand knives were drawn between them, but they kept the sheaths. Meanwhile, the bridal couple lay snugly in bed, each planning how to escape in order to please the other. The innocent pretended to feel upset; what it was, he did not know, but he declared he would like to go out of doors. His virgin wife urged him to take a stroll in the moonlight; to which he agreed, deploring the necessity of leaving her all alone even for a few minutes. Then, both in turn rose quickly from the conjugal bed and sped off to seek wisdom from their mentors, who, as may be imagined, were waiting impatiently. They were put through an excellent course of instruction. How? I cannot tell because everyone has his own method and practise and, of all sciences, this is the most shifting in principles. But you may be certain that never did scholars more readily take to heart the precepts of any language, grammar, or indoctrination of any sort. Then they fluttered back to their bridal nest, delighted at being able to communicate to each other the discoveries of their scientific peregrinations.

"Ah! darling," the bride sighed, "already you are more up in it than my master!"

Out of these curious tests came their domestic joy and perfect fidelity for from their very entrance into the state of wedlock, they undertook to prove how much better equipped they were for the sport of love than anyone else, including their master. For the rest of their lives, they confined themselves to the legitimate substance of their own persons. And in his old age the Lord of Moncontour used to remark to his friends:

"Do as I did; be cuckolds in the blade and not in the sheaf."

Which is the true morality of the conjugal stock-in-trade.

The Costly Night of Love

*T*HE *WINTER* of the first religious uprising—the Riot of Amboise, history calls it—an advocate called Avenelles lent the Huguenots his house in the Rue des Marmousets for their interviews and conventions. He was of their persuasion but he did not know that the Prince de Condé, La Régnaudie and others were already planning to abduct the King.

This Avenelles wore a nasty red beard, shiny as a stick of liquorice; he was devilishly pale, like all pettifoggers buried in the dark regions of the law courts; he was the most blackguardly brute that ever lived, laughing at hangings and selling everybody, like the true Judas he was. According to certain authors, this arch-intriguer was half-knave half-fool in the affair. The present narrative abundantly proves it.

He had married a very comely lady of Paris and was so jealous of her that had there been one crease for which she could not account in her sheets, he would have slain her. Wrong, it would have been: plenty of honest wrinkles may be found in a bed. Anyhow, she folded her sheets nicely, and that was that. Knowing his wicked, murderous nature, she took care to remain faithful to him, standing always at hand like a candlestick, drawn up for duty like a chest which never moves and opens to order. Nevertheless, the advocate placed her under the hawk-eyed protection of an old servant, a duenna as ugly as a cracked pot, who had brought him up and who loved him. Poor wife! The only pleasure in her chill domestic existence was to go to the Church of St. Jean, on the Place de Grève, the rendezvous of the world of fashion. As she prayed to God, she would feast her eyes on all the young bloods, curled, adorned, starched, fluttering to and fro,

253

frisky as so many butterflies. In time, from among the lot, she singled out one cavalier and fell madly in love with him. He was an Italian, a particularly handsome man, the lover of the Queen Mother. Madame Avenelles lost her heart to him because he was in the springtime of his age; because he was nobly attired and proud of carriage; and because he possessed every quality a gallant needs to inflame a virtuous woman with passion, oblivion and a wild desire to fling off the chafing harness of matrimony. Nor was it long before he became enamored of this lady whose mute adoration spoke secretly to him without themselves or the Devil knowing how it was done. To begin with, she now dressed solely for church and was always arriving in sumptuous new finery. Then, instead of thinking of God, she annoyed Him by thinking only of her handsome gentleman. Forsaking her prayers, she surrendered to the fire which moistened her heart, her lips and everything else, since such fire invariably resolves itself into water. Often she thought:

"Ah, I would give my life for a single rapture with this courtly lover who worships me!"

Often, too, instead of saying her litanies to Our Lady the Virgin, she thought:

"To feel the exquisite youth of this sweet lover, to taste the full joys of love, to savor all in one moment, little would I mind the stake at which heretics perish!"

The gentleman, surveying her charms and her heightened color when she knew he was watching her, kept coming close to her stool and addressing such requests to her as ladies understand thoroughly. Then, to himself, he would mutter:

"By the double horn of my father, I swear to have that woman, though I die for it."

When the duenna turned her head, the pair squeezed, pressed, sniffed, breathed, ate, devoured, and kissed each other with glances fit to set a musketeer's wick on fire, had a musketeer been present. It was inevitable that a love so far advanced in the heart should have an end.

The gentleman, disguised as a scholar of the Sorbonne, made the acquaintance of Avenelles' clerks; he treated them to drinks and joked with them in order to learn the husband's habits, absences, journeys and so forth, biding his time to clap a pair of horns on him. Though Avenelles had decided secretly to betray the plot to the Guises, if opportune, he was for the present obliged to follow its course. This made a journey to Blois imperative, as the Court sat there at the moment, in great danger of being carried off. Our gentleman, apprised of Avenelles' intentions, went to Blois before him and set a master ambush into which despite his cunning the lawyer was to fall and from which he was not to emerge before he had been steeped in a crimson cuckolddom. The Italian, crazed with love, summoned all his pages and servitors; then he posted them about so that when advocate, wife and duenna arrived, at every hostelry they went to they were told there was no room because of the Court's sojourn in town. He made an arrangement with the host at the *Sign of the Royal Sun* whereby he should have the whole inn to himself without any of the usual servants remaining there. For greater security, he sent landlord and varlets to the country and put his own servants in their places. Everything was done with order and dispatch; the lawyer had no way of knowing anything about the stratagem. My Lord's friends came to Court and moved into his inn; for himself he reserved an apartment above that in which he intended to lodge his lovely mistress, her lawyer and the duenna. Nor did he neglect to have a trap-door cut through the boards. His butler was charged to play the part of the landlord, his pages were dressed like guests, his women as servants of the hostelry. Then he waited till his spies ushered in the chief actors in this farce.

Wife, husband and duenna did not fail to arrive. Considering the vast crowds of lords, merchants, soldiers, servitors and others brought to Blois by the presence of the young King, two Queens, the Guises and all the Court, nobody had cause to wonder at or to discuss either the ingenious trap or the confusion at the *Sign of the Royal Sun*, whose rays warmed our gallant and brought his desires to boiling point. The advocate lodged, the lover walked about in the courtyard, hoping and watching for a glance from his lady. Nor did he dally long: almost at once Madame Avenelles surveyed the courtyard, as woman will, and, with fluttering heart, recognized her gallant, adorable admirer. Happiness surged through her. If, by some lucky chance, the pair had been left alone for one ounce of time, the gentleman would have enjoyed his good fortune then and there. Madame Avenelles was afire from her soles to the crown of her head.

"Oh, how hot it is in the rays of this lord!" she murmured, meaning to say, "in the rays of this sun." Indeed, it was shining down very brightly.

The husband, hearing her, ran to the window, spied our gentleman:

"Ha, my love, so it's lords you want now, eh?" As he spoke, he drew her away by the arm and flung her like a sack on the bed. "Remember this: though I carry a pencase instead of a sword, I have a penknife in this pencase; and that penknife will go straight through your heart on the slightest suspicion of marital plumage. I believe I have seen that gentleman somewhere."

The lawyer was so fierce in his cruelty that she rose, and:

"Very well, kill me. I long to deceive you. Never touch me again after threatening me as you have. From now on, my sole thought will be to sleep with a lover more gentle than you are."

"Come, come, darling," he said, bewildered, "I went too far. Kiss me, my love, and forgive me."

"I will neither kiss nor forgive you," she answered. "You are a wicked man."

Avenelles, enraged, sought to capture forcibly what his lady withheld; a combat ensued from which the husband emerged clawed all over. Worse still, covered with scratches, he was expected at a meeting of the conspirators. He had therefore to withdraw from the field and leave his wife in the hands of the old duenna.

The pettifogger gone, the gallant detailed one of his servants to mount guard at the street-corner, sped off to his blessed trapdoor, raised it noiselessly and called his lady with a gentle *pst! pst!* heard and understood by the all-hearing, all-comprehending heart. The lady raised her head to see her handsome lover about four flea-jumps above her. He lowered two cords of heavy silk; at a sign from him she passed her arms through the loops and in the twinkling of an eye she was translated by two pulleys from her bed through the canopy into the room above. Then the trapdoor closed as soundlessly as it had opened, leaving the old duenna utterly flabbergasted when she turned around to behold neither feather nor beak and to realize that the bird had flown. But how? With whose help? Through what outlet? And where? . . . *Hocus, pocus, malus, locus!* The alchemists, standing over their stoves and reading Herr Trippa, knew just about as much. Yet the old woman was familiar with the work at hand and the crucible: the former spelled cuckoldry, the latter the prettiest chattel of the lady's person. The duenna was completely abashed as she sat awaiting the arrival of the Sieur Avenelles—or, in other words, death—for he would rend everything to bits in his fury. Nor could she escape now, the luckless female, for the jealous husband had very prudently taken the keys away with him.

At first glance, Madame Avenelles found a dainty supper, a warm fire in the fireplace, but one warmer still in the heart of her lover. He seized her and with tears of joy kissed her on the eyes, to begin with, to thank them for their sweet glances during devotion in the Church of St. Jean en Grève. Far from refusing her sweet mouth to love, the lawyer's ardent spouse allowed herself to be adored, hugged and caressed, rejoicing to experience a rapt worship, an iron embrace and ineffable blandishments, after the fashion of famished lovers. They both agreed to belong to each other all night long, no matter what came of it, she considering the future not worth a fig against the bliss of this night, he counting upon his wits and his sword to obtain many more. Both, then, heedless of life so but they consummated a thousand lives at one stroke, partook of a thousand delights, each giving the other double his own pleasure. Were they not falling into an abyss, he and she? And must they not roll over its depths clasping and clinging together, knit close as one, putting all their souls' passion ragefully into a single ecstasy? Ah, theirs was a passionate conjunction! What do they know of love, the poor townsmen who sleep regularly with their worthy wives? Have they ever experienced the fierce pulse of the heart, the hot gush of life and the vigorous tautness of two lovers, joined flesh to white flesh, radiant with desire and *accoupled* in the very teeth of death? Our lady and her gallant scarcely touched the supper; then they retired to bed early. Here they may be left at their task since no tongue save that of a paradise unknown to us, could describe their delighted anguish and their anguished delights.

Meanwhile the husband, so well hornified that all memory of

this marriage was effaced by love, found himself in a parlous predicament. The Prince de Condé, accompanied by all the chiefs and bigwigs, came to the council of the Huguenots, where plans were laid for a *coup d'état:* the Queen Mother, the Guises, the young King and the young Queen were to be abducted and the government changed. The game having become serious, the advocate saw his head was in danger but he did not feel the antlers being planted there. He hastened off to divulge the conspiracy to My Lord Cardinal of Lorraine, who took the rogue to his brother, the Duke. The trio held a consultation; many splendid promises were made to the lawyer and at last, at about midnight, he was reluctantly allowed to issue secretly from the château. At this moment the gentleman's pages and servants were holding a merry midnight banquet to celebrate their master's fortuitous espousals. Arriving at the height of the festivities, amid drunkenness and happy cheers, Avenelles was greeted with a volley of jokes, raillery and laughter, at which he turned pale as a ghost when, reaching his room, he found the duenna alone. The luckless woman sought to speak, but Avenelles promptly planted his fist in her gullet, and, by a gesture, enjoined silence. Then he rummaged about in his bag and brought out a good dagger. As he drew it from its sheath and began to sharpen it, a frank, ingenuous, joyous, amorous, tender, celestial burst of laughter, followed by certain words of easy comprehension, floated down through the trap. Recognizing the voices of his wife and the courtier, the sly advocate blew out his candle. Then, through the cracks in the ceiling, if not through the extrajudiciary door itself, he saw a glimmer which vaguely shed light upon the mystery. Seizing the duenna by the arm, he tiptoed up the stairs, sought and found the door behind which the lovers were rejoicing. With a single terrific forensic lunge, he knocked down the door; one bound brought him on the bed where he fell upon his wife half-naked in her lover's arms.

"Ah!" she gasped.

The lover, having avoided the blow, tried to wrench the dagger from the scoundrel's hand; the other held on to it with a grip of iron. In this life-and-death struggle, the husband felt both his lieutenant and his wife hindering him: the former squeezed him tight as in a vise, the latter bit him, tearing away at his flesh with furious fangs, gnawing away as a dog gnaws at a bone. Immediately he imagined a better way of satisfying his rage. This devil new-horned, with all the malice in the world told the chamberwoman in her patois to tie up the lovers in the silken cords of the trap. Throwing his dagger away, he helped her bind them fast

in the snare. The thing finished in a turn of the wrist, he stuffed linen in their mouths to gag them, and, without a word, ran to his good dagger.

At precisely this moment, several officers of the Duc de Guise entered the room. During the struggle, no one had heard them turning the house topsy-turvy as they searched for the Sieur Avenelles. These soldiers, suddenly warned by a cry from the pages of the lord who lay trussed up, gagged and half-killed, threw themselves between the man with the dagger and the lovers.

Having disarmed him, they discharged their duty by arresting him and leading him off to the prison of the château, with his wife and the duenna as well. In the rescued lover, the henchmen of the Duc de Guise had recognized a friend of their master, a gentleman whom the Queen wished immediately to consult and whom they had been sent to summon to the council. They invited him to come with them. Then, swiftly unbound, the gentleman, while he dressed, whispered to the leader of the escort that, on his account and for love of him, he should be careful to keep husband and wife separated. He promised the soldier his favor, good advancement and even much money if he looked personally to the enforcement of this request. For greater security, he explained the reason for the whole affair, adding that if the husband found his pretty wife within reach, he would assuredly rip her up. Finally, he ordered the officer to place Madame Avenelles in the château jail in a pleasant spot, level with the gardens, but to clap the advocate in a safe dungeon and chain him up hand and foot. The officer promised to obey; he managed matters according to the will of the gentleman, who accompanied his mistress as far as the courtyard of the château, assuring her that this business would make her a widow and that he would perhaps espouse her in lawful wedlock. Indeed, Avenelles was thrown into a damp airless hole; his comely wife was placed in a little room above him, out of consideration for her lover, who was Scipio Sardini, a lord of Lucca, a man extremely wealthy and, as has been said above, lover to Queen Catherine who at that time did everything in concert with the Guises. Sardini went quickly to the Queen's apartment where an important secret council was being held; here he learned what was afoot and how the Court was in danger. He found the privy counsellors surprised and at a loss how to cope with this menace; but he soon made them all agree, urging them to turn it to their own advantage. To his advice was due the skilful trick whereby the King was moved to the Château d'Amboise and the heretics, caught like foxes in a bag, were all put to death. Indeed, everyone knows how the Queen Mother and the Guises lay low and how the Riot of Amboise ended. The account of it is no wise the object of the present writing.

When all their plans were laid and the counsellors left the

Queen Mother's apartment in the morning, Sardini did not forget his love for Madame Avenelles, although he was much smitten with the lovely Limeuil, a daughter of the Queen Mother's and related to him through the house of La Tour de Turenne. At once he asked why the good Judas had been clapped in a cage. The Cardinal de Lorraine assured him that he had not the slightest intention of harming Avenelles; he had put him out of the way to guard against the scoundrel's possible remorse and to ensure silence until the whole affair was concluded. He would, he assured Sardini, free Avenelles at the proper time and place.

"Free him!" the Italian gasped. "God forbid! Sew him in a sack for me: throw the old black gown into the Loire! To begin with, I know him; he will never forgive you his sojourn in jail; he will go back to the heretics. Besides, if you do away with him, no one will know your secrets; and none of his friends would dare ask what became of him, because he is a traitor. Let me arrange for his wife to escape and do whatever else is needful; I will rid you of him!"

"Ha, ha, ha," the Cardinal laughed, "a good idea, that! Before distilling your counsel, I will have both of them more securely guarded. Ho there!"

An officer of justice appeared; he was ordered to allow no one to communicate with the prisoners. Then My Lord Cardinal begged Sardini to say at his inn that the advocate had left Blois to return to his lawsuits in Paris.

The men detailed to arrest the advocate had been specially warned to treat him as a person of importance; they therefore neither stripped nor robbed him. Thus he had kept thirty crowns in gold in his purse. These he resolved to spend in order to slake his vengeance; they would prove sound arguments in convincing his jailors to allow him to visit a wife whom he adored and from whom he craved a legitimate embrace. Now Sardini, nervous about his mistress and afraid that a dangerous proximity to the red-headed chicaner might spell damage to her, resolved to carry her off by night and put her in a place of safety. He planned to hire a boat and some men and ambush them near the bridge; then he would get three of his most alert servants to file the bars of the cell, seize the lady and bring her to the garden wall where he would be waiting.

Having made the proper preparations and procured some sharp files, he obtained an audience with the Queen Mother that morning. Her Majesty's apartments were situated above the dungeons where the lawyer and his wife languished; Sardini believed that the Queen would willingly lend her aid in the projected flight. She received him; he besought her to countenance his liberating Madame Avenelles unknown to the Cardinal and Monsieur de Guise. He again begged her most urgently to advise My Lord Cardinal to toss the man into the river. To all of this Her Majesty breathed Amen. Then the lover sent his lady a letter concealed in a dish of cucumbers, congratulating her upon her approaching widowhood and telling her the hour of the flight. At which she rejoiced mightily. At dusk the Queen drew the soldiers of the watch aside and sent them off to investigate a ray of moonlight that frightened her, while the Italian's servants raised the grating, beckoned the lady who promptly appeared, and led her to the wall where Sardini was waiting.

But, the postern closed and the Italian outside with the lady, suddenly the lady threw off her cloak and there she was, changed into an advocate; and there the advocate seized his horner by the collar, choked him and dragged him toward the water to throw him to the bottom of the Loire. But Sardini put up a good front, defended himself, shouted and struggled, without being able, despite his dagger, to shake off this long-robed devil. In the moonlight, by sudden breaks in the fiendish struggle, Sardini caught sight of Avenelles' face, stained with his wife's blood. Then he fell into a slough and lay quite still under the feet of the advocate. Avenelles ran wildly away believing the Italian dead; at that moment some servants armed with torches came rushing up. But he found time to jump into the boat and row off at top speed.

Thus poor Madame Avenelles alone paid with her life. Sardini was picked up, half-strangled; subsequently he recovered. Later, as everyone knows, he married the lovely Limeuil, after this sweet girl had been brought to bed in the Queen's room —a great scandal which, through affection, the Queen Mother wished to conceal and which from great love Sardini covered. Queen Catherine gave him the splendid domain and château of Chaumont-sur-Loire.

But he had been so furiously smitten, mauled, buffetted and trampled by the husband that he did not make old bones; the fair Limeuil was left a widow in the springtime of her life. Despite her wrath, the advocate was not pursued. On the contrary, he was crafty enough to get himself included among those who were freed from persecution by an Edict of Grace; he returned to serve the Huguenots in Germany.

Poor Madame Avenelles, pray for her soul. She was thrown none knows where, without church prayers or Christian burial. Alas! remember her, ye ladies whose loves run smoothly.

The Jocund Curé of Meudon and His Sermon

HE LAST visit Master François Rabelais paid to the Court of King Henry the Second occurred in that winter when Nature's inevitable decree bade him put off his fleshly garb and don the eternal life of his books— those radiant works of a philosophy to which we must needs forever return! By then, the good man had counted near threescore and ten flights of the swallow. His Homeric head was somewhat scant of hair, but his beard still retained its erstwhile majesty, April still shone in his quiet smile and all wisdom sat upon his ample brow. A handsome old man, according to those fortunate enough to gaze upon his face, in the features of which Socrates and Aristophanes, once enemies, had become reconciled and mingled their traits.

Hearing the knell of his last hour tinkling in his ears, he resolved to go and pay his respects to the King of France. His Majesty had just arrived at his château of Les Tournelles; his Court was therefore but a stone's throw from our blessed philosopher who lived in the gardens of St. Paul. An audience granted, he was ushered into Queen Catherine's apartment. Others present included Madame Diane (whom Her Majesty tolerated from motives of high policy) the King, My Lord Constable, the Cardinal de Lorraine, the Cardinal du Bellay, Messieurs de Guise, the Sieur de Birague and various Italians who were then rising to prominence at Court under the Queen's protection, My Lord Admiral Montgomery, the officers of the household and a few poets such as Melin de St. Gelais, Philibert de l'Orme and the Sieur Brantôme. Perceiving the good man, His Majesty, who relished his wit, conversed with him a while. Then: "Have you ever delivered a sermon to your parishioners of Meudon?"

Rabelais believed the King was joking, for he had never troubled about his incumbency beyond collecting its emolument.

"Sire, my flock is everywhere," he replied, "and my homilies are heard throughout Christendom."

He looked up at all these courtiers, who with the exception of Messieurs du Bellay and de Châtillon considered him but a learned buffoon, whereas he was the king of wits and a better king far than him they worshipped solely for the benefits of the Crown. As his glance travelled over their faces, a malicious desire came into the good man's head. What a satisfaction, before giving life the slip, to piddle philosophically over their heads precisely as the excellent Gargantua was pleased to sprinkle the Parisians from the turrets of Notre Dame.

"If you are in a merry mood, Sire," he went on, "I can offer you a splendid sermon. It is appropriate on all occasions; I have been storing it under the tympanum of my left ear, in order to deliver it in a fit place, by way of an aulic parabola."

"Gentlemen," cried the King, "Master François Rabelais has the floor and our souls' salvation is at stake. Be silent, then, and listen carefully: he is rich in evangelical comicalities."

"Sire," said the good man, "I begin."

All the courtiers ceased speaking and drew up in a circle, supple as osiers before the father of Pantagruel. And Rabelais proceeded to unfold the following tale in words whose illustrious eloquence it would be impossible to match. Since the narrative has been only verbally preserved, the Author may be forgiven for writing it in his own way.

"In his old age Gargantua was given to curious eccentricities which amazed his household but which were forgiven him. Was he not seven hundred and four years old? Ay, he was, in spite of the statement made by St. Clement of Alexandria in his *Stromates* to the effect that he was then a quarter of a day younger— which matters little to us. Now this very paternal master, perceiving that everything was at sixes and sevens in his house and that he was being fleeced and plundered by everybody, became terrified at the idea of being left destitute in his last hour. He therefore resolved to perfect the management of his domains. And he did rightly, too.

"In a storeroom of his Gargantuan mansion, he laid by a fine

heap of red wheat, twenty jars of mustard and a few delicacies
such as prunes and early Touraine peaches, pies, forcemeat, pat-
ties of pork, cheeses from Olivet near Orléans, goat-cheeses and
other varieties famed from Langeais to Loches, tubs of butter,
pâté of hare, aspic of duck, pig's feet in bran, crocks and pots full
of crushed peas, attractive little boxes of Orléans quince jam,
hogsheads of lampreys, kegs of green sauce and much river game
such as francolin, teal, sheldrake, heron, phenicoptera, all preserved in brine; dried raisins, tongues smoked in the manner invented by Hapmouche, his celebrated ancestor; then sweetmeats
for Gargamelle his mother on her good days; and a thousand
other things which are detailed in the code of the Ripuarian
Laws and in certain folios taken from the Capitularies, Pragmat-
ics, Royal Establishment, Ordinances and Institutions of the period. This done, our great Gargantua put his spectacles on his
nose or his nose in his spectacles and set out to look for some rare
flying dragon or unicorn who might be entrusted with the guardianship of this precious treasure. He would have nothing to do
with a Cocquesigrue because the Egyptians fared ill with them,
as the Hieroglyphics fully prove. He rejected the cohorts of
the Caucquemarres, because the Emperors were disgusted with
them, as were the Romans, according to the reports of that sly
fox Tacitus. He would not hear of the men of Pichrochole in
council assembled; he set his back upon Magi by the spadeful,
Druids by the basketful, the legion of Papimany and the Masso-
rets, who, as his son Pantagruel told him when he returned from
his travels, grew as thick as couchgrass and overran the land. The
old stager out-Gauled a Gaul in his knowledge of the ancient stories: he had not the least faith in any race, and had it been lawful, he would have implored the Creator of all things for a brand-
new one. Not daring to bother Him with such trifles, poor
Gargantua did not know whom to choose and was thinking how
cumbersome his opulence was when on the road he met a handsome little shrew-mouse, of the noble race of the Musaranea,
who bear all gules on a field of azure. By the Prophet's belly! you
may be sure he was a fine virile specimen with the finest tail of
the whole family. There he was, strutting about in the sunlight
like one of God's brave shrew-mice, very proud of having been

in this world since the post-diluvian creation, as proved by letters-patent of incontestable nobility registered by the parliament
of the universe. It is indeed established in œcumenical proceedings that there was a shrew-mouse in Noah's Ark.

"Here Master Alcofribas touched his cap and said reverently:

" 'I salute Noah, My Lords, who planted the vine and first
knew the happiness of getting drunk on its rich, red blood!'

" 'For it is certain,' he went on, 'that there was a shrew-mouse
in the vessel whence we all originated. Unfortunately, men have
married beneath them. But not shrew-mice: they are more jealous of their bearings than any other beast and would not dream
of receiving a common field-mouse among them, even if the
churl possessed the special gift of transmuting grains of sand into
choice fresh hazel-nuts.'

"This splendid nobleman's virtues pleased our blessed Gargantua; he resolved to appoint Master Shrew-Mouse custodian of
his granaries with the amplest concomitant powers of justice,
Committimus, Missi Dominici, clergy, men-at-arms and the rest.
The shrew-mouse promised to discharge his office satisfactorily
and to do his duty as a loyal steward provided he were allowed to
live upon the heap of wheat—a condition Gargantua considered
perfectly legitimate. So the shrew-mouse started capering about
his vast domain, happy as a prince who is happy, reconnoitring
his immense kingdoms of mustard, his principalities of confectionery, his provinces of hams, his duchies of raisins, his coun-
ties of forcemeat and his baronies of every description, climbing
on his heap of wheat and sweeping everything with his tail.
Everywhere he was received with honor by the pots, which stood
at attention in a respectful silence, except a few golden goblets
which knocked together like church bells in a sort of holy tocsin.
This pleased him mightily; and he thanked them, right and left,
with a nod of the head as he marched under the ray of sunlight
which was glittering down upon his realm. His tawny hair
gleamed so brightly that he looked for all the world like some
Emperor of the North clad in a cloak of sable marten. Having
toured about, jumped and caracoled to his heart's content, he
munched two grains of wheat, sat on his heap like a king in
plenary court and considered himself the loftiest of shrew-mice.

"At this moment the gentlemen of the Noctambulant Court, who scamper with their little feet over the floors, emerged from their accustomed holes; there were rats, mice, and every other kind of gnawing, plundering, good for nothing beasts that harass a thrifty housewife. Seeing the shrew-mouse, they were frightened and stood stock-still on the threshold of their dens. In spite of the danger, one old miscreant of the trotting, nibbling race of mice thrust out his head from amid this sea of small pates. Poking his muzzle at the window, he had the audacity to stare boldly at My Lord Shrew-Mouse, who was proudly squatted on his bum with his tail in the air. Eventually the daring beast came to realize that he was a Devil from whom only a good clawing was to be gained. This is how the thing occurred.

"In order that all the shrew-mice, cats, weasels, martens, field-mice, domestic mice and other rascals of the same kidney should recognize the authority of his lieutenant, Gargantua had lightly dipped his muzzle, pointed as a larding pin, into oil of musk. Since then all shrew-mice have inherited the odor, because this particular one disregarded Gargantua's sage advice and rubbed shoulders with others of the race. Great troubles arose therefrom in Musaranea and I would give a full account of them in a historical work, if time were not lacking.

"Then an old mouse or rat—the Rabbis of the Talmud have not yet agreed about the species—recognized from this scent that the shrew-mouse had been appointed to watch over Gargantua's grain, inured to virtue, invested with sufficient power and armed at all points. This old mouse was much upset; he feared that he would no longer be allowed to live, after the ancestral fashion of mice, upon crumbs, scraps, crusts, bits, slips, fragments and a myriad oddments of this Promised Land for rodents. In this quandary, with all the guile of an old courtier who has lived under two regents and three kings, he resolved to test the mettle of the shrew-mouse and devote himself to the salvation of the jawbones of all his race. This would have been admirable enough in a man. How much more admirable in a mouse belonging to a most selfish race of beasts who live brazenly and shamelessly for themselves alone and who, in order to attain their end, would befoul a consecrated wafer, gnaw a priest's stole without the least compunction and drink from a holy chalice without giving a thought to God. Our mouse advanced, bowing gracefully; the shrew-mouse suffered him to draw quite near, because, to tell the truth, shrew-mice are naturally short-sighted. Then this Curtius of nibblers spoke not in the vulgar jargon of ordinary mice but in the elegant Tuscan of shrew-mice:

" 'My Lord,' he said, 'I have heard many things about your glorious family, to which I am the most faithful of servants. I know the hallowed legend of your forefathers; I know how of yore the ancient Egyptians respected, worshipped and adored them like other sacred birds. Nevertheless your furry robe is so regally perfumed, and its color is so supersplendiferously tanned that I find it difficult to recognize you as belonging to this race. Never have I seen one of the latter so brilliantly adorned. Yet I observed you devour the grain after the antique fashion. Your proboscis is one of high sapience; you have laid about you like a savant shrew-mouse. But, if true shrew-mouse you are, in I know not what part of your ear you must certainly possess I know not what hyperauditive channel, closed at your secret command by I know not what wonderful door (I know not when or how), in order to enable you (I know not wherefore) to shut out I know not what sounds which are displeasing to you—because with your perfection and omniperception, certain things might pain you.'

" 'Quite so,' said the shrew-mouse. 'The door you refer to has just closed down. I hear nothing.'

" 'Oh!' exclaimed the old rapscallion. 'So much the better!'

"And he pounced headlong upon the heap of wheat from which he began to levy his provision for the winter.

" 'Can you hear anything?' he asked.

" 'I hear the pit-pat of my heart.'

" 'Quweek! Quweek!' all the mice squeaked. 'We shall fool him easily!"

"The shrew-mouse, believing he had met a loyal servant, opened the trap of his musical orifice. At once his ear rang with the patter of the grain rolling toward the mouse's hole. Without having recourse to the justice of bailiffs, he leaped upon the old mouse and ripped open his throat. It was a glorious death; the hero perished in the thick of the grain; he was canonized as a martyr. The shrew-mouse seized him by the ears and nailed him

to the door of the granary, after the method of the Ottoman
Porte, upon which my excellent Panurge came near to being
spitted.

"The dying cries of the victim sent all the rats, mice and their
allies scurrying off to their holes amid great trepidation. Then,
at nightfall they assembled in the cellar, having been summoned
to a council to consider public affairs. To this meeting, by virtue
of the *Lex Papiria* and other laws, their legitimate wives were
admitted. The rats demanded to pass before the mice and the
ageless quarrel over precedence almost spoiled everything. But
a fat rat offered his arm to a mouse and gaffer rats pairing off
with gammer mice soon they were all sitting on their scuts,
their tails in air, their muzzles to skyward, their whiskers crisp,
their eyes bright as falcons'. Then began a deliberation destined
to finish up with insults and an uproar worthy of the best councils of the Fathers Œcumenical. Some said black, others white;
a passing cat fled away in terror before these strange strident
sounds of *Boowe, boowe, fruwh, whu, whu, whouic, whouicc,
briff, briffnac, nac, owhix, frowx, trr, trr, trr, razza, za, za, zaa,
brr, brrr, raaa, ra, ra, ra, ra, fouix.* These squeaks blended together in a babel of stridulous clamor that aldermen in a Town
Hall could not have matched.

"In the midst of this tempest, a little mouse too young yet to
enter parliament thrust her curious head through a crack, offering a dainty snout with all the soft, virgin down of an animalcule
hitherto uncaptured. As the turmoil increased, her body gradually followed the snoutlet; presently the wench slipped onto
the hoop of a barrel and balanced herself on it so gracefully that
she might have been a delicate work of art chiselled in antique
bas-relief. An old rat raised his eyes to Heaven to implore a wise
remedy for the misfortunes of the State; he caught sight of this
winsome, shapely mouse and declared that she must bring about
the State's salvation. Every muzzle turned toward the Lady of
Good Succor; all grew mute and agreed to loose her upon the
shrew-mouse. Then, in spite of the ire of certain envious rodents,
she was marched triumphantly round the cellar. The old rats
watched her tripping jauntily along, moving the springs of her
chine, shaking her sly little head, wiggling her diaphanous ears
and running her pink, slight tongue over her chops and the new-

born fur on her lips. They lost their hearts to her; and, with hoary, wrinkled jaws, they began to chant and warble her praises, just as the old Trojans did of yore, lost in admiration of the lovely Helen returning from her bath.

"Then they let the fair virgin loose in the granary with instructions to debauch the heart of the shrew-mouse and save the gnawgrain race. Even so the fair Hebrew Esther went forth to save the Chosen People by lying with the Sultan Ahasuerus, as it is written in the Master Book—for *Bible* comes from the Greek *Biblos,* as who might say the only book. The mouse promised to deliver the granaries, for, as it happened, she was the queen of mice . . . a delicate, plumpish, blond young mouse, the most entrancing little lady that ever scampered merrily over the floors, trotted friskily between the walls and uttered rapt, dulcet cries of joy when she found nuts, crumbs, and bits of bread on her way . . . a true sprite, comely and playful, with a glance limpid as a white diamond, a small head, glabrous skin, an amorous body, rosy feet and a tail of velvet . . . a highborn mouse, fair-spoken with a natural love for lying abed and for the pleasures of indolence . . . a merry mouse, shrewder, withal, than an old doctor of the Sorbonne with Papal decrees at his fingers' ends . . . lively, white-bellied, streaked faintly on the back . . . with high, firm breasts, as pointed as a suggestion, with pearly teeth and a fresh nature, a morsel fit for a king!"

This description was so bold—all of them recognized the true portrait of Madame Diane, who was present—that the courtiers stood aghast. Queen Catherine smiled; but the King was in no joking mood. Cardinal du Bellay and Cardinal de Châtillon, terrified for the good man, sought to attract his attention. But he went on blithely:

"The pretty mouse dispensed with lengthy circumbilivaginations; she went straight to the point. The first evening she trotted before the shrew-mouse, she enslaved him forever with her coquetries, mock-modesty, blandishments and dalliance . . . with deft, provocative refusals, melting glances and all the soft impeachments of a virgin who desires but dares not . . . with amorous oglings, semi-caresses, preparatory stratagems . . . with the pride of a mouse who is conscious of her value . . . with brangling born of laughter and laughter of brangling . . . with fond triflings, gentle, ensnaring conversations and other lush, treacherous feminine manœuvres . . . with every snare that the females of every land make capital use of. After much wriggling, pawing and rubbing of snouts, after all the gallantries of a love-sick shrew-mouse, after much knitting of brows and heaving of cavernous sighs, what with serenades, snacks, dinners and suppers on the grain heap and all manner of other entertainments, the steward of the granaries triumphed over the scruples of his beautiful mistress. What pleasure they took in this incestuous, illicit love! The mouse, having caught her shrew-mouse on the fly, held on fast and became queen of everything. She would demand mustard on her wheat, sweetmeats for dessert; she foraged everywhere. And, though uneasy at this betrayal of his vows to Gargantua and his shrew-mouse duties, her lord permitted the empress of his heart to do as she willed.

"She pursued her biblical advantage with the pertinacity of woman. One night when they were in the throes of joy, the mouse remembered her dear old father and wished him, too, to be given an opportunity to feed upon the grain occasionally. Unless the shrew-mouse suffered her to indulge her daughterly piety, she threatened to leave him alone and forlorn in his domain. With a sweep of the paw he granted his strumpet's father letters-patent, duly stamped with a broad seal of green wax and tagged with ribbons of crimson silk, authorizing him to enter the Gargantuan palace at all hours, to visit his beloved and virtuous daughter, to kiss her brow and to eat his bellyful but only in one corner. A venerable rat appeared, an oldster weighing at least twenty-five ounces and dragging a long white tail behind him. He moved like the President of a Court of Justice, wagging his head sagely from side to side. He was followed by fifteen or twenty nephews, with teeth sharp as saws. By all manner of little observations and suggestions, they demonstrated that they, his relatives, would be his loyal vassals; they would wear themselves out helping him make an inventory of his stock, sorting it out systematically and labelling it properly so that when Gargantua came to inspect it, he would find provisions and accounts in ship-shape order. This assurance bore a semblance of truth. Yet despite their arguments, the poor shrew-mouse was tormented by certain ideas from on high and no uncertain prick-

ings of his shrew-mousish conscience. Noticing that he found
pleasure in nothing, but went about listlessly and half-heartedly,
the mouse, now pregnant by his instrumentality, began to worry
over the worries of this master who was her slave. One morning,
while playing with him, it occurred to her that an official consultation with the pundits of the Sorbonne might ease his
doubts. She therefore summoned the learned doctors of the
tribe.

"During the day, she brought before him a certain Sieur
Evegault, freshly emerged from a cheese, where he lived in utter
abstinence. An old confessor, basted with the choicest grease, a
personable enough rascal, with fine black skin, standing firm
as a tower and slightly tonsured on the head by the sweep of a
cat's paw. A grave rat, too, with a monastical paunch; he had
studied and digested the best scientific authorities by nibbling
at parchments, decretal briefs, mountains of clementine documents and tomes of all sorts, fragments of which had clung to
and discolored his gray beard. In reverent honor of his exalted
virtue, sapience and cheesy life, he was accompanied by a dark
troop of rats each paired off with his own comely, attractive
privy mouse, for the Canons of the Council of Chézil had not
yet been adopted and it was lawful for them to have respectable
women for concubines. These prebendary and beneficiary rats
and their mice lined up in double file so that they looked exactly
like a university procession going to the historical Lendit ceremony. They sniffed eagerly at the victuals.

"When all were properly placed for the ceremony, the old
Cardinal of the rats took the floor and in choice rat-Latin delivered an oration in which he pointed out that none was superior
to the shrew-mouse save God alone and that to God alone he
owed obedience. The lush phrases rolled out sonorously in a
speech glittering with biblical quotations, beautifully calculated
to dazzle an awed audience and to obscure the issue. Then there
were telling arguments interlarded with sound common sense.
The address wound up with a peroration thickly studded with
highfalutin' phrases in honor of all shrew-mice, among whom
this exemplar was the most illustrious and best that ever drew
breath. Such brilliance completely blinded the custodian of the
granaries. Poor dear gentleman, his head was utterly turned,

and he installed these silver-tongued rats in his realm. Night and day there were showers of golden eulogies and mellifluous canticles in his honor; nor did they omit to celebrate his lady. All kissed her frail paw and sniffed at her joyous crupper.

"Finally the mistress, knowing that certain young rats were still fasting, desired to crown her achievement. So she wielded her charming snout to perfection, kissing the shrew-mouse, moaning for love and practising a thousand strategies any single one of which suffices to damn a beast's soul. He was, she told him, wasting the precious moments of their love by scouring the country on tours of inspection; he was perpetually on highroad and byway, while she pined away for loneliness, unable ever to get her fill of him and when she desired him most poignantly, he was clearing the leads in pursuit of cats. Alas, no! to please her, he should be ready to her hand as a lance and gentle in it as a bird. In the midst of this heartrending plaint, the mouse pulled out a gray hair, and, believing herself the unhappiest creature in the world, she fell to weeping. In vain the shrew-mouse objected that she was mistress of everything; in vain he sought to resist. A shower of tears melted his will and brought him to his knees imploring a truce, craving to know her desires. This soon dried her tears. Offering him her paw to kiss, she advised him to arm some experienced mercenaries, veterans all, who could be relied upon to keep watch and go the rounds. Everything was prudently arranged in this wise. The shrew-mouse had the rest of the day to sport, dance, and amuse himself, to hear such roundels and ballads as the poets indited in his honor, to play the lute and the mandola, to compose acrostics, to eat, drink and make merry.

"At last his mistress rose from her confinement, having hatched the most delectable mousified shrew or shrewified mouse. The name they gave this product of amative alchemy, I do not know. But you may be sure the pundits of the law legitimatized it."

As Rabelais said this, My Lord Constable of Montmorency, who had married his son to a legitimatized bastard of the King's, clapped his hand to his sword, gripping the hilt viciously.

"That day," Rabelais went on, "the granaries witnessed a feast unparalleled by any Court festival or gala including the celebrations following the Field of the Cloth of Gold. The mice gambolled in every nook and cranny. Everywhere there were dances of all kinds, concerts, banquets, toasts, sarabands, music, happy songs, epithalamia. The rats gutted the pots, opened the jars, overturned the demijohns and ransacked the stores. Rivers of mustard flowed over the floors; hams were slashed to bits; what had once been tall heaps of food were reduced to scattered pulps. Everything piddled, streamed, rolled, tumbled to the ground: the small rats were splashing about in puddles of green sauce, the mice waded through pools of sweetmeats, the oldsters made off with the pies and *pâtés*. There were wood-mice riding astride salted tongues of beef; there were field-mice swimming about inside the pots while the canniest were busy carting off the grain to their private holes, making the most of the hub-bub to lay up a rich store. No one passed by the Orléans quince without paying it the tribute of a nibble, if not two. It was one gay Roman carnival. Anyone with a sharp ear could not have helped hearing the sizzle of frying-pans, the sundry cries and clamors in the kitchens, the roaring of ovens, the pounding of mortars, the seething of stewpans, the wheezing of turnspits, the creaking of hampers and baskets, the susurration of pastries, the click of meat-jacks and the echo of small feet pattering down like hail upon the floor. It was one vast wedding-feast, with a tumult of retainers coming and going, stewards and cooks, footmen, ostlers and grooms—not to mention the musicians, the turns of the tumblers, the general applause, the drums of the militia and the choirs of the three Orders. In a word so great was their delight that they organized a general ball to celebrate this auspicious occasion.

"Suddenly they heard a blood-curdling footstep as Gargantua climbed the stairs of his house: the beams shook, the floor trembled, the ceiling swayed. Certain venerable rats inquired what this noise might be, and, as nobody knew the lordly step, many rats decamped. They did well, for a moment later the master entered. As his eyes fell upon the bear garden the gentlemen rats had made of his granaries, as he saw his stores plundered, his preserves swallowed, his mustard strewn over the place, everything befouled and ruined, he brought his foot down upon these revelling vermin and crushed them without giving them time to squeal. Thus their rich garments of satin, their pearls and velvets and rags were spoiled and the feast blotted out."

"What became of the shrew-mouse?" asked His Majesty, emerging from a brown study.

"Ah, Sire," Rabelais answered, "here is where the Gargantuan race proved unkind. The shrew-mouse was put to death, but, being a gentleman, he was beheaded. That was unjust, for, after all, he had been tricked and misled."

"You go rather far, my good man," the King said.

"Not far, Sire, but high. Have you not raised the pulpit above the crown? You asked me to preach a sermon: I gave you one which is gospel."

"Eh, my fair Court Preacher, suppose I were spiteful?" Madame Diane whispered in his ear. "What then?"

"Madame," Rabelais said, "was it not necessary to warn your royal master against the Queen's Italians who are thick here as cockchafers?"

"Wretched orator," Cardinal Odet said under his breath, "be off to a stranger land!"

"Ha, My Lord Cardinal," the good man replied, "ere long I shall be in a stranger land than you dream."

"God's truth, Master Scribbler," growled My Lord Constable. (His son, as everyone knows, cravenly jilted Mademoiselle de Piennes in order to marry Diane de France, a daughter born to the King by a lady from this side of the Alps.) "What gives you the audacity to attack persons of such lofty station? So, wretched poet, you like to soar high, eh? Well, I promise to raise you to a very high place indeed!"

"We shall all come to it, My Lord Constable," the good man said. "But if you are a friend to State and King, you will thank me for having warned His Majesty against the tricks of Lorrainers—a band of rats apt to ruin everything."

"Look here, my good man," Cardinal Charles de Lorraine murmured, "if you happen to need a few gold crowns to bring out your fifth book of Pantagruel, you shall have them from my privy purse. Hum, hum! That old hound-bitch who has bewitched the King . . . you told her off properly . . . and her pack, too!"

"Well, gentlemen, what is your opinion on this sermon?" asked the King.

"Sire," said Melin de St. Gelais, perceiving that the company was merry, "I never heard a better Pantagruelian prognostication. It was well worthy the poet who created these leonine verses in honor of the Abbaye de Thélème:

" *'Should ye who enter here profess in jubilation*
Our gospel of elation, then suffer dolts to curse!
Here refuge shall ye find, and sure circumvallation
Against the protestation of those whose delectation
Brings false abomination to blight the universe.' "

All the courtiers applauded their fellow; everybody celebrated Rabelais. The latter beat a retreat accompanied with great pomp by the King's pages who, by express command, lighted him home.

François Rabelais, the imperial honor of our country, has been charged by certain persons with malicious tricks and apish pranks unworthy of this philosophical Homer, of this prince of wisdom, of this paternal centre which, since the rising of his subterranean light, has given issue to a vast number of wondrous works. Fie upon such as have fouled upon his divine head! May such as have misrepresented his wise, moderate nourishment be condemned to find grit between their teeth all their lives long!

Beloved drinker of pure water, loyal observer of monastic abstinence, O mine of knowledge, what rollicking gusts of sempiternal laughter would seize you if, returning for a little moment to your blessed Chinon, you were vouchsafed a chance to read the incongruous balderdash, the unconscionable tomfoolery and the learned farrago of those dolts of every water who have interpreted, commentated, torn, shamed, misunderstood, betrayed, murdered, adulterated and vitiated your matchless book! As many dogs as Panurge found busy at his lady's dress in church, so many academic drivellers, so many biped snouters have arisen, with no meninx in their brains, no life in their diaphragm, yet spoiling to excrete upon that high marmoreal pyramid of yours which holds forever locked in it not only every seed of phantasy and comedy, but also the most magnificent instructions. Rare though such pilgrims be as have the breath to follow your vessel in its sublime peregrinations over the ocean of ideas, methods, vanities, religions, wisdom and human superstitions, at least their incense is unalloyed, unadulterated, pure, at least they bravely recognize your omnipotence, omniscience, omniloquence. Therefore a humble son of our glad Touraine desired to do you honor, however inadequately, by magnifying your image and glorifying your works of eternal memory, your works so dearly cherished by all who love concentrative writing wherein beyond theatrical mummeries and jest they can find not only the entire moral universe but also, pressed like fresh sardines in their boxes, all conceivable philosophical notions, all sciences, all arts and all eloquences. . . .

The Succubus

Prologue

CERTAIN scions of the noble land of Touraine, vastly edified by the Author's vigorous research in the antiquities, adventures, jokes and amenities of that blessed country, supposed that he must certainly know everything. They therefore asked him (after they had been drinking together, of course) whether he had discovered the etymological reason for which a certain street in Tours is called the Rue Chaude. This point, they added, intrigued the ladies considerably. The Author expressed his amazement that old inhabitants had forgotten the great number of convents in this location, where the austere continence of monks and nuns must have burned the walls so fiercely that several respectable women had become pregnant because they had strolled down that street a trifle too slowly of an evening. One troublesome fellow, a would-be scholar, averred that formerly all the brothels of the town were situated there. Another, embrangling himself in the labyrinthine byways of science, spoke golden words without being understood; he qualified vocables and harmonized the melodies of ancient and modern civilization, he compared customs, distilled roots and alchemized all languages since the Flood, citing the Hebrews, Chaldeans, Egyptians, Greeks, Latins, and then Turnus, the founder of Tours. Finally, the good man wound up by stating that *Chaud* was, in Old French, *Chauld* which, minus the *h* and *l,* came from the Latin *Cauda* and that there was therefore some tail in the affair. The ladies understood nothing save the end. Then an old man declared that years ago there was a thermal spring on the site; in fact his great-great-grandfather had drunk from it. Thus in less time than it takes a fly to seize his paramour by the neck, there was a pocketful of derivations. But the truth of the matter was to be found less readily than a louse in the filthy beard of a Capuchin friar.

Now a really learned man was present. Everybody knew that he had set foot in sundry monasteries, consumed much midnight oil, gutted more than one volume and heaped up more documents, diptychs, record-boxes, charter-chests and registers concerning the history of Touraine than a farmer stores hay in August. This gouty, broken-down old man sat drinking in his corner without uttering a word, but smiled a scholar's smile and knitted his brows. Then this smile resolved itself into a roundly articulated *Pish!* The Author heard the exclamation: he understood that it must be fraught with a richly historical adventure and foresaw the possibility of including its delights in this charming collection.

On the morrow, this old rheumatic said to him:

"By your poem, which is called *The Venial Sin,* you have forever conquered my esteem, because everything in it is true from start to finish—which I believe a precious superabundance in like matters. But I doubt if you are aware of what happened to the Mooress whom the Sieur de La Roche Corbon placed in the lap of our holy religion. As for me, I know quite well. So if the etymology of the street vexes you—not to mention your Egyptian nun—I will lend you a curious and antique parchment which I found in the *Olim* of the Archbishopric, whose libraries were somewhat upset at a period when none of us could tell of an evening if his head would still be on his shoulders in the morning. Now then—won't this give you perfect contentment?"

"Absolutely!" said the Author.

So this worthy collector of truths gave the Author certain precious and dusty parchments, fragments of the record of a very old ecclesiastical trial. These he has not without great pains, translated into French. He believed that nothing could be droller than the true resurrection of this ancient affair, a very monument to the crass ingenuousness of the good old times. Therefore, lend him your ears.

The writings, which the Author has made use of in his own way, for the language was devilishly difficult, appeared in the following order.

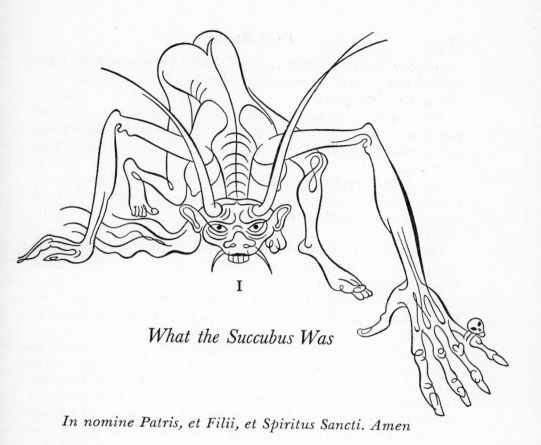

I

What the Succubus Was

In nomine Patris, et Filii, et Spiritus Sancti. Amen

IN THE year of Our Lord one thousand two hundred and seventy-one, before me, Jérôme Cornille, Grand Inquisitor and Judge Ecclesiastical (commissioned to this office by the honorable members of the Chapter of St. Maurice, the Cathedral of Tours, they having deliberated in the presence of My Lord Jean de Montsoreau, Archbishop),

Concerning the grievances and complaints of the inhabitants of the town, whose request will be hereto appended,

There appeared certain noblemen, townsmen and villeins of the diocese who stated the following facts anent the misconduct of a demon suspected of having assumed the shape of a woman, who sorely afflicts the souls of the diocese and is at present a prisoner in the jail of the Chapter,

In order to establish the truth of the said grievances, we have opened the present inquiry, this Monday, the eleventh day of December, after Mass,

Thereby to make known the evidence of each witness to the said demon, to question her on the charges brought against her and to pass judgment upon her according to the laws enforced *contra dæmonios.*

In this inquiry, in the writing of the whole body of evidence, Guillaume Tournebouche, rubrician of the Chapter, a learned man, has vouchsafed me his assistance.

Firstly, appeared before us Jean, surnamed Tortebras, a citizen of Tours, duly licensed landlord of the *Hostelry of La Cigogne,* in the Place du Pont, who swore by the salvation of his soul, his hand upon the Holy Book, that he would utter no other thing than himself had heard or seen. He then deposed as follows:

"I declare that about two years ago before the Feast of St. Jean, upon which day are bonfires and illuminations, a nobleman, at first unknown to me, but undoubtedly a vassal to Our Lord the King, visited me. He was at that time newly returned to our country from the Holy Land. He proposed that I let him at rental a country-house, built by myself in the quit-rent of the Chapter, near the place called St. Étienne. This house I leased to him for nine years in return for three bezants of fine gold.

"In this house, the said lord placed a fair wench of his, having the appearance of a female and clad in the stranger fashion of the Saracen and Mahometish women. Nor would he suffer any man to draw nearer to her than the reach of a bowshot, nor to look upon her more closely: but by my own sight I saw her with a weird feather in her hair, a supernatural complexion and eyes more flaming than I can possibly describe. Out of these eyes shot a fire of Hell. . . .

"The deceased nobleman, having threatened with death whoever should appear to spy upon the house, I, Jean Tortebras, through great fear, abandoned it. And to this day I have kept to myself certain presumptions and doubts concerning the evil mien of the foreign woman who was so rampant that I have never seen her like.

"At that actual time several persons of all conditions reported the nobleman to be dead but kept on his feet by virtue of certain charms, philtres, spells and diabolical sorceries administered by this seeming woman. In this connection I hereby affirm that whenever I saw the lord he was so deathly pale that I was wont to compare his face to a Paschal taper. Also, to the knowledge of all the folk of my inn, which is *At the Sign of the Stork,* this knight was committed to the grave exactly nine days after his arrival. In regard to the statement of his groom, namely that the deceased had been shut up in my house scaldingly accoupled with the Mooress during seven whole days without withdrawing from her, I hereby affirm that I heard him horribly confess the same upon his deathbed.

"At the time, several persons alleged that this she-devil held the nobleman bound to her by her long hairs. These would seem to be furnished with certain fiery properties capable of communicating the flames of hell to Christians in the guise of a passion which makes them moil away until their souls are strained from out their bodies and thus won to Satan. As to this, I declare that all I saw was the aforesaid deceased lord lying bowelless, drained, unable to move yet craving, despite his confessor, still to go to his paramour. He was recognized to be the Sieur de Bueil, a Crusader; according to some townsmen, he was bewitched by a demon he had encountered in the Asiatic lands of Damascus or elsewhere.

"Thereafter, pursuant to the clauses set down in the deed of lease, I left my house to the said unknown lady. My Lord of Bueil being deceased, I nevertheless went to my house to ascertain from the foreigner whether she wished to remain on the premises. After great trouble, I was led into her presence by a queer, half-naked, black man with white eyes. Then I beheld the Mooress in a brilliantly lighted apartment shining with gold and precious stones. She was sitting in scanty attire, on an Asiatic carpet, beside another gentleman who was even then losing his soul to her. I did not feel strength enough in my heart to look upon her, for her eyes would have incited me to yield to her forthwith. Already the music of her voice was cramping the pit of my belly, filling my brain and debauching my mind. Perceiving this, through fear of God, and of Hell, too, I made myself scarce, leaving her my house as long as she cared to retain it. For very dangerous, it was, to gaze upon this Moorish complexion that exhaled such diabolical heat, very dangerous to see a foot so much slighter than that a real woman may lawfully possess, very dangerous to hear her voice which gripped the heart. From that day forth, I have eschewed going to my house, being in mortal terror of plunging into Hell. I have said my say."

The witness Tortebras was then confronted with an Abyssinian, Ethiopian or Nubian, black from his crown to his soles, in whom were found wanting such virile appurtenances as Christian males usually possess. Having been lashed and tortured several times, albeit he groaned much, he persisted in his silence and was presumed to be ignorant of the language of our land. This heretical Abyssinian, who is suspected of aiding and

abetting the witchcraft, was certified by Tortebras as having dwelled in his house in company with the demoniac spirit. Finally Tortebras proclaimed his earnest faith in the Catholic religion, denying knowledge of aught else except certain rumors, known to everyone, which he had witnessed only in so much as he had heard them repeated.

In obedience to a summons served upon him, next appeared Mathieu, surnamed Cognefêtu, a day-laborer in the acreage of St. Étienne, who, after taking his Bible oath to speak the truth, avowed:

That he had always seen a bright light in the Mooress's dwelling, and heard much wild and diabolical laughter as though a great number of people were within, both by day and night on Feast Days and Fasts, particularly during Christmastide and Holy Week.

That he had seen by the windows of this dwelling, green buds of all kinds in the midst of winter, roses, in especial, during a season of frost, besides other plants which would require great heat;

That this had in no wise astonished him because the foreigner burned so ardently that she had walked along his wall one evening and on the morrow he found his salad grown; further, that on certain occasions, the mere brushing of her skirts against the trees had brought forth sap and hastened the buds;

Finally, that he knew nothing more, because he rose with the sun and went to bed with the fowls.

Next, Cognefêtu's wife was requested by us to disclose, also on oath, such events as she knew might have a bearing upon this case. Witness steadfastly refused to profess aught but praise of the Mooress since whose coming Cognefêtu, her husband, had treated her better. The improvement in his conduct she attributed to the proximity of this good lady who distilled love in the air as the sun distils its rays. She added much other incongruous nonsense which we have not committed to writing.

The aforesaid Cognefêtu and his wife, having been confronted with the unknown African prisoner, admitted that they had seen him in the gardens of the house and certified that he undoubtedly belonged to the demon.

Thirdly, we heard the testimony of Messire Harduin V, Lord of Maillé, who, being reverently besought to us to acknowledge the religion of the Church, expressed his willingness to do so. Furthermore, he pledged his word as a loyal knight to tell nothing other than what he had actually seen.

He asserted that in the army of the Crusaders he had known the demon in question and that in the city of Damascus, he saw the Sire de Bueil, since deceased, fight in single combat for sole possession of her. This wench or demon belonged at the time to Geoffroi IV, Sire de la Roche Pozay, who frequently said that he had brought her from Touraine, although she was a Saracen. This fact made the French knights marvel as much as did her beauty, which created a great stir and wrought a thousand scandalous ravages in the camp. During the voyage, the wench was the occasion of more than one death: La Roche Pozay killed several Crusaders who sought to win her for themselves because, according to certain lords whom she had cockered secretly, she bestowed unparalleled joys upon a lover. At length the Sire de

Bueil slew Geoffroi de la Roche Pozay and became lord and master of this murderous sheath whom he hid away in a convent or harem, after the Saracen fashion. Previously, however, during entertainments she had given, she was often heard to chatter in

a thousand outlandish dialects such as Arabian, Greek of the
Latin Empire and Moorish, but, what is still stranger, she could
speak French more fluently than those in the Christian host who
knew the language best. This circumstance gave rise to the belief that she was essentially demoniacal.

My Lord Harduin went on to avouch to us that he had not
tilted for her in the Holy Land. It was not through fear or
frigidity or for any other reason of the sort. He believed, rather,
that such a blessing had fallen upon him because he carried a
piece of the true Cross and also because he had a noble lady of
his own in the Greek land, who saved him from any such peril
by extorting all his love, day and night, taking substantially
everything from him and leaving nothing in his heart or elsewhere for others.

My Lord Harduin assured us beyond doubt that the female
living in Tortebras' country-house was in reality the said Saracen, come thither from the land of Syria. To prove it, he told
how he had been invited to a great entertainment given at her
house by the young Sire of Croixmare who, according to Madame de Croixmare, his mother, perished the seventh day thereafter, ravaged at all points by the same wench, her commerce
having sapped his vital force and her strange whims squandered
his crowns.

Next, we questioned him in his quality as a man full of wisdom, knowledge and authority in this country, asking him to
disclose his personal conviction about the Mooress and calling
upon him to unburden his conscience. In so doing, we were
sedulous to point out that here was a most abominable case of
Christian faith and divine justice. The said lord made answer
that, in the opinion of certain Crusaders, this she-devil was ever
a virgin to who bestrode her and that Mammon was patently
astir within her to create a fresh virginity for each of her lovers.
My Lord cited a thousand other foolish sayings of drunken men
which were not of a nature to form a fifth Gospel. But this much
was certain; himself an old knight in the decline of life and no
longer a practician of amour, had felt himself a young man
again during that last supper with which the Sire de Croixmare
had regaled him. The voice of this demon had struck straight
at his heart before flowing into his ears; it had awakened such

consuming love in his body that his life began to ebb away by
the place whence man creates life. At length, but for the wine
of Cyprus (he drank it in order to dim his vision and enable him
to lie under the table lest he look again into the eyes of his
demoniacal hostess and find death in her), he would beyond a
shadow of doubt have slain young Croixmare so but he might
enjoy this supernatural female one single time. Since then, My
Lord had been punctual to seek absolution of this evil thought
in the confessional. Then, by counsel from on high, he had
taken back his relic of the true Cross from his wife and had
stayed at his manor. These Christian precautions notwithstanding, the unearthly voice still fired his brain at certain times; in
the morning, he would remember that she-devil mammarily ardent as tinder. And because the wench's gaze was so volcanic
that she made him, a man half-dead, burn like a youngster, and
because it cost him many wasteful transpercolations of vital
forces, My Lord requested us not to confront him with this empress of love, to whom if not the Devil, then God the Father had
vouchsafed monstrous liberties with the properties of man.

Then he withdrew, but not before hearing this statement
read over and identifying the African prisoner as the lady's servant and page.

Fourthly—upon our faith pledged in the name of the Chapter
and of My Lord Archbishop that he would not be tortured, tormented or pursued by us in any form or manner nor again cited
after this testimony, considering the voyages of trade that he was
bound to make—and upon further assurance of being suffered to
withdraw in all liberty—there appeared a Hebrew Jew named
Salomon al Rastchild, who, despite the infamy of his person and
his Judaism was heard by us to the sole end of our knowing all
concerning the misconduct of the said demon. The witness
Salomon was not required to take any oath seeing that he is beyond the pale of the Church and separated from us by the blood
of Our Savior *(trucidatus Salvator inter nos)*.

Questioned as to why, counter to the Royal and Ecclesiastical
Ordinances, he appeared without the green bonnet on his head
and the yellow wheel sewn clearly on his garment over his heart,
the said al Rastchild produced letters-patent of dispensation

granted by His Majesty the King and recognized by the Seneschal of Touraine and Poitou.

Then this Hebrew Jew revealed to us that he had transacted considerable business for the lady residing in the innkeeper's house: he had sold her chandeliers of gold with many branches minutely engraved, plates of vermilion silver, cups mounted richly with precious stones, emeralds and rubies; for her he had imported from the Levant a number of priceless materials, Persian carpets, silks, fine linens, and other objects of such magnificence that no queen in Christendom could consider herself so amply provided with jewels and household possessions. The Mooress, for her part, had paid him three hundred thousand pounds Touraine for the rarities he had undertaken to purchase, namely Indian flowers, popinjays, outlandish birds and most costly feathers, spices, Greek wines and diamonds.

We, the judge, then challenged him to state whether he had ever furnished her with the ingredients of magical exorcism— the blood of newborn babes, conjuring books or any tool whatsoever generally used by witches. We granted him full license to admit his guilt without ever being sought or arraigned therefor. The witness al Rastchild pledged his Hebraic faith that he had never in any wise transacted such business. He was, he affirmed, involved in interests too lofty to admit of his trifling with such nonsense. Was he not agent of many puissant lords? Did he not number among his clients the Marquis of Montferrat, the King of England, the King of Cyprus and Jerusalem, the Count of Provence, the Lords of Venice and many lords sovereign of Germany? Did he not own all manner of merchant galleys plying to Egypt, by permission of the Sultan? In point of fact, it was his vast traffic in precious gold and silver that brought him so often to the Mint at Tours.

The witness went on to state that he held the accused to be a highly loyal and natural woman, the comeliest and shapeliest ever he saw. Insofar as her reputation for diabolatry was concerned, he had been inspired, by a wild imagination and by his keen lust of her, to offer her his company one day she happened to be husbandless. To this the Mooress had not been unwilling.

For a long time after he had felt his bones dislocated and his loins crushed. But he had not felt, as certain people reported, that who ventured therein never returned but was molten down like lead in an alchemist's crucible.

These words proved conclusively that the witness Salomon held commerce with the Devil, since he had fared with impunity where all Christians succumbed. Nevertheless we gave him his liberty, in accordance with the terms of the safe-conduct he bore. Before retiring, he submitted an agreement to us concerning the said demon, to wit: if this seeming woman were condemned to be burned alive he would redeem her with a ransom sufficient to defray the expenses of completing the highest towers of the Church of St. Maurice, at present in the course of construction. This offer we duly recorded in order that it may be deliberated upon at an opportune season by the Chapter assembled.

The witness Salomon then withdrew, refusing to name a residence but assuring us that the Chapter might communicate the result of its deliberations to him through a Jew in the ghetto of Tours, Tobias Nathaneus by name. Salomon having, before his departure, been confronted with the African, identified the latter as the demon's page. He added that the Saracens were wont thus to mutilate the serfs they appointed to guard their women, following an ancient usage as recorded by profane historians in the case of Narsez, General of Constantinopolis, and others. . . .

Fifthly, on the morrow, appeared before us the most noble and illustrious Lady of Croixmare. Swearing her faith in the Holy Book, the witness tearfully recounted how she had buried her eldest son who perished through his excess in love with the female demon. The deceased lord was three and twenty years of age, in perfect health, manful and heavily bearded, like his late father. His robust physique notwithstanding, within a period of ninety days he was gradually worn down and ruined by the Succubus of the Rue Chaude, as the common folk say. Her maternal authority, the noble witness lamented, was unavailing. During his latter days, he looked like a poor dried-up worm—the sort housewives find in a corner when they clean out a lodging. And always, so long as he had the strength to bear him, he sped to that cursed woman who finished off his life and drained his purse.

In the end, when he lay in his own bed and knew his last hour was at hand, he swore, cursed, threatened and insulted the entire family, his brother, his sister, even herself, his mother. He rebelled in the face of his chaplain, he denied God; he wished to

die the death of the damned, at all of which the retainers of the family were so much afflicted that to save his soul and snatch it from the jaws of Hell, they had founded two annual Masses at the Cathedral. To assure the lad burial in consecrated ground, the house of Croixmare had undertaken for one hundred years to furnish the Chapter with tapers for chapels and church on Palm Sunday. Finally, except for the wicked words heard by that reverend person, Dom Louis Pot, a monk of Marmoûtier who had come to stand by the Baron de Croixmare in the hour of death, the aforesaid noble witness affirms that she never heard the deceased proffer any words regarding the demon that held him in her grip.

Thereupon the noble and illustrious lady retired in great mourning.

Sixthly, appeared before us, after adjournment, Jacquette, called Old Greasy, a kitchen mopsy, who goes to houses to wash dishes and is now resident in the Fishmarket. After having pledged her word to utter no single thing she did not hold for true, the witness made the following statement, to wit:

One day, having gone to the Mooress's house—she was not in the least afraid because the demon was wont to feed upon males only—she chanced to see this female fiend, superbly clad, walking in the garden with a gentleman and laughing like any normal person. In this demon, the witness recognized the true likeness of the Mooress placed as a nun in the Convent of Notre Dame de l'Égrignolles about eighteen years ago, by the late Messire Bruyn, Comte de La Roche Corbon and Seneschal of Touraine and Poitou, under the following circumstances.

The image of Our Lady the Virgin, Mother of Our Blessed Savior, had been stolen by certain Egyptians who left this Moorish wench in Her niche and stead. Because of the parlous times arisen in Touraine, no record of these facts is available. But it is known that this wench, aged about twelve years, was baptized and thus saved from the stake at which she was to have burned. The aforesaid deceased Seneschal and his lady, likewise deceased, stood as sponsors at the baptismal font to this daughter of Hell.

The witness, then laundress in the convent, remembered not only the arrival of the Mooress but also, some twenty months after, her flight, so skilfully contrived that by what means or by whose agency it was effected has never come to light. Everyone at the time believed that, with the aid of the Devil, she had flown through the air because, despite a thorough search, no trace of her evasion was found in the convent. On the contrary, everything remained in its accustomed order.

The scullion, having been confronted with the African prisoner, affirmed that she had never seen him, though very curious to do so, because he was committed to guard the place where the Mooress luxuriated with those whom she drained through the spigot.

Seventhly, appeared before us the Sieur de Bridoré, bringing into our presence his son, Hugues du Fou, twenty years of age and placed under caution of his estates in the custody of his father, on whom he depends, until he be duly convicted and attainted for having, with the assistance of several unknown ruffians, attacked the jail of the Archbishop and of the Chapter and attempted to obstruct the force of ecclesiastical justice by abducting the demon. Despite his reluctance, we commanded the said Hugues du Fou to testify truthfully concerning such information as he must possess about the Mooress, with whom he is vehemently reputed to have had commerce. We conscientiously objected to him that his salvation and the life of the said demon were at stake. The witness, having taken the oath, said:

"I swear, by my eternal salvation and by the Holy Gospels here present under my hand, that I consider the woman charged with deviltry, a very angel, a perfect woman, even more so in mind than in body, living in all honesty, fraught with subtle strategies and superexcellencies in love, nor in any way evil but rather generous, having often helped the poor and the afflicted. I aver that I saw her shedding veritable tears over the death of my friend the Sire de Croixmare. Because that day she made a vow to Our Lady the Virgin that she would never again receive in amorous mercy such young noblemen as proved too weak for her service, she denied me constantly and with great courage the enjoyment of her body, granting me only the love and possession of her heart, of which she made me sovereign. Since this gracious gift, despite my increasing ardor, she remained alone in her house, where I spent the greater part of my days, happy at merely seeing and hearing her. Oh, but I fared well at her side, partaking of the air that entered her lungs, of the light that gleamed in her lovely eyes; and in this occupation I tasted greater joy than falls to the high lords of Paradise. I elected her to be forever my lady, I chose her to be my sweetheart some day, my wife, my only love; and, poor madman that I am! I received no advance from her against the joys of the future, but, on the contrary, a thousand virtuous counsels. She urged me to win fame as a gallant knight, to grow into a handsome, strong man, to fear naught but God, to honor the ladies, serving but a single one but loving all in memory of her. Then, she said, when I should be strengthened by the endurances of war, if her heart still pleased mine, then and then only she would belong to me. She said she would be able to wait for me because she loved me so much. . . ."

At these words, the youthful Sire Hugues wept, and, weeping, added:

"As I thought of this graceful, weak woman, whose arms I always believed too frail to bear the light weight of her golden chains; as I thought of the irons that bruised her, of the miseries traitorously heaped upon her, I could bear it no longer! Thence came my rebellion. And I have full license to proclaim my sorrow in the face of justice, because my life is so utterly bound in the life of my blessed mistress and sweetheart that on the day evil comes to her, I shall most surely die."

The young nobleman gave vent to a thousand other praises of the demon, thus exemplifying the merciless witchcraft practised upon him and proving conclusively the abominable, shameless, incurable life and the fraudulent sorceries to which he is now subject. Of these My Lord Archbishop shall duly judge in order, through exorcism and penitence, to rescue this youthful soul from the snares of Hell, if the Devil has not gained too firm a footing in it.

Then we returned the young witness into the hands of the noble lord, his father, after the said Hugues had recognized the African to be the servant of the accused.

Eighthly, before us, the footguards of My Lord Archbishop led in great state the MOST EXALTED AND MOST REVEREND LADY JACQUELINE DE CHAMPCHEVRIER, ABBESS OF THE CONVENT OF NOTRE DAME under the invocation of Mount Carmel, to whose government the late Lord Seneschal of Touraine (father of the

Comte de La Roche Corbon, present patron of the convent) entrusted the Egyptian, named at the baptismal font Blanche Bruyn.

To the noble Lady Abbess we summarily exposed the present case, which touches not only the Holy Church, the glory of God, the eternal happiness of the diabolically afflicted folk of this diocese but likewise the life of a creature who might conceivably be quite innocent. Having elaborated the proceedings, we begged the Lady Abbess to impart what she knew concerning the magical disappearance of her daughter in God, Blanche Bruyn, espoused to Our Savior under the name of Sister Claire.

Then, the most noble, most high and most illustrious Lady Abbess deposed as follows:

Sister Claire, of origin to her unknown, but suspected to be of heretical parents hostile to God, had indeed been placed in religion in the monastery whose government had fallen canonically to herself, despite her unworthiness. The said Sister completed her novitiate equably and took her vows according to the holy laws of the Order. But, her vows taken, she was plunged into profound sadness and began to pine away. She, the Lady Abbess, having questioned Sister Claire upon her melancholiac malady, the Sister wept and answered that she was unaware of its cause . . . that a flood of tears rose to her eyes because she no longer felt her beautiful hair upon her head . . . that, worse, she hankered after fresh air . . . that she could not quell a mad desire to leap on trees, to climb, and to tumble about as she had done all the days of her life in the open . . . that she spent her nights weeping, dreaming of the forests under whose leaves she had slept in the old days . . . that, recalling these, she abhorred the quality of the cloister air, which stifled her . . . that evil vapors exuded deep down within her . . . and that often in church she was inwardly diverted by thoughts that put her out of continence and countenance. . . .

Then the noble witness further attested:

"To the poor creature's objections, I sedulously opposed the holy teachings of the Church; I reminded her what eternal felicity a sinless woman enjoys in Paradise, how transitory our life here below and how certain God's goodness which, in return for the loss of a few bitter pleasures, maintains us in infinite love. Such wise maternal counsel notwithstanding, the evil spirit still haunted Sister Claire. During the offices and services, she was forever gazing through the chapel window on the leaves of the trees and the grass in the meadows. Next, with deliberate obstinacy, she persisted in turning pale in order to be allowed to stay in bed. At other times, she would career through the cloister like a goat broken loose from its tether. At last, she sickened, lost her great beauty and withered away to a mere shadow.

"Seeing her in this plight and fearing lest she die, we the Abbess, her mother, had her placed in the infirmary of the convent. One winter's morning, Sister Claire vanished without leaving the slightest trace: no door was found broken, no lock forced, no window opened nor any tell-tale mark of her flight. This terrible act was generally believed to have been effected with the help of the demon who tortured and tormented her. Ultimately the authorities of the metropolitan church came to the conclusion that this daughter of Hell had been sent to divert the nuns from their holy practices. But, dazzled by their beautiful lives, she had winged her way back through the air to the Sabbath of the witches who, in mockery of our holy religion, had first left her in the stead of Our Lady the Virgin."

Having given testimony, the Lady Abbess was escorted amid great honor and in obedience to My Lord Archbishop's orders, to the gates of the Convent of Mount Carmel.

Ninthly, before us appeared Joseph, surnamed Leschalopier, a money changer, living on the Bridge at the *Sign of the Gold Bezant*. Who, having pledged his Catholic faith, to say nothing save what he knew to be true concerning the case now before the ecclesiastical tribunal, testified as follows:

"I am an unhappy father, grievously afflicted by the sacred will of God. Before the advent of the Succubus of the Rue Chaude, I had, for dearest possession, a son, handsome as a nobleman and learned as a holy clerk. Had he not fared on more than a dozen voyages to foreign lands? He was a good Catholic, too, resisting the prickings of love, and balking at marriage, because he knew that he was the staff of my old age, the love of my eyes, the constant delight of my heart. He was the sort of a son a King of France might be proud of; he was a good, courageous man, the light of my business, the joy of my dwelling. Above all, he was an inestimable blessing, for I am alone in the world, having had the misfortune to lose my wife, and being too old to take another unto myself. Now, My Lord Judge, this peerless treasure

was taken from me by that demon and plunged into the abyss of hell. Ah, My Lord Judge, that sheath for a thousand blades, that she-fiend in whom everything is a mill of perdition, a nesting-place of pleasure and lust, that devil whom nothing can satiate! . . . No sooner did my poor boy see her than he was caught fast in the lime of his love. And there he stuck, to live only between the columns of Venus, but not for long, because so consuming a heat permeates this place that nothing can slake the thirst of its maw, though you were to thrust in the seed of all the world. Alas! then, my poor boy, his wealth, his generative hopes, his eternal happiness, all of him and more than himself were lost in this chasm like a grain of corn in the jaws of a bull.

"Thus I, who am become an orphan in my old age, shall know no single joy hereafter save that of witnessing the calcination of this demon fed on blood and gold, this Arachne who has scooped and sucked up more marriages, more families in the seed, more hearts, more Christian beings than there are lepers in all the lazarets of Christendom. Burn and torment this ghoul, this vampire who feeds on human souls, this tigerish nature that drinks blood, this amorous cauldron that boils up the venom of all vipers! Close up this abyss whose depths no man can plumb! I offer the Chapter my money to pay for the pile and my arm to set fire to it. Have a care, My Lord Judge, keep this devil safe prisoned, she darts a fiercer flame than any blaze on earth. All the fires of Hell burn in her lap, all the strength of Samson bristles in her hair, all the echoes of celestial music thrill in her voice. She charms to kill body and soul in one blow; she smiles to bite; she kisses to devour; she would bewitch a saint and make him deny God! Oh, my son, my son! Where is he at this hour, the flower of my life, a flower cut by this female sheath as by a pair of scissors. Ah, My Lord Judge, why did you call me here? Who shall restore my son to me? How shall I recover him whose soul was swallowed by a womb that gives death to all and life to none? Only the Devil copulates and engenders not.

"Such is my testimony which I pray Master Tournebouche to set down without omitting one jot or tittle and then to give me a schedule of it that I may repeat it to God daily in my prayers, that I may make the blood of innocence ring in His ears, that I may obtain from His infinite mercy the pardon of my son."

Here followed seven-and-twenty other statements whose transcription, in their true objectivity and vast qualities of space, would prove over-fastidious, draw out to great length and divert the thread of this curious inquest. This story, in obedience to the ancient precepts, must march straight to its conclusion like a bull to his principal office. Therefore here, in a few words, is the gist of this evidence.

A great number of worthy Christians, townsmen and towns-women, residents of the noble town of Tours, stated:

That this demon had held festivals and royal revels every day . . . that she had never been seen at any church, that she had cursed God, mocked His priests, nor ever made the sign of the cross in any place . . . that she had spoken all the languages of the earth, a gift granted by God to none save the Holy Apostles . . . that she had been met in the fields many times riding upon an unknown animal who went before the clouds . . . that she

never grew old but always retained a youthful face . . . that she unloosed her girdle for both a father and his son on the same day, saying that her portal was without sin . . . that she had visible malign influences which flowed out from her, because a baker who was seated on his bench at his door saw her one eve-ning and received such a gust of hot love that, on going home, he retired immediately to bed and manhandled his wife with such amorous fury that he was found dead the next morning, still busily engaged . . . that the oldsters of the town went to spend the remainder of their days and money at her forge, tasting the pleasures of their sinful youth and dying like flies, belly-down, some of them having turned black as Moors . . . that this demon did not show herself at dinner, breakfast, or supper, but ate alone, because she fed on human brains . . . that several had seen her go into the cemeteries at night there to drain young dead men, because only thus could she slake the demon rampant in her entrails and there raging like a tempest . . . that thence proceeded the compressive, caustic, corrosive, shooting, precipitant and diabolical movements, clutches, swirls and writhings of love and voluptuousness from which several men had emerged contused, distorted, bitten, pinched and crushed . . . that, since the coming of Our Savior who had imprisoned the master devil in the body of the swine, no malignant beast had ever been seen in any place on the face of the earth, so noxious, so venomous and rapacious to such a degree that if the city of Tours were tossed into this field of Venus, it would there be transmuted into small grains of stone for the demon to swallow like so many strawberries.

A thousand other affirmations, statements and affidavits clearly established the infernal generation of this woman—daughter, sister, granddaughter, spouse, niece or brother of the Devil—and yielded abundant proofs of the mischief and calamities she visited upon all families. If it were possible to transcribe these documents from the rolls preserved by the excellent man to whom we owe their discovery, they would seem like a sample of the horrendous lamentations the Egyptians uttered on the day of the seventh plague.

The proceedings of this trial reflect great credit upon Master Guillaume Tournebouche, who drew up all the legal instruments.

Thus in the tenth vacation this inquest was concluded, having arrived at a maturity of proof, furnished with authentic testimony and sufficiently augmented by particulars, complaints, interdicts, rejoinders, charges, assignments, verifications, public and private confessions, oaths, adjournments, appearances and controversies to which the demon must reply.

And the townspeople said everywhere that, if the accused were really a devil furnished with internal horns planted in her nature to drain and crush men, she was due to swim a long time in this sea of writings before landing, safe and sound, in Hell.

II

What Proceedings Were Instituted
Against This Female Devil

i

In nomine Patris, et Filii, et Spiritus Sancti. Amen

*I*N THE year of Our Lord one thousand two hundred and seventy-one, before us, Jérôme Cornille, Grand Inquisitor and Judge Ecclesiastical, to this office canonically appointed, there appeared:

The Sire Philippe d'Idré, Bailiff of the town and city of Tours and province of Touraine, resident in his mansion in the Rue de la Rôtisserie, in Châteauneuf;

Master Jean Ribou, Provost of the Guild and Brotherhood of Drapers, resident in the Quai de Bretagne, by the image of St. Peter-of-the-Chains;

Master Antoine Jean, Alderman, head of the Brotherhood of Changers, resident in the Place du Pont, by the image of St. Mark-counting-the-Touraine-pounds;

Master Martin Beaupertuys, Captain of the Town Archers, resident in the Château;

Jean Rabelais, ship's caulker and boatmaker, resident at the Port of the Île St. Jacques and Treasurer of the Brotherhood of the Mariners of the Loire;

Marc Jérôme, known as Mâchefer, hosier, at the *Sign of St. Sebastian*, President of the Trades' Council;

Jacques, called de Villedomer, master tavern-keeper and vine-dresser, resident at the *Sign of the Fir Cone* in the High Street;

And to the Sire d'Idré, Bailiff, and to these townsmen of Tours we read the following petition, by them drawn up, signed and deliberated, to be brought to the attention of the Ecclesiastical Tribunal.

PETITION

We, the undersigned, all townsmen of Tours, are hereby as-

sembled in the mansion of My Lord the Sire d'Idré, our Mayor
being absent, and have requested him to hear our plaints and
grievances concerning the following facts, which we assume ourselves to bring before the tribunal of My Lord Archbishop, the
judge of ecclesiastical crimes, to whom the prosecution of the
case we herewith expose should be deferred.

A long time ago, into this our town came a wicked demon in
the shape of a woman, who lives in the acreage of St. Étienne,
in the house of the innkeeper Tortebras, situated in the quit-
rent of the Chapter and under the temporal jurisdiction of the
archiepiscopal domain. This foreign female practises the commerce of a harlot in treacherous, abusive fashion and with such
increase of evil that she threatens to destroy the Catholic faith in
this town, because such as go to her return with the utter loss of
their souls and refuse the assistance of the Church with a thousand scandalous speeches.

Now, whereas a great number of those who yielded to her are
dead . . . and, arrived in our town with no possession other than
her nature, she now has, according to public clamor, infinite
riches and royal treasures . . . and the acquisition of these is
violently suspected of witchery if not theft, committed with the
help of the magical attractions of her supernaturally amorous
person;

Whereas the honor and security of our families are at stake . . .
and never in this our land was there seen a woman wild of body
or a daughter of pleasure plying her strumpet's trade with such
general hurt, and so frankly and fiercely menacing the savings,
morals, chastity, religion and total possessions of the inhabitants
of this city;

Whereas an investigation of her person, her property and her
misconduct is necessary in order to establish whether these re-
sults of love are legitimate or whether they proceed, as her deeds
would seem to indicate, from witchcraft of Satan, who often visits
Christendom under a female form (as appears in the Holy Book,
where it is written that Our Blessed Savior was carried away to
the top of a mountain whence Lucifer or Ashtaroth showed him
the fertile domains of Judæa);

Whereas in diverse places succubi have appeared or demons
with female faces who bear an insatiable fire within them and

who, unwilling to return to Hell, attempt to refresh and sustain themselves by sucking in human souls;

Whereas in the case of the said woman there are a thousand evidences of deviltry which certain citizens discuss quite openly, and whereas it is needful for the repose of the said woman that this case be probed lest she be assailed by certain persons who have been ruined as a result of her malefactions;

Therefore we pray that it please you to submit to the consideration of Our Lord Spiritual, father of this diocese, the most noble and holy Archbishop Jean de Montsoreau, the sorrows of his afflicted flock.

By so doing, you will fulfill the duties of your office, as we do those of preservers of the security of this town, each according to the matters he has charge of in his locality.

And we have signed the present petition, in the year of Our Lord one thousand two hundred and seventy-one, on All Saints' Day, after Mass.

Master Tournebouche having completed the reading of this document, we, Jérôme Cornille, addressing the petitioners:

"Gentlemen, do ye this day persist in these statements? Have ye proofs other than are come to our knowledge? Do ye warrant to bear out the truth of this before God, before man and before the accused?"

All, save Master Jean Rabelais, persevered in their belief, the aforesaid Rabelais withdrawing from the complaint, saying that he held the Mooress to be a natural woman and a good trollop whose only fault lay in keeping up a very high temperature of love.

Accordingly, we, Judge, canonically appointed, after mature deliberation found matter upon which to grant the foregoing petition and commanded that the woman now in the jail of the Chapter be proceeded against by all legal ways and means as written in the canons and ordinances *contra dæmonios*.

The said ordinance, embodied in a writ, shall be published by the town crier in all parts and to the sound of the trumpet, in order that all may have knowledge of it and that each, testifying according to his conscience, may be confronted with the said demon.

Finally we commanded that the accused be provided with a

defender, according to custom, and that the inquest and the process be congruously conducted.

signed

(And, below:)
JÉRÔME CORNILLE
TOURNEBOUCHE

ij

In nomine Patris, et Filii, et Spiritus Sancti. Amen

In the year of Our Lord one thousand two hundred and seventy-one, on the tenth day of February, after Mass, by order of us, Jérôme Cornille, Judge Ecclesiastical;

There was brought from the Chapter jail and led before us the woman seized in the house of the innkeeper Tortebras, situated in the domain of the Chapter of the Cathedral of St. Maurice,

Who is thus subject to the temporal and seignorial jurisdiction of the Archbishopric of Tours,

Besides which, pursuant to the nature of the crimes to her imputed, she is liable to the Tribunal and dependent upon the ecclesiastical justice,

All of which facts we brought to her notice in order that she might have full knowledge of the matter.

Then, after a solemn and unabridged reading, clearly understood by her of: in the first place, the Petition of the townsmen; in secundo, the statements, complaints, charges and proceedings which comprise four-and-twenty quires written by Master Tournebouche and which are herebefore related;

With the invocation and assistance of God and Church, we determined to ascertain the truth, by questions directly put to the accused.

In our initial query, we requested the accused to tell us in what land or town she was born? By her it was answered: "In Mauritania."

Next, we asked if she had a father, a mother or any other relatives? To which she replied that she had never known them.

We then challenged her to declare her name. Whereupon she said: "Zulma—in the Arabian tongue."

Q. Why do you speak our language?

A. Because I came to this land.

Q. At what period?

A. About twelve years ago.

Q. How old were you then?

A. Fifteen years old or thereabouts.

Q. Then you admit you are twenty-seven years of age?

A. Ay.

Q. Then you are the same Mooress found in the niche of Our Lady the Virgin; baptized by the Archbishop; held at the font by the late Lord of La Roche Corbon and the Lady of Azay, his wife? You are the same Mooress placed as a nun by them in the Convent of Mount Carmel, where you took vows of chastity, poverty, silence and love of God, under the divine assistance of St. Claire?

A. It is true: I am.

Q. Do you acknowledge the truth of the declarations made by the most noble and illustrious Lady Abbess of the Convent of Mount Carmel? Do you acknowledge the truth of the statement made by Jacquette, called Old Greasy, a kitchen mopsy?

A. Their words are for the most part true.

Q. Then you are a Christian?

A. Ay, father.

We accordingly called upon her to make the sign of the Cross and to take holy water from a vessel placed in her hand by Master Guillaume Tournebouche. This being done and witnessed by us, it was admitted as an indisputable fact that Zulma the Mauritanian, known in our land as Blanche Bruyn, a nun of the convent under the invocation of Mount Carmel, and there named Sister Claire, and suspected to be a demon in the false appearance of a woman, had, in our presence, qualified as a Christian, thereby recognizing the justice of the Ecclesiastical Tribunal.

Then we:

Q. My daughter, the manner of your escape from the convent was supernatural in every way; it gave rise to the vehement suspicion that you had recourse to the Devil.

A. The accused rejoined that she had gained the fields quite naturally by the street door after Vespers, concealed under the robes of Dom Jean de Marsilis, visitor to the convent; the same had hidden her in a hovel belonging to him, situated in the Ruelle de Cupidon (Cupid's Lane, close to a tower of the town wall). There this priest had at great length and very systematically taught her the delights of love, of which she had previously been ignorant in all points. To these delights she took a great taste, finding them of excellent use.

Q. Where did you go thereafter?

A. To the Sire d'Amboise. One day, this nobleman caught sight of me at the window of our retreat and fell deeply in love with me. Then, loving him more heartily than the monk, I fled from the hovel where Dom Marsilis had detained me to his pleasure's profit. I went to Amboise in great haste, where I dwelled in the château of the said lord, enjoying a thousand pastimes: hunting and dancing and clothes fit for a queen.

One day having invited the Sire de la Roche Pozay to sup and make merry, My Lord of Amboise allowed him to look at me (I had no knowledge of it) as I was coming out of my bath. Seeing me, the Sire de la Roche Pozay fell deeply in love with me; on the morrow he killed the Sire d'Amboise in single combat; and with great violence, despite my tears, he took me into the Holy Land.

Here she had led the life of women who are much beloved and revered because of their great beauty. Eventually, after numerous adventures, she had returned to this country, in spite of her forebodings of misfortune; such had been the will of her lord and master, the Baron de Bueil, who was pining with grief in Asiatic lands and hankered to return to his ancestral manor. In view of her apprehensions, he had promised to shield her from all danger; she had put her faith and trust in him, the more since she loved him deeply. But on their arrival in this country, the Sire de Bueil was stricken with illness and died deplorably, refusing to take any remedies in spite of her fervent prayers, because he loathed physicians, master doctors and apothecaries. This was the whole truth.

Q. Do you concede the veracity of the statements sworn to by the good Lord Harduin and by the innkeeper, Tortebras?

A. I recognize them as evidence for the most part; but certain portions of them are malicious, slanderous and idiotic.

We then inquired whether she had had pleasure and carnal

commerce with all the noblemen, townsmen and others whom the complaints and charges cited.

To this question she countered with great effrontery:

"Pleasure, yes. Commerce? I do not know."

Q. Did they not all die through your instrumentality?

A. Their deaths cannot be my fault: always I refused myself to them and the more I fled them, the thicker they swarmed about me to assault me with infinite fury. When I was taken by them, I went to work with all my power, by the grace of God, because I felt infinite, matchless sweet joys in the thing.

The accused added that she divulged her secret thoughts solely because we had called upon her to tell the truth about everything. For her part, she said, she stood in great fear of the torturers' engines.

Q. Then under penalty of torture, explain what was your frame of mind when a young nobleman died as a result of his traffic with yourself?

A. I was plunged in grief; I wished to destroy myself; I implored God and the Virgin and the Saints to receive me in Paradise. For never, never have I met with any but true noble hearts in which no vice could dwell. When I beheld them perish, I fell into a profound gloom, considering myself a maleficent creature or the victim of an evil lot which I communicated like the plague.

Q. Where did you say your prayers?

A. I prayed in my oratory, on my knees, before God, Who, according to the Gospel, seeth and heareth all things and dwelleth everywhere.

Q. Why did you never frequent the churches nor observe offices or feasts?

A. Those who came to have love of me chose feast days for their pleasure. I bowed to their will in all respects.

In Christian fashion, we remonstrated that by so doing she submitted to the will of man rather than to the commandments of God.

She made answer that, for such as loved her well, she would have flung herself into a burning, fiery furnace, having never followed any course in her attachments other than that of her nature. Not for the weight of the world in gold, would she have lent either her body or her devotion to a king, unless she had previously loved him with the heart, feet, head, hair and all of her. In short, furthermore, the accused had never performed harlotry by selling one single sip of love to any man she had not chosen to be hers: whosoever had held her in his arms an hour or for a fleeting moment kissed her mouth, possessed her for the rest of her days.

Q. Whence came the jewels, the gold plate, the silver, the precious stones, the regal furniture, the carpets, *et cetera,* valued at two hundred thousand doubloons, according to the inventory found in your house, and placed in the custody of the Treasurer to the Chapter?

A. I do pin all my hope on yourself, as much as on my very God; but I dare not answer this question, for it involves the sweetest raptures of love, which I have always lived upon.

Then, in reply to our judicial query, the accused proposed that if we, Judge Ecclesiastical, knew in what fervor she held her lover, with what loyalty she followed him for better or for worse, with what zeal she submitted to him, with what happiness she inclined to his desires, with what aspiration she hung upon his lips waiting the sacred words he spoke, in what adoration she held his person, we, ourself, a venerable Judge, would believe with her paramours that no sum could pay for this priceless affection all men pursue.

"From no man whom I have loved did I at any time solicit reward or gift. I was ever content to abide in the heart of my lover; I wound myself about it with joy ineffable and inexhaustible, deeming myself wealthier therein than in aught else. At all times my only thought was to lavish a richer pleasure upon him and a rarer bliss, even, than I received at his hands. Notwithstanding my repeated proscriptions, my lovers were forever bent upon rewarding me graciously.

"Now one would come with a necklace of pearls, saying: 'This is to show my sweetheart that the satin of her skin is really whiter than pearls!' And he would clasp it about my neck kissing me passionately the while. Then I would grow angry at such follies, but how could I refuse to wear a jewel he had put on my person and liked to see there?

"Each had a different whim. Now one enjoyed stripping me of

the costly garments I donned to please him; now another took pleasure in decking my arms, legs, neck or hair with sapphires. Still another was happy when he stretched me out on a carpet, clad in a shroud of black velvet or silk; for days at a time he would sit in rapt ecstasy before the perfections of my body. Whatever my lover desired gave me endless contentment because it delighted him.

"Furthermore, since we love nothing so much as our own pleasure and desire everything both within and without the heart to shine forth in beauty and harmony, they all wished to see the house I lived in adorned with the loveliest things; and all of them were no less happy than I to decorate the place with flowers and silks and gold. What harm was there in it? What did such handsome objects spoil? What power had I, what authority to prevent a knight or even a wealthy townsman who happened to love me, from gratifying his whims? Thus I found myself compelled to accept precious perfumes and other presents which made me very angry. Such and such only is the source of that gold plate, these carpets, and these jewels seized at my house by the bailiffs."

This concluded the first hearing of Sister Claire, suspected to be a demon, because we, Judge Ecclesiastical, and Guillaume Tournebouche were too greatly fatigued by the sound of her voice in our ears and because we found our understanding confused in every way.

We, Judge Ecclesiastical, have called the second inquest for three days from today, in order that proofs may be sought for of the demon's obsession and presence in the body of the accused,

Who, by order of the Judge, was returned to her cell under conduct of Master Guillaume Tournebouche.

iij

In nomine Patris, et Filii, et Spiritus Sancti. Amen

On the thirteenth day following of the said month of February, in our presence, Jérôme Cornille, *et cetera,*

The aforementioned Sister Claire was produced in order to

be questioned upon the deeds and acts to her imputed, and of
them to be convicted.

We, the Judge, addressing the accused, contended that from a
consideration of the divers answers she had given at the preceding inquiry, it was established that:

Even were it lawful to authorize a female to lead the life of a
harlot and give pleasure to all—which it is not—it has never lain

in the power of a simple woman to bring about so many deaths
and to practise sorceries so perfect without the assistance of a
special demon, who lodged within her body and to whom her
soul had been sold by a specific compact.

Therefore it was clearly proven that beneath her outward
form a demon lay and moved, the author of these calamities.

Q. You are now solemnly challenged to avow at what age you
received the said demon, to confess the terms of the agreement
entered upon by this demon and yourself, to tell the truth anent
your joint maleficence.

A. I am prepared to answer you, a man, as I would answer
God, Who must be judge to all of us. I have never known this
demon, I have never spoken to him, nor have I in any way desired to see him. I have never followed the harlot's calling, because I never practised the manifold delights of love's invention
for other profit than the pleasure Our Sovereign Creator has put
in the thing. And I have always been incited thereto more by a

desire to be docile and gentle to the dear lord I loved than by a lust incessantly rampant.

Yet had such been my will, I would implore you to remember that I am a poor African girl through whose veins God has made a torrid blood to flow; and in my brain is so ready an understanding of the delights of love that if a man but looks at me, I feel a troublous pressure on my heart.

The accused went on to explain that if an amorous gentleman, moved by a desire of connection, should happen to touch her on any portion of her body, merely brushing it with his hand, she fell completely under his sway, in spite of anything she might do, because her heart failed on the spot. By this contact, the apprehension and remembrance of all the heavenly bliss of love awakened in her centre, kindling an intense heat which rose thence to course flaming through her veins and quicken her with love and joy from top to toe. Since the day when Dom Marsilis had first stirred her to the comprehension of these things, she had thought of nothing else. In that moment she had realized that love was a gift supremely concordant with her special nature; and ever since, she had had proof that, short of a man and natural humectation, she would have withered and died at the said convent. As evidence of this affirmation, she earnestly assured us that after her flight from the said convent, it was certain that she never passed a single day or the tiniest fraction of a day in sadness or melancholy. On the contrary, she was always joyous, thus following God's sacred will in reference to her, from which she believed she had been diverted during the whole time she wasted in this convent.

Thereto, we, Jérôme Cornille, objected to the demon:

Q. In this your answer there is open blasphemy against God, because we have all been created to His greater glory and sent into this world to honor Him and serve Him. Do you not know we must forever keep His blessed commandments before our eyes and walk in holiness that we may win eternal happiness? Is it not wrong to lie forever supine doing that which the very beasts themselves do only in a certain season?

A. I have honored God much; in whatsoever land I was, I comforted the poor and the afflicted, giving them both money and raiment and weeping at the sight and knowledge of their misery. And on the Day of ultimate Judgment, I dare hope to find around me a goodly company of holy works acceptable to God and meet to intercede for me.

She added that but for her humility, her fear of reproach and her dread of displeasing the gentlemen of the Chapter, she would joyfully have spent her wealth to complete the building of the Cathedral of St. Maurice and to found Masses for the welfare of her soul, sparing neither her pleasure nor her person. Indeed, with this high aim in view, she would have found a double relish in her nights, because each of her amours would have added one stone to the building of the basilica. Also to this end, and for the eternal welfare of the accused, all those who love her would cheerfully have given of their wealth.

Q. How can you justify the fact that you are barren, since, despite abundant copulation, no child has been born of you? Does this not prove the presence of a demon in your womb?

Again, only Ashtaroth or a blessed Apostle can speak in all tongues. Does not your conversing in the manner of all countries prove the presence of a demon within you?

A. For the languages, I know naught more of Greek than *Kyrie Eleison!* a phrase I made much use of. And of Latin, only *Amen,* which I said to God when I prayed to obtain my liberty.

For the rest, I have been much aggrieved at my barrenness; and if the worthy housewives have children, I believe it must be because they take so little pleasure in the thing while I, for my part, take a whit too much. Doubtless, it is the will of God, who fears lest from excess of happiness the world would be in danger of perishing.

In due consideration of the above, as well as for a thousand other reasons which sufficiently established the presence of a demon in the body of Sister Claire, since it is characteristic of Lucifer always to conjure up plausible arguments of heresy;

We gave orders that the accused be subjected in our presence to torture and severe bodily hurt in order to reduce the said demon by suffering to submit to the authority of the Church;

We therefore summoned to our assistance François de Hangest, master surgeon and doctor to the Chapter, charging him, by a schedule herewith appended, to investigate the qualities of the female nature (*virtutes vulvæ*) of the aforesaid woman in order that our religion might be enlightened as to the methods the demon employed to suck in souls through its instrumentality and to ascertain if any artifice were therein apparent.

Then the Mooress wept and groaned very bitterly in anticipation; and, her irons notwithstanding, she fell to her knees, imploring the revocation of this order with cries and clamor, objecting that her limbs were in so feeble a state and her bones so brittle that such torture would shatter her like glass. Finally, she offered to purchase her dispensation therefrom by the gift of her wealth to the Chapter and her immediate departure from the country.

Q. Do you of your own free will allow that you are a demon of the nature of the Succubi, who are female fiends employed in corrupting Christians by means of blandishments and flagitious delights of love?

A. No, no, no! Such a thing would be an abominable falsehood! I have always felt myself a perfectly natural woman.

Her irons having been removed by the torturer, the accused proceeded to take off her dress and maliciously and with intent, to obscure, confound and destroy our understanding by offering us the sight of her body, which, in truth, exercised upon man a host of supernatural coercions.

At this place, Master Guillaume Tournebouche, by force of nature, laid down the pen and retired, objecting that he could not be a witness to this torture without incredible temptations working upon his brain because he felt the Devil violently gaining his person.

This concluded the second inquiry. As the Apparitor and Janitor of the Chapter reported that Master François de Hangest was in the country, the torture and inquiry were appointed for the morrow, at the hour of noon, after Mass.

These last paragraphs were set down by myself, Jérôme, in the absence of Master Guillaume Tournebouche, in token of which we have signed

JÉRÔME CORNILLE
Grand Inquisitor.

iv

PETITION

On this day, the fourteenth of the month of February, in the presence of the undersigned, Jérôme Cornille, there appeared:

The said Masters Jean Ribou, Antoine Jean, Martin Beaupertuys, Jérôme Mâchefer, Jacques de Villedomer and the Sire d'Idré, in the stead and place of the Mayor of the City of Tours, temporarily absent, all plaintiffs designed in the act of process made at the Town Hall,

To whom at the request of Blanche Bruyn (now acknowledging herself a nun of the Convent of Mount Carmel named, in religion, Sister Claire) we made known that the above, accused of demoniacal possession, appealed to the judgment of God and offered to suffer the ordeal of water and fire in the presence of the Chapter and the City of Tours, thereby to prove her reality as a woman and her innocence.

To this appeal, the said accusers have for their part agreed, undertaking, on condition the city stand as security for it, to prepare a suitable place and pile, to be approved by the sponsors of the accused.

Then, by us, Judge Ecclesiastical, the term of the ordeal was appointed for the first day of the new year—which will be Easter Day—at the hour of noon, after Mass, each of the parties having conceded this delay to be amply sufficient.

Therefore, the present decree shall be cried, at the suit of each of them, in all the towns, boroughs and châteaux of Touraine and of the land of France at their request, costs and suit.

JÉRÔME CORNILLE

III

What the Succubus Did to Suck Out the Old Judge's Soul and What Came of Such Diabolical Delectation

*H*EREWITH *is the act of extreme confession made on the first day of the month of March, in the year one thousand two hundred and seventy-one after the coming of Our Blessed Savior, by Jérôme Cornille, priest, Canon of the Chapter of the Cathedral of St. Maurice, Grand Inquisitor, of all recognizing himself unworthy;*

Who, finding his last hour at hand and repenting of his sins, depravities, crimes, iniquities and wickedness desired that his avowal be made public to serve to establish the truth, the glory of God and the justice of the Tribunal, and also to ease him of his punishment in the next world.

The said Jérôme Cornille, being upon his deathbed, the following were summoned to hear his declaration:

Jean de la Haye (de Haga) Vicar of the Church of St. Maurice;

Pierre Guyard, Treasurer to the Chapter, appointed by My Lord Jean de Montsoreau, Archbishop, to write his words;

Dom Louis Pot, monk of the maius monasterium *(Marmoûtier) chosen by him for his spiritual father and confessor;*

The three assisted by the great and illustrious Doctor Guillaume de Censoris, Archdeacon of Rome, at present sent into our diocese (Legatus) *by His Holiness the Pope.*

Finally in the presence of a great number of Christians assembled to witness the passing of the said Jérôme Cornille, upon his known wish to make an act of public repentance, insomuch as he required shriving and hoped that his words might open the eyes of such Christians as were about to slip into Hell.

And before him, Jérôme, who, by reason of his great feebleness, was unable to speak, Dom Louis Pot read the following confession, to the great agitation of the said company:

"My beloved brethren, until the seventy-ninth year of my life, in which I now am, save for such lesser sins as a Christian, however holy, incurs toward God—which sins he may lawfully redeem by penitence—I believe I led a Christian existence. And I believe I deserved the praise and renown bestowed upon me in this diocese, where I was raised to the most lofty office of Grand Inquisitor, whereof I am unworthy. At present, seized by apprehension at the infinite glory of God and terrified at the anguish awaiting evildoers and prevaricators in Hell, I have hoped to mitigate the enormity of my crimes by the severest penance I can possibly make in the ultimate hour which I now reach. Wherefore of the Church, whose privileges and whose renown for justice I abused, betrayed and sold, I have craved the blessed boon of publicly accusing myself, in the manner of the ancient Christians. To betoken even deeper contrition, I would wish there were still life in me to permit of my going to the Cathedral portal, to be reviled by all my brethren as I remained a whole day there on my knees, barefoot, a taper in hand and a rope around my neck. For I have much followed the errings of Hell to the prejudice of the sacred interests of God. But amid the catastrophe of my frail virtue (may it prove a warning to you to eschew vice, to flee the toils of the demon and to take refuge in the Church wherein is all succor!) so hopelessly did Lucifer bewitch me that Our Lord Jesus Christ will take pity upon me, a miserable abused Christian whose eyes are dimmed with tears. To this end I implore your intercession and help and prayers. So would I wish to have another life to spend in works of penitence. Now, therefore, give heed and tremble in great fear!

"I was elected, by the Chapter assembled, to investigate, sift and draw up the evidence in the suit instituted against the demon appeared in female form in the person of a relapsed nun, an abominable creature who denied God and who, in her infidel country of origin, was named Zulma. This demon (known in the diocese as Claire of the Convent of Mount Carmel) had sorely afflicted the city by lying under an infinite number of men, by winning their souls to Mammon, Ashtaroth and Satan, Princes of Darkness, by making them quit this world in a state of mortal sin, by dealing death to them in the place whence life proceeds.

"Then, I, I, a Judge, in the evening of my life, fell into this snare; I lost my senses; I acquitted myself traitorously of the functions by the Chapter committed in great trust to me in my chill old age. Give heed, then, how artful is the demon; steel yourselves against her artifices!

"While hearing the first answer given by the said Succubus, I saw with terror that the irons placed about her hands and feet had left no mark there; I was dazed at her hidden strength and her apparent weakness. Then, of a sudden, my mind was troubled as I beheld with what perfections of nature the devil was armed. I listened to the music of her voice, which warmed me from top to toe and made me long to be young again in order to yield to her. Alas! for one brief hour spent in her company, I deemed my eternal happiness was but scant payment for the amorous pleasures savored in her slender arms. I lost that firmness which is the attribute of judges. The demon, by me questioned, argued so effectively that at the second interrogatory, I was firmly convinced I would be committing a crime to mulct and torment a piteous little creature who wept like an innocent child. Then I was warned by a voice from on high to do my duty: these golden words, this music of celestial sweetness were diabolical mummeries; this body, so delicate and so inviting, would transmute itself into a horrible, bristly beast with rending claws; her melting eyes would turn into brands of hell, her chine into a squamous tail, her rosy, fair mouth and soft lips into the jaws of a crocodile. I returned, intending to submit the said Succubus to torture until she should avow her mission, as that practise has been heretofore followed in Christendom. But when the demon bared her naked body to be tortured, I was suddenly placed, by magical conjurations, in her power. I felt my old bones crack; my brain reeled under a hot radiance; my heart overflowed with young, boiling blood; I felt my body light and buoyant; and by virtue of a charmed philtre thrown into my eyes, the snows upon my brow melted away. I lost all conscience of my Christian life; I was a school boy, scampering about in the fields, escaped from class and stealing apples. I had not the strength to make the sign of the Cross: I was utterly oblivious of the Church, of God the

Father, of the blessed Savior of Mankind. A prey to this design, I roamed through the streets, recalling the delights of the demon's voice, seeing her abominable fair body everywhere, and repeating a thousand iniquities to myself. Then, pierced and drawn by a blow of the Devil's fork, already sinking into my head like a bill in an oak, I was pulled by its sharp prong to the jail. From time to time, my guardian angel plucked me by the arm and defended me against these temptations; but his holy advice and his aid notwithstanding, I was dragged away by a million claws fastened on my heart. Soon I found myself in the demon's cell.

"The moment its door swung open before me, all outward semblance of a prison vanished. With the aid of evil genii or spirits, the Succubus had constructed a pavilion of purple and silk, filled with perfumes and flowers, in which she frolicked, superbly clad, without either an iron collar about her neck or chains at her feet. I suffered myself to be stripped of my ecclesiastical vestments; I was placed in a perfumed bath. Then the demon covered me with a Saracen robe and regaled me with a repast of rare delicacies served upon precious vessels and wines of Asia poured in goblets of gold. There were songs and wondrous music and a myriad sweet sounds that, passing through my ears, lulled my soul to ecstasy. The Succubus remained constantly beside me; her detestable, lush commerce distilled new ardors in my loins. My guardian angel abandoned me. Then I lived only by the terrible light of the Mooress's eyes, craving the perfervid embrace of her adorable body and pining always to feel of her red lips which I believed natural; nor did I in the least fear the bite of her teeth which draw men to the very depths of Hell. I thrilled to the unparalleled tactile ravishment of her hands, without thinking that these were obscene claws. In a word, I seethed like a husband desiring to go to his bride, without realizing that this bride was eternal death. None of the things of this earth mattered; I was indifferent to the interests of God; but dreamed of love only, of the grateful breasts of this woman consuming me, and of her portal to Abaddon into which I longed to sink. Alas, my beloved brethren, three days and three nights long, I was compelled to toil and moil without being once able to exhaust the stream flowing from my veins, into which the Succubus plunged her hands like two pikes, while she communi-

cated I know not what amorous sweat to my poor senescence and
to my avid bones. In the beginning, to draw me to her, the demon caused a fluid to run through me that was mild as milk;
next, came poignant thrills that pricked their hundred needles
into my bones, my marrow, my brain, my sinews. At this sport,
the obscure springs of my head caught fire; my blood, my nerves,
my flesh, my frame blazed; whereupon I burned with the true
fire of Hell, which, amid a wrenching of my joints and an incredible, intolerable, all-rending voluptuousness, loosened the
bonds of my life. The demon's hair, coiled about my wretched
body, poured a river of living flame upon me; each tress I felt
searing into me like a bar of iron, red-hot. In this mortal trans-
port, I saw the ardent face of the said Succubus, she was laughing
as she spoke a thousand exciting words, saying I was her knight,
her lord, her lance . . . I was her day and her night . . . her thunder, her life . . . her good, her best rider . . . she would weld herself even closer unto me . . . to dwell beneath my skin . . . or to
have me grafted in hers. . . . Hearing this, under the goad of the
tongue that was sucking that soul out of me, I sank, I toppled
headlong ever deeper into the chasm of Hell without striking
the bottom. When I had no drop of blood in my veins, when my
heart had ceased beating in my body, when I was completely
shattered, the demon, her flesh still cool, white, roseate, shining:

" 'Poor madman,' she said with a laugh, 'so you thought me a
demon, eh? If I asked you to sell me your soul for a kiss, would
you not grant it me with all your heart?'

" 'Yes,' I said.

" 'And if, to ply this pleasure, always, I had to feed upon the
blood of newborn babes? If thus alone I could obtain new life to
spend in my bed, would you not suck it up for me willingly?'

" 'Yes,' I said.

" 'To be my gallant rider, forever in the saddle; to be gay as
a man in his prime; to feel life pulsing through you; to drink in
pleasure and to dive into depths of joy like a swimmer into the
Loire, would you not deny God? Would you not spit in the face
of Jesus?'

" 'Yes,' I said.

" 'If twenty years of monastic life were still to be granted you, would you not fling them away for two years of this consuming love and this rapturous glamor?'

" 'Yes,' I said.

"I felt fivescore fierce claws ripping up my diaphragm as if the beaks of a thousand vultures were pecking at it, shrieking. The Succubus spread her wings. I was lifted upon them high above the earth, while the Succubus cried in my ears:

" 'Now ride you, ride you, my rider, ride! Hold fast to your mare, hug her crupper and flanks; grip her mane, clasp her neck and ride you, ride you, my rider, ride! All creation is riding! Ride you, ride!'

"I glimpsed the towns of earth, distant as a mist, and by special gift, I saw the sons of man, each accoupled to a female demon, writhing about, rampaging, engendering amid great concupiscence, shrieking hoarse words of love, gasping and panting, all united, locked together in an orgy of progeneration. Then my mare with the Moorish head, still flying and galloping through the clouds, pointed out the earth intervolved with the sun in a commotion whence sprang a seed of stars: and there each female sphere was joyously belaying a male sphere. But instead of the words we humans speak, the spheres were straining to utter storms, to shoot forth lightning and to roll out thunder. Now, still soaring upward, above the congeries of spheres, I saw the female nature of all things in love-throes with the Prince of Movement. To mock me, the Succubus placed me in the pit of this frightful, perpetual convolution wherein I was lost like a grain of sand in the ocean. And my white mare kept urging: 'Ride you, ride you, fair rider, ride! . . . All creation rides!'

"Realizing how infinitesimal a mere priest was in this torrent of the seed of worlds, where metals and stones, waters, airs and thunders, fishes, plants and animals, men, spirits, worlds and planets were forever nature to cod, writhing in fury, I did deny the Catholic faith. The Succubus showed me that vast conglomeration of stars in the heavens and:

" 'This milky way is a drop of celestial seed,' she said, 'escaped from the huge flow of the worlds in conjunction.'

"Whereupon, I again bestrode the Succubus furiously by the light of a thousand million stars; and I would, astraddle, have wished to feel the nature of all these thousand million creatures. At last, exhausted by this titanic effort of love, I fell, impotent in every limb. I heard loud diabolical laughter. Then I found myself in my bed, surrounded by my servants, who had dared struggle with the demon, throwing a full pail of holy water in my bed and offering fervent prayers to God. Despite their assistance, I had to sustain a terrific combat with the Succubus, whose claws still clutched my heart and caused me infinite anguish. Brought to my senses by the voices of my servants, relatives and friends, I at once strove to make the sign of the Cross; but the Succubus, sprawled over my bed, at the head, at the foot, on my bolster, everywhere, kept relaxing my nerves, laughing, grimacing, presenting a thousand obscene pictures to my sight and arousing a thousand evil desires in me. Nevertheless, taking pity upon me, My Lord Archbishop sent for the relics of St. Gatien. At last, when the shrine touched my bed, the said Succubus was compelled to escape, leaving behind her an odor of sulphur and Hell, which made my servants, friends and others hoarse for a whole day. Then the divine radiance of God enlightened my soul; I knew that through my sins and my struggle with the evil spirits, I stood in great danger of perishing. Objecting the infinite merits of Jesus dead upon the Cross for the salvation of Christians, I implored of God's mercy the signal boon of living a short spell more in order to render glory to God and to His Church. By this prayer, I obtained the favor of recovering sufficient strength to accuse myself of my sins and to impetrate of all the members of the Church of St. Maurice their help and assistance so I may be delivered from purgatory, whither I go to redeem my sins through infinite agonies.

"Lastly, I hereby declare to be a subterfuge my decree, wherein the said demon appealed to the judgment of God by the ordeals of fire and water. I confess that it was inspired by the said demon's nefarious will to enable her to escape the justice of My Lord Archbishop's Tribunal, she having secretly admitted to me that another demon, inured to this test, would be substituted in her place.

"In conclusion, to the Chapter of the Church of St. Maurice I give and bequeath my property of all kinds, to found a chapel in the said church, to build and to adorn it and to place it under the invocation of St. Jérôme and St. Gatien, of whom the one is my patron, the other the savior of my soul."

This, heard by all the company, was submitted to the Ecclesiastical Tribunal by Jean de la Haye (Johannes de Haga).

We, Jean de la Haye (Johannes de Haga) elected Grand Inquisitor of St. Maurice by the Assembly General of the Chapter, according to the usage and custom of this Church, and appointed to pursue afresh the trial of the demon Succubus, at present in the jail of the Chapter,

Hereby order a new inquest for the hearing of all those of this diocese who have cognizance of the facts thereto relating.

In the name of the members of the Church, in general and sovereign Chapter assembled, we declare null and void all past proceedings, interrogations and decrees and disallow the appeal to God treacherously made by the demon, in view of the said demon's notorious perfidy in its obtainment.

The said judgment shall be published to the sound of the trumpet by the town crier in all parts of the diocese in which the false ordinances were proclaimed one month ago, these being patently due to the instigations of the demon, as proven by the confession of the late Jérôme Cornille.

May all Christians lend their aid to our Holy Church and to its commandments.

JEAN DE LA HAYE.

IV

How the Mooress of the Rue Chaude Proved So Tortile That Great Efforts Were Needed to Burn and Broil Her Alive in the Teeth of Hell

This was written in the month of May, in the year 1360, after the manner of a testament.

M Y VERY dear and well-beloved Son,
"When it shall be lawful for you to read this, I, your father, shall be lying in the grave, imploring your prayers and beseeching you to conduct yourself in life as ordered in this rescript. These instructions I bequeath to you for the wise government of your family, for your happiness and for your security; I have drawn them up at a time when my senses and understanding were still freshly affected by the sovereign injustice of men.

"In my virile age, I nourished the great ambition of rising in the ranks of the Church and attaining the loftiest ecclesiastical dignities, because no life appeared to me more enviable. With this earnest purpose, I learned to read and to write; then, with great trouble, I managed to fit myself to qualify for the clergy. Because I lacked protection and prudent counsel to speed me on my way, I conceived the notion of offering my services as scribe, tabellion and rubrician to the Chapter of St. Martin which comprised the richest and most illustrious personages of Christendom, since the King of France is but a simple canon in this foundation. There, I thought, I would be best able to find services to render certain lords; this would win me masters and patrons who could assist me to enter into religion; eventually I might be mitred, like anyone else, and ensconced in an archiepiscopal throne somewhere or other. But this early vision proved too rosy and a whit too ambitious, as God gave me clearly to recognize in the process of time. As a matter of fact, Master Jean de Villedomer, who later became a Cardinal, was appointed to the post, and I rejected, to my great discomfiture.

"In this unhappy hour, I was in a measure consoled by the advice of good old Jérôme Cornille, Inquisitor of the Cathedral, whom I have often mentioned to you. This dear man in his kindness prevailed upon me to become rubrician to the Chapter of St. Maurice and the Archbishopric of Tours, a position I held with honor, for I was reputed a capital scrivener. In the year I contemplated entering the priesthood, the celebrated trial of the demon of the Rue Chaude occurred. Today, still, of an evening, the old folk entertain the youngsters with the story, which, in its time, was told at every fireside in the realm of France.

"Arguing that it would prove of great advantage to my ambition, and that, to reward my assistance, the Church would raise me to some dignity, my beloved master had me appointed to record everything subject to writing in this momentous case.

"From the very outset, Monseigneur Jérôme Cornille—a man close to eighty years of age, of great sense, justice, and sound understanding—suspected some malice in this suit. Though he was never partial to wenches wild of their bodies, though he had never copulated in his life, though it was his very probity and sanctity that won him his judicature, nevertheless, having taken all the depositions and heard the wretched wench, he was convinced of her innocence. Obviously, the lusty trollop had broken her monastic vows; but she was guiltless of all deviltry and it looked very much as though her great fortune was coveted by her enemies and by other people whom, from motives of prudence, I will not name. At the time, everyone believed her so amply furnished with gold and silver that she could, some reckoned, have bought the whole County of Touraine, had she desired to do so. A thousand lies and slanders were therefore invented about the wench, whom all the respectable ladies envied; such falsehoods spread from mouth to mouth, and eventually were accepted as gospel truths. In these circumstances, Monseigneur Jérôme Cornille, having recognized that no demon possessed her save that of love, made her consent to spend the remainder of her days in a convent. Having been assured by certain gallant knights, brave in war and rich in domains, that they would do everything to save her, he invited her secretly to request of her accusers the appeal to God's judgment. But be-

fore, to silence gossip, he persuaded her to give all her goods to
the Chapter. By these means, the stake was to be cheated of the
most delicate flower Heaven ever suffered to fall upon our earth,
a blossom of womanhood that erred only through excessive tenderness and compassion before the malady of love her eyes instilled in the hearts of all her pursuers. But the real devil, in
the guise of a monk, took a hand in the affair; and in this wise.

"An arrant foe of virtue, wisdom and sanctity, whose name
was Jean de la Haye, knew that the poor girl was being treated
like a queen in the jail. He maliciously accused the Grand In-
quistor of connivance with her, charging that Monseigneur
Jérôme Cornille was her servitor because she made him young,
happy and amorous. In a single day the unfortunate old man
died of chagrin, knowing that Jean de la Haye had coveted his
dignities and sworn his ruin. When My Lord Archbishop visited
the jail, he found the Mooress lodged in a pleasant apartment
and comfortably bedded, with no sign of any irons in her cell.
To tell the truth, she had concealed a diamond in a place where
none would have believed she could have held it; with it, she
had bought the clemency of her jailer. At the time, others said,
her jailer was infatuated with her and, through affection or probably through great fear of her young noblemen lovers, was planning her escape. Poor old Cornille was at the point of death.
What with the accusations and intrigues of Jean de la Haye, the
Chapter deemed it imperative to annul the proceedings and decrees drawn up by the Inquisitor. Jean de la Haye, then a mere
vicar of the Cathedral, pointed out that to obtain their end they
required no more than a public confession from the good man
on his deathbed. Then the moribund was hounded and tormented by the gentlemen of the Chapter, by those of St. Martin,
by those of Marmoûtier, by My Lord Archbishop and by the
Papal Legate, who were bound that he retract to the profit of the
Church. This, Jérôme Cornille refused to countenance. But,
after a thousand tribulations, his public confession was drawn
up; the most noteworthy people in the town attended; it spread
more horror and consternation than I can possibly convey. The
churches of the diocese held public prayers for the grievous calamity; everyone in town was terrified, expecting to see the Devil
tumble down into his house by the chimney. The truth of the

matter is that when they obtained this recantation from him my dear master Jérôme was delirious and seeing cows and God knows what else striding across the room. His fever over, the poor saint wept bitterly as I told him of their trickery. He died in my arms, in the presence of his physician; heartbroken at this mummery, he assured us he was going to the feet of God to implore Him not to suffer the consummation of this lamentable iniquity.

"The tears and repentance of the Mooress had moved him deeply since, before having her appeal for the judgment of God, he had privily confessed her. Thus the divine soul that dwelled within this body found vent; he spoke to us of it as of a diamond worthy, after she should repent her sins and quit life, of adorning the holy crown of God. Then, my dear son, having weighed the talk in town and that poor wretch's guileless answers, I knew what lay at the bottom of the whole business. So I decided, on the advice of Master François de Hangest, physician to the Chapter, to feign an illness and abandon the service of the Church of St. Maurice and of the Archbishopric; for I was unwilling to dip my hand in innocent blood which still cried and will forever cry out to God, until the day of the last judgment.

"The jailer was banished; they appointed the torturer's younger son in his place. This man immediately threw the Mooress into a dungeon; and not only mercilessly locked her hands and feet in irons weighing fifty pounds, but also crushed her in a wooden girdle. The jail was guarded by the crossbowmen of the town and My Lord Archbishop's men-at-arms. The wench was tormented and tortured; her bones were broken. Beyond herself with pain, she made a confession to suit Jean de la Haye, and was incontinently condemned to be burned in the acreage of St. Étienne, having previously been stationed at the Church portal, clad in a shirt of sulphur. Her possessions were given to the Chapter, *et cetera*.

"Her sentence was the cause of a great riot and much fighting in the town, because three youthful knights of Touraine swore to deliver the hapless girl by fair means or foul, or else to die in her service. They came to town escorted by a good thousand sufferers, laborers, old soldiers, fighting-men, artisans and others whom the wench had succored and saved from trouble, hunger and misery; they rummaged all the hovels of the town where lay those whom she had befriended. These were roused and assembled at the foot of Mont Louis under the protection of the lords' soldiers; the throng was swelled by all the scapegraces within a radius of twenty leagues. One fine morning they advanced to lay siege to My Lord Archbishop's prison, demanding that the Mooress be delivered to them, as though they sought to put her to death but in reality to set her free and secretly place her on a swift charger. In this way, she could undoubtedly have gained the open country, for she rode like a groom. Then amid a tremendous tempest of men, between the buildings of the Archbishopric and the Bridge, we saw more than ten thousand people swarming to the fray, besides all those who were perched on the housetops and those who clambered to every floor and window to watch the sedition. The grisly cries of the Christians who were laying on with a vengeance and the harrowing yells of those surrounding the jail to free the hapless victim could easily be heard across the Loire, beyond St. Symphorien. The immense crowd surged forward, thirsting for the blood of this ill-starred creature at whose feet all would have fallen, had they had the good fortune to behold her. So heavy was the press and suffocation that seven children, eleven women, and eight townsmen were crushed and squashed beyond recognition, like so many clots of mud. The huge jaws of this popular Leviathan, of this ghastly monster, gaped so widely that its clamor was audible as far away as at Montils-les-Tours. 'Death to the Succubus!' they cried, 'Hand over the demon!'—'Ha, I'd like a quarter!'—'I'll take her nap!'—'Her foot is mine!'—'Mine, her mane!'—'I spoke for the head!'—'I'll have the socket . . . is it crimson?'—'Shall we see it? . . .'—'Will they broil it?'—'Death to her, death to her!' Each had his say. But the cry 'Largess to God! Death to the Succubus!' was uttered in unison by the mob so hoarsely and so cruelly that the ears and heart bled for it; it drowned out the other cries which were scarce heard in the houses.

"In order to calm this storm threatening to overthrow everything, My Lord Archbishop decided to sally from the church with great pomp, bearing the host. This move saved the Chapter from ruin, for the ruffians and young lords had vowed to destroy and burn the cloister and to slay all the canons. By My Lord

Archbishop's stratagem, the mob was forced to disperse, and, for lack of provisions, to return home. That night the monks of Touraine, the noblemen and townsmen, in great fear of pillage on the morrow, held an assembly and resolved to side with the Chapter. Thanks to them, men-at-arms, archers, knights and townsmen, in vast numbers, mounted guard and killed a band of shepherd boys, freebooters and bandits, who knowing the confusion in Tours, came to swell the ranks of the malcontents.

"Messire Harduin de Maillé, an old nobleman, reasoned with the young knights, who championed the Mooress, and argued sagely with them. Were they willing to put all Touraine to fire and sword for the sake of one pretty little face? And even were they victorious, could they remain masters of the lawless rabble they had mustered? Having razed the manors of their enemies, would not these pillagers turn upon those of their leaders? Their insurrection was already an accomplished fact; yet what success had attended their first effort? Was not the Archbishopric still unscathed? What hope had they of besting the Church of Tours, when the latter could invoke the aid of the King? To this logic, he added a host of conclusive points.

"The young knights replied that it was easy for the Chapter to allow the girl to escape secretly by night, thus removing the cause of the sedition. To which wise and humane request, Monseigneur de Censoris, Legate of the Pope, objected the imperative necessity of force remaining with Church and Religion. So the poor wench paid for the lot, it being agreed that no inquiry should be made concerning the sedition.

"Then the Chapter had full license to proceed with the wench's execution, to which act and ecclesiastical ceremony people came from a distance of twelve leagues round. On the day appointed, after divine satisfaction, for the delivery of the Succubus to secular justice to be publicly burned at the stake, not for a gold pound could a varlet, let alone an abbot, have found lodging in the town of Tours. The night before, crowds camped in tents or lay on straw outside the city walls. Provisions were sorely lacking; many who came with bellies full returned with empty bellies, having seen nothing but a vague blaze in the distance. The footpads did a rushing business on the road.

"The wretched courtesan was all but dead. Her hair had

turned white. She was, truth to tell, no more than a skeleton, thinly covered with flesh; her chains weighed more than she did. If ever she had tasted joy in her life, she paid heavily for it in this moment. Those who saw her pass said that her tears and cries were enough to move her most relentless pursuers to compassion. In the church, they were compelled to put a gag in her mouth; she bit on it as a lizard bites at a stick. Then the executioner tied her to a stake, to hold her up, because at times she sagged and fell from lack of strength. But suddenly she recovered a vigorous handful, for she was actually able, they say, to shake off her chains and escape in the church, where, remembering her former calling, she climbed with great ability into the upper galleries, flying like a bird along the little columns and friezes. She was about to escape over the leads, when a crossbowman took careful aim and sent his arrow clean through her ankle. In spite of her foot, half amputated, the poor wench was so terrified of the flames at the stake that she ran on through the church, heedless of her broken bones and bleeding freely. At last, she was seized, bound, tossed into a tumbrel and taken to the stake, without a single cry having been heard from her thereafter. The account of her flight through the church confirmed the mob in its belief that she was a devil; some even reported that she had flown away through the air. As the executioner of the town flung her into the flames, she gave two or three horrible leaps, then fell into the middle of the pyre, which flamed all that day and the following night. On the morrow, in the evening, I went to see if anything remained of this gentle, sweet, loving girl; but I found nothing save a poor fragment of ventral bone, in which, this intense fire notwithstanding, there still clung a little moisture and which, some said, still quivered like a woman in the thrill of amour.

"I cannot possibly express, my dear son, what numberless and unequalled sorrows haunted me for the next ten years. I could not banish the memory of this angel destroyed by the wickedness of men; always I saw her eyes, alive with love; the supernatural gifts of this guileless child shone day and night before me; I prayed for her in the very church where she had been martyred. At length I lacked both strength and courage even to look upon the Grand Inquisitor, Jean de la Haye, without shuddering. Leprosy did the bailiff's task on him; he died eaten up by lice.

Fire burned his house and mate; and all those who had a hand in that pyre drew out flame therefrom.

"Such, my well-beloved son, was the cause of a thousand thoughts which I have here set down in writing to be the rule of conduct in our family forever.

"I left the service of the Church; I married your mother, from whom I received infinite blessings and with whom I have shared life, possessions, soul and all. She, too, was of my mind in the following precepts. To wit:

"Firstly, in order to live happily, it is imperative to dwell far from churchmen, honoring them much but never giving them leave to enter your house, any more than you would all those who by right, just or unjust, are supposed to be our superiors.

"Secondly, to maintain a modest condition and to remain therein without ever seeking to appear in any way rich. To be scrupulous to excite the envy of none, nor in any way to strike anyone, whosoever he be. For, if you would break envious heads, you must be strong as an oak which kills the plants at its foot. But even then, you would succumb, because human oaks are exceedingly rare and no Tournebouche, being a real Tournebouche, must flatter himself that he is an oak.

"Thirdly, never to spend more than a quarter of your income; to conceal your wealth; to hide your property; to undertake no office; to go to church like your neighbor; to keep your thoughts always to yourself, inasmuch as they belong to you and not to others, who assume them, embrangle them and twist them to their guise into the grossest calumnies.

"Fourthly, always to endure in the condition of Tournebouches, who are drapers, now and for evermore. To marry your daughters to worthy drapers; to send your sons to be drapers in other towns of France, having first furnished them with these sage precepts, brought them up to honor the draper's calling, and quelled any dream of ambition they might nourish. *A draper like a Tournebouche* should be their glory, their armorial bearings, their title, their motto, their life. So, being ever drapers, they will ever be Tournebouches, to live on inglorious but comfortable like the wise little insects who, once lodged in a beam, make their holes there and in all security go to the end of their ball of twine.

"Fifthly, never to speak any language other than the idiom of the draper's trade; and never to dispute about religion or politics. Though the government of state, province, religion and God should swerve and incline capriciously now one way, now the other, always in your quality of Tournebouche to stick to your cloth! Thus utterly inconspicuous, the Tournebouches will live peaceably with their little Tournebouchekins, duly paying tithes, taxes and whatever else they shall be forcibly required to pay to God, King, town or parish, to whom they must never offer the least resistance. Remember that to have peace, it is essential to save your patrimonial treasure, in order to keep and purchase peace, to owe no man aught, to have grain in your house, and to enjoy yourself behind barred doors and blinded windows.

"If you live thus, none will have a hold on the Tournebouches, nor State nor Church nor lords to whom, in the event of forcible pressure, you shall lend a few crowns without nursing the fond hope of seeing them again—the crowns, I mean.

"Thus, in all seasons, all men will love Tournebouches, and, the while, laugh at these Tournebouches of small means, these Tournebouches with cramped vision, these Tournebouches of such limited understanding. Let ignoramuses talk away, the Tournebouches will neither burn nor hang to the profit of King, Church or anyone else; the prudent Tournebouches will have money tucked away in their pockets and joy in their households, hidden from all.

"Do you, my beloved son, follow this counsel and lead a mediocre, middle-class life. Maintain this rule in your family as a county charter; and may you, dying, have your successor maintain it as the sacred gospel of the Tournebouches, until God will there be no Tournebouches left in this world."

This letter was found at the time of the inventory made in the house of François Tournebouche, Lord of Veretz, Chancellor to My Lord Dauphin, and condemned, by reason of the said Lord's rebellion against His Majesty, to lose his head and to suffer the confiscation of all his goods, by order of the Parliament of Paris. The above letter has been handed to the Governor of Touraine as a historical curiosity and appended to the records of the suit in the Archbishopric of Tours by me, Pierre Gaultier, Alderman, President of the Trades' Council.

The Author, having completed the transcription and deciphering of these parchments, and having translated them from their strange jargon into French, was informed by their donor that the Rue Chaude in Tours was probably so called because the sun remained there longer than elsewhere.

But in spite of this version, people of lofty understanding will ascribe the said name of the said place to the warm passage of the Succubus.

This teaches us not to abuse our bodies, but to use them wisely in view of our salvation.

Despair in Love

HEN King Charles the Eighth conceived the notion of decorating the Château d'Amboise, he brought in his train certain Italian artists, master sculptors, excellent painters, masons and architects, who adorned the galleries with marvelous works. These, through neglect, have since been thoroughly spoiled. The Court, at the time, was staying in this attractive spot; as everybody knows, our keen young monarch took great pleasure in watching his artists work out their designs.

Among the foreign gentlemen was a Florentine, Master Angelo Cappara, a most estimable man, who, in spite of his youth, was the finest sculptor and engraver of all. Since he was still in the April of his life, with scarcely a flutter of down on his face there where a luxuriant growth of hair endows a man with virile majesty, many people wondered how he had so soon acquired such mastery of his craft. The ladies were all greatly smitten: Angelo was charming as a dream and melancholy as a dove alone in its nest, bereft of its mate.

The reason for his solitude was not far to seek. The luckless sculptor was a prey to the evil of poverty, which haunts and troubles all the actions of life. He lived wretchedly, ate almost not at all and felt ashamed of his penury; he devoted himself to his art with a sort of rageful despair, seeking by any means to win that life of idleness which is the richest of all lives to those whose minds are busy. Out of bravado, he came to the Court brilliantly attired; out of youthful shyness and unhappiness, he dared not ask for his pay. The King, seeing him thus clad, believed him to be amply provided with the goods of this world. Courtiers, ladies, everyone admired his beautiful craft and the craftsman,

too; but of money, never a copper! Everybody (especially the ladies), finding him rich by nature, deemed his eager youth, his
long black hair and his bright eyes an ample gift, nor dreaming
of these, ever gave a thought to lucre. They were quite right, too,
for such advantages brought many a Court friggler his fine estates, golden crowns and all the rest of it.

In spite of his youthful appearance, Master Angelo was twenty
years of age, and no fool; he had a noble heart, a head full of poetry and a mind pulsing with lofty imagination. But he was excessively humble, like all the poor and afflicted; and the success
of ignoramuses dazzled him. Further, he believed he was ill-
fashioned in body or soul; he kept his thoughts to himself—or
rather not quite to himself, for during his lone, chill nights he
would speak them to the shadows, to God, to the Devil, to everything about him. He would curse his luck for having a heart so
ardent that women doubtless recoiled from him as they would
from a red-hot iron; he would tell himself over and over again
with what fervor he would welcome a comely mistress, on what a
pedestal of honor he would set her in his life, with what loyalty
bind himself to her, with what devotion serve her, with what dili-
gence follow her commandments and with what sport scatter the
light clouds of her melancholy on days when the sky was over-
cast. Conjuring up such a woman in his artist's soul, he would
roll at her feet, cover them with kisses, and caress, fondle, bite
and cling to her with all the reality of a prisoner scampering
away to liberty across the green fields he glimpses through a cleft
in the prison wall. He would speak eloquently and melt her
heart; then, in rapturous abandon, stifle her in his embrace, hurt-
ing her a little despite his respect, and furiously biting his bedclothes as he sought her absent body. How boiling of courage
when alone, how shamefaced on the morrow if a woman so much
as brushed by him! Aflame with these amorous fancies, he ham-
mered away again at his marble figures, engraving lovely breasts,
fit to make the mouth water for such sweet fruits of love. And the
other things he raised, rounded and caressed with his chisel, softened with his file, and moulded so perfectly that a greenhorn
could not fail to understand their perfect uses and lose his virgin
illusions in a single day! The ladies recognizing themselves in
these beautiful figures, all set their caps at Master Angelo. And

the sculptor sweeping his eyes lovingly over their forms, vowed that the day one of them gave him her little finger to kiss, he would have all of her. . . .

Among these highborn ladies, one came to the Florentine personally, inquiring why he was so bashful and whether no lady of

the Court could overcome his reserve. Very graciously she invited him to her house that evening.

Master Angelo at once perfumed himself, purchased a mantle of velvet fringed and satin-lined; from a friend, he borrowed a wide-sleeved cloak, a slashed doublet and silken hose; and away he sped. As he climbed the steps with hasty feet, his gizzard was choking for hope, his heart was unmanageable, leaping and cavorting about like a goat; in a word, he had fallen head over heels in love, a feat which made the perspiration trickle down his back.

For the lady was indeed beautiful. Master Angelo appreciated it the better since his profession had taught him the joining of arms, the lines of the body, the secret contours of the seat of love, and other mysteries. This lady satisfied the technical rules of art; besides, she was fair and slender, with a voice fit to quicken life at its mainspring, to set fire to the heart, the brain and all the living body. She stirred in the imagination the most delicious arabesques of love, without appearing to dream of it—which is characteristic of these cursed women.

The sculptor found her seated in a high chair by the fire. Then she began to converse, wholly at her ease while Master Angelo dared utter no syllable save "Yes" and "No," finding never a word on his lips, never an idea in his brain. He would cheerfully have beaten his head against the fireplace, had he not experienced such bliss as he watched and heard his lovely mistress frisking like a young fly in a beam of sunlight.

Because, amid this mute admiration, both stayed up half the night, advancing step by little step down the flowery paths of love, the good sculptor went away happy. As he walked home, he argued to himself if a noble lady kept him rather close to her skirts during four hours at night, there was no earthly reason why she should not keep him there until morning. Drawing various charming corollaries from these premises, he resolved to request of her, as he would of any ordinary woman, no uncertain consummation. He determined to kill everybody—the husband, the lady or himself—unless he were allowed to spin a single hour of joy on this exquisite distaff. He was so utterly infatuated that he reckoned life but a trumpery stake in the game of love, one single day of which was worth a thousand drab existences.

The Florentine hewed away at his statues, dreaming of his evening and ruining many a nose as he thought of something else. Realizing how badly he was working, he flung away his tools, perfumed himself and went to sit at his lady's feet, basking in a conversation which he hoped soon to translate into action. When he was in her sovereign presence, her womanly majesty dazzled him.

Poor Angelo, a very lion in the street, suddenly grew very lamb-like as he faced his victim.

Nevertheless, towards the hour when desires strike fire, he had edged up to the lady; now he was all but on top of her and clasping her tightly. He had bargained for a kiss and, much to his delight, taken it; for when they give one, women reserve the right of refusing another, but when they allow one to be stolen, a lover may snatch a thousand more. That is why they usually allow kisses to be stolen. The Florentine had had a good many; things were already shaping themselves to perfection when the lady, who had doled out her favors rather frugally, cried:

"Here is my husband!"

In point of fact, My Lord was returning home after a game of tennis. The sculptor had to take to his heels, not, however, without first receiving the ardent glance a woman lavishes upon her lover when they have been interrupted in the midst of pleasure.

Such was to be his sole profit, pittance and enjoyment for a whole month. Always on the brink of Angelo's rapture, My Lord husband arrived; always he timed his advent nicely between a flat refusal and the gentle caresses with which women spice their denials—so many pretty blandishments to revive and redouble the passion in a lover's heart. Angelo began to exhaust his patience. If he essayed, immediately upon his arrival, to open fire point-blank in the battle of the skirt, hoping to see victory arrive before the husband (how profitable these disturbances proved to him Angelo could only guess!), My Lady reading the desire written in her sculptor's eyes, launched into interminable recriminations and quarrels. First she would pretend to fly into a fit of jealousy for the sole pleasure of hearing herself revile love. Did the little god grow angry? Then she would drown the fire of wrath with the holy water of a kiss, and proceed to monopolize the conversation. Her lover, she kept saying, must remain gentle, mild and docile to her will; he must do her bidding else she could not grant him her life and soul. What a trifling thing it was for a man to offer his mistress his desire! She, for her part, was the braver of the two since, loving more deeply, she made the greater sacrifice. If the occasion rose, she would exclaim: "That will *do!*" with the air of a queen. And to reply to Angelo's reproaches, she would, in the nick of time, assume an irate air:

"If you are not as I would wish you, I shall cease to love you."

At length, somewhat later, the poor Italian realized that hers was not a very noble love. It was, rather, a love that squeezed out joy as a miser his crowns. His lady delighted in allowing him to be master of everything and jump about the periphery of love all he pleased so long as he did not touch its charmed centre.

At this business, Angelo conceived a deadly rage. He unburdened himself to some friends, stout lads whom he posted on the road, charging them to seize the husband as he came home that night after his game of tennis with the King. Then he went to his lady's at the usual hour. When their sweet amorous dalliance was under way—the sport consisted of ardent kisses, hair twisted and untwisted, hands and ears bitten ragefully, in brief the entire operation minus that special thing good authors rightly deem abominable—our Florentine, between two kisses that went somewhat far, cried:

"Darling, do you love me more than aught else?"

"Ay," she replied, since words are cheap.

"Well then," the lover urged, "give yourself to me . . . entirely!"

"But my husband is coming home," she objected.

"Is that the only reason?"

"Ay!"

"I have friends who can seize him. They will let him pass only if I show a light at this window. If he complains to the King, my friends can say they thought they were playing a joke on one of our lot."

"Ah, my dear," she sighed, "let me see if everyone has gone to bed . . . if everything is quiet."

She rose—and held the light to the window. Seeing this, Master Angelo blew out the candle, seized his sword, and, facing this woman whom at last he knew in all her scorn and perfidy:

"I shall not kill you, Madame," he cried, "but I shall so disfigure you that never again shall your damnable coquetting make havoc of a wretched lover's life. You have abused me shamelessly; you are no decent woman! Now you shall learn that a kiss may never be wiped out of a true lover's life. Nay, a mouth kissed calls for the rest. My existence you have rendered forever burdensome and joyless. Now shall I make you think eternally upon my death, which you have caused. Never again shall you look at yourself in the glass without seeing my face in it, too!"

He raised his arm and swung his sword as though aiming to slice off a morsel of the fair cheeks upon which the traces of his kiss still lingered. She screamed.

"Wretch! You are a disloyal, dishonorable wretch!"

"Enough!" he cried. "You told me you loved me more than all else. Now you deny it. Every evening you raised me a little higher toward Heaven; then, at one blow, you throw me into Hell. Can you imagine your skirts will save you from a lover's wrath? Never!"

"Ah, Angelo, my love," she sighed, marvelling at this man aflame with rage, "I am yours . . . yours. . . ."

But he stepped back three paces:

"Back, you skirt of the Court! Back, lewd heart! You love your face better than your lover, eh? Very well: take that!"

She turned pale then and humbly offered her cheek to his blow. For she understood that in this hour her past treachery was wronging the love she bore him now. With one swing, Angelo slashed her face. Then he left the house and cleared out of town.

His compatriots, having seen the light in the window, did not molest the husband. My Lord returned to find his wife minus her left cheek. In spite of the great pain she felt, she would not breathe a word concerning her wound; since Angelo had inflicted it, she loved him better than her very life. The husband persisted in his efforts to ascertain what had happened. Since the Florentine had been the only caller at his house, he complained to the King, who had the artist pursued and condemned to hang. This was accomplished at Blois.

The day of the execution a noble lady wished to save this brave man, for she was convinced that he was a lover of true mettle. She begged the King to grant him to her; this His Majesty did willingly. But Angelo declared that he belonged heart and soul to his lady, whose memory he could never banish. He became a monk, then a Cardinal and a great savant. In his old days he used to say that he had existed upon the remembrance of his joys during those bitter hours of suffering when his lady had treated him both very well and very badly. There are authors who hold that afterward he went all lengths with the lady, whose cheek healed. But I do not believe this, for he was a man of heart, with a lofty notion of love's holy delights.

This teaches us nothing of advantage, save that there are unlucky meetings in life. For this story is true in every detail. If, elsewhere, the author had haply overreached the truth, this tale would earn him indulgence in the conclaves of lovers.

Epilogue

THOUGH, from the date-line of the frontispiece, this second series would appear to have been completed in a season of frosts and snow, it comes in the glad month of June, when all is green and fragrant, because the poor Muse who rules the Author was more capricious than the love of queens and wished mysteriously to bear her fruit in the sweet time of flowers.

No man can boast of mastering this sprite. Let but a grave thought occupy his mind, giving his brain no rest, and here comes the laughing wench, whispering her charming fancies in the Author's ear, tickling his grave lips with her feathers, dancing a saraband and raising the devil's tattoo all over the house! If perchance the Author, abandoning science for pleasure, cries: "Wait, my love, I come!" and rises hurriedly to play with the madcap, hi presto! she has vanished, she has scurried back to her lair, she has hidden there, she is writhing on the floor, groaning. Take a domestic poker, a church crosier, a rustic staff or a lady's cane, raise it, strike the wench and revile her, what does she do? She moans! Strip and flay her, she moans! Caress her and fondle her, she moans! Kiss her, cry "Hey, love!" and she moans!

Now she is cold; now she is on the point of death: adieu to love, adieu to comedy, joy and good tales, adieu, adieu! Put on deep mourning for her passing, weep her devoutly and fancy her dead, moan over her fate, what happens? She raises her head, bursts out laughing, spreads her white pinions and flutters away no one knows whither . . . wheels about in the air, capers and caracoles . . . displays her elfin tail, her woman's breasts, her nervous loins, her angel's face . . . shakes out her scented tresses; rolls about in the rays of the sun . . . shines forth again in all beauty, changing her colors like the throat of a dove . . . laughs until she weeps and spills her tears into the sea, where fishermen find them transmuted into lovely pearls and save them to adorn the brows of queens. Like a colt broken loose, she turns and twists about, exposing her virgin crupper and a thousand charms delectable enough to make a pope invoke damnation at the mere sight of them.

Amid this wild beast's hurly-burly, friends appear and dolts and tyrants, taunting the poet: "Where is your work? Where are your stories? You are a pagan prognosticator! Oh yes, we know you! You go to galas and feasts and you do nothing between meals. Where is your work?"

Though I am naturally inclined to mildness, I would like to see one of these folk impaled after the Turkish fashion and then send him thus equipped on a love-chase.

Here endeth the second series. May the devil give it a lift with his horns and it will be welcomed by a smiling Christendom.

Prologue to Third Ten Stories

CERTAIN people have inquired of the Author why these tales were so much the rage that no year could pass without his producing a supply. How did he account for this? And why, after all, did he bother to mix up commas and wretched syllables which the ladies publicly kept at arm's length?

The Author declares that these treacherous words, strewn like stones in his path, have touched the very depths of his heart. More, he protests that he is too keenly aware of his duty to fail to offer his distinguished audience arguments differing from those in the preceding prologues. Alas! it is forever necessary to reason with children until they grow up, understand things and hold their peace. Besides, among the infinite multitude of grumblers, he perceives plenty of mischievous fellows who wilfully ignore what these tales are about.

To begin with, you must know that if certain respectable ladies. . . .

(I break off to explain that I used the adjective "respectable" advisedly: lewd wenches and common women avoid these folios, preferring to live unpublished adventures. On the contrary, noble ladies and solid townswomen, being conventional and God-fearing, are doubtless disgusted at what happens, but they read on piously in order to satisfy an evil spirit. Thus they remain perfectly virtuous. Do you hear, my good reapers of horns? Better far to be made cuckold between the covers by a book than under the covers by some pretty gentleman. You escape the damage, poor cods, and, what is more, often your lady grows enamoured and applies to you to quell the fecund excitement this tome has aroused in her. Accordingly, these tales add some capital seeds to the gestation of our land, which they maintain in mirth, honor and health. I say mirth, because you may find it aplenty here. I say honor, because you save your nest from the claws of the perennially youthful demon yclept Khuckholdum in the language of the Celts. I say health, because this treatise incites you to the gentle relaxation prescribed by the Church of Salerno as a preventive to cerebral plethora. Now I challenge you to derive a similar profit from other typographically blackened folios. Ha, ha! Where are the books that produce children? Search high and low, you will not find them. What you will find, by the bushel, is children producing books that beget much boredom.)

But to go back to my phrase: you must know that if certain respectable ladies, virtuous of nature and foolish of mind, deliver themselves publicly to recriminations on the subject of these tales, on the other hand, a pleasantly large number of ladies, far from condemning the Author, confess that they prize him very dearly. He is, they say, a valiant man, worthy to be a monk in the Abbey of Thélème. For as many reasons as there are stars in the firmament, he refuses to lay down the magic flute with which he trills these lays. On the contrary, he allows himself to be impugned and goes straight to the goal, knowing that our noble France is a female who will not countenance you know what; rather, she screams and squirms about, crying:

"No, no, never! Ho, sir, what are you about there? I couldn't possibly . . . you would ruin me!"

Then, when the book is finished and done:

"Oh, sweet master!" she sighs, "will there be some more soon?"

So you may consider the Author a joyful rogue, who will not heed the lamentations and writhings of the lady you name glory, fashion or public favor. He knows her to be very much a harlot and by nature ready to make the best of a good rape. He knows that in France her war-cry is *Mount Joy!* A fine cry, undoubtedly, although certain scriveners have disfigured it; it means: "Joy is not of the earth, it is there; make haste or farewell!" This interpretation the Author holds from Rabelais, who told it to him. If you ransack history, has France ever uttered a word when she was joyously mounted, bravely mounted, furiously mounted and mounted full tilt? She is rageful in all things: she much prefers horsemanship to banqueting. What! Don't you see that these tales are French in their joy, French in their riding, French before, French behind, everywhere French? Stand back then, churls; a flourish of trumpets! Silence, bigots! Step forward, my noble wags, my gentle pages, put your fair hands in the hands of your ladies and scratch them in the centre (of the hand, naturally). Ha, ha, ha! These are tintinnabulary and peripatetic reasons or the Author is no judge of bell-ringing and Aristotle. On his side, he has the arms of France, the King's oriflamme and My Lord St. Denis, who, having lost his head, cries: "Mount-my-Joy!" What, ye quadrupeds? Do ye pretend this word is false? Never! Of yore, several persons undoubtedly heard it; but in these utterly wretched days, you believe in nothing that concerns our good Churchmen.

The Author is not done. So then, know all ye who read these tales with hand and eye, who feel them in the head alone and love them for the joy with which they fill your hearts, know that the Author, in an evil hour, misplaced his axe, *id est,* his heritage. As it was never recovered, he found himself stripped of everything. So, like the woodcutter in the prologue of his beloved master Rabelais, he sought to make himself heard by the Gentleman on High, Lord Suzerain of all things, and to obtain another axe. This said Most High, still busy with the Congresses of the times, had Mercury throw the Author an inkstand with two cups, on which was engraved by way of a motto the three letters: *Ave.* The poor lad, perceiving no other help, took great pains to work upon this inkstand, to seek its hidden meaning, to construe its mysterious letters and to find a sense in them. At the outset he realized that God was polite, like the great Lord He is, since He owns the world in fee to no one. But as the Author recalled the days of his youth, he could think of no special service he had rendered God; he was therefore in deep perplexity about this hollow civility and he pondered long without drawing any tangible profit from this celestial tool. Then, by dint of turning the inkstand first one way, then the other, by dint of studying and examining it, filling and emptying it, knocking it with an interrogative rap, polishing it, setting it up on one end, then on another, then upside down, he read backwards *Eva.* And the Divine Voice commanded the Author:

"Think of woman; woman will heal your wound and replenish the yawning void of your bag of tricks. Woman is your wealth. Have but one woman only; dress and undress her, fondle and coddle her, exploit her. Woman is everything. She has an inkstand of her own; drive your quill deep into this bottomless well. Woman loves Amour; make love to her, quill in inkwell; tickle her fancies and, for her sake, portray pleasurably the thousand aspects of love in its million blissful variations. Woman is generous; all for one and one for all; she will pay the painter and furnish the hairs for his brush. Finally elaborate upon the written theme: *Ave,* Hail, lo!—*Eva,* woman. Or *Eva,* woman—*Ave,* hale, high! Ay, truly, she makes and unmakes. Here is the quill, then; give me the inkwell. What is it woman loves best? What is it she craves? Love, in all its specialties. And quite right she is, too! To bear children, to reproduce is to imitate nature, which is forever arutting. Then heigh-ho, woman, this way! Come here, Eva, to me!"

Thereupon the Author settled down to plumb this fertile inkstand, which held a cerebral mash, concocted in talismanic fashion by virtues from above. Out of one inkwell came earnest subjects which wrote their thoughts in brown ink; out of the other, frisky maggots which shed a roseate hue over the pages of the folio. Pity the Author! How often has he mixed the inks through sheer carelessness, spilling one here, the other there. But no sooner had he completed the weighty phrases of some work suitable to the taste of the day and arduous indeed to smooth, brighten and adorn, than he longed to make sport. Despite the small amount of merry ink in the left inkwell, he boldly stole a few penfuls, delighting as he did so. This theft, then, represents these same Droll Stories, whose authority is above suspicion since it flows from a divine source. Does not the Author's naïve confession prove it?

Certain malevolent persons will still cry out at this. But where will you ever find a limb of man who is perfectly contented with this clod of mud? Is it not iniquitous? In this the Author has sagely behaved for all the world like God; he proves it by *atqui.* The wise and learned have had ample cause to know that the sovereign Lord of worlds has made an infinite number of grave, weighty and cumbersome machines with huge wheels, heavy chains, terrible expansion springs and horrendously complicated systems of screws and weights on the principle of the turnspit. But He has likewise taken pleasure in delicate trifles and grotesqueries, light as air; He has incontrovertibly produced guileless and agreeable creations which make you laugh as you look at them. Therefore, in all concentric works such as the very spacious edifice undertaken by the Author, it is necessary to follow the laws set down by the aforesaid Lord. In other words, the Author must fashion certain dainty flowers, charming insects and noble dragons, imbricated, brilliantly colored and even gilt, though all too often he has no gold to gild them with. Then he must toss these at the feet of his snowy mountains, his craggy heaps and other cloud-capped philosophies, lengthy and terrible works, marble colonnades and genuine precepts graven in porphyry.

Well then, ye unclean beasts who decry and repudiate jocularity, phantasy, puns and verbal gymnastics, all the tunes and roulades of the sweet muse of drollery, will ye not gnaw away your claws and give over rending her white flesh, the azure network of her veins, her amorous reins, her flanks so supremely elegant, her feet that stay so demurely abed, her satin countenance, her lustrous features and her heart, innocent of gall? Ha, blockheads, what shall ye say as ye see this blithe wench springing from the heart of France, agreeing with womanly nature, receiving the tribute of the angel's courteous *Ave!* in the person of their spokesman Mercury and finally representing the clearest quintessence of Art? This work embodies necessity, virtue, imagination, the desire of woman, the oblations of a stout Pantagruelian—everything! Hold your tongues, cheer the Author and let his double-barrelled inkstand endow the Gay Science with one hundred glorious Droll Stories.

Stand back, then, churls; a flourish of trumpets. Silence, bigots! numbskulls, avaunt! Step forward, my noble wags! my gentle pages! give your fair hands to the ladies, scratch theirs in the centre in your prettiest ways and bid them: "Read to laugh!" After, you can give them some other more delightful counsel and make them explode! For, when they are laughing, their lips are spread wide and they offer but the slightest resistance to love.

Perseverance in Love

URING the first years of the thirteenth century after the coming of Our Divine Savior, a man of Tours enacted an amorous adventure which was the talk of town and of His Majesty's Court as well. As for the clergy, the part it played in the business appears in this story. It was the clergy, too, that preserved the account of what happened.

This man, called Le Tourangeau by the common people because he was born in our blessed Touraine, was in reality named Anseau. Towards the end of his life, he returned to his birthplace and became Mayor of St. Martin according to the chronicles of abbey and town. But in Paris he was a famous goldsmith.

In his prime, through his great honesty, his labors and so on, he became a citizen of Paris and subject of the King, whose protection he bought, according to the custom of his times. He built himself a house free of all quit-rent, close to the Church of St. Leu, in the Rue St. Denis, where his forge was well known by those who sought lovely jewels. Though a scion of Touraine, with plenty of spirit to spare, he remained as virtuous as a saint in spite of the blandishments of the city; he spent the days of his green season without ever setting foot in a stew. Many will say that this surpasses the faculties of belief with which God has graced us as a help toward that faith due the mysteries of holy religion. It is therefore necessary to establish clearly the recondite motives of this goldsmith's chastity. In the first place—an important point—he had come into town on foot and poorer than Job, the old people said. Then, unlike the people from our part of the country, who flare up and burn out, Anseau had a character of iron and persevered in his ends like a monk in his vengeance. As a workman, he labored incessantly; become a master, he toiled on, forever learning new secrets, seeking new receipts, and discovering new inventions of all sorts in the process. Belated passers-by, men of the watch and ruffians could always see a demure light shining through his window and the good goldsmith working with some apprentice, tapping, sculping, clipping, chiselling, filing and modelling away, his door closed, his ears open. Poverty engendered hard work, hard work engen-

dered his notable virtue, which, in turn, engendered great riches. Ponder this, ye children of Cain, who devour doubloons and spirt water. If the excellent man was seized by such wild desires as assail a lonely bachelor now and then, when the Devil seems about to triumph over a sign of the cross, he would hammer away at his metal again, sublimating the unruly spirits as he set to fashioning the exquisite masterpieces, the delicate engravings, the golden figures and silver moulds which cooled the fury of his Venus. Furthermore, he was no slyboots but rather a man of simple understanding, fearing God first, next thieves, then noble-men and a row above all else. He had two hands, but he never did more than one thing at a time; he was as soft-spoken as a bride before marriage. Though clergy, officers and others did not deem him learned, he knew his mother's Latin and spoke it to the point without waiting to be asked. Life among the Parisians had taught him to walk straightforwardly, not to beat the bush for others, to measure his passions by the yardstick of his reve-nues, to suffer none to make a cat's paw of him, to feather his nest, to look at both sides of the shield, never to say what he did but always to do what he said, to shed nothing but water, to be more mindful than flies usually are, to hug his sorrow—and his purse!—to himself, to eschew sky-gazing when he walked down a street, and to sell his jewels for more than they cost him—sage counsels all, which, as he observed them prudently, gave him enough wisdom to transact his business agreeably and profit-ably. Which he did, without bothering a soul. And as they watched this worthy little man living his life, many said:

"Upon my faith, I wouldn't mind being in that goldsmith's shoes though I had to wade up to the knee in the sewers of Paris for a century."

They might as well have wished to be the King of France, for Anseau had great, sinewy, powerful arms and so wondrously strong a grip that when he closed his fist a pair of pincers worked by the most brawny bravo could not have made him open it. Thus anything he ever caught hold of was indisputably his. More, he had teeth fit to chew iron, a stomach to dissolve it, in-testines to digest it, a sphincter to expel it again without wrench-ing, and shoulders stout enough to bear the burden of the world, like that pagan nobleman to whom this duty was of yore en-trusted and whom the advent of Jesus Christ relieved in good time. He was, truth to tell, one of those men who were made at one stroke. They are the best; the others, who need retouching, are useless, because they are patched up and finished off at odd times. In a word, Maître Anseau was a man, dyed in the grain, with the face of a lion and, under his shaggy brows, a glance ar-dent enough to melt gold, if his forge ever failed him. But a limpid moisture dropped in his eyes by the Moderator of all things tempered this great ardor, without which Anseau would have burned everything up. Was he not a splendid specimen of manhood?

Given this sample of his cardinal virtues, some critics will persist in asking why the good goldsmith remained as celibate as an oyster, seeing that such properties of nature are highly useful in all places? But do these opinionated censurers really know what to love is? Ho, ho! A plague on them! The business of a lover is to come and go, to listen, to watch, to hold his tongue, to talk, to creep into a corner, to make himself big, to make himself little, to make himself nothing; to be pleasant, to make music, to toil and moil, to fetch the Devil wherever he lodge, to count gray peas on a sorting-board, to find flowers under the snow, to say paternosters to the moon, to stroke the pet cat and pat the pet dog, to greet family friends, to flatter the maiden aunt's gout or her catarrh and to tell her at opportune times:

"What splendid health is yours! Ah, you will still live to write the epitaph of humankind."

The business of a lover is to sense what will please his sweetheart's relatives, to tread on no one's toes, to break no glasses, to square the circle, to make bricks without straw, to whisper pleasant nothings, to hold ice in his hands, to enthuse over gew-gaws, to cry: "Ah, that is excellent!" or "Truly, Madame, you are very lovely thus!" And he must vary this in a hundred thousand ways. It is likewise his business to ruffle and starch himself up like a nobleman, to have a ready and prudent tongue, to endure with a smile all the evils the Devil visits upon him, to stifle his anger, to hold his nature in leash, to have the finger of God and the tail of Satan, to make gifts to the mother, to make presents to the cousin, to reward the servant, in a word, always to put his best foot forward. Otherwise the wench vanishes, leaving him high and dry, without so much as a Christian reason. Indeed, take the lover of the sweetest maid God ever created in a moment of great good humor, let him talk like a noble book, hop like a flea, spin like a die, strum like King David, execute the hundred thousand turns of Hell and build her the Corinthian order of the columns of Beelzebub, if he fails in the radical and secret thing which most pleases his lady (often she herself does not know it, however much she may need to) then she flees him as she would flee red leprosy. That is her privilege; no man could brook objec-

tion. When this occurs, some men become cross, irate, more infatuated than you can possibly imagine. Several have actually
slain themselves over the recoil of a petticoat. Here man distin-
guishes himself from the beast, since no animal ever yet lost his
senses through despair of love, which proves conclusively that
beasts have no souls. Accordingly, the business of a lover is a job
for a mountebank, a swashbuckler, a charlatan, a buffoon, a
prince, an oaf, a king, a loafer, a monk, a dupe, a gallows' bird, a
liar, a braggart, a sycophant, a nincompoop, a giddyhead, a gaby,
a noodle or a rapscallion. It is an occupation from which Jesus
abstained; people of lofty intelligence follow His example. It is a
pursuit in which a man of worth is required to expend, before
all else, his time, his life, his blood, his noblest eloquence, not to
mention his heart, his soul and his brain. For women are cruelly
avid of all these things because, no sooner their tongues start
wagging than they tell each other that short of possessing the
whole of a man, they have none of him. You may be sure that
there are vixens who glower and grumble when a man moves
Heaven and earth and raises very Hell for them. Can he do no
more, they wonder, as their lust of conquest and their spirit of
tyranny demand the absolute limit? This exalted jurisprudence
has always flourished among the customs of Paris, where women
receive more wit at their baptism than anywhere else in the
world, and are thus malicious at birth.

Our goldsmith, always busy burnishing gold and melting silver in his shop, had never a chance to melt a maiden's heart and
burnish or polish his desires. Nor could he dress like a fop, parade about, waste his substance in mischief or seek a mould with
ears. In Paris virgins do not fall into the beds of young men any
more than roasted peacocks fall into the streets, even when these
young men are royal goldsmiths. Anseau thus was fortunate
enough, as has been said before, to find a greenhorn under his
shirt. Yet when the excellent man was debating the price of his
jewels, he could not close his eyes to the advantages of nature
which his clients—ladies or townswomen—possessed generously
and valued highly. Often after having listened to the sweet
wheedling of women who wished some favor of him, Anseau
would stroll home through the streets, dreamy as a poet and
more desperate than a vagrant cuckoo. At such times: "I ought

to take a wife unto myself," he would muse, "she would keep the house clean, have the plates hot for me at mealtime, look after my linen, sew my clothes, sing blithely about the house, tease me until I did everything to her taste. And she would tell me as all of them tell their husbands when they want a jewel: 'Eh, but darling! Look at this one! Isn't it pretty?' And everyone in the quarter, thinking of my wife, then of myself, would exclaim: 'There's a happy man for you!' "

He saw himself married, enjoying the wedding festivities, caressing Madame Goldsmith . . . dressing her superbly, fastening a chain of gold about her neck, loving her from crown to toe . . . granting her entire government of the household (money excepted), settling her in his fine upstairs room, with splendid windows, good carpets, handsome tapestries and a marvellous chest in it . . . laying her in a huge bed with twisted columns and curtains of lemon-colored sendal . . . buying her the most beautiful mirrors. . . . By the time he reached home, there were always ten or twelve children, born effortlessly to them. But, when he crossed the threshold, wife and children vanished as he set to work. His melancholy imaginings he would transform into fantastic designs; his dreams of love assumed the shape of curious jewels which delighted his customers. How could they know what armies of women and children were lost in the poor man's handicraft? How could they guess that the more talent he threw into his art, the more he grieved? Had God failed to take pity on him, he would have left this world without knowing what love was; though he would of course have learned it in the next world without that metamorphosis of flesh which spoils it, according to Master Plato, a man of considerable authority who erred in that he was not a Christian. But la! this preparatory confabulation is but an idle digression and a fastidious commentary which miscreants force a man to wrap around a tale as a mother wraps swaddling clothes around a child instead of letting it run about stark naked. May the mighty Devil give them an enema with his triple red fork! I shall proceed to tell my story without further circumlocution.

This is what happened to the goldsmith in the forty-first year of his life. One Sunday, while he strolled on the left bank of the Seine, musing of marriage, he ventured as far as the meadowland, which has since been called the Pré aux Clercs, but which in those days lay in the domain of the Abbey of St. Germain and not in the University's. Sauntering on, Anseau found himself in the open fields. Presently he met a poor young girl, who, observing that he was well-dressed, curtseyed and said: "God preserve you, My Lord." Such heartfelt sweetness was in her tone that the goldsmith's senses reeled at the girlish melody. Then and there he conceived a love for her which proved the more intense since, craving marriage as he did, he found everything propitious to that end. But, having already passed her, he dared not go back, for he was shy as a maid who would die in her petticoats rather than raise them for her own delight. Still, when he was about a bowshot off, he decided that a master goldsmith of ten years' standing, a citizen of Paris and a man twice the age of an old dog might permissibly confront a woman. Besides, his imagination egged him on. He therefore veered back, as if he had changed the objective of his stroll and was soon face to face with the girl again. She held her wretched cow by a frayed cord; the animal was cropping the grass that had grown up along the green bank of a ditch by the roadside.

"Ah, my dear," he said, "how very ill-provided you are with the goods of the world to be doing such handiwork on the Lord's day! Are you not afraid of being thrown into prison?"

"My Lord," she replied, looking down meekly, "I have nothing to fear: I belong to the Abbey. My Lord Abbot gave us leave to walk the cow after Vespers."

"Then you hold your cow dearer than the salvation of your soul?"

"Ah, My Lord, our beast is worth at least half our miserable lives."

"I am amazed, my girl, to see that you are so poor and ragged . . . out at elbows and barefoot . . . traipsing through the fields of a Sunday. . . . For you carry about you more treasures than ever you pass by in the whole estate of the Abbey. Surely the townsmen must pursue you and plague you with love?"

"No, no, My Lord: I belong to the Abbey," she explained, as she showed him a circlet around her left arm. It was the kind of band a beast wears, but without the bell attached. As she did so, she cast such a pathetic glance at Anseau that he was filled with melancholy. Are not contagions of the heart, when they are strong, communicated through the eyes?

"What does that mean?" he asked, wishing to know all about her.

"My Lord, I am the daughter of a bondsman. Thus any man

bound to me in wedlock would fall into bondage; were he even a townsman of Paris, he would belong body and goods to the Abbey. If he loved me otherwise, our children would still belong to the Abbey. That is why everyone shuns me and I am abandoned like a poor dumb beast of the fields. But what hurts me most is that I may be coupled with a bondsman at any time or place at

My Lord Abbot's good pleasure. Alas! were I less ugly than I am, the mere sight of my band would put the most ardent suitor to flight as surely as the black death."

She tugged at her cord, drew the cow on.

"How old are you?" asked the goldsmith.

"I cannot tell your worship. But My Lord Abbot has a record of it."

Such profound misery touched the heart of the good man, who had long broken the bread of misfortune in his own life. He swung into step with the girl and the pair moved towards the river amid a pregnant silence. The townsman observed all the purity of the maiden's brow, her red, lithe arms, her queenly figure and her feet, dusty but shaped like those of a Virgin Mary; fondly he gazed upon her gentle countenance. Here was the living image of St. Geneviève, patroness of the city of Paris and protectress of such maids as dwell in the fields. To be sure, this Simon-pure greenhorn did not fail to divine the exquisite, white beauties of her breasts, which, in modest grace, were covered by a mean cloth. Very longingly he coveted them as a schoolboy covets a rosy apple on a hot day. Nor was there any doubt possible but that these charmed slopes of nature denoted a wench fashioned in delicious perfection, like everything the monks possess. So the more strictly forbidden this lush fruit of love was to his touch, the more his mouth thirsted for it. The mere thought brought his heart leaping to his throat.

"That's a fine cow of yours!" he remarked.

"Would you like a little milk? It's very warm these early May days! And you are far from town."

In point of fact, the sky was blue, cloudless, and fiery as a forge; everything—leaves, air, maids and greenhorns—was radiant with youth; everything was aglow, verdant and redolent of balm. The goldsmith felt his heart melt at this naïve, utterly disinterested offering (how could even a bezant of gold requite the extraordinary grace of her speech?). Then her modesty of gesture as she turned made him long to place this bondsmaid in a queen's skin and lay all Paris at her feet.

"No, no, my dear, it is not milk I thirst for, but you! I would I had leave to free you!"

"That may not be and I shall die the chattel of the Abbey.

Very long we have lived so from father to son, from mother to daughter. Ay, I shall spend all my life on this land, just as my poor forefathers before me and my children, after, for the Abbey will not suffer us to go childless."

"What!" cried the goldsmith, "have your bright eyes moved no gallant to try buying your freedom, just as I bought mine from the King?"

"No, it would cost too dear! So those whom I please at first sight go away even as they came."

"And you never dreamed of escaping to another land with a lover on a fiery steed?"

"Yes, I have dreamed. . . . But if I were caught, My Lord, I would hang for it at the very least. And even were he a nobleman, my gallant would lose more than one estate for it, not to mention the rest! I am not worth such riches. Besides, the Abbey's arm is more far-reaching than my feet are swift. So I live on in perfect obedience to God, Who has willed this existence for me."

"What does your father do?"

"He tends the vines in the Abbey grounds."

"And your mother?"

"She is a laundress."

"What is your name?"

"I have no name, dear My Lord. My father was baptized Étienne, my mother is l'Étienne and I am Tiennette, at your service."

"My love," said the goldsmith, "never has woman pleased me as you do; I believe your heart is a mine of riches. Now since you appeared before me just as I was earnestly deliberating upon taking a mate, I am convinced that I am vouchsafed a sign from Heaven. If I am not displeasing to you, I beg you to accept me as your lover."

Tiennette again lowered her glance. The words were proffered so gravely, in so earnest a tone and so compelling a manner that she burst into tears.

"No, My Lord," she replied, "I would cause you a thousand misfortunes. . . . I would bring about your unhappiness! With a wretched bondsmaid, let words suffice you."

"Ho, my child!" cried Anseau, "you do not know what manner of man you are dealing with!"

Anseau crossed himself, joined his hands and said:

"I hereby make a vow to My Lord St. Éloi, patron saint of goldsmiths, to fashion two niches of vermilion silver, adorned with the finest workmanship I am able to muster. One shall be for a statue of Our Lady the Virgin as a thanks-offering for the freedom of my beloved wife; the other shall house my said patron, if I am successful in my undertaking to liberate the bondsmaid Tiennette, here present—an undertaking in which I rely upon his assistance. Furthermore, I swear by my eternal salvation to pursue this quest bravely, to spend all I possess therein, and to abandon it only with my life. God has undoubtedly heard me," he added, "and so have you, my love."

He turned towards the girl.

"Oh, look, My Lord! . . . there goes my cow . . . she's running away!" The girl clung to Anseau's knees, sobbing. "I will love you all my life, but take back your vow."

"Let us catch the cow," answered the goldsmith raising her to her feet but afraid, still, to kiss her, though she was quite disposed to it.

"Yes!" Tiennette answered, "they would beat me if . . ."

Anseau darted after the cursed cow, which cared little for lovers; soon he held her by the horns in a vise of iron and would for a snap of the fingers have tossed her cheerfully through the air like a straw.

"Farewell, my love. If you go to town, come to my house, close to St. Leu. I am called Maître Anseau; I am goldsmith to the King of France, at the *Sign of St. Éloi*. Promise me to be in this field next Lord's Day. I shall not fail to come though it rain pitchforks."

"Ay, good My Lord; for this I would leap over the hedges! And, in gratitude, I would be yours without mischief, nor cause you prejudice, at the price of my future salvation. Until that blessed hour, I shall pray God for you with all my soul."

She remained standing there like a stone saint, never moving until Anseau, who went off slowly, and turned frequently to gaze at her, was out of sight. Long after he had disappeared and was far off, she stood on until nightfall, in rapt meditation, wondering if she had not dreamed the things that had befallen her. When at last she returned home very late, she was thrashed for tarrying in the fields. But she felt never a blow.

Anseau meanwhile could neither eat nor drink. Desperate with love, he shut up shop, his every step haunted by the thought of Tiennette.

On the morrow, his first move was to rush in great apprehension to the Abbey to speak to the Lord Abbot. But, on the way, he very wisely decided to seek the protection of some favorite of

the King's, and, with this purpose in view, returned to Paris, where Court was then being held.

Anseau was esteemed by all for his prudence and much loved for his delicate talent and his pleasant ways. He went to the King's Chamberlain, for one of whose mistresses he had recently fashioned a golden casket set with precious stones and unique in its way; My Lord promised his help, and a horse saddled for himself and a hackney for Anseau, and proceeded forthwith to the Abbey. Here he asked for the Abbot, Monseigneur Hugon de Senecterre, who was then ninety-three years old. Having been admitted into the prelate's presence, with a very breathless, nervous goldsmith in his wake, My Lord Chamberlain begged the Abbot to grant him in advance a favor both easy and pleasant to vouchsafe. The prelate shook his head and replied that the Canons definitely and formally forbade him thus to pledge his word.

"Here, my dear Father," said the Chamberlain, "here stands the Court goldsmith who has conceived a great love for a bonds-maid belonging to your Abbey. In return for my promise to grant any service you may care to ask of me, I do entreat you to free this girl."

"Who is she?" the Abbot asked Anseau.

"Her name is Tiennette," the other answered meekly.

"Humph!" said old Hugon smiling, "there's bait that has drawn us a good catch! This is a serious case; I could not possibly pass upon it alone."

"I know what these words mean, Father," said the Chamberlain, with a frown.

"My Lord," the Abbot asked, "do you know what this maid is worth?"

The Abbot sent for Tiennette, telling his clerk to dress her in her finest clothes and show off her radiant beauty.

"Your love is in great danger," the Chamberlain told Anseau as he drew him aside. "Forgo that vain whim! Everywhere, even at Court, you can meet women of position—young and pretty ones, too—who would gladly marry you. If necessary His Majesty will help you to acquire some title, which, in time, would allow you to found an excellent family. You have money enough to become the head of a noble house?"

"I could not, My Lord," Anseau replied, "I have made a vow!"

"Well then, try and buy the girl's freedom. I know the monks. With them, money does anything."

"My Lord," the goldsmith advanced toward the Abbot, "your charge and office is to represent God's mercy here below, Who is often clement towards us and Who possesses infinite treasures of loving-kindness against our wretchedness. Now I shall remember you in my prayers, day and night, for the rest of my life, nor shall I ever forget how it was your charity brought about my happiness, if you will aid me to enjoy this maid in lawful wedlock, without maintaining in bondage the children born of our union. For this, I will make you a casket for the holy Eucharist so elaborate, so rich with gold, precious stones and winged angels that it shall not have its match in all the length and breadth of Christendom. It shall remain unique, it shall delight your sight, it shall bring such glory to your altar that townsmen and foreign lords shall rush to behold it in all its magnificence."

"My son," cried the Abbot, "have you taken leave of your senses? If you are determined to have this girl as your lawful wife, then both your possessions and your person belong to the Chapter of the Abbey."

"Ay, My Lord; I am madly in love with this unfortunate maid; her very misery and her gentle Christian heart move me even more poignantly than her perfections do. Yet," he added, as the tears rose to his eyes, "I am still more amazed at your harshness; and I say so though I know that my fate lies in your hands. Alas! My Lord, I know the law. But if my possessions must needs fall to your domain, if I become a bondsman, if I forfeit house and citizenship, I will not give up the talent I have acquired through long study and labor. It rests there," he struck his forehead, "in a place none save God may be lord of . . . none save God and myself! Nor could your whole Abbey begin to pay for the original creations it can produce. My body, my wife, my children—these you shall have; but nothing shall bring you my skill, not even torture, since my strength is greater than the sharpest iron and my patience greater than the bitterest suffering."

As Anseau observed the Abbot's calm and realized how firmly the latter resolved to turn all his hard-earned doubloons into the Abbey treasury, a fierce rage came over him. He punctuated the climax of his speech with a vigorous bang of his fist on an oaken chair, which burst into a thousand fragments as surely as though he had struck it with a mace.

"There, My Lord," he concluded, "that is the sort of servant you shall have, when, out of a craftsman of divine masterpieces, you will have made a mere beast of burden."

"My son," the Abbott answered, "you have wrongfully broken my chair and lightly passed judgment on my soul. This girl belongs to the Abbey, not to me; I am but a faithful servant to the rights and customs of this glorious monastery. Even though I might grant this woman's loins the right to bear free children, I still stand responsible on this head both to God and to the Abbey. Now ever since an altar, bondsmen and monks have existed here, *id est*, from time immemorial, no townsman has ever been known to become the property of the Abbey through marriage with a bondswoman. We must therefore strictly adhere to our privilege of exercising this right; we must never allow it to lose its strength, to fall into decay, to fail by growing obsolete—which would occasion a thousand difficulties. This is of far greater advantage to the State and to our Abbey than your caskets, be these ever so beautiful, for we possess a treasure wherewith to purchase costly jewels, whereas no treasure can possibly establish customs and laws. I call upon His Majesty's Chamberlain to bear witness to what infinite trouble our sovereign takes in fighting for the establishment of his decrees."

"That's said to close my mouth!" murmured the Chamberlain.

Anseau, who was no deep thinker, remained pensive. Then Tiennette came, bright as a housewife's prize silver, her hair gathered up around her head; she wore a white woolen dress with a sky-blue girdle, dainty shoes and white stockings. So regally beautiful she was, and so stately her bearing, that Anseau stood there in sheer ecstasy before her and My Lord Chamberlain vowed that he had never laid eyes on so perfect a creature. The mere sight of the girl, he thought, was too fraught with danger for the luckless goldsmith; he bundled Anseau off to town in short order begging him to think the matter over again very seriously since My Lord Abbot would never give up a bait so enticing to the townsmen and lords of the body Parisian.

The Chapter soon conveyed its decision: if he married Tiennette, the wretched swain must not only yield his goods and his house to the Abbey, but also recognize himself a bondsman and bondsmen, too, any children that might be born of this union. By special favor, however, My Lord Abbot permitted Anseau to remain in his house, provided he supplied an inventory of his furniture and paid a yearly rent. Furthermore, in order to qualify by action as a bondsman, Anseau must each year spend one week in a hovel belonging to the Abbey. Everybody spoke to the goldsmith of the monks' obstinacy; he realized that the Abbot would incommutably maintain this decree; he despaired to the point of losing his mind. Now he wished to set fire to the monastery; now he proposed to lure the Abbot to a lonely spot and there torture him until he had signed an order freeing Tiennette. A thousand schemes stormed his imagination and evaporated into so many futile fancies. After much grieving, he decided to abduct the girl and fly with her to some safe place whence nothing could draw him; he went so far as to make the necessary preparations, certain that, with him out of the kingdom, his friends or the King could dress the monks better and bring them to reason. But the good man was reckoning without his Abbot. When he went to the fields, Tiennette was not there; he learned that they had so thoroughly confined her in the Abbey that he would have had to storm the monastery to get at her. At this Maître Anseau filled the air with tears, complaints and lamentation. In town, goodmen and housewives spoke much of the adventure; rumor of it actually reached the King, who summoned the aged Abbot to Court. His Majesty inquired of the prelate why he would not yield under the circumstances before Anseau's great love and thus put the tenets of Christian charity into practise.

"Sire," the Abbot answered, "all rights are knit together as close as the various pieces of a suit of armor. Loose one and all collapse. Were this maid taken from us against our will, were tradition defied, your subjects would very soon be taking your crown from off your head and rising everywhere in rebellion against the dues and taxes that burden the populace."

The King's lips were sealed. Everyone anxiously awaited the outcome of the adventure. The general curiosity reached fever point; some lords wagered that Anseau would abandon his love-quest and the ladies wagered the contrary. Our goldsmith went to the Queen and complained tearfully that the monks kept his sweetheart hidden away from him. Her Majesty found the act merciless and detestable. At her command, My Lord Abbot allowed Anseau to see Tiennette in the Abbey parlor every day, but always under the supervision of an old monk and always Tiennette appeared clad in great splendor like a noblewoman. The lovers could do no more than see and speak to each other; never a chance was vouchsafed them to snatch the tiniest crumb of pleasures. Their love waxed all the more ardent for it. One day Tiennette said to her lover:

"My blessed Lord, I have determined to make you a gift of my life in order to lighten your suffering. This is how I shall do it. By making inquiries about everything, I have found a loophole through which I can cheat the Abbey of its rights while giving you all the joy you expect of my furniture. The Judge Ecclesiastical declared that, as you are not a bondsman by birth but only by accession, your servitude will cease with the cause that made you a serf. Now if you love me more than all else, give up your goods for the sake of our happiness and let us get married. After, when you have had joy of me, when you have loved and whelmed me to your heart's content, before I have offspring I will kill myself. Thus you will become free again. At least in such a plea you would have the King on your side: and His Majesty, they say, wishes you well. God, certainly, will forgive me for having brought about my own death in order to deliver my lord husband."

"My dear Tiennette," the goldsmith cried, "the matter is settled: I will be a bondsman; you will live to make my happiness as long as I live. With you beside me, the heaviest chains will weigh but lightly on me; and little I care about being penniless, since all my wealth lies in your heart and all my pleasure in your sweet body. I pin my faith on My Lord St. Éloi, who will deign to look pitifully upon us in our misery and keep us safe from every harm. I am going to the scrivener's forthwith to get contracts and deeds drawn up. At least, O blessed flower of my days, you will be nobly clad, comfortably lodged and served like a queen throughout your lifetime, since My Lord Abbot allows us to enjoy what I have earned."

Tiennette wept, laughed, struggled against her own happiness and wished to die rather than reduce a free man to bondage. But the excellent Anseau whispered such soft-sweet words and threatened so steadfastly to follow her to the grave that she agreed to the marriage, remembering that she could always kill herself after she had tasted the bliss of love.

When news of Anseau's submission spread through the town and the citizens learned that the goldsmith was abandoning possessions and liberty for his sweetheart's sake, everyone sought to see him. For a chance to talk to him, the ladies of the Court encumbered themselves with jewels; enough women now fell as from the clouds upon him to make up for all the long days he had gone without them. But if some may possibly have matched Tiennette in beauty, none had her heart. At last, when the hour of love and bondage was at hand, Anseau melted all his gold into a royal crown, studded it with all his pearls and diamonds, and gave it secretly to the Queen, saying:

"Madame, I know not where to place this fortune you behold. Tomorrow everything that is found in my house will belong to those cursed monks who have had no pity on me. Deign, therefore, to keep this for me. It is but scant return for the happiness I obtained when, through your kindness, I was able to see the maid I love. For never a treasure is worth a single glance from her eyes. What will become of me, I cannot tell. But if some day my children were to be freed, I trust in your queenly generosity."

"Well spoken, goodman," said the King. "Some day the Abbey will need my help; nor shall I forget this!"

A huge crowd filled the Abbey on their wedding-day. The Queen presented Tiennette with the bridal dress; the King granted her leave to wear golden earrings every day of the year. When the pretty couple proceeded from the Abbey to St. Leu, to the house where Anseau—a serf, now—lived, there were torches at every window to light him on his way and the streets were lined with rows of people as though for a royal entry. The luckless groom had forged himself a silver band, which he wore on his left arm, as a symbol of his bondage to the Abbey of St. Germain. But despite his servitude, the populace cried, "Noël, Noël!" as though to hail a new-crowned king. Very gracefully the bridegroom bowed to them, happy as only a lover can be, and overjoyed at the tributes one and all paid to his wife's modesty and grace. Green boughs and blue cornflowers hung in crowns over the sign of his shop. The leading townsmen of his quarter were all there, and, as a great honor, made music for him and cried:

"You will always be a noble man in spite of the Abbey."

Need you ask whether the couple waged love's sweet warfare to the very death? Our goldsmith fleshed many a doughty lance against his sweetheart's buckler and, like a fine country maiden, Tiennette was of a nature to give as good as she got. For a whole month they lived on thus, tender as doves, who, in the springtime, build their nest twig by twig. Tiennette was deliriously happy, both with her new house and with the clients who came to see her and went away marvelling. This month of flowers past, one day the worthy old Abbot Hugon, their lord and master,

came to see them amid great pomp. As he entered the house—
no longer the goldsmith's, now, but the property of the Abbey—
the prelate said:

"Children, you are quit, free, and exempt from everything. I
must add that from the very first, I was greatly struck by the love
which bound you together. The rights of the Abbey once recognized, I had privately resolved to make you utterly happy after
I had tested your loyalty in God's crucible. Nor shall this manu-
mission cost you a penny."

So saying, he gave each of them a little tap on the cheek. They
fell to their knees, weeping tears of joy for reasons obvious
enough. The goldsmith informed his neighbors of the good Abbot's largess and benediction; they assembled in the streets to do
him honor. Then, with a great show of respect, Maître Anseau
led My Lord Abbot's mare by the rein as far as the gate of Bussy.
On the way, the goldsmith who had picked up a bag of silver,
threw pieces to the poor and suffering, crying: "Largess, largess
to God! God save and guard the good Abbot! Long live My Lord
Abbot Hugon!"

Returning to his house, he banqueted his friends and gave a
new wedding entertainment that lasted a full week. Of course
the Abbot's clemency was much censured by a Chapter whose
jaw was opened to snap up such a splendid prey. So when Hugon
fell ill about a year later, the Prior assured him that here was a
punishment from Heaven because he had betrayed the sacred
interests of Chapter and God.

"If I have judged this man rightly," the Abbot replied, "he
will remember what he owes us."

In effect, that day happening to be the anniversary of Anseau's
marriage, a monk came to announce that the goldsmith craved an
audience of his benefactor. Anseau was duly admitted, bearing
two marvellous shrines, which no workman has since surpassed
in any place in Christendom and which were accordingly named
"The Vow of Perseverance in Love." As everyone knows, these
two treasures stand on the master altar of the church; they are
considered to be an inestimable work, for the goldsmith had
spent all his wealth upon them. Nevertheless, this offering, far
from emptying his purse, filled it to overflowing—his fame and
profits increased so speedily that he actually bought a patent of

nobility, acquired many estates, and founded the house of Anseau which has since been held in great honor in the fair land of Touraine.

Which teaches us always to rely on the saints and on God in all the undertakings of this life, and to persevere in all such things as are recognized to be good. It teaches us, further, that a great love triumphs over everything, which is an ancient maxim; but the Author has set it down because it is a most pleasant one.

Of the Provost's Poor Memory for Things

IN THE days ere he laid aside the quest of pleasure to conquer a kingdom—and conquer it he did—our monarch used to wanton in the good town of Bourges. At this period, a provost lived there, charged by His Majesty to maintain order and known as the Provost Royal. (Later, under this said King's glorious son, the office became that of Provost of the Household; it was somewhat too harshly filled by the Seigneur de Méré, Tristan by name, whom these tales mention though he was anything but a merry blade. I supply this information for such friends as pilfer from ancient manuscripts in order to piddle out novelties and I thereby show how learned these tales are though they may not appear so.)

Well, then, this Provost was called Picot or Picault, whence people manufactured the words *picotin* (a peck of oats), *picorer* (to plunder) and *picoter* (to prick, peck or tingle). Some knew him as Pitot or Pitaut, whence came the word *pitance* (a pittance); others in the Provençal tongue, as Pichot, from which nothing worthwhile has come. Others, again, named him Petiot or Petiet, as in the Langue d'Oil, the language which became modern French; still others, Petitot, Petinault or Petiniaud, the current appellation in Limousin, the country about Limoges. But at Bourges he was called Petit, a name eventually adopted by his family which bred very freely, since everywhere you find *des Petit*—people called Petit—not to mention *des petits*—children. So Petit he shall be in this adventure. I have established this etymology in order to cast light upon our language and illustrate how townsmen and others finally acquired their names. But enough of science! . . .

This official, who had as many names as there were provinces

represented at Court, was by nature, too, a little squirt of a man,
dusted off so poorly by his mother that, when he tried to laugh,
he pursed up his chops as cows truss themselves up preparatory
to making water. At Court, they called this facial manœuvre the

Provost's smile. Hearing certain lords proffer this proverbial expression one day:

"You err, gentles," the King said jokingly, "Petit is not laughing; the trouble is that he's short of hide below the lips."

This false laugh of Petit's made him all the more suited to
play the policeman and catch evildoers. He was, on the whole,
worth the labor he had cost. For all malice, he was a mite cuckold; for all vice, he used to go to Vespers; for all wisdom, he be-

lieved in God when he could; for all joy, he had a wife at home; for all recreation from joy, he looked for a man to hang. Nor, when requested to produce one, did he ever fail. But when he lay abed, slumbering behind the curtains, he never bothered his head about thieves. I defy you to find a less maleficent provost in all constabulo-justiciary Christendom. No, all provosts hang either too much or too little; this exemplar hanged just as much as was necessary to be a provost.

Now this excellent petty Justiciar or this excellent Justiciar Petit held in lawful wedlock one of the most beautiful women of Bourges—a circumstance which amazed him as much as it did everybody else. Often, then, on his way to the gallows, he would ask God the same question as many a man in town asked, namely, why he, Petit, Justiciar and Provost Royal, had to himself, Petit, Provost Royal and Justiciar, a female so wondrously formed and so richly endowed with charms that a very donkey brayed with delight to see her pass by? To this, God vouchsafed no reply and doubtless had His reasons. But the slanderous tongues of the town replied for God that an interval of a span separated the wench from perfect maidenhood when she became Petit's wife. Others added that she was not his exclusive property. The wags suggested that asses often got into the prettiest stables. Each brought a few drams of banter and the lot would have made a good ton of ridicule had anybody taken the trouble to gather them. From this ton, however, nearly twenty hundred-weight would have to be deducted, inasmuch as Petit's wife was a virtuous housewife with a lover for pleasure and her husband for duty. How many can you find in town as chary of heart and lip? Produce one for me and I'll give you pence or punce, whichever you like. For you will undoubtedly find some women who have neither husband nor lover; others have a lover and no husband; ugly women have a husband and no lover. But verily, to meet with a woman who, possessing both a husband and a lover, keeps to the deuce without trying for the trey, there is a miracle, do you hear, you ninnies, you gabies, you oaves! Therefore inscribe the name of Madame Petit upon the tablets of your memory in raised and golden characters; then go your ways, let me go mine.

Our worthy Madame Petit was not one of those women who are forever on the go, hurrying and scurrying hither and yon, unable to keep still a moment, flittering and fluttering about, boiling and spoiling, helter-skelter, holus-bolus, with nothing to hold them down or steady them; she was not one of those women who are so light that they rush after the winds of flatulence as after their quintessence. No, on the contrary, Madame Petit was a good housewife, always sitting in her chair or reclining on her bed, handy as a candlestick, waiting for her lover when the Provost went out, waiting for the Provost when her lover departed. The dear woman never dreamed of dressing herself up to make the other goodies cringe. Pooh! she had found a better use for the merry time of youth; she put life in her joints in order to have the best time possible. Now you know the Provost and his excellent wife.

The Provost's lieutenant and aide-de-camp in the business of matrimony—a duty so heavy that it takes two men to discharge it—was a great lord and landowner who detested the King. This circumstance must be borne in mind, for it is one of the most important features of this story.

Now the Constable, a Scotsman and a rough customer, chanced to meet Madame Petit and conceived a desire to see and behold her (others said to seize and hold her) informally, towards morning, just long enough to tell his beads—which is Christianly honest or honestly Christian—in order to converse with her on the things of science or the science of things. Believing herself quite learned enough, and being, as has been said before, an honest, wise and virtuous wife, Madame Petit refused to listen to My Lord Constable. Suggestion after suggestion, argument upon argument, feint, ruse, reasoning, messenger and message, one and all fell wide of the mark. At last My Lord Constable swore by his great black cockadoodle that he would disembowel the lover, mighty lord though the latter was. But he swore nothing about the lady. This is characteristic of a good Frenchman, for in such a quandary certain other nationals, likewise offended, would lay to right and left, killing four souls where only three were involved. My Lord Constable, then, pledged his great black cockadoodle in the presence of His Majesty and Madame de Sorel, who were playing cards before supper. His Majesty was well pleased at the prospect of getting rid of a vexatious lord, without so much as a royal prayer.

"And how will you manage the thing?" Madame de Sorel asked saucily.

"Ho, ho!" replied the Constable, "you may take my word for it, Madame, I've no desire to lose my great black cockadoodle."

"And what was the great cockadoodle in those days?" I hear the reader asking.

Ha, ha! This point is clouded and obscure enough to ruin your eyesight if you scan the books of old; but the object was certainly one of considerable importance. No matter, let us put on our spectacles and ferret out what the word means. *Doodle* is a corruption of the Breton word *douille,* meaning a wench. *Coque* is not, as one might suppose, from the Latin *coccus,* a domestic animal with a red crest, but derives from *coquus,* a cook, and thence a burner, a heater, a tool or frying pan. From this word comes the French *coquin,* used to denote a rascal who is always guzzling, licking and lapping, always in a state of coction, afry and afriggle, in and out of stews, aboil and asimmer, bottoms-up, bottoms-down, tucking in and forever gorging, therefore an idler, utterly useless for any job between meals—a rascal who consequently becomes wicked and poor, which incites him to beg or to steal. From all this, the scholars must needs conclude that the great cockadoodle is a household utensil shaped like a skillet and suitable for warming up the wenches.

"Well then," went on the Constable, who was My Lord of Richmond, "I shall have the Provost sent out of town overnight to apprehend in the King's name certain rustics suspected of plotting treasonably with the English. When they hear he is to be absent, my love-birds will be happy as soldiers on furlough; then, if they indulge in a certain, particular delectation, I'll loose my Provost on the house to search it in the King's name. And I've no doubt he will arrive in time to slay our friend who pretends to have this holy friar all to himself."

"What do you mean?" Agnès de Sorel asked.

"Friar . . . fryer . . . an equivoke!" said the King, smiling.

"Let us go to supper," said Madame Agnès. "You are lewd fellows who with a single word insult citizens' wives and worthy monks."

For many a moon Madame Petit had been pining to taste pleasure for a whole night long and to cut capers at her lover's house, where she could shout at the top of her lungs without rousing the neighbors. At her own place, of course, she was afraid to make the slightest noise; she had to content herself with sippets of love, hugger-mugger snacks, cantlets and roguish morsels. She dared at most amble down amour's flowery path; she longed to be able to gallop along full-speed, nimble-legged, and heels to skyward. On the morrow, at noon, she sent the welcome tidings to her lover through her maid, whom he had frequently rewarded and who scarcely had cause to dislike him. He was, she said, to make all due preparations for their enjoyment and supper; he might be certain that the Mistress of the Provost's Rolls would be with him that evening, hungry and athirst.

"Good!" said the Lord, "tell your lady that I shall not leave her wanting in any respect."

The pages posted about the house by the villainous Constable saw the lover preparing for his gallantries and setting out viands and flagons. They hastened to their master to tell how splendidly every circumstance was running parallel to his spite. The Scotsman rubbed his hands for joy as he thought of the Provost's coup. He sent for the latter immediately, by express command of the King, bidding him return to Bourges; the Provost was to enter the nobleman's house, and there to seize an English lord, for the pair were vehemently suspected of hatching a plot of black villainy. But before executing this order, the Provost must come to the King's palace to learn what courtesy must be exercised in this case.

The Provost, happy as a king at the thought of speaking to the King, hastened home with such dispatch, that he reached town just as the first strokes of the organ pealed for the lover's Vespers. My Lord of Cuckolddom and lands adjacent—a droll liege if ever there was one—managed things so well that Madame Petit was communicating in the best of all possible fashions with her lover at exactly the time when the Provost was, to his great joy, conversing with King and Constable. Thus both husband and wife were happy—a rare thing in marriage.

As the Provost entered the King's chamber:

"I was just telling His Majesty," the Constable said to the Provost, "that every man in the kingdom has a right to kill his wife and her lover if he catches them astraddle. But our monarch, who is clement, argues that he has a right to kill the cavalier only, not the mount. Now then, you tell us, my dear Provost: what would you do if perchance you met a lord strolling in that sweet meadow whose blossoms all laws, divine and human, enjoin you alone to besprinkle and cultivate."

"I would kill both," said the Provost, "I would crush everything to atoms—the five hundred thousand devils of nature, the flower and seed, the bag, balls and skittles, the pips and the apple, the grass and the meadow, the woman and the man."

"You would be in the wrong," said the King. "That is contrary to the laws of Church and State: of the State because you would be depriving me of a subject, of the Church because you would be sending an innocent unshriven to limbo."

"Sire, I admire your profound wisdom. I clearly see you are the fountainhead of all justice."

"Then we may slay the cavalier only? Amen," cried the Constable. "Slay the cavalier! Now, Provost, go quickly to the house of the suspected lord. But, without letting yourself be hoodwinked, take care you do not fail in your duty towards him."

The Provost, confident he would be appointed Chancellor of France if he accomplished his mission satisfactorily, hastened from the château into the town, took his men-at-arms, proceeded to the nobleman's house, posted them around it, closed up every avenue of escape, opened noiselessly in the King's name, inquired of the servants where their master was and declared the latter under arrest. Then he walked upstairs alone, knocked at the door behind which the lovers were jousting with no uncertain weapons, and cried:

"Open, in the name of His Majesty the King."

The woman recognized her husband's voice; she could not but smile as she reflected that she had not waited for the King's order to do this. But terror followed swiftly on the heels of laughter. The nobleman picked up his cloak, threw it over him and went to the door. There, unaware that his life was in danger, he declared that he belonged to the Court and to His Majesty's household.

"Bah!" said the Provost, "I have strict orders from His Majesty. Under pain of being punished as a rebel, you are required to admit me instantly."

The nobleman came out into the corridor, his hand on the doorknob.

"What are you seeking here?"

"An enemy of His Majesty the King. We have received orders to deliver him up. What is more, you must come with us to the château."

"This," mused the lover, "is a piece of treachery on the part of My Lord Constable, whom my beloved sweetheart repelled. I must get us out of this scrape."

Then, turning to the Provost, he staked double or quits on the outcome.

"My friend," he reasoned with the cuckold, "you know that I hold you to be as gallant a man as a Provost possibly can be in the discharge of his duty. Now, look here: can I trust in you? The fairest lady of the Court is in there, in bed. As for Englishmen, I've not enough of one to make the breakfast of My Lord Constable who sent you here. To be frank with you, all this is part of a bet I made with My Lord Constable, and the King. They wagered they knew the lady of my heart; I wagered to the contrary. No man on earth hates the English more than I, for, as you know, they seized my estates in Picardy. Well then, Provost, is it not a dastardly trick to set justice in motion against me? Ho, ho, My Lord Constable, a Chamberlain is worth two of you: I shall make you look foolish yet. So, my dear Petit, I give you leave to rummage in every nook and cranny of my house, night and day. But come in here alone. You may look through my bedroom, move the bed about and do as you will. Only allow me to throw a cloth or a snottinger over this beautiful lady—she is in the costume of an archangel—lest you discover who her husband is."

"Willingly," said the Provost. "But I'm an old fox and I'll let no man pull my tail with impunity. I want to be certain it's really a lady of the Court and not an Englishman. For those Goddams have flesh as white and soft as women. I ought to know: I've hanged enough of them."

"Very well," the lover answered. "I am basely suspected of a crime; I needs must clear myself of it. I shall therefore implore my lady and mistress to consent to abandon her modesty for a moment. She bears me too much love to refuse to save me from

reproach. I shall beg her to turn over and thus show you a physiognomy which, compromising her, will yet suffice for you to recognize her as a noblewoman, although she be downside-up!"

"Agreed!" said the Provost.

The lady, who was listening with both ears, folded up her

clothes and hid them under the pillow; then she took off her
chemise lest her husband recognize the material, twisted her
head up in a sheet and displayed two fleshy hummocks divided
by the pearly line of her roseate spine.

"Come in, my good friend," said the lover.

The Provost looked up the chimney, opened wardrobe and
clothes chest, rummaged under the bed, through the sheets and
everywhere.

"My Lord," he said gazing at his lawful appurtenances, "I have seen young English lads with backs like that. Forgive me for discharging my duty, but I must see otherwise."

"How do you mean: otherwise?"

"Eh, but the other physiognomy, or, if you prefer, the physiognomy of the other."

"Well then, allow Madame to cover herself; she can manage to show you the minimum of what constitutes our happiness," said the lover, knowing that his sweetheart had several moles easy to recognize. "Turn your back a moment, I beg you, so that my dear lady may satisfy the conventions of decency."

The wife smiled at her lover, kissed him for his cunning, and concealed herself skilfully. The husband, confronted for the first time with what the wench never suffered him to see, was entirely convinced that, on the face of it, no English person could be so moulded short of being a charming Englishwoman.

"Ay, My Lord," he whispered in his lieutenant's ear, "that was surely a lady of the Court, for no townswoman was ever of nature so downy in leafage, so savory in the bud."

Then having searched the house and found no sign of an Englishman, the good Provost returned to the King's residence, according to orders.

"Is he dead?" asked the Constable.

"Who?"

"The man who hornified you."

"I saw only a Court lady in this nobleman's bed . . . they seemed to be enjoying themselves very thoroughly!"

"You confounded wittol, you saw this woman with your own eyes and you did not slay your rival?"

"It was not a common woman; it was a lady of the Court."

"You saw her?"

"I verified the whole at all events—and in either particular."

The King burst out laughing:

"What do you mean by that?"

"Saving your Majesty's presence, I mean to say that I verified the over and the under."

"Then you don't know the features of your own wife's physiognomies? You witless old dolt! You deserve to be hanged!"

"I hold my wife's appurtenances in too great respect to view them. Besides, she is so modest of nature that she would die before showing me the barest speck or tittle."

"Quite right!" said the King, "it was not made to be shown."

"You old cockadoodle, it was your wife!"

"My Lord Constable, she is sound asleep, poor maid!"

"Up and away, then! To horse! Let us speed to your house, and if she be there, I'll let you off with fivescore blows of the bull's pizzle."

So the Constable and the Provost rode to the latter's house in less time than a pauper would have required to empty a poor-box.

"Hallo there. Hi!"

At the noise of the men, who threatened to bring the walls down about their ears, a maidservant, yawning and stretching her arms, opened the door. Constable and Provost rushed into the room, where, with great trouble, they managed to rouse the wife. Madame Petit pretended to be vastly frightened; she had been sleeping so soundly that a little gum still clung about her lids. At which the Provost crowed triumphantly assuring My Lord Constable that he must necessarily have been fooled and that Madame Petit was a virtuous woman. In point of fact, the lady appeared to be utterly stupefied. The Constable scowled, turned and left the house.

Our excellent Provost quickly undressed; he was anxious to get to bed speedily for this adventure had brought his dear wife to his memory. While he was unharnessing, and peeling off his breeches, the wife, still astonished, asked:

"Eh, my darling husband, whence comes all this hullabaloo, what with My Lord Constable and his pages? Why did you come to see if I were sleeping? Is it to be part of the Constable's duties to see how we go about . . . ?"

"I don't know," said the Provost, interrupting to tell her what had happened to him.

"And you saw a Court lady's without my permission?" she demanded. "Oh, oh, oh. . . ."

She began to moan, lament and cry so grievously and so loud that the Provost was utterly at a loss.

"Eh, but what's the matter, my sweet? What is it? What do you want?"

"Alas, you won't love me any more now you've seen how the Court ladies are!"

"Nonsense, my love, they are great ladies. I don't mind telling you confidentially, they're devilishly great in every particular, those women!"

"Honestly?" she smiled. "Am I nicer?"

"Much nicer!" he said adaze. "There's a difference of a full span between you."

"Then they must taste deeper joys," she said, sighing, "when I—poor little thing!—yet have so much."

Thereupon the Provost sought a better argument to put to his wife and he put it so cogently that she finally allowed herself to be convinced of the great pleasure Heaven has planted in small things.

Which shows us that nothing here below can prevail against the Church of Cuckolds.

Of the Monk Amador Who Was a Glorious Abbot of Turpenay

*I*T WAS a drizzly Sunday, during the sort of weather that makes the ladies glad to stay at home because they like a certain dampness and because the men, to whom they are not averse, cling close to their skirts. In her chamber in the Château d'Amboise, the Queen sat back in her chair against the window-curtains, amusing herself by working at a piece of tapestry. But she plied her needle listlessly, preferring to watch the rain fall into the Loire and to abandon herself to silent *rêverie*. Her ladies followed her example. The King had just returned from Vespers and was chatting with the courtiers who had accompanied him from the chapel. Having finished exposing his objections, arguments and views, he turned to the Queen. She was melancholy, he thought, and her ladies also; he noted that one and all were married women.

"Heigh-ho!" he sighed. Then: "Did I not see the Abbot of Turpenay here just now?"

The prelate came forward. It was this same monk whose pleas for justice years ago so pestered King Louis the Eleventh that the monarch harshly commanded the Provost of his Household to remove Turpenay from his sight. How the petitioner escaped through Messire Tristan's fault has been related in an earlier tale which deals with that sovereign.

By this time, Turpenay's qualities had developed vigorously and fully—so much so that his wit spread a high jovial crimson over his face. He was a great favorite with the ladies, who stuffed him with wines, pastries and delicacies at the dinners, suppers and entertainments to which they invited him because every host likes such hearty guests of God, with lusty jaws and a word for every snack they put away. He was a pernicious rascal, too;

under cover of his monkish garb he slipped many a joyous tale to the ladies, who, for their part, were annoyed only after they had heard them, for things must be heard ere they are judged.

"My reverend Father," said the King, "here is the twilight hour, in which feminine ears enjoy certain pleasant stories, for the ladies may laugh without blushing or blush while they laugh to their heart's content. Tell us a good story then: I mean a truly monkish story. Upon my faith, I'll listen gladly, for I crave amusement and so do the ladies."

"We incline only in order to please Your Majesty," the Queen said, "because the Abbot goes a little too far."

"Good!" the King answered as he turned to Turpenay. "Read us some Christian admonition, Father, to amuse Madame."

"Sire, my sight is weak and night is falling."

"Give us a tale then that stops at the girdle."

"Ay, Sire," said the monk, smiling, "the one I am thinking of stops there, certainly. But it begins at the feet."

The lords present remonstrated with the Queen and her ladies so gallantly, and implored them so winningly, that Her Majesty, like the good Breton she was, smiled graciously upon the monk.

"Do your worst, Father," she said, "but you must answer for our sins to God."

"Right willingly, Madame. If it be your good pleasure to assume mine, you will be the gainer."

Everybody laughed, even the Queen. His Majesty moved over beside his wife whom, as everyone knows, he loved dearly. The courtiers received permission to sit down—the old lords, of course, for the young ones stood, by the ladies' leave, beside their chairs, to laugh softly whenever they did.

Then the Abbot of Turpenay gave graceful utterance to the following story, gliding over the scabrous passages in the soft, mellow, piping tones of a fluteplayer.

"About a hundred years ago, at least, great quarrels arose in Christendom because there were two Popes at Rome, each of whom claimed that he had been lawfully elected. It all proved very prejudicial to the monasteries, abbeys and bishoprics, since in order to secure a wider recognition than his rival, each of these two Popes granted incumbencies, titles and rights to his own followers. This made a pair of appointees for every office.

Under these circumstances, such monasteries and abbeys as had legal difficulties with their neighbors could not recognize both Popes; the unacknowledged prelate thereupon immediately gave his verdict in favor of the Chapter's enemies. This wicked schism created infinite mischief; it also proved that Christendom knows no plague more malevolent than the adultery of the Church.

"Now in those days, while Satan wrought havoc among our unhappy possessions, the very illustrious Abbey of Turpenay, whose unworthy governor I now am, had a weighty suit concerning the settlement of certain rights against the much-feared Sire de Candé, an idolatrous infidel, a heretic, a renegade and a most iniquitous lord. This devil, appearing on earth in the shape of a nobleman, was, truth to tell, a good soldier and in high favor at Court. He was also a friend of the Sieur Bureau de la Rivière, a vassal whom King Charles the Fifth, of glorious memory, prized very highly. Under the shelter of this puissant courtier's wing, My Lord of Candé rode roughshod over the Indre valley; he was undisputed master of everything from Montbazon to Ussé. You may be certain that his neighbors were terrified of him and that to save their hides they let him go his own way. But they would have preferred to see him six feet underground than walking the face of earth. They wished him a thousand ills; at which he snapped his fingers. . . . Throughout the valley, the noble Abbey alone stood up to this fiend. Has it not always been part of the Church's doctrine to gather the weak and the afflicted to breast and to strain every sinew to protect the oppressed, especially when Church rights and privileges are menaced?

"Hence this fierce warrior loathed monks, but especially those of Turpenay, who refused to be robbed of their rights by force, ruse or any other means. Naturally My Lord of Candé was delighted at the ecclesiastical schism: he waited only for our Abbot to acknowledge one Pope before himself recognized the other and ravaged the Abbey. Since his return to his château, he had made a practise of vexing and tormenting any priests he met on his estates. So brutal was he that one poor religious, caught by this devil on the road that follows the river bank to Candé, perceived no other hope of safety than to throw himself into the river. There, by a special miracle of Heaven, which the good man had fervently invoked, his robe held him up in the water and he floated easily across the Indre. Indeed, he reached the other side under the eyes of My Lord of Candé, who, far from being ashamed of himself, gloated and laughed over the terrors of a servant of God. Such, then, was the material of which the blackguard was fashioned.

"The Abbot to whom our glorious Abbey was then entrusted led a most holy life and prayed to God devoutly; but he would have saved his own soul ten times, so sterling was his faith, before finding a chance to rescue the Abbey from the clutches of that fiend. Though the old Abbot was greatly perplexed and saw disaster staring him in the face, he relied upon God for future aid. The Almighty, he said, would not suffer the property of His church to be impaired; He Who had raised up the Princess Judith for the Hebrews and Queen Lucretia for the Romans would succor His most illustrious Abbey of Turpenay. He crowned these arguments with other highly sagacious observations. But his monks who, to all our prejudice, I must confess, were miscreants, reproached him for his nonchalance. They held, on the contrary, that to ensure the timely arrival of the chariot of Providence, all the oxen of the province should be yoked to it at once; again, that the trumpets of Jericho were no longer manufactured anywhere in the world; again that God had been so direly plagued by His creation that He had washed His divine hands of it. In brief, they made a thousand and one worldly remarks that were so many doubts and contumelies against God.

"Very strangely, at this deplorable juncture, there arose a monk called Amador. He had been given this name by way of a joke, for his person offered a spitten image of the false god Ægipan. He was, like his model, ventripotent; like him he had crooked legs. His were powerful, hairy arms like a hangman's, a back created to carry a scrip, a face red as a drunkard's mug, eyes glistening like coals of fire, a tangled beard and a shaven pate. He was, further, so richly basted with lard and suet that you would have sworn he was with child. Matins he used to sing on the cellar stairs. Vespers in the vineyard of the Lord. When he was not lying flat on his back like a beggar with sores, he was going about the valley fuddling and footling, blessing the bridals, plucking the grapes and even draining the wenches, despite My Lord Abbot's prohibitions. A plunderer, he was; a wastrel, a bad soldier of the ecclesiastical militia; none of the monks paid any attention to him, but, through Christian charity, let him go his own idle way, deeming him mad.

"When Amador heard that Turpenay was in danger—the home in which he wallowed like a pig in his sty—he reared his bristles, bustled about in every direction, visited every cell, kept his ears open in the refectory, shivered in his boots and vowed that he would attempt to save the Abbey. He took cognizance of the points at issue, obtained My Lord Abbot's permission to settle the suit and a spontaneous promise from the whole Chapter that, if successful, he could have the vacant office of Sub-Prior. Then he set out across the country. Little he cared for the harshness and brutality of Messire de Candé; he protested that under his gown he bore the means to confound him. Indeed he departed on foot with that same gown for sole *viaticum;* but you must remember it was sufficiently pinguid to feed a Paulist father. He chose to go on a day when it rained hard enough to fill the tubs of all the housewives; he arrived in sight of Candé without meeting a soul and looking for all the world like a drowned dog. Very bravely he stepped into the courtyard and calmly took shelter under the roof of a pigsty until the fury of the elements abated. Then he planted himself fearlessly before the hall where he supposed the nobleman was tarrying.

"A servant, on his way from hall to pantry, took pity on Amador and advised him to make himself scarce, else My Lord would give him a hundred lashes, by way of beginning the conversation. What, he asked, made Amador so bold as to enter a house where monks were about as welcome as red leprosy?

" 'Ha,' said Amador, 'I am bound for Tours on My Lord Abbot's business. If the Sire de Candé were not so harsh towards poor servants of God, I should not be kept in the courtyard during such a downpour but rather invited into his house. I hope he may find mercy in his hour of need.'

"The servant having reported these words to his master, the latter at first wished to toss the monk into the moat. A filthy thing, he said, belonged in a sewer. But Madame de Candé—an authoritative woman whom he feared because through her he expected to inherit much property and because she was a petty tyrant—called him sharply to order. This monk, she objected, might well be a true Christian; in such weather, thieves, even, would house a constable; besides, they should treat him decently in order to learn what decision the monks of Turpenay had taken with respect to the schism. Incidentally, her advice was to settle amicably and not by force such differences as had arisen between the Abbey and the domain of Candé, because no lord since the coming of Christ had proved stronger than the Church, and, sooner or later, the Abbey would best the manor. In conclusion she offered the myriad sage arguments ladies put up in the midst of life's tempest when these grow unbearable.

"Amador's face looked so piteous, his utterly wretched appear-

ance provided so perfect a butt for ridicule, that My Lord, bored
by the rain, decided to make merry at his expense, to torment
him, to play practical jokes on him and to give him a lively recol-
lection of his welcome to Candé. He therefore charged Perrotte,
his wife's maid, with whom he had secret relations, to carry out
his evil designs upon the luckless Amador. To please her master,
the good wench of course detested all monks. As soon as they had
hatched the plot between them, she went out to this one, who
stood under the eaves of the pigsty, and, affecting a courteous demeanor in order to hoax him completely:

"'Father,' she said, 'the master of this place is ashamed to
leave a servant of God out in the rain when there is room aplenty
in the hall, a good fire in the chimney, and a table spread for supper. In his name and in My Lady's, I invite you to follow me in.'

"'I thank My Lord and My Lady, not for their hospitality,
which is a Christian duty, but for having sent as envoy to me,
poor sinner that I am! an angel of such delicate beauty that I
fancy I am seeing the Virgin over our altar.'

"So saying, Amador raised his nose in the air and gazed out at
the comely maidservant through two flakes of fire that sparkled
in his ardent eyes; nor did she, for her part, deem him so ugly,
or filthy or bestial. But as he climbed up the stairs in Perrotte's
wake, Amador suddenly felt the vicious cut of a whip across his
face. Messire de Candé, who was busy lashing his greyhounds and
feigned not to see the monk, dealt the blow with such telling effect that Amador's brow, nose, cheeks and chin smarted and his
closed eyes saw all the lights of the Magnificat. Immediately the
nobleman begged him to pardon this accident and ran after the
hounds that had knocked down his guest. The laughing wench,
who knew the trick, had neatly stepped aside. Putting two and
two together, Amador suspected how things lay between My
Lord and Perrotte, how things stood between Perrotte and My
Lord; perhaps, too, the wenches of the valley had dropped a hint
at their washing. As the man of God went into the hall, not one
of those present made room for him; he stood freezing in the
draught between door and window until the noble family entered. First came the Sire de Candé with My Lady; then his
aged sister, Mademoiselle de Candé; then the younger Mademoiselle de candé, the heiress of the house, who was about sixteen

and whom her aunt had in charge. They took their places at the head of the table, far from the common people, according to the old custom which—more's the pity!—the noblemen of our day have unwarrantedly abandoned.

"The Sire de Candé paid not the slightest attention to the monk, allowing him to squeeze in at the extreme end of the table, in a corner, between a pair of scapegraces who had instructions to crowd and hustle him as much as possible. These varlets proceeded to stamp on his feet, squeeze his body and pin down his arms like professional torturers. Hoping to befuddle him and make better sport of him, they poured white wine into his goblet instead of water; but though they had urged him to drink seven large jugs of it, he never once gagged, belched, hiccoughed, piddled or broke wind. What horrified them even more was that his gaze remained clear as crystal. Egged on, however, by a glance from their lord, they set blithely to work again, throwing gravy into his beard as they bowed, and wiping it dry solely in order to pull it violently for him. The scullion serving a caudle baptized his head with it, taking great care to let the burning liquid trickle down poor Amador's spine. This agony he endured serenely, for the spirit of God was in him and also, as you may imagine, the hope of finishing the litigation by holding out in the château. Nevertheless, the mischievous varlets burst into such explosions of laughter and jeers at the sopping monk and his greasy baptism—the scullion vowing he had thus sought to slake his thirst—that Madame de Candé could not but look down the table to see what was going on. She perceived Amador sponging his face, wearing a look of sublime resignation and endeavoring to get something out of the huge beef bones in his pewter platter. Just then the unhappy monk, having jabbed his knife skilfully into a great, wretched bone, took it up between his hairy paws, snapped it clean in two, sucked out the hot marrow and found it to his taste.

" 'Verily,' Madame de Candé mused, 'God has put great strength in this monk.'

"Forthwith she seriously admonished the pages, servitors and others to cease tormenting Amador, who, at the moment, was being served with worm-eaten apples and maggoty nuts. Fully aware that the old spinster, her charge, My Lady and the maids had seen him manœuvring the bone, Amador drew up his sleeve, displayed the muscles prominent on his arm, placed the nuts exactly on the bifurcation of the veins over his wrist, and crushed them, one by one, pressing them so powerfully with the palm of his hand that they looked like so many ripe medlars. Then, under teeth white as a hound's, he crunched them, husk, shell, fruit and all; in less than no time, he had made a paste which he swallowed like syrup. When only the apples stood before him, he made a mortise of two fingers and, using the latter like scissors, snapped the apples in half without a moment's hesitation.

"You may imagine how quiet the women were, how the varlets believed the Devil lodged in this monk and how, but for his wife and the darkness of the night, Messire de Candé would, in great fear of God, have turned him out of doors. Everyone vowed that the monk was the sort of man to turn the château inside out and hurl it into the moat. So when they had all wiped their chins, the master was careful to imprison a devil whose strength was so perilous to behold. He had Amador conducted to a foul, stinking hole, where Perrotte had used all her cunning to prepare a horrible night for him. The tomcats of the region had been incited by aphrodisiac herbs to retail their sins to him; the swine, too, had been summoned and, lest they become monks (a conversion they earnestly desired), great platterfuls of tripe had been placed under Amador's bed. These, coupled with the monk's litany of liberation, would be enough to keep them contented with hogdom. Cut horsehair was placed in his sheets; and at every move the luckless man made, he would bring down a shower of cold water on his bed. A thousand other torments such as practical jokers play in châteaux were arranged for Amador's benefit.

"Everybody went off to bed, looking forward to the monk's riotous discomfiture. Certainly nothing could go wrong: Amador had been lodged under the eaves at the top of a little tower, the door to which was carefully committed to the dogs who howled for a bite of him. To make sure of knowing in what language Amador would converse with cats and swine, My Lord came to spend the night with his mistress Perrotte who slept in the next room.

"When he saw how they were treating him, Amador drew a knife from his bag and nimbly unbolted himself. Next, he listened carefully in order to learn what went on in the manor. Presently he heard the master laughing softly as he slipped into the servant's bed. Suspecting their revels, he allowed My Lady time to dismiss her servants and retire; then, removing his sandals, lest they share his secrets, he crept barefoot to her room. He appeared before her by the dim light of the lamp in the manner in which monks generally make their nocturnal apparition—that is, in a strange and wonderful manner, which the laity find it difficult to sustain long. The thing is a trick of the robe, which magnifies everything. Having given her an opportunity to make sure he was every inch a monk, he spoke softly to her as follows:

" 'God save and preserve you, Madame! I am sent to you by Jesus and the Virgin Mary to bid you put an end to the shameless perversities that are being practised here to the prejudice of your virtue. Your virtue, Madame, is being treacherously defrauded of your husband's dearest largess, which he lavishes upon your chamberwoman. What boots it to be a mighty lady if the seigniorial fine, diverted from its proper channel, is being spent elsewhere? At this rate, your servant is the lady and you are the servant. Are not all the pleasures My Lord showers upon her your due entail? Well, you will find them all amassed in our Holy Church, which is the consolation of the afflicted. Behold in me the messenger prepared to liquidate this debt in full—unless, of course, you prefer to let it stand.'

"As he finished, the good monk gently loosened his girdle, which hampered him, so greatly was he moved by the sight of those beauties Messire de Candé disdained.

" 'If you speak truly, Father, I shall place myself under your guidance,' she said, leaping lightly up from her bed. 'You are undoubtedly a messenger from God, because in a single day you have seen what I have not noticed here in a long time.'

"Then she went off with Amador, whose most holy robe she did not fail to graze offhand; and so deeply stirred was she by its outstanding authenticity that she hoped to find her husband guilty. In effect, she heard him moving about in her maid's bed, discussing the monk. Faced with this felony, she flew into a towering rage, opened her mouth to give vent to it in words (as women will do) and wished to raise the devil's tattoo before delivering the wench to justice. But Amador observed how much wiser it was to avenge herself first, and to cry out afterwards.

" 'Quick, Father, avenge me at once,' she said, 'for I am dying to cry out!'

"Whereupon the monk avenged her most monastically with a fine, powerful sweet vengeance which she indulged in greedily, bolting it down like a drunkard with his lips on the bunghole of a barrel, for when a lady has a rod in pickle, she must be overcome and drunk with vengeance or she does not taste it at all. And avenged she was—with a vengeance!—so thoroughly that she was unable to move, since nothing chokes, knocks up and exhausts a woman like rage and revenge. But though she settled her score, though she was manifoldly and multifariously avenged in regular progression to nth power without extraction of root, still she refused to forgive, wishing, as she did, to retain the right to keep the wound alive now here, now there, with this blessed monk. Perceiving her love for unrelenting counterstrokes, Amador promised to help her wreak vengeance as long as her passion endured. Indeed, he confessed that in his position as a monk, constrained to dwell at length upon the nature of things, he knew an infinite number of modes, methods and fashions of practising revenge. Then canonically he impregnated her with the realization that to revenge oneself was a highly Christian action.

" 'In the Holy Writ,' Amador pointed out, 'from end to end, God Himself asseverates that, above all other things, He is a God of vengeance; furthermore, by creating a Hell, where His vengeance is eternal, He has made manifest how royally divine a thing is vengeance. It therefore follows that women and monks should take revenge or they fail in their duty as Christians and loyal servants of the celestial doctrines.'

"This dogma proved infinitely pleasing to the lady, who admitted she had never really understood the commandments of the Church; she invited her well-beloved monk to come as often as possible and, to the top of his bent, impart them regularly to her. Then the lady, whose vital spirits had been excited and refreshed by this vengeance, stormed into the room where the trollop was frolicking with her lord. As luck would have it, she entered just as Perrotte settled her hand where My Lady's glance often rested, much as a merchant's does on a precious commodity he would not be robbed of. The pair was caught—to quote Judge Lizet when he was in a gay mood—'in fragrant delight.' They looked abashed, shamefaced, and foolish. The spectacle before her proved ineffably displeasing to My Lady, as her speech plainly showed; her words were as turbulent as the waters of her big pond when the sluice-gate was opened. It was a sermon in three heads, accompanied by music of a high gamut, with variations on every tone, and many a sharp among the keys.

" 'Gramercy for virtue, My Lord; I've had my share of it. You have shown me that religion in conjugal faith is an abuse. So this is the reason why I have no son, eh? How many children have you dumped into this common teaze-hole, this poor-box, this bot-

tomless alms-poke, this leper's porringer, this perfect cemetery
for the house of Candé? For my own satisfaction, I will find out
if I am barren by a trick of my nature or through your fault.
The servants, I leave to you; for my part, I will have handsome
knights, so we may produce an heir. The bastards to you; I shall
have legitimate children!'

" 'My dear!' The bewildered lord hemmed and hawed. 'Don't
shout so!'

" 'Not at all!' the lady persisted. 'I *will* shout! I *will!* I'll shout
loud enough to be heard distinctly by the Archbishop, by the
Papal Legate, by the King, and by my brothers. They will all
help me avenge this infamy!'

" 'Madame, do not dishonor your husband.'

" 'Dishonor, eh? This is a dishonor? You are right: yes! But,
My Lord, such shame could not proceed from you—no! It is this
harlot's doing! I'll have her sewn up in a sack and tossed into the
Indre, I swear it. That will wash away your dishonor! Ho, there!'
she cried.

" 'H-h-h-ush, Madame,' the lord stammered, with his tail between his legs and humble as a blind man's dog.

"Under his wife's glance this doughty warrior, so prompt to
kill his neighbor, was like a helpless child. Soldiers are not unaccustomed to this sort of thing; for they have no more than
force and heavy physical bulk, while women, on the contrary,
possess a subtle wit and a spark of the fragrant flame that illu-
mines Paradise. This is apt to dazzle the male. That is how certain women rule their husbands, for mind is the master of matter."

(As the Abbot of Turpenay propounded this aphorism, the
ladies burst out laughing. So, too, did the King. The Abbot
paused a moment, cleared his throat and continued.)

" 'I shall not hush!' Madame de Candé persisted, 'I have been
too grievously outraged. So this is my reward for the great wealth
I brought you? This is how you requite my virtuous conduct?
Did I ever refuse to obey you, even in Lent and on days of fasting? Am I so chill as to freeze the sun? Do you suppose I give myself by force, from a sense of duty or in sheer kindness of heart?

Have I a sacred pyx? Am I a holy shrine? Do you need a Papal brief to approach me? God's truth, have you had so much of me that you are *blasé?* Do I not suit you? Have chambermaids a deeper fund of knowledge than ladies? Ha! doubtless they have, since she let you dibble the plot without sowing. Teach me the trick, I'll practise it with those I take into my service, for it's quite settled now: I am free. And a good thing, too! Your company was really too wearisome; too dear you made me pay what wretched scraps of pleasure you doled out. God be praised, I am quit of you and your whims! I shall retire to a monastery and there, among the monks—'

"She meant to say 'to a convent' and 'among the nuns,' but this avenging priest had perverted her tongue.

" '. . . Yes,' she pursued, 'I shall be better served in this monastery with my daughter than here, in this pit of shame and iniquity! You can inherit from your chambermaid. Ha, ha, ha! A fine Madame de Candé *she* is! Look at her!'

" 'What ever is the matter?'

"Amador suddenly appeared on the threshold.

" 'The matter is, Father,' she said, 'that here is a wrong that cries out for vengeance. To begin with, I shall have this bawd sewn up in a sack and tossed into the river, for having diverted the seed of the house of Candé to her own end. 'Twill save the hangman trouble. As for the other, I intend—'

" 'Lay aside your wrath, my daughter,' the monk said. 'Does not the Holy Church command us in the Lord's Prayer to forgive those who trespass against us, if we look to Heaven? God will not pardon such as have not pardoned others; He wreaks eternal vengeance on the wicked who take vengeance into their own hands and He welcomes into His Paradise those who have been merciful. Thence comes the Jubilee, which is a day of great rejoicing, because all debts and offenses are wiped out. Forgiveness brings supreme happiness. Pardon! pardon! to pardon is a most holy work. Pardon My Lord of Candé, who will bless you for your gracious mansuetude and love you much thereafter. Clemency will give you back the flowers of youth; and remember, my dear fair young lady, forgiveness is, in certain cases, the best of all possible vengeances. Pardon your maid, too; she will pray Heaven for you! Thus God, invoked by all, will have you in His keeping and, for your pardon, bless you with a line of noble sons.'

"Taking the husband's hand, he put it in the lady's, adding:

" 'Go and talk over this pardon.'

"Then he whispered this wise counsel in the husband's ear:

" 'My Lord, pull out your trump argument: she'll be quiet when you put it to her. For a woman's mouth is full of words only when she is elsewhere empty. Out with your argument, join the issue, lay stress on it and you will always make head against a woman.'

" ' 'Oddsbody, there's good in this monk,' My Lord murmured as he withdrew.

"As soon as he was alone with Perrotte, Amador spoke as follows:

" 'You are at fault, my dear, for having attempted to torture a poor servant of God. By that deed, you incurred the thunder of Heaven's wrath, which will surely strike you. Wherever you may hide, it will follow you always; it will gripe you in every limb, even after your death; it will bake you like dough in the oven of Hell, where you will parch for all eternity. And never a day shall pass but you will receive seven hundred thousand million lashes of the whip for the one I received through you.'

" 'Alas, Father!' the maid cried as she cast herself at the monk's feet, 'you alone can save me, for if I don your holy robe, I shall be shielded from God's wrath.'

"With these words, she raised the robe as though to find protection under it. Then:

" 'By my faith!' she exclaimed, 'monks are far greater than noblemen.'

" 'By the sulphur of Satan, has no monk ever come into your ken?'

" 'No,' Perrotte answered.

" 'And you've no inkling of the services monks chant without uttering a word?'

" 'No,' she repeated.

"Whereupon the monk solemnized this function for her with all due magnificence, as it is celebrated on great feast days, with all the grand flourishes used in monasteries, the psalms beautifully chanted in F major, the flaming tapers and the choristers;

he explained the *Introit* and the *Ite, Missa est,* bodily to her; and, when he departed, he left her so exhaustively hallowed that the wrath of Heaven could not have discovered a single atom of her that was not most amply monasticated.

"This service done, Amador commanded Perrotte to conduct

him into the presence of Mademoiselle de Candé, the lord's sister. Appearing before the spinster, he inquired whether she did not wish to confess to him, since monks came so rarely to Candé. Mademoiselle was delighted, as any good Christian would be, at this chance of furbishing up her conscience. Amador requested her to show him the latter, and the poor lady having shown him what he considered the seat of old maid's consciences, he found it very much in need of attention.

" 'It is here, Mademoiselle,' he explained, 'that all the sins of women are perfected. In order to be sinless in the future, you must have your conscience probed and stopped up by a monk's indulgence.'

"As the poor, ignorant lady replied that she had no idea where these indulgences were to be had, Amador explained that he bore a treasure of indulgence—nothing on earth, in fact, was more indulgent, since without uttering a syllable it produced infinite pleasures. Was this not the true, eternal and primary character of an indulgence? The sight of this treasure, of which she had been wholly deprived, dazzled the poor spinster; her brain reeled and her senses grew confused; she was so eager to pin her faith on the monk's relic that she finally indulged as fervently in these indulgences as her sister-in-law had indulged in vengeances. Presently the noise of this contrition and confessioning awakened the younger Mademoiselle de Candé, who came to watch the proceedings. This consummation our monk had hoped for, you may be certain; his mouth had watered for this luscious fruit; in the twinkling of a bedpost he devoured it. Nor could the guardian aunt prevent him from showing the eager niece the surplus of his indulgences. But, after all, this pleasure was certainly due him for the trouble he had taken.

"At dawn, the swine had eaten their tripe and the cats become disenchanted with love after flooding the places where Perrotte had rubbed herbs. Amador went off to rest in his bed, which the maid had put straight again. Thanks to the monk, everybody slept so soundly that none of the family rose before noon. The servants were convinced that the monk was a devil who had carried off the cats, the swine and their masters. Nevertheless, everyone appeared in the hall at mealtime.

" 'Come, Father,' said the lady of the manor, giving the monk her arm and placing him beside her in the baron's chair. To the amazement of the flunkeys, Messire de Candé did not breathe a word.

" 'Page, give some of this to Father Amador,' Madame commanded.

" 'Father Amador wants some of that,' said the excellent Mademoiselle de Candé.

" 'Fill Father Amador's tankard,' said My Lord.

" 'Father Amador needs some bread,' the younger Mademoiselle de Candé exclaimed.

" 'What will you have, Father Amador?' Perrotte asked.

"It was Father Amador here, and Father Amador there, on the slightest provocation. They treated him like a little virgin on her wedding night.

" 'Eat, Father,' said Madame, 'you fared so poorly yesterday at supper.'

" 'Drink, Father,' said her husband. 'By the Blood, you're the bravest monk I ever clapped eyes on.'

" 'Father Amador is a handsome monk,' said Perrotte.

" 'An indulgent monk,' said the spinster.

" 'A beneficent monk,' said her niece.

" 'A mighty monk,' said My Lady.

" 'A monk who lives up to his name,' said the clerk of the castle.

"Amador munched and champed, wallowed in the dishes, lapped up the hippocras, licked his chops, sneezed, snorted, grunted, reared, swelled and battened like a bull in a field, while the servants watched him in terror, certain that he was a wizard.

"Dinner over, with a myriad fine arguments Madame de Candé, Mademoiselle de Candé and the little niece wheedled the Sire de Candé into settling the suit. Madame spoke at length pointing out how useful a monk was in a manor; Mademoiselle, who from now on wished her conscience furbished up every day, waxed very eloquent; the little Mademoiselle kept pulling her father's beard and begging him to let this monk reside permanently at Candé. To begin with, if their differences were ever to be ironed out, it would be done through this monk; again, Amador was a man of high parts, gentle and virtuous as a saint; thirdly, what a misfortune it was to be at daggers drawn with a monastery that contained such brethren! Next, My Lord must realize that if all the monks were of a piece with Amador, the Abbey would inevitably triumph over the château at all points and ruin it utterly. And how strong, how powerful the monk was! In brief, they brought a host of reasons to bear upon him, amid showers of words that pelted down so diluvially that My Lord threw up the sponge. What peace, indeed, could the poor man have known so long as he did not settle matters to the satis-

faction of his womenfolk? He sent for his clerk. To his amazement, Amador showed him charters and letters of credit which
prevented lord and clerk from delaying the agreement.

"Seeing them at work putting an end to this suit, Madame de
Candé went to the linenroom to get some fine, soft cloth to make
a new robe for her dear Amador. Everyone in the château had
noticed how worn his was; surely it would have been a great
shame to leave so splendid an instrument of vengeance in such
a horrid garb? They vied with each other in working on the
gown. Madame cut it, Perrotte made the hood, Mademoiselle
sewed it on, the little demoiselle did the sleeves. Then all of
them set so eagerly to work to adorn the monk that the robe was
ready by suppertime, as was also the charter of agreement, drawn
up and sealed by the Sire de Candé.

" 'Ah, Father,' sighed Madame, 'if you love us, you will refresh yourself after your great labor by taking a bath which I
have had Perrotte heat for you.'

"Amador was bathed in scented water; then, when he came
out, he found his new robe of fine linen and handsome sandals
laid out for him. They made him appear the most glorious monk
in the world.

"Meanwhile the monks of Turpenay, trembling for Amador,
had ordered two of the brethren to scout around the castle.
These spies rounded the moat just as Perrotte threw Amador's
greasy robe, with a lot of potsherds, into it. From this, they at
once concluded that it was all over with the poor madman, and,
hastening back to Turpenay, they reported that Amador had undoubtedly suffered the cruelest martyrdom for the sake of the
Abbey. At this news, the Abbot ordered them to assemble in the
chapel, where they implored God's mercy on this devoted servant amid his torments. Amador, meanwhile, calmly finished his
supper, tucked his charter under his girdle and prepared to depart. At the foot of the steps, he found Madame's mare, bridled
and saddled, and a groom holding it ready for him. My Lord,
for his part, had commanded his men-at-arms to see the good
monk safely home. Before such kindness, Amador, forgiving the
persecution of the night before, gave his benediction to all ere he
departed from this regenerated home. You may be certain that
Madame's glance followed him and that she proclaimed him a

splendid rider. Perrotte said that, for a monk, he held himself stiffer and more upright in the saddle than any of the men-at-arms. Mademoiselle de Candé sighed. The young heiress wished him for her confessor.

" 'He has sanctified the manor,' they all said as they returned to the hall.

"When Amador and his escort rode up to the Abbey gate, confusion and terror burst out among the monks, for the warden believed that Amador's tragic death had whetted the nobleman's appetite and that the latter was now come to sack the Abbey. But Amador's great booming voice rang through the night, was unmistakably recognized and secured them admittance to the courtyard: and, when he dismounted from Madame's hack, there was hubbub enough to make the monks wild as April moons. In the refectory, Amador waved the charter in the air; they burst into tumultuous cheers and all of them came to congratulate him. The men-at-arms were regaled with the best wine in the cellar— a present from the brethren of Marmoutier, who owned the vineyards of Vouvray. After the good Abbot had had the charter read to him, he went about repeating:

" 'In these diverse vicissitudes, we never fail to see the finger of God! Oh, let us render thanks to Him!'

"The good old Abbot, in his speech of thanks to Amador, kept harping on this finger of God. It annoyed the monk to see his mainspring thus diminished.

" 'Call it the arm of God, Father,' he said, 'and let's say no more about it.'

"The settlement of this suit between the Sire de Candé and the Abbey of Turpenay was followed by a blessing which made him devoted to the Church: nine months after, he had a son. Two years later, Amador was elected Abbot by the monks, who looked forward to a merry régime under such a madcap. But Amador, become Abbot, proved righteous and austere, because he had conquered his evil desires by his labors and recast his nature at the female forge. Ay, friends, that forge burns with a fire that scorifies all impurities, for is it not perforce the most persevering, persistent, perfectioning, perturbing, perfusing, perfervid, peritoneal and perineal thing there ever was on the face of earth? It is a fire to ruin everything; so well it ruined what was evil in Amador that it left only what it could not devour: to wit, his spirit that shone forth clear as a diamond, which, as everyone knows, is a residue of the great fire that carbonized our globe. So Amador was the instrument chosen by Providence to reform our illustrious Abbey. He put everything to rights again, watched over his monks night and day, made them all rise at the hour appointed for prayers, counted them in chapel as a shepherd counts his sheep, held them well in hand and punished them so sternly for their faults that he made excellent monks of them.

"This teaches us to devote ourselves to woman, more to the end of being chastened than of deriving pleasure. For the rest, this story teaches us that we should never pit our strength against the Churchmen."

The King and Queen found his tale highly to their taste; the courtiers confessed that they had never heard a better one; and the ladies would all have gladly played a part in it.

Bertha the Penitent

How Bertha Remained a Virgin in the Married State

BOUT the time of the Dauphin's first flight, which sorely grieved our good King Charles the Victorious, a great misfortune fell upon a noble house of Touraine. The dynasty being extinct in every branch, the highly deplorable story may now be brought to light. To aid him in this work, the Author invokes the Holy Confessors, Martyrs and other heavenly Dominations who, by God's command, were the promoters of good in this adventure.

Through some flaw in his character, the Sieur Imbert de Bastarnay, one of the chief landholders in our realm of Touraine, possessed not the slightest confidence in the mind of the female of man. Her circumbilivaginations made her, he thought, too restless; perhaps he was right. At all events, ruled by this evil thought, he reached a ripe age without taking a mate—which in no wise profited him. Except for his warlike expeditions and the hurly-burly he set up with rough lads who did not exactly stand upon ceremony, he had always led a solitary life, without dreaming of putting himself out for anybody. Thus he remained very foul in his clothes, and sweaty in his equipment, his hands were forever grimy, his face that of an ape; in short, with respect to his person, he was quite the ugliest man in Christendom. On the other hand, so far as his head, heart and sundry secret places were concerned, he had properties which redounded greatly to his credit. A messenger from Heaven—and I beg you to believe this —would have tramped many a mile before meeting an old warhorse firmer at his post and a nobleman more scrupulous about his honor, more curt in his speech and more loyal in spirit.

Certain witnesses, who actually heard him, report that he was sound in judgment and very profitable to consult. But what a deliberately strange whim of God's to endow so filthy a form with such illustrious perfections!

At last, having made a sexagenarian of himself in every particular though he was still but fifty, Messire de Bastarnay resolved to take a wife unto himself in order to have issue. Then, having searched about for a suitable mould, he heard people enthusiastically citing the sterling merits and charms of a daughter of the illustrious house of Rohan, which then held certain fiefs in Touraine. The young lady was named Bertha. Imbert visited her at the Château de Montbazon and was so overwhelmed by her beauty and innocence that he determined then and there to marry her, convinced, as he was, that a maid of such lofty lineage could not possibly fail in her duty. This wedding took place very soon, for the Sire de Rohan had seven daughters and found it hard to provide for all of them at a time when people were recovering from the wars and mending their fortunes.

Rumor had not lied: good old Bastarnay was overjoyed to find Bertha a genuine virgin—a sign of her excellent bringing up and perfect motherly correction. Accordingly, on the very first night he could lawfully enjoy her, he proceeded to get her with child so roughly that he had ample proof of it within two months. This made him as happy as a king.

In order to complete this part of the story, we may add that from this legitimate seed sprang the Sire de Bastarnay whom King Louis the Eleventh appointed duke, chamberlain and even his personal envoy at large in Europe, for this fearsome monarch prized Bastarnay highly nor did the latter ever prove unfaithful. This loyalty he inherited from My Lord Imbert, his father, who had been fond of the Dauphin from the very beginning and had followed his fortunes even in the rebellions. Imbert was the sort of friend who would have crucified Christ all over again, had Louis required it of him. What a noble flower of steadfastness and how seldom found blooming in the neighborhood of princes and among the mighty of the earth!

From the beginning, the fair lady of Bastarnay behaved so loyally that her presence dispelled the dense vapors and black clouds overcasting the glory of woman in the goodman's mind. Soon, as sceptics will do, he passed from intense distrust to the completest confidence, abandoning the government of his house to her and appointing her mistress of his every deed and action. She was un-disputed sovereign of all things, queen of his honor, guardian of his white hairs; he would instantly have brained any man rash enough to whisper a word of evil against this mirror of virtue—a mirror over which no breath had passed, save that issuing from his martial and husbandly (and cold and withered!) lips. To tell the whole truth, we must add that the existence of the little boy favored her virtuous conduct considerably, since for six years his mother busied herself with him. Her first care was to give him her own milk in suck, making a lover's lieutenant of him; she of-fered him her sweet breasts and he gnawed at them avidly, as often as he would, being forever at them like a lover. This ideal mother knew no titillation other than his rosy lips afforded, no caresses other than those of his little hands running over her like the feet of playful mice; she read in no other book than those pure, clear eyes of his that mirrored the blue sky; she heard no other music than his cries floating into her ear like angels' whis-pers. And you may be sure she was forever coddling him. From earliest morning, she was wanting to hug him; her last act in the evening was to embrace him; she was said to rise in the middle of the night in order to eat him up with kisses, making herself a child like him and rearing him in the perfect religion of mother-hood. In fine, she behaved as the best and happiest mother who ever lived (with all due respect to Our Lady the Virgin, Who surely had scant trouble bringing up Our Savior, since He was God!).

This tutelage and Bertha's disinclination for the function of matrimony delighted her goodman: for one thing, he would have been hard put to it to stand up to too amorous a mate; for an-other, at present he could barely make both ends meet and was husbanding his resources in order to have the wherewithal for a second child.

At the end of six years, Bertha was compelled to deliver her son into the hands of grooms and other servants chosen by Mes-sire de Bastarnay to mould him manfully, since Imbert wished his heir to inherit not only the estates and titles of his dynasty but also its virtues, its merits, its nobility and courage. Poor Ber-tha wept bitterly, with her happiness gone. What was it, for the

great heart of this mother, to have her adored son only after
others had finished with him and then but for a few, swift, fleeting hours? She fell into deep dejection. Her goodman, perceiving her melancholy, strained every nerve to produce another
child for her; but alas! he did not come off successfully. It was
torture to Bertha! As she herself said, she was sore-pressed by the
introduction to childmaking, which demanded untold efforts of
her and invariably rubbed her up the wrong way. True words,
these were, or no doctrine on earth is true; if you do not believe
her naïve remark, then you must burn the Gospels as a tissue of
falsehoods.

Now certain ladies (I exclude men because they are crack
practitioners of the science) will persist in holding this to be an
untruth. That is why the Author has been careful to supply the
mute reasons for this strange phenomenon—I mean Bertha's
aversion to what her sex adores supremely—thus explaining how
the want of pleasure did not make her face any the older or torment her heart. Will you ever meet a scribe as deferent and as
fond of the ladies as I am? No, of course not. Certainly I have
loved them very much, yet not so often as I would wish. The nib
of my goose-quill is more frequently in my hand than the barbs
with which to tickle their lips, to move them to laughter, and to
sport in all innocence—with their coöperation, of course. . . .
Here, then, is how matters stood.

Goodman Bastarnay was not a lusty lad, ready to meet all comers in the lists of love and up to all the roguish variations of the
thing. He did not trouble his head about how he laid an enemy
low, so long as he did it; he was ready to send souls to Paradise
right and left, without so much as a word—in the thick of battle, of course. Such arrant heedlessness in the matter of death
matched his nonchalance in the matter of life and extended to
birth and to the technique of *souffléing* children in the pretty
oven you know of. In other words, My Lord was crassly ignorant
of the thousand litigious, dilatory, interlocutory and prelusive
amenities . . . of the little faggots slipped through the teaze-hole
to warm up the oven . . . of the balmy branches gathered up stalk
by stalk in the dingle of love . . . he never dreamed of the nuz-
zling and fondling . . . the charming artifices of cosseting and
cockering . . . the shy reciprocal peckings . . . the joint bites at

love's fruit . . . the catlicking and other tricks and traffic of love that ruffians employ, lovers dulcify and ladies love above their salvation because there is more of the cat than the woman in them. How clearly this stands forth in all their female ways! If

you think them worth watching, observe them carefully while they eat. Not a single one (I refer to noble and well-bred women) will ever plunge her knife into the victuals and gobble them down suddenly, as brutal men do. They will, on the contrary, fritter about with their food, take the bits they fancy and sift them like gray peas on a sorting-board, sip at the sauces, leave the large cuts untouched and—so heartily do they detest going straight to the point—ply their knife and fork as though condemned to by order of the police. Again, they employ every sort of circumbendibus, finesse and refinement in everything. It is characteristic of them; they do things differently from men (and rightly, too!). Therefore the sons of Adam dote upon them. You agree? Good: we are friends!

Well then, Imbert de Bastarnay, an old soldier but an ignoramus in the glandojuggleries of amour, rushed into the sweet garden named after Venus as into a stronghold taken by storm; he had not the slightest regard for the clamors of the poor tearful inhabitants; he drove his child home as who might plant an arrow in the bull's-eye. Though our gentle Bertha was not used to such treatment (poor child! she was just fifteen) she believed, in the candor of her virgin faith, that the happiness of motherhood required this fearsome, horrible, painful and objectionable operation. Throughout the whole gruesome business, she would fervently implore God's assistance, recite *Aves* to Our Lady and consider the latter fortunate indeed to have had but the Holy Dove to endure. Having therefore undergone nothing but pain in wedlock, she never asked her husband to repeat the function; and since, as we have said before, the goodman was scarce up to it, Bertha lived in perfect solitude, like a nun. She hated the commerce of man, never suspecting that the Creator of Earth had rooted so much pleasure in a thing from which she had received only infinite wretchedness. But she loved her son the more, because he had cost her so much before being conceived. It is not surprising, therefore, that she set her face against that charming tourney where it is the hack masters the rider, guiding, exhausting and, if he falter, abusing him. Such is the true history of not a few unhappy marriages, according to the statements of old men and old dames. It undoubtedly accounts for the follies some women commit when, late in life, they somehow discover that they have been disappointed. In order to have their fair share of life they at once strain to crowd into a single day more time than it can hold. There's high philosophy for you, my friends! Therefore study this page in order to look wisely to the government of your wives, sweethearts and any other sort of female you may chance—God help you!—to have in your care.

Thus a virgin indeed, although a mother, Bertha was, in her

one-and-twentieth year, the flower of the manor, the glory of her goodman and the honor of the province. Imbert de Bastarnay delighted in seeing this child come and go. She was as lissom as a willow-reed, as lively as an eel and as innocent as her own child, yet at the same time so sensible and intelligent that he never embarked in any enterprise without first consulting her. How true it is that, if the minds of such angels have not been disturbed in their purity, they answer every querying knock with the clearest of sounds. Bertha, at this time, lived in her lord's manor near the town of Loches; she knew no other desire than to look after her household affairs in the hallowed fashion of prudent housewives. From such admirable constancy, the ladies of France were led astray when Queen Catherine and her Italians came with their banquets and feasts. Francis the First and his successors put the finishing touches to the demoralization of the French housewife; their pleasure-loving ways harmed France as direly as the wickedness of the Protestants. But this is beside the point.

At about this time the King summoned Messire de Bastarnay and his wife to the good town of Loches, where he was tarrying with the Court. Bertha's extraordinary beauty had been much bruited about. When she came to Loches, His Majesty received her with much kindness and praise; she at once became the object of homages from very youthful lords, who feasted their eyes on this apple of love, and from the oldsters, who basked in the radiance of this warm sun. All of them, young and old, would gladly have suffered a thousand deaths in return for an opportunity to utilize these splendid pleasure-making tools that dazzled the sight and muddled the brain. In the district of Loches, Bertha was cited at greater length than God in the Bible. This naturally infuriated a vast number of ladies who were not so richly dowered with attractions and who, for ten nights with the ugliest courtier, would have wished to send this exquisite gatherer of smiles back to her château.

From one such—a young lady who, inevitably recognizing the infatuation of a lover of hers for Bertha, became a spiteful fiend —proceeded all the misfortunes that befell Madame de Bastarnay; but from the same source rose her supreme happiness and her discovery of the smiling, undreamed-of shores of love.

This wicked lady had a kinsman, Jean de Saché, who confessed to her straightway, the moment he saw Bertha, that if he might become her lover and have joy of her for a month, he would be perfectly willing to forfeit his life. Jean was delicately handsome as a girl and innocent of hair on chin and cheeks; he would have won pardon from an enemy by simply asking; he was scarcely twenty years old.

"Fair coz," the traitress told him, "leave the room and go to your house; I will try to afford you this joy. But be careful not to let her see you . . . and look out for the owner of this sprite of beauty, look out for that old baboon grafted, by error of nature, on a Christian stem!"

Jean having lain low, the lady came fawning around, rubbing her treacherous nose against Bertha's, calling her "my love," "my treasure," "star of beauty," striving to please her in a thousand ways, only the better to wreak vengeance upon the poor child! Alas! all unwittingly Bertha had offended the spiteful lady by making the latter's lover unfaithful of heart—which, for a woman ambitious in love, is the direst of infidelities. After a short conversation, the jealous lady suspected that poor Bertha was still virgin in amour: a limpid moisture filled her eyes, her brow and temples showed never the slightest wrinkle nor did the point of her little snow-white nose—a feature usually betraying the ravages of pleasure—reveal the faintest hint of a black speck. In short, no habit of passion marred her face, which shone pure as an innocent maid's. Bertha's answers to a few insidiously feminine questions convinced her enemy that, if Bertha had reaped the profit of motherhood, she had unmistakably foregone the ecstasies of copulation. For her cousin's sake, the traitress rejoiced, like the good soul she was.

She told Bertha about a young noblewoman of the house of Rohan, who needed the help of a lady of position to reconcile her to Messire Louis de Rohan. If Bertha's charity matched the beauty God had given her, she would take Sylvia de Rohan home with her, make sure of the sanctity of her life and bring about her reconciliation with the head of the house, who at present refused to receive her. Bertha consented without the least hesitation, since she had heard about Sylvia's misfortunes, though she did not know her personally and, indeed, had believed her to be in a foreign land.

It is here necessary to explain why the King had been so cordial to the Sire de Bastarnay. His Majesty had a suspicion of the Dauphin's first flight into Burgundy; he wished to deprive his son of as excellent a counsellor as Bastarnay. But the old man was loyal to young Louis; his mind was made up, he was ready to go the whole hog. So he took Bertha back to his château. When she informed him that she was bringing a companion home with her, and that the latter was none other than Sylvia de Rohan, Imbert was rather annoyed. But he was touched, too, by Bertha's generosity and he congratulated her upon undertaking to bring an errant lamb back to the familiar fold. Having regaled his wife aplenty during the long last night, he left a guard at the château and set off next morning for Burgundy with the Dauphin. How was he to know that Sylvia was none other than the amorous lord, disguised as a girl and vouchsafed this opportunity by his cousin, who was jealous of Bertha, vexed by her virtue and determined to deprave her? How was he to guess what a cruel enemy he fostered in his very bosom? He had never before laid eyes on the lover, a knight-bachelor in the service of Cardinal Dunois (who had brought him up) and a lad but lately come to Loches to see the King's Court.

Old Bastarnay believed Jean to be a girl, and a very pious, timid one at that, for the lad mistrusted the language of a lover's eyes and always kept his glance meekly lowered. He lived in constant fear of being recognized and slain ere he had had joy of his sweetheart. And when Bertha kissed him full on the mouth, he would tremble lest his skirt prove indiscreet and he would quickly move away to the window. . . .

So when the portcullis was lowered and the old nobleman galloped away across country, Jean was blissfully happy, as any lover would have been in his place. He had suffered such terrors that he vowed to build a pillar at his own expense in the Cathedral of Tours, in gratitude at escaping the perils his mad scheme involved. In point of fact, he gave fifty marks of silver to pay God for his delight. But, by chance, he had to pay for it all over again to the Devil, as appears in the following facts—if you find the tale amusing enough to persuade you to follow the narrative. It will be succinct, as all good narratives should be.

II

How Bertha Behaved Knowing the Business of Love

*T*HIS bachelor-knight, Jean de Saché, was the cousin to the Sieur de Montmorency who, at Jean's death, inherited the fiefs of Saché and various other estates by deed of tenure. Jean was twenty years old and fiery as a live coal; had a hard time of it getting through the first day. While old Imbert was speeding away across the fields, the two cousins perched themselves on the lookout of the portcullis to watch him as long as they could and to wave him a fond farewell. When the cloud of dust raised by the horses disappeared on the horizon, they came down to the hall.

"What shall we do, dear coz?" Bertha asked the counterfeit Sylvia. "Do you like music? We will play together! Let us sing a lay by some ancient sweet minstrel. Eh, tell me, would you like that? Come to my organ, come along; do please, if you love me. Let us sing."

She took Jean by the hand and drew him to the keyboard of the organ, at which the rascal seated himself gracefully after the fashion of women.

"Ah, sweet cousin," Bertha cried when they had tried the first notes and he brought his head close to hers so they might sing together, "how exceedingly piercing your glance is! You move a strange, unknown spring in my heart."

"Alas, fair coz," the false Sylvia answered, "that was what proved my undoing. A charming milord from the land across the sea kept telling me that I had beautiful eyes; he kissed them so much and so well that I felt ineffable delight at the kissing, and I yielded. . . ."

"What, Sylvia? Has love its being in the eyes?"

"They are the forge of Cupid's bolts, my dear Bertha," said the lover, casting fire and flame at her.

"Let us sing, Sylvia," Bertha put in quickly.

Then, at Jean's desire, they sang a love-plaint by Christine de Pisan, every note of which thrilled with desire.

"Oh, cousin, the depth and power in your voice! It pierces me through and through!"

"Where?" Sylvia asked impudently.

"Here," Bertha replied, pointing to her pretty diaphragm—an organ which registers the harmonies of passion more acutely than the ears. Why? Because it lies closer to the heart and to another organ which is indisputably the first brain, the second heart and the third ear of the ladies. I say this with all due respect and honor, for physical reasons and no other.

"Let us leave off singing," Bertha said suddenly, "it stirs me too deeply! Come to the window; we will ply our needles until evening."

"Alas, dear cousin of my soul, I couldn't hold a needle in my fingers. To my perdition, I have been accustomed to employ these for other tasks."

"What did you do then, all day long?"

"I let myself drift down the current of love, which turns days into seconds, months into days, and years into months. Could it but last, 'twould make you gulp down eternity like a strawberry, for it is all coolness and fragrance, sweetness and infinite joy."

Then the rascal closed his fair eyelids over his shining eyes and remained as melancholy as a poor jilted lady who weeps for her gallant, longs to embrace him and is ready to forgive his treachery if he but return down the rosy path to the once-loved fold.

"Does love blossom in the married state, cousin?"

"No, no," Sylvia explained. "In the married state, everything is duty; in love everything is done in perfect freedom of heart. This difference communicates an indefinable soft balm to those caresses which are the flowers of love."

"Come, let us talk of something else; this conversation grips me more poignantly than the music did."

She called a servant hastily and bade him bring her son. As the lad entered:

"He is as beautiful as love!" Sylvia sighed. And she kissed him passionately on the brow.

"Come, darling," the mother said, as the child climbed on to her lap. "Come, you are your mother's love, her unalloyed happiness, the joy of her every hour, her crown, her jewel, her own pure pearl, her stainless soul, her treasure, her star by night and day, the one and only white flame of her heart. . . . Give me your hands, that I may eat them; give me your ears, that I may peck at them; give me your head, that I may kiss your hair. Be happy always, little flower of my body, if you would have me happy."

"There, cousin, you are speaking the language of love to him."

"What? Is love a child?"

"Certainly, sweet coz. That is why the Pagans have always portrayed him as a little boy."

And with much further conversation permeated with the spirit of love, the pretty pair played with the child till suppertime.

"Would you not like to have another child?" Jean whispered into Bertha's ear at an opportune moment, grazing her flesh with his hot lips as he did so.

"Oh, Sylvia, for that, I would cheerfully undergo a hundred years in Hell, if only it pleased God to vouchsafe me such a joy! But despite the efforts, swink and labor of my husband, which pain me very much, my girdle will not slip a single notch. Ah, wellaway! to have one small child is nothing, nothing. . . . If I hear but one cry in the manor, my heart is ready to burst: I tremble for my innocent angel, I fear beast and man alike, I dread volts, passes and the handling of weapons, I am in terror of everything. I have ceased living in myself in order to live wholly in him and alas! I revel in my misery, because my worrying is a sign that my offspring is safe and sound. I implore the saints and apostles for him alone. To be brief—for I could go on talking of this until tomorrow—I believe that my breath is in him, not in me."

So saying she hugged him to her breasts, as only mothers know how to hug children, with a spiritual force that crushes the heart only. Should you entertain the least doubt on this score, watch a cat carrying her kittens in her mouth: not one will utter a single mew. Our youthful rogue had feared it would be wrong to shower joy upon this fair, unfruitful plot; but Bertha's words reassured him. To win over this soul to love would be no more, he thought, than following the commandments of God; and he thought rightly.

At nightfall, according to the old custom which the ladies of our day have forsaken, Bertha invited her cousin to keep her company in the great seigniorial bed. To which Sylvia, who was bound to keep up her part as a maiden of lofty birth, replied with a delighted acceptance. The curfew rang. They proceeded to a bedchamber richly adorned with carpets, hangings and royal tapestries. Bertha, assisted by her women, began to undress with a charming grace. Need you ask whether the gallant chastely refused to allow strange hands to touch his body? Blushing a deep crimson, Sylvia told her bedfellow that she was accustomed to undress all by herself, ever since she had lost the services of her lover, whose tender ministrations had disgusted her with the hands of women. How vividly these preparations recalled his delicate flattery and the pranks he played as he stripped her naked! To her great loss, the mere memory made her mouth water.

These words proved more than puzzling to Bertha; she let Sylvia say her prayers and make her other preparations for the night behind the curtains of the bed. Jean de Saché, spoiling with passion, leaped quickly under the sheets. From the vantage of this hiding-place, he looked out at her, thrilling with each chance glimpse at the wonder of her immaculate charms. Convinced that she was with an experienced girl, Bertha omitted none of her usual practises: she washed her feet, heedless of raising them high or not, she bared her delicate shoulders and did as all ladies do before retiring. At last, she came to bed, stretched out comfortably, and kissed her cousin on the lips. Incidentally, she found these extraordinarily warm.

"Are you ill, Sylvia, that you burn so?" she asked.

"I always burn like that in bed," Sylvia replied, "for that is when I remember the heady, sweet tricks my lover invented to please me. Oh, they burned me even more!"

"Eh, Sylvia, tell me all about this '*he*' . . . tell me about the delights of love . . . tell me, who live beneath the shadow of a hoary head with snows enough to keep me from such ardors . . . tell me, you who are cured, now. It will serve as a good warning to me, and your misfortunes will have been a salutary lesson to two poor womanly natures."

"I do not know if I should obey you, sweet coz," the rascal demurred.

"Tell me why not?"

"Ah, deeds are better than words!" Sylvia uttered a sigh deep as *ut* of an organ. "Besides I fear that this lord showered so much joy upon me that if I imparted but a mite of it to you, it would prove potent enough to give you a daughter, since my own faculty for childmaking would grow weak within me."

"But between you and me," Bertha objected, "would it be a sin?"

"No, on the contrary, it would spell joy both here and in heaven; the angels would shed their fragrance about you and make sweet music in your ears."

"Out with it then, sweet cousin!" Bertha urged.

"Well then, here is how my blessed lover warmed the cockles of my heart."

With these words, Jean put his arms about Bertha and, straining her to his breast, thrilled with immeasurable desire. In the dim light of the lamp and clad in cool white linen she lay in this soft bed like the delicate nuptial appurtenance of a lily in the depths of its virgin calyx.

"When he held me as I hold you now," Sylvia went on, "he would whisper in a voice far gentler than my own: 'Oh, Sylvia, you are my eternal love, my priceless treasure, my joy by day and by night; you are whiter than the day is day and fairer than anything on earth. I love you, Sylvia, I love you more than God, and I would wish to endure a thousand deaths for the happiness I ask of you.' Then he would kiss me, not after the brutal fashion of husbands but in a heavenly, dovelike manner."

To prove on the spot the superiority of a lover's method, he sucked all the honey from Bertha's lips, teaching her to use her pretty tongue, small and rosy as a cat's, and to speak volumes to the heart without uttering a single syllable. Then, catching fire at the game, Jean communicated the flame of his mouth to Bertha's neck, and thence to the most divinely lactescent fruits that ever woman gave a babe to slake his thirst upon. And anyone in his place would have esteemed himself a wicked man not to imitate him.

"Ah," sighed Bertha, stuck fast in the quagmire of love without knowing it, "this is better! I must tell Imbert about it!"

"Are you mad, cousin? No, never tell your old husband a

thing! How could he make his hands as suave and caressing as mine? His are hard as washerwomen's beetles, and that old pie-bald beard must certainly rasp this centre of delights, this rose that encloses all our feeling, our good, our substance, our love and our fortune. Do you know that it is a living flower demand-ing to be fondled thus and not grappled like a catapult of war? This, now, was the gentle way of my lover the Englishman."

So saying, the handsome rascal comported himself so manfully that a salvo of shots exploded. Suddenly, poor ingenuous Bertha exclaimed:

"Ah, God! the angels are come! But so beautiful is their mu-sic, that I can hear naught else, so flaming their luminous darts, that my eyes are closing."

In effect, she swooned under the burden of love's pleasures: they burst forth within her like the highest notes of the organ, they dazzled like the most magnificent aurora, they coursed through her veins like the rarest musk, and they loosened the bonds of life by giving life to a child of love—progeny which in lodging itself sets up a rather more tumultuous confusion than any other. Presently Bertha believed that she must be in the high heaven of Paradise, so ecstatic did she feel. She awakened from this nonpareil dream in the arms of Jean, crying:

"Ah, would that I had been married in England!"

"My darling mistress," said Jean, who had never savored such supreme rapture, "you are married to me in France, where things are even better ordered, and I am the man to lay down a thousand lives for your sake if I had them."

With a shriek shrill enough to pierce the very walls, the un-fortunate Bertha flew from her bed, much as a locust of the plagues of Egypt might have done. She flung herself on her knees before her *prie-dieu* and wept more pearls than ever Mary Mag-dalen wore.

"Ah, I am slain!" she moaned. "I am deceived by a devil who has assumed an angel face. I am lost, for I am surely mother to a fine child, without being any guiltier than you, O Lady Virgin! Implore God's grace for me, if I lack the grace of men upon earth; or let me perish, that I need not blush before my lord and master."

Hearing that she spoke no evil of him, Jean rose, amazed that

Bertha should be taking on so about this entrancing duet. But, as she heard her Gabriel stir, she sprang to her feet, facing him with tear-stained cheeks and eyes ablaze with holy wrath. This made her all the more beautiful to behold.

"If you take one step towards me," she cried, seizing a small dagger—obviously a woman's, "I shall take one toward death."

So heartrending was the tragic spectacle of her sorrow that Jean answered:

"It is I must die, not you, O blessed love, more dearly cherished than ever woman shall be on this earth!"

"If you had really loved me, you would not have killed me as you did. For die I shall, rather than face my husband's reproach."

"You will die?"

"Without fail!"

"No!" he protested. "If I am pierced, here, with a thousand blows, you will win your husband's pardon. You need but say that when your innocence was surprised, you avenged his honor by killing the deceiver. What greater happiness for me than to die for your sake the instant you refuse to live for mine?"

Before the tender, tearful tone of these words, Bertha dropped the dagger. Jean pounced upon it, pointed it to his heart and thrusting it into his flesh:

"Only death can repay such happiness!" he groaned.

And he fell, stark as a corpse.

Bertha, terrified, called for her maid, who was much frightened too as she beheld a wounded man in Madame's chamber, and Madame holding him up, gasping:

"What have you done, my love? Oh, what have you done?"

For Bertha, believing him dead, was thinking how immeasurable her joy had been and how beautiful Jean was, since everyone, even Imbert, took him for a girl. In the throes of her grief, she kept telling her maid everything, weeping and crying out that a child's life on her conscience was enough without adding a man's death. At which the poor lover tried to open his eyes but could show no more than a thin white patch of the pupils.

"Be careful, Madame, let us not shout!" the maid advised. "We must keep our heads and save this pretty gentleman. I'll send for La Fallotte; we need not even confide in a physician. She is a witch; to please Madame, she will miraculously heal this wound and leave never a trace behind!"

"Run," said Bertha, "I will love you and befriend you for this help."

But before doing anything else, lady and servant agreed to be silent about this adventure and to hide Jean from every eye. The maid went out into the night to fetch La Fallotte, her mistress saw her as far as the postern because the guard could not raise the portcullis without special orders from My Lady. When Bertha returned, she found that her handsome lover had fainted away from exhaustion; the blood kept flowing ceaselessly from his wound. Piously she kneeled and drank a little of this blood, grieving at the thought that Jean had spilled it for her sake. Moved by his great love and by his present peril, she kissed this pretty varlet of pleasure on the face, bound up his wound, bathed it with her tears, implored him not to die and promised to love him with all her heart if he would only live. Naturally Bertha grew still more enamored of him as she observed the various differences between a white, smooth, downy young lord like Jean and a yellow, bristly, wrinkled old battler like Imbert. These differences reminded her of the further difference she had found in the ecstasy of amour, and, under the sway of the memory, her kisses became so honeyed that Jean returned to consciousness, his glance grew clearer, he could see Bertha and implore her forgiveness in a feeble voice. But Bertha forbade him to speak until La Fallotte had come. Both spent the interval loving each other with their eyes. Bertha's were brimful with compassion and in these circumstances compassion is akin to love.

La Fallotte was an old humpback, vehemently suspected of dealing in necromancy and of riding a broomstick to the Witches' Sabbath, like the weird sisters. Certain people had seen her harnessing her broom in the stable, which, as everyone knows, is under the eaves. To tell the truth, she possessed some mysterious medical secrets, and she served ladies in certain things and lords in others so well that she was allowed to live her life in perfect tranquillity. Far from yielding up her soul on a pyre of faggots, she slept on a feather bed; and although the physicians tormented her, declaring that she sold poisons (which was strictly true, as this story will prove) she earned money hand over fist. The servant and La Fallotte rode to the manor on the same ass, having sped so quickly that they arrived before daybreak.

"Now then, children, what's the matter here?" the old humpback croaked as she entered the room.

This was her best bedside manner; she treated the mighty with a great deal of familiarity, for to her they appeared quite small. Putting on her spectacles, she probed the wound very adroitly, saying:

"Fine blood this is, my sweet! But you've tasted it, eh? Things will be all right; he has bled outwardly."

Next, she washed the wound with a fine sponge, under the nose of lady and maid, who watched breathlessly. Finally La Fallotte vouchsafed her doctoral verdict: the knight would not die of this wound.

"But," she added as she scanned the lines of his hand, "he shall die a violent death and you'll have this night's work to thank!"

This decree of chiromancy horrified Bertha and the servant. La Fallotte prescribed the urgent medicaments and promised to return the following night. Subsequently, she nursed Jean's wound for a whole fortnight, always coming secretly by night. The folk of the manor were told that Mademoiselle Sylvia de

Rohan was at death's door, as a result of an abdominal swelling, which must remain a secret for the honor of Madame, her cousin. This yarn satisfied everyone; the servants' mouths were so full of it that they retailed it to their friends.

The good people believed that the illness was fraught with danger, but not at all! It was really the convalescence that proved parlous! Fast as Jean gathered strength, Bertha lost it, becoming so weak, indeed, as to allow herself to slip back into that Paradise Jean had opened up for her. In a word, she loved him more and more. But, at the height of her happiness, she was always stabbed by her apprehension at La Fallotte's dire prophecy, by the self-reproach of her deeply religious conscience and by her terror of My Lord Imbert.

She had been compelled to write to the latter announcing that he had given her a child who would be there to delight him on his return. Poor woman! to lie out like that hurt her far more than ever lying-in!

The day she wrote the dishonest letter, she avoided her lover sedulously and sat alone, crying her eyes out. Usually, of course, they were as inseparable as the flame and the log it burns through. Jean, seeing himself neglected, concluded that she had begun to hate him. And he, too, wept bitterly. That evening, Bertha saw traces of tears about his eyes despite his efforts of concealment. Deeply affected, she told him the cause of her grief; unconsciously she went on to confess her terrors for the future and to point out how much they were both to blame. She appealed to him with much noble, Christianly eloquence; she adorned her plea with contrite prayers and divine tears. Her zeal pierced Jean's heart. This love, so ingenuously bound up with repentance, this magnanimity in sin; this compound of weakness and strength, would, as the old authors say, have soothed the fury of a tiger and melted it to pity. Small wonder, then, that Jean was compelled to pledge his knightly word to obey her in whatever she might command for her salvation in this world and in the next.

Such proof of his trust and his fundamental goodness brought her prone at his feet, which she covered with kisses, as:

"O lover, lover," she cried, "I needs must adore you though it be a mortal sin; you are so good, so compassionate toward your unhappy Bertha! If you would always have her think of you kindly, if you would stem the torrent of her tears, whose source is so grateful and so pleasurable . . ."—to prove her sincerity, she suffered him to steal a kiss—". . . O Jean," she went on, "if you would make the remembrance of our celestial bliss, our angel music, and our balms of love a consolation in my loneliness rather than a burden of guilt, then do what the Virgin bade me command you. I dreamed a dream in which I besought Her to enlighten me on our present plight, since I had implored Her so fervently and She was come in answer to my prayer. I confessed to Her what excruciating torment I would endure . . . how I would tremble for this child already stirring in my womb . . . and for its real father, left at the mercy of the other and liable to expiate his fatherhood by a violent death. . . . (Alas! La Fallotte may well have read aright into the future.)

"And the beautiful Virgin, smiling, told me that the Church offered us the forgiveness of our sins if we followed her commandments, and She told me that we must save ourselves from Hell fire by mending our ways early, ere God waxed wroth. Then She pointed, and, following Her finger, I saw a Jean, like you but clad as you should be, and as you will be, if you love me with an eternal love."

Jean protested his perfect obedience, lifted her up, seated her on his knee and kissed her fondly. Then Bertha explained that the garment she had seen in the vision was a monk's robe. Trembling lest he refuse, she entreated him to enter the Church and retire to Marmoutier, beyond Tours. Would he do it? If so, she swore to grant him one last night—after which she would never again belong to him or to any other man on earth. In return for this, she would let him come to her one day every year to see his child.

Jean, bound by his promise, declared that he was willing to abide implicitly by his sweetheart's will. Thus he would remain forever faithful to her, experiencing no joys in love excepting those savored in her divine embrace; and he would go on living only in the blessed remembrance of these. Hearing his magical words, Bertha vowed that, great though her sin and however dire the fate God held in store for her, this hour would enable her to brave the worst, since she believed she had yielded not to a man but to an angel.

Then they lay down in the nest where their love was hatched, but only to bid all its sweet flowers a supreme farewell. Beyond doubt, My Lord Cupid had a hand in this feast, for never was woman given such joy anywhere in the world and never did man take so much. The quintessence of true love lies in a certain concordance through which the more one gives, the more the other receives, and conversely, as in certain mathematical equations where things multiply themselves to infinity. This problem can be explained to unscientific people by likening it to Venetian glasses which reproduce thousands of faces from a single model. Similarly in the hearts of two lovers, the roses of pleasure multiply themselves further and further down blissful depths, while they marvel that the latter can hold such funds of ecstasy without anything bursting. Bertha and Jean would have wished this night were the last of their lives; adaze at the rapt languor that oozed through their veins, they believed that love had resolved to charm them away on the wings of a deathly embrace. But they held out, despite these infinite multiplications.

On the morrow, since Imbert's return was imminent, Mademoiselle Sylvia de Rohan was forced to depart. As she left her cousin, the poor girl covered her with tears and kisses; it was always the last, and the last kiss stretched out until evening. Finally he must needs go, and go he did, though his heart's blood coagulated like the wax fallen from a Paschal taper. According to his promise, he went off to Marmoutier, entering the monastery towards the eleventh hour of the day. They placed him among the novices.

The Sieur de Bastarnay was told that Sylvia had returned to the Lord—but whether to an English lover or to a divine master was not explained. At all events, Bertha did not lie in her statement.

Imbert's joy when he saw that Bertha had grown too big to wear a girdle, was the first nail in this unhappy woman's cross. She did not know how to deceive; for each false word she uttered, she would go to her *prie-dieu*, weep tears of blood, break into piteous prayer and commend herself to the mercy of the Lord's Saints in Paradise.

It happened that she clamored so loudly to God that He heard her, because He hears everything: He hears the stones that roll beneath the waters, the poor who moan and the flies that buzz

through the air. It is just as well that you should know this, or
you might not believe what followed. God ordered the Archangel Michael to give this penitent a Hell upon earth so that
she might indisputably enter into Paradise. St. Michael winged

his way down from the skies, stood at the gate of Hell and delivered this triple soul to the Devil; pointing out the mother,
the lover and the child, he informed Satan that he might lawfully torment Bertha for the rest of her days. The Devil, who, by
God's good will, is lord of all evil, assured the Archangel that he
would perform this office.

While these supernatural arrangements were being concluded, life moved here below according to its earthly rhythm. The sweet lady of Bastarnay presented Messire Imbert with the prettiest child in the world, a lad of lilies and roses, as highly gifted as an infant Jesus, merry and pert as a pagan Eros, growing handsomer day by day. He was bright as a star; he took after his father and mother; their bodily and spiritual perfections had produced a compound of illustrious graces and marvellous intelligence. Meanwhile his brother was turning more and more into a baboon like his father: the resemblance he bore to Imbert was downright uncanny. As My Lord observed his younger son, he thrilled at this perpetual miracle of flesh and spirit blended with the quintessential condition. For his eternal salvation, he said that he would like to be able to make the younger the elder and vowed to arrange the matter with the King's protection. Bertha was at a loss: what could she do? She adored Jean's child and could love the other only feebly; but she nevertheless shielded him from the evil intentions of old Bastarnay. In time, Bertha grew satisfied with the way things were going, and stilled her conscience with falsehood. Surely all their troubles were over?

Twelve years passed, cloudless save for the doubt which at times poisoned her joy. Every year, according to her pledged word, the monk of Marmoutier, whom none but the maid knew, would come to the château and spend a whole day with his child. Even then, Bertha had begged her friend Brother Jean several times to forgo his right. But Jean, pointing to the child, said:

"You see him every day of the year; I have but one day only."

What answer could the poor mother make to such an appeal?

A few months before the Dauphin's last rebellion, the child was treading closely on the heels of his twelfth year. He seemed likely to become a great scholar, so learned was he in all the sciences. Never had old Bastarnay been happier in his fatherhood. He resolved to bring his son to the Court of Burgundy, where Duke Charles, who was never averse to intelligent men, promised to give the lad a post which princes would envy. Seeing matters thus settled, the Devil judged the time ripe for his mischief. He took his tail and whipped it right into the middle of this happiness, in his most approved manner. Then he stirred up everything to his liking.

Horrendous Chastisement and Penance of Bertha, Who Died Pardoned

MADAME DE BASTARNAY'S chambermaid, then thirty-five years old, fell in love with one of My Lord's men-at-arms. What is more, she was foolish enough to let him bake a few loaves in her oven—an operation that left her with a natural swelling which the wags in these parts call the nine months' dropsy. The unfortunate woman implored her kind mistress to intercede with My Lord and compel the wicked man to complete at the altar what he had begun in bed. Madame de Bastarnay easily obtained this favor from Imbert; the maid was delighted. But the old warrior, as ever devilishly gruff, summoned the culprit to his pretorium, hauled him over the coals and ordered him under pain of the gallows to marry the maid. This the soldier agreed to, since he preferred his neck to his peace of mind.

Unfortunately Imbert also sent for the female, judging it seemly for the honor of his house to sing her a litany, spangled with abusive epithets and adorned with horrisonant invective. By way of punishment, she should believe that she was not to achieve marriage but, rather, to be clapped into jail. The maid concluded that Bertha was trying to get rid of her in order to bury the secret of her dear son's birth. So when the old ape reviled her outrageously—he said, for instance, that he must have been a half-wit to keep a harlot in his house—she thought only of her spite and her safety, and replied that he must have been a raving lunatic not to know that his wife had for a long time played the harlot. And with a monk, too, which, for a soldier, is the bitterest extremity.

Think of the fiercest tempest you ever saw in your born days, and you will have but a faint adumbration of the furious passion into which the old man flew as he heard her assail him in a portion of his heart that sheltered a triple life. He seized her by the throat and was about to strangle her incontinently. But she, to prove her point, cited the how, the when and the why. If he did not believe her, he could surely rely upon his own ears; very

well, let him hide some day when Dom Jean de Saché, Prior of Marmoutier, came. He would then hear the father's words, observe him making up for his year's fast, hear him kiss his son enough in one day to compensate him for his twelve months' loneliness.

Imbert ordered the woman to leave the château forthwith: if her accusation was true, he would kill her as surely as if she had invented a tissue of falsehood. In a trice, he gave her a hundred crowns, besides her man, and enjoined them not to bed in Touraine. For greater security, he had one of his officers conduct them into Burgundy. Then he informed his wife curtly of their departure, adding that the maid was a damaged article whom he had judged it politic to get rid of, but that he had given her a hundred crowns and found employment for the man at the Burgundian Court. Bertha was surprised to hear that the maid had left the château without receiving her dismissal from herself, her mistress; but she held her peace. Soon after she had other fish to fry: she had cause for grave apprehensions when Imbert's attitude changed completely. He began to comment upon the resemblances between his first-born and himself; but he could find nothing of his nose, his brow, or this, or that, in the youngster he loved so dearly.

"He takes entirely after me," Bertha rejoined one day when Imbert was making these equivocal comparisons. "Don't you know that in well-ordered households, sons favor the father and mother in turn, or often both together because the mother mingles her nature with the vital forces of the father? Surely you have heard that certain physicians boast of knowing many children born without resemblance to either father or mother? These are, they say, mysteries due to the whims of God."

"You have become very learned, my sweet," Imbert replied, "but I, an ignoramus, would imagine that a child who resembled a monk—"

"—was born of a monk, eh?" Bertha interrupted. She looked him fearlessly in the eye though ice rather than blood filled in her veins.

The goodman decided he was mistaken and cursed the maid heartily; but he was none the less eager to establish the truth.

As the day of Dom Jean's visit drew near, Bertha, alarmed by Imbert's behavior, wrote to the monk that she was unwilling to receive him this year, reserving the right to withhold her reasons. Then she went to Loches in search of La Fallotte, who was to deliver her letter. For the present, anyhow, everything seemed safe. Later, she found further grounds for congratulating herself on having warned him. In the past, towards the time when the luckless monk's visit fell due, Imbert had invariably taken a journey into the province of Maine, where he owned great estates. This year, however, he decided not to; he would be too busy helping in the preparations for the rebellion My Lord Dauphin was then planning against his poor father, who, as everyone knows, died of a broken heart because of it. Imbert's excuse was so plausible that poor Bertha, caught in the web, did not bother about it.

On the appointed day, the Prior arrived as usual. Bertha seeing him turned pale as a ghost. Had her message failed to reach him?

"What message?" Jean asked.

"Oh, we are lost then! . . ." Bertha moaned, "the child, you and I. . . ."

"Why should we be lost?" the monk demanded.

"I do not know," she said, "but our last day has dawned."

She asked her blessed son where Bastarnay was. The lad informed her that his father had been summoned to Loches by special messenger. He was not to return before night. Against his sweetheart's will, Jean insisted on remaining with her and his beloved son: what mischief could possibly come of it when twelve years had passed safely?

On previous occasions, when they celebrated the adventurous night you know of, Bertha always remained in her room with the ill-starred monk until suppertime. But now, when Bertha retailed her apprehensions, which Jean shared the moment he heard them, they decided that, under the circumstances, they had best dine early. Still, the Prior reassured Bertha as he cited the privileges of the Church and pointed out how Bastarnay, already in bad odor at Court, would undoubtedly be afraid to attack a dignitary of Marmoutier. As they sat down at the table, their youngest happened to be playing; he was riding around the courtyard of the château, exercising a fine Spanish jennet that the Duke of Burgundy had given Bastarnay. In spite of his mother's repeated prayers, he refused to abandon his sport. And as youths like to appear older (varlets play the bachelor, bachelors play the knight) this lad was delighted at being able to show his friend the monk that he was almost grown-up. He made the horse jump like a flea in the bedclothes, keeping as firm a seat, the while, as a veteran knight.

"Let him have his way, darling," the monk told Bertha. "Disobedient children often turn into great characters."

Bertha ate sparingly, for her heart swelled within her like a sponge in water. At the first mouthful, the monk, a man of considerable science, felt a burning in his stomach and an acrid aftertaste on his palate. Was it some deadly bane? Had the Sire de Bastarnay sought to dispatch them with poison? Ere he made this discovery, Bertha had already eaten. Suddenly Jean pulled off the table cloth, flung everything into the hearth and imparted his suspicions to Bertha, who gave thanks to the Virgin that her son had been so intent on his sport. But Dom Jean kept his wits about him. Remembering his early training as a page, he leaped into the court, lifted his son off the horse, swung into the saddle and sped across the country like a shot out of a gun. He rode at lightning pace, crushing his mount's flanks with his heels as though he would disembowel it. He reached La Fallotte's house at Loches so soon that only the Devil could have matched his time. Telling her of the accident in two words, for the poison was already gnawing at his entrails, he begged her for an antidote.

"Alas!" said the witch, "had I known it was for you I gave this poison, I would sooner have bared my throat to the dagger they threatened me with . . . I would sooner have forfeited my sorry life to save that of a man of God and of the sweetest woman ever blossomed on this earth. . . . Oh, my poor friend, I have only the few drops of counter-poison you see in that phial."

"Is it enough for her?"

"Ay, but make haste," urged the old hag.

The monk hurried back even more quickly than he had come; as he rode into the courtyard, his horse died under him. He rushed to the room where Bertha, believing her last hour at hand, was kissing her child and writhing like a lizard in the fire. Over her own fate, she uttered never a cry; all her lamentation was for her child, abandoned to the fury of Bastarnay. All consciousness of her own torment fell away as she thought of this cruel future.

"Take this!" cried the monk. "My life is saved!"

Dom Jean had the superb courage to speak these words without flinching, though he felt the claws of death gripping his heart. He kissed his son, saw Bertha drain the potion, levelled a glance upon his sweetheart that did not alter even after he had sighed his last, and fell, dead, at her feet. This sight turned her cold as marble; it terrified her so much that at first she stood rigid before the corpse stretched at her feet. If she moved, it was to press the hand of her weeping child; herself gazed with eyes as dry as the Red Sea when Baron Moses led the Hebrews over it. She seemed to feel sharp grains of sand rolling under her eyelids. Pray for her, O ye charitable souls, for never was woman so bitterly harrowed as Bertha, when she divined that her lover had saved her life at the cost of his own. Presently, with her son's help, she laid the monk in the middle of her bed and stood by the bedside, praying. Then she told the lad that Jean was his real father. In this state, she awaited her evil hour. . . .

Nor was the interval long before it struck. At about eleven o'clock, Bastarnay returned; at the portcullis, they informed him that the monk was dead, but not Madame, nor yet the child. Crossing the courtyard, he saw his beautiful jennet lying across the cobbles, dead. Seized with a rageful lust to kill Bertha and the monk's bastard, he sprang up the stairs with one bound. But as he took in the scene—the corpse on the bed, his wife and the boy repeating endless litanies, with no ears for his virulent abuse, no eyes for his menaces and swordmills—he dared no longer perpetrate the dastardly outrage. These first paroxysms of his fury spent, he had not the faintest idea what to do: he paced up and down the room like a coward, like a thief caught in the act. And these prayers, said over and over again, stung him to the quick. Night passed amid tears, groans and prayers.

Bertha had ordered her maid to go to Loches to buy her the attire of a young noblewoman and her poor child a horse and the arms of an esquire. When these arrived, the Sieur de Bastarnay was much surprised; he sent for Bertha and the monk's son, but neither mother nor child returned any answer. They donned the clothes the maid had brought, while the latter, at Bertha's order, balanced the accounts of Madame's household, and arranged her clothes, pearls, jewels and diamonds as a widow's property is usually arranged when she renounces her rights. Bertha bade her even put her alms-bag over the lot, in order that the ceremony might be perfect. Reports of these preparations ran rife through the house; everyone knew then that Madame was about to forsake it; no heart but was filled with sorrow including even a little scullion's, who had been there less than a week and who wept because Madame had already said a kind word to him.

Appalled by these preparations, old Bastarnay came into Bertha's room; he found her weeping by Jean's corpse, for her tears had come at last. But, seeing Imbert, she dried them hastily. To his numberless questions, she replied briefly by the confession of her fault, explaining how she had been tricked, how the poor page had stabbed himself (she showed him the scar on the corpse) and how long he had been convalescent . . . how, in obedience to her and out of penitence towards God and man, he had entered the Church, abandoned the glorious career of knighthood and—worse than death—suffered his name to perish . . . how she, while avenging her honor, had believed that God Almighty Himself would not have refused this monk one day in the year when he might see the child for whom he was sacrificing everything . . . how, not wishing to live with a murderer, she was about to quit his house, leaving all her possessions there . . . Further, she observed, if the honor of the Bastarnays was besmirched, it was he, not she, who had brought down the shame upon them, because amid this misfortune she had managed things in the best possible way. Finally she made a vow to go over mountain and valley, she and her son, until all was expiated, for she knew how to expiate all.

Very pale she looked, and very noble as she spoke these proud words. Then, taking her child by the hand, she went forth in great mourning, more magnificently beautiful than was My Lady Hagar setting out from the house of the patriarch Abraham. And so superb she was, that all the servitors and menials fell to their knees as she passed by, imploring her with joined hands like Notre Dame de la Riche. It was piteous to see the Sieur de Bastarnay following her, shamefaced, weeping, proclaiming his guilt, and despairing like a man on his way to the scaffold.

But Bertha paid no attention whatever. So great was the general desolation that she found the drawbridge lowered; she hastened to escape from the castle, fearing it might suddenly be raised again. But no one had either the right or the heart to do

so. She sat down at the edge of the moat, in view of the whole
castle, while they all besought her tearfully to stay. The unfortunate lord stood there with his hand on the chain of the portcullis,
as silent as the stone saints carved above the gate; he watched
Bertha stop at the end of the bridge, bid her son shake the dust
from his shoes lest he take anything belonging to Bastarnay with
him, and herself do likewise. Then pointing earnestly at Imbert,
she turned to her son and said solemnly:

"Child, behold the murderer of your father, who was, as you
are aware, the unfortunate Prior. But you have taken the name
of this man. Give it back to him, here, just as you left the dust
your shoes took from his manor. As for the food you have eaten
in his house, we will settle that score too, by God's help."

As he heard this complaint, old Bastarnay would gladly have
abandoned a whole monastery of monks to his wife to retain her
and a young squire capable of becoming the glory of his house.
He stood motionless, his head bowed over the chains.

"O Satan," Bertha cried, without knowing what part the Devil
had played in this business, "are you content? Then may God,
His Saints and His Archangels, whom I have so fervently invoked, bear us help amid the ruin of our lives."

Suddenly Bertha's heart was filled with consolation as she beheld the banner of the great monastery turning down the road
and appearing in full view, accompanied by holy chants which
burst forth like heavenly music. Informed of the murder perpetrated upon their beloved Prior, the monks had come procession-
ally, with the ecclesiastical justice, to claim the body. My Lord
of Bastarnay had barely time to rush through the postern with
his people and speed off to the Dauphin, leaving everything in
confusion.

Poor Bertha, in the saddle behind her son, went to Montbazon
to take leave of her father, whom she assured that this blow
would spell her death. Her family tried their utmost to console
her, but in vain. The old Sire de Rohan presented his grandson
with a splendid suit of armor, and urged him to win such great
glory and honor by his doughty deeds as must turn his mother's
fault into eternal glory. Madame de Bastarnay had instilled but
one thought in her son's mind: he must atone for the harm done

in order to save her and Jean from eternal damnation. Accordingly they both made for the centre of the rebellion in order to render services to Bastarnay more precious than life itself.

Now the core of the revolt was, as everyone knows, in the neighborhood of Angoulême and of Bordeaux in Guyenne, though

in other parts of the kingdom fierce battles and violent encounters were likely to take place between the rebels and the royal forces. The principal one, which finished the war, was waged between Ruffec and Angoulême, where all the prisoners were tried and hanged. This battle, in which old Bastarnay led the rebel host, was fought some time in November, exactly seven months after the murder of Dom Jean. Imbert knew that he had been specially marked for execution as the Dauphin's chief adviser. When his men began to retreat, he found himself hemmed in by six men-at-arms who were determined to seize him. He realized that they had instructions to take him alive, so that the King might proceed against his house, dishonor his name and confiscate his goods. The unfortunate lord preferred to die on the field, thus saving his family and preserving his estates for his son; he defended himself like the brave old lion he was. In spite of their number, these soldiers, seeing three of their comrades bite the dust, were compelled to attack Bastarnay even at the risk of killing him. They laid low his two equerries and a page, then threw themselves together upon him.

In this extreme danger, a squire, wearing the arms of Rohan, fell upon the assailants like a thunderbolt and downed two of them. "God save the Bastarnays!" he cried. The third man-at-arms, who had already clutched old Imbert, was so hard pressed by this squire that he was forced to loose his hold on the old man. Turning to face his assailant, he plunged his dagger through the gap between the squire's gorget and breastplate. Imbert was too loyal a comrade to flee without assisting the liberator of his house, especially as he saw the squire was wounded. With a blow of the mace, he brained the soldier; then he lifted the squire from the ground, threw him across his horse and galloped off for the open country, following a guide who led him to the Château de La Roche Foucauld.

He entered the place by night, to find Bertha de Rohan in the great hall. It was she who had prepared this retreat and posted the guide for him. As he lifted his rescuer's visor, he recognized Jean's son. The lad died upon the table, having with a supreme effort kissed his mother and cried in a loud voice:

"Mother, we have paid him our debt!"

Hearing these words, the mother threw her arms about his body and joined her love-child for all eternity: she died of grief without hearing or heeding Imbert's pardon and repentance.

This extraordinary tragedy hastened the last days of the poor old man; he did not live to see the coronation of his master the Dauphin as King Louis the Eleventh. Imbert founded a daily Mass at the Church of La Roche Foucauld, where he placed mother and son in the same grave, with a large tombstone on which their lives were illustriously celebrated in Latin.

The diverse morals which everyone may deduce from this tale are very profitable for the conduct of life. To begin with, it shows us how gentlemen should be courteous towards the lovers of their wives. Further, it teaches us that all children are blessings visited upon us by God Himself and that their fathers, whether in name or fact, have no right of murder over them. To be sure, this was formerly the case in Rome according to a heathen and abominable law; but it does not befit Christianity, wherein we are all sons of God.

How the Pretty Maid of Portillon Confounded Her Judge

*T*HE MAID of Portillon, who as everyone knows, later married Tâchereau, was a laundress before becoming a dyer's wife. She lived at Portillon, whence her name. If there be anyone who does not know Tours, it may be well to explain that Portillon is down the Loire on the St. Cyr side, as far from the bridge which leads to the Cathedral of Tours as again the bridge is from Marmoutier. In other words the bridge is on the embankment exactly half-way between Portillon and Marmoutier. Now, do you follow? . . . Yes? . . . Good!

This girl, then, had her washhouse at Portillon; she could run down to the Loire in no time at all, do all her washing, then cross on the ferry-boat to St. Martin. She delivered most of her laundry at Châteauneuf and places nearby.

About Midsummer day, seven years before marrying goodman Tâchereau, she was just ripe for love. Being of a merry disposition, she allowed herself to be wooed without making a choice from among the lads who pursued her with their attentions. Though the bench under her window saw such occupants as Rabelais' son, who had seven boats on the Loire, the first-born of the Jeans, Marchandeau the tailor and Peccard the church gilder, she made fun of them all. She firmly intended to be led to the altar before being trammelled by a man, which proves that she was an honest wench until her virtue was drabbled. She was one of those girls who put up a brave front against contamination but who, if they chance to be scotched, let everything go to sixes and sevens.

"A pretty kettle of fish!" they think. "Besides, a thorough furbishing is just as necessary for one blot as for fifty!"

Such characters implore our Christianly indulgence.

One day a young courtier saw her as she crossed the river in the glare of a noontide sun that made her charms shine forth in all their ample beauty. He inquired who she was. An old man, working on the riverbank, informed him that she was the pretty maid of Portillon, a laundress renowned for her merry wit and her virtue. This lordling had no mean ruffs to starch, as well as many linens and precious draperies. He determined to give the belle of Portillon his trade and stopped her to tell her so. Very grateful she was and very heartily she thanked him, for he was none other than the Sire du Fou, Chamberlain to the King. The encounter went to the sweet maid's head; his name was forever on her lips. She prattled about him to the folk of St. Martin; returning to her washhouse, she babbled away, nineteen to the dozen; on the morrow she still kept harping upon him as she did her washing by the river. Thus My Lord du Fou was more frequently invoked at Portillon than God is in a pulpit—which is rather too much.

"Ef she didders thataways in cold water, what'll she do when she's blood-hot?" an old scarecrow asked her fellow washerwomen. "Du Fou'll fool her and foul her, too! Oh, ay! Hark at 'er! All them du Fous'll foozle her proper!"

The first time this madcap with her mouth full of My Lord du Fou had linen to deliver at his mansion, the Chamberlain asked to see her. He sang her praises, loaded her with compliments upon her charms, wound up by telling her that she was not foolish to be beautiful and that he would accordingly do the needful on the spot. The deed followed the word, for, the moment his servants left them, he began cockling the pretty maid. She, for her part, expected to see him take some shining crowns from his purse and, like a girl ashamed of accepting wages, she dared not look at it.

"This will be the first time. . . ." she murmured.

"The first stroke is half the battle," he said.

Some people report that he had untold difficulties in imposing the punctilio and that he barely forced her at all; others insist that she was shockingly forced, because she emerged like a routed army fleeing, sobbing bitterly and reviling him. In any case, she went straight to the Judge's house. The man of law happened to be out; the laundress waited for him to return, and, amid a shower of tears, told the servant that she had been robbed, because My Lord du Fou had given her naught but his mischief, whereas a Canon of the Chapter used to give her large sums for what Du Fou had stolen ... that if she loved a man, she would deem it wise to offer him this pleasure scot-free because she her-

self would enjoy it ... but that the Chamberlain had jostled and tumbled her about, instead of caressing her gently, as he should have done ... and that he therefore owed her the thousand crowns of the Canon. The Judge came in, saw the fair wench and tried to wanton with her; but she put herself on guard and said she had come to make a complaint. The Judge replied that he would certainly hang the offender, if she wished it, because he was ready to go all lengths for her sake. But the belle pointed out that, far from desiring her man to die, she wanted him to pay her a thousand gold crowns, because she had been forced against her will.

"Ha, ha!" laughed the Judge. "The fruit he stole is worth more still."

"I'll let it go for a thousand," she said, "because then I can give up my washing."

"Is the culprit rich?" the Judge asked.

"Yes, very!"

"Well then, he shall pay through the nose. Who is it?"

"My Lord du Fou."

"Hm! that alters the case," said the Judge.

"And justice?" she demanded.

"I said 'the case' not 'justice'," the man of law replied. "I must know exactly how it happened."

Naïvely, the fair maid related how she was arranging My Lord's ruffs in his wardrobe, when he began to play with her skirts, and how she turned round and said:

"Have done, My Lord!"

"You have no case!" cried the Judge. "Obviously he thought those words urged him to go the whole hog. Ha, ha!"

The belle objected: she had defended herself fiercely, she had wept and cried out. Here was a clear case of rape.

"Pooh!" said the Judge, "a virgin's tricks to egg him on!"

She protested: on the contrary, she had suddenly felt herself seized by the waist and backed up against the bed; she had struggled and shouted; at last, seeing no help at hand, she had lost courage.

"Good! Good!" the Judge opined. There was a pause. Then: "Did you experience any pleasure?"

"No," she said, "nothing less than a thousand gold crowns could compensate me for my anguish."

"My dear, I cannot possibly allow your complaint, because I hold that no girl can be violated without her enthusiastic coöperation."

"Oh, oh, oh, Judge," she sobbed. "You ask your servant and see what she tells you!"

The servant affirmed that there were pleasant assaults as well as highly unpleasant ones and that if the laundress had received neither cash nor pleasure, then either pleasure or cash was due her. This wise counsel left the Judge vastly perplexed.

"Jacqueline," he said, "before I have my supper, I want to look into this. Here, go fetch my bodkin and the red thread I use to sew up my legal wrappers."

Jacqueline returned, bearing a piece of metal with a dainty, perfectly fashioned hole in it, and a thick red thread such as magistrates use. Then she stood by to watch how her master would deliver judgment. She was all agog at these mysterious preparations. The laundress, too, was breathless.

"My dear," said the Judge, "I shall hold up this bodkin: its eye is easily large enough for this thread to go through without trouble. If you manage to put it in, I will take up your case and make My Lord du Fou come across in a fair composition."

"What's that?" she said. "I'll not have him come in any position!"

"No—a composition is a legal word; it means a compromise—a part for the whole!"

"Whew!" she whistled. . . . "Then that's why they say the 'body of the law'?"

"My dear, I see that rape has given you great mental penetration as well. Are you ready?"

"Yes," she cried.

The artful Judge gave the nymph fair play by holding the eye

steady for her; but when, having twisted the thread straight, she
sought to slip it in, he moved it a whit, and her first effort proved
unavailing. Suspecting the Judge's argument, she wetted the
thread, stretched it and returned to the fray. The magistrate
moved, squirmed and wiggled about like a virgin who dares not;
still the cursed thread would not go in. The maid kept aiming at
the hole, the Judge kept fidgeting. The marriage of thread and
bodkin could not be consummated; the eyelet remained virgin,
while the servant roared with laughter, assuring the laundress
that, so far as violation was concerned, she knew more about playing a passive part than an active or instrumental. The waggish
Judge laughed too; the maid of Portillon wept for her golden
crowns.

"If you won't keep still," she said losing patience, "if you keep
moving about, how can I ever slip this in?"

"Just so, my dear. If you had done likewise, My Lord could
not have come off successfully. Consider, moreover, how easy this
orifice is and how tight-closed a maiden should be."

The self-styled victim remained thoughtful, searching for some
means to convince the Judge. She must prove to him that she
had been forced to yield; was not the honor of all poor girls open
to violation at stake?

"My Lord, to make things fair, I should do exactly as the Sire
du Fou did. Were it but a question of moving, I should be moving still! But he went through other ceremonies."

"Let us hear all about it," said the Judge.

The belle drew out the thread and rubbed it in the wax of the
candle to make it stand firm and straight, poised it in the air
and stabbed at the bodkin which the Judge held before her a moment, then moved always to the right or to the left. As she
worked, she made a thousand mock-amorous remarks:

"Ah, the sweet little bodkin! . . . What a delightful mark to
pink! . . . never have I seen such a jewel! . . . What a cosy little
inlet! . . . let me put this persuasive bit of thread in it! Oh, oh!
you will hurt my poor thread, my delicate thread! . . . keep still,
do! Come, my love of a judge, judge of my love. . . . Eh, won't
this thread go nicely into this iron gate . . . aye, the gate wears it
down, for it comes out quite bedraggled! . . ."

She burst out laughing, for she was already a better hand at this game than the Judge, who laughed too, so saucy and mischievous and arch she was as she pushed the thread backwards and forwards. She kept him bodkin in hand until seven o'clock, bobbing up and down friskily as a marmot. But, as she continued trying to get the thread in, he could not help getting tired. Meanwhile his roast was burning in the kitchen. He was compelled to rest his fatigued wrist against the table for a moment. At once, very skilfully the fair maid of Portillon drove the thread home, saying:

"That is how it happened."

"But my meat was burning!" the Judge protested.

"So was mine," she said.

The Judge, utterly confounded, promised her that he would arrange to speak to My Lord du Fou and himself carry the matter through, because he was now convinced that the young nobleman had forced her against her will. But, he added, for valid reasons, he would keep the business dark. On the morrow he went to Court, saw Du Fou, cited her grievance and told him how she had set forth her case. This juridical complaint pleased the King mightily. Young Du Fou having confessed that there was some truth in it, His Majesty asked him if he had found her of difficult access. The Sieur du Fou replied naïvely that he had not, to which His Majesty rejoined that the operation seemed certainly worth a hundred gold crowns. These the Chamberlain gave the Judge in order not to appear niggardly, adding that starch would net her a good income. The Judge returned to Portillon and, with a smile, informed the maid that he had collected a hundred crowns for her. If, however, she desired the balance of the thousand, there were at that moment in the King's apartments certain lords who, knowing the case, volunteered to raise the sum if she wished.

She did not refuse; in order to do no more public washing, she did not mind a little in private now. She rewarded the good Judge handsomely for his pains, went to town and earned her thousand crowns in a month. Thence rose the falsehoods and jokes about her: out of these ten lords or so, the jealous hussies made a hundred, whereas, unlike most slatterns, the maid of Portillon took to virtue as soon as she had won her thousand gold crowns. Short of five hundred, even a duke would have found the wench rebellious; this alone proves that she was chary of her works. To be sure the King summoned her to his retreat in the Rue Quincangrogne, on the Mail du Chardonneret. He found her extremely attractive and bubbling over with affection; he enjoyed her society and forbade the sergeants to molest her in any way whatsoever. Seeing how beautiful she was, Nicole Beaupertuys, His Majesty's sweetheart, gave her a hundred gold crowns to go to Orléans and find out whether the color of the Loire was the same there as at Portillon. She went all the more willingly because she did not care a scrap for the King. When the holy man came who confessed the King in his last hours and was afterwards canonized, the fair wench went to him to have her conscience furbished, did penance and founded a bed in the leper-house of St. Lazare-lez-Tours. A number of ladies whom you know, have, of their own accord, been violated by more than ten lords without founding any other beds than those in their own homes. This fact bears citing in order to wash the honor of this fair maid, who herself once washed the ordures of others and who afterwards won renown for her charm and her wit. She gave proof of her merits when she married Tâchereau, whom she cuckolded cheerfully to the happiness of both of them, as has been related in the story of *The Wife's Appeal.*

This proves conclusively to us that with strength and patience a human can violate Justice herself.

Which Proves That Fortune Is Always Female

ON THE island of Sicily, which, as you doubtless know, is tucked away in one corner of the Mediterranean Sea and which enjoyed a great celebrity of yore, two chevaliers happened to meet in a wood. It was in the days when knights used courteously to help and assist each other in the quest of fortune.

One of these chevaliers looked like a Frenchman. He was presumably stripped of everything, since he went on foot, without esquire or following, and so miserably attired that, but for his princely mien, he might have passed for a villain. Possibly his horse had perished of hunger or fatigue on disembarking from overseas, whence this lord had journeyed in the hope of such good luck as befell French chevaliers in Sicily. A justly confident hope, as examples might prove.

The other knight, a Sicilian named Pezare, had emigrated from the Republic of Venice a long time before; nor had he the least desire to return, since he had obtained a footing in the Court of the King of Sicily. Being a younger son and therefore impecunious, he had no taste for a commercial career at home; for this reason, he was eventually cast off by his family, a most illustrious one. So he had settled at the Sicilian Court and won the King's abiding affection.

Pezare was riding a splendid Spanish mount and thinking to himself how lonely he was in this foreign capital without a single friend he could rely upon, and how, in such cases, fortune was harsh to helpless people and turned treacherous. Suddenly he met the poor French knight. How bitterly bereft he looked! Much more so than he, Pezare, equipped with excellent arms, a

449

noble steed and servants aplenty who were even then busy preparing a sumptuous supper in an inn nearby.

"You must have come a long way to have so much dust on your
feet?" said Pezare.

"My road is longer and dustier than ever my feet can show."

"If you have travelled so much," Pezare went on, "you must
be a learned man."

"I have learned to take no heed of those who heed me not,"
said the Frenchman. "I have learned that, however high a man's
head was, his feet were always level with mine. And I have learned

to put no trust in the warm days of winter, in the sleep of my enemies and in the words of my friends."

"Then you are richer than I am," the Venetian exclaimed in astonishment, "for here you are telling me truths I had never dreamed of."

"Everyone must think for himself," the stranger replied. "As long as you addressed me, I may beg you kindly to point out the road to Palermo or to some inn, for night is falling apace."

"Do you know any French or Sicilian lord at Palermo?"

"No."

"Then you are not certain of being received there?"

"I am disposed to forgive those who deny me. The road, My Lord?"

"Like yourself, I am lost," Pezare told him: "Let us seek our way together."

"To do so, we needs must go together. But you are on horseback, I am on foot."

Pezare took the French knight up behind him.

"Have you any idea whom you are with?" he asked.

"With a man, apparently."

"Do you think you are safe?"

"Were you a highwayman, it is you would have to look to safety," said the Frenchman, pressing the hilt of his dagger against the other's heart.

"Well, my brave Frenchman, you appear to me to be a man of great learning and sound sense. Know that I am a nobleman established at the Court of Sicily, that I am very much alone and that I seek a friend. You seem to be in the same plight: judging from appearances, you are scarce friendly with your lot. You look as though you needed everybody."

"Would I be happier if all the world had dealings with me?"

"You are a devil who turn my every word against me. By St. Mark! My Lord Chevalier, are you to be trusted?"

"More so than you, who began our federal friendship by deceiving me. You told me you had lost your way; but you ride like a man who knows very well where he is going."

"You, too, deceived me," Pezare replied, "by making a sage of your years walk and by making a gallant knight look like a serf! Here is the hostelry: my servants have prepared supper for us."

The Frenchman jumped off the horse, went into the inn with Pezare and accepted his invitation to supper. Both sat down at the table. The Frenchman fought so well with his jaws and twisted the joints with such dispatch as to establish that he was equally experienced in supping; he again proved it by draining the flagons neat, without his eye dimming or his senses wandering. Assuredly Pezare congratulated himself on meeting a proud son of Adam, sprung from the proper rib, on the good side. While they chatted together, Pezare tried to find some joint through which to probe the secret depths of his new friend's meditations. But he soon realized that the Frenchman would cast his shirt away before he would his prudence; so the host judged it opportune to win his guest's esteem by opening his doublet to him.

Pezare therefore proceeded to tell him of conditions in Sicily . . . of the sovereign, Prince Leufroid and his gentle wife . . . how gallant their Court was and what courtesy flourished here . . . what a multitude of lords of lofty plumage, from Spain, France, Italy and elsewhere, lived here in high feather . . . how many princesses there were, as rich as noble, and as beautiful as rich . . . how Prince Leufroid nourished the loftiest ambitions, aspiring to conquer Morea, Constantinople, Jerusalem, the lands of Soudan and other Afric places . . . how certain eminent men managed his affairs . . . how he summoned vassals of every degree from the very flower of Christian chivalry . . . how he upheld this splendor, intent upon making of that island, so opulent of yore, the queen of the Mediterranean, to the ruin of Venice, which had not an inch of land. These designs had been implanted in the King's mind by him, Pezare; but though he was high in Leufroid's favor, he felt himself weak, had no assistance from the courtiers and desired to make a friend. In this quandary, he had decided to ride out to the country and ponder his problem. While doing so, he had been fortunate enough to meet a man as sensible as the chevalier had proved himself to be. Why should they not swear brotherhood therefore? Why should not Pezare open his purse to him and place his palace at his disposal? They would follow the path of honor together through pastures of pleasure; each would help the other on all occasions, just as Crusaders did. Was the Frenchman seeking fortune and did he require assistance? Very well, help him Pezare would, nor for a moment brook the other's refusal of this offer of mutual solace.

"I need no help whatever," the Frenchman affirmed, "because I pin my faith upon a point which will win me all I wish. Nevertheless, I should like to acknowledge your courtesy, my dear Chevalier Pezare. You will soon find yourself obliged to the Chevalier Gauthier de Montsoreau, a gentleman of the fair land of Touraine."

"Have you some relic that assures you success?"

"A talisman given me by my dear mother," the knight from Touraine explained. "With it, castles and citadels are razed to the ground. It is a hammer to strike coin, a nostrum for every ill, a traveller's staff, a security which may be impawned at a profitable rate, a master tool that operates marvellous embossing in forges of all sizes, without making the slightest sound."

"Ha! By St. Mark, you've some mystery hidden under your coat-of-mail!"

"No," answered the Frenchman, "it is a perfectly natural thing. Here it is!"

Suddenly, as he rose from the table to go to bed, Gauthier exposed the finest implement for the fashioning of pleasure that Pezare had ever laid eyes on.

"This," Gauthier announced as, after the custom of the age, they both got into bed together, "this smooths down all obstacles by making itself master of female hearts. As the ladies are queens of this Court, your friend Gauthier will soon reign there."

Pezare viewed Gauthier's privy charms with boundless amazement. Indeed the Frenchman had been generously fettled by his mother (perhaps, too, by his father) and endowed with such bodily perfections that he could not but go far, especially as to them he joined the wit of a young page and the wisdom of an old devil.

They swore eternal friendship, reckoning a woman's heart a negligible factor in such a partnership; they vowed to be of one and the same mind, as if their heads had been under the same helmet; and they went to sleep on the same pillow, vastly pleased with their compact. That was how things were ordered in those days.

On the morrow, Pezare presented his friend Gauthier with a

splendid steed, a purse full of money, fine silken hose, a velvet doublet worked with gold, and an embroidered cloak. This costume enhanced Gauthier's proud appearance and accentuated his beauties so prominently that Pezare was confident he would charm all the ladies. The servants received orders to obey Gauthier as they would Pezare and began wondering among themselves about this catch their master had fished up. Then the two friends made their entry into Palermo at the hour when the Prince and Princess took their stroll.

Pezare presented his French companion proudly, vaunting his merits and procuring him so gracious a welcome that Leufroid invited him to supper. Meanwhile Gauthier kept a sharp eye on the Court and learned a great many curious and secret practises. If His Majesty was a handsome and valiant prince, his consort was a Spaniard of high temperature, the fairest and worthiest lady of his Court. But she seemed somewhat disposed to melancholy. Gauthier, a true son of Touraine, decided that she was inadequately served by the King, for the law of Touraine is that an expression of joy on the face comes from an impression of joy elsewhere. Pezare frankly pointed out several ladies who were open and prone to Leufroid's pleasure, who were exceedingly jealous and who fought for his possession in a tourney of gallantries and marvellous female inventions. From all of this, Gauthier concluded that though he had the loveliest wife in the world, the Prince ran rampant, taxing all the ladies in Sicily in order to groom and water his charger in their stables, vary his fodder and learn the technique of equitation as practised in many lands. The Sire de Montsoreau was certain that, in spite of Leufroid's infidelities, no one had dared enlighten the Queen. He resolved to plant his staff at one blow, by a master stroke, in the heart of the fair Spaniard's field. He went about it in this wise.

In order to show the foreign knight a courtesy, the King was careful to place him beside the Queen at supper. Gallantly, Gauthier offered her his arm to take her into the hall; but he rushed her off at top speed, in order to get away from the others and at once whisper a word concerning matters which please the ladies, whatever their condition. Imagine what this word was and how, piercing stubble and shrub, it flew straight into the warm thicket of love.

"I know the reason why Your Majesty is so pale."

"Why?" she asked.

"You are so fair to mount that His Majesty bestrides you night and day. But you abuse of your beauties; the King will surely die of love."

"What must I do to keep him alive?"

"Forbid him to say more than three full Masses daily at your altar."

"You are cracking a French joke at my expense, Chevalier. The King himself told me that the height of his devotions could be but one low Mass per week, on pain of death."

"You are deceived," said Gauthier, sitting down at the table, "I can prove to you that love should celebrate the whole Mass, Vespers, Complines, and an occasional *Ave* as well, for queens just as for simple women. Besides, this function must be gone through every day, as monks do in their monasteries, with fervor. But, for you, these litanies should never end."

The Queen favored the handsome Frenchman with a glance that was anything but angry. She smiled, shook her head.

"In this," she said, "men are great liars."

"I bear a monstrous truth which I will show you whenever you please," the knight answered. "I warrant I can serve you a queen's fare and give you joy choke-full up to the eyes! Thus you will make up for lost time, especially as His Majesty has ruined himself on other ladies, whereas I shall reserve my parts for your service."

"If the King hears of our compact, he will bring your head rolling to your feet."

"Even should this calamity befall me, after the first night, I would esteem that I had lived a hundred years, considering what joy I had received. For though I have visited all the Courts of Europe, never have I laid eyes on a princess fit to hold a candle to your beauty. In a word, if I die not by the sword, I shall die at your hands, for I am resolved to spend my life in our love, if life ebbs out on that same tide that brings us life."

Never had Her Majesty heard such a speech; it was sweeter music to her ears than the most perfectly sung Mass. Her pleasure showed in her face, which turned purple. These words made her blood boil fiercely in her veins: the strings of her lute throbbed and struck a high-pitched chord that echoed in her ears, for, by an exquisite artifice of their sensitive natures, this lute imbues the brains and bodies of ladies with its music. What a shame to be young and beautiful, to be a queen, to have Spanish blood spoiling within one and yet to be betrayed! She conceived a mortal disdain for those of her Court who, through fear of the King, had kept their lips tight-closed over this treachery. She resolved to avenge herself with the help of this handsome Frenchman, who cared so little for life that, with his first words, he had hazarded it. What gallant recklessness to make a proposal to a queen, who, if she did her duty, would have had him put to death! Far from doing so, however, she pressed his foot with hers in no uncertain fashion, and said aloud:

"Let us change the subject, my dear Chevalier. It is wrong of you to attack a poor queen in her weak spot. Tell us the customs of the ladies at the Court of France."

Thus Gauthier received the sweet assurance that matters were settled. He proceeded to talk of mad and pleasant things which kept the King, the Queen and all the courtiers in such good spirits that, as he rose, Leufroid vowed he had never laughed so heartily. The company proceeded to stroll in the gardens (the most beautiful in the world) where the Queen used the chevalier's words as an excuse to walk with him beneath a grove of blossoming orange trees which exhaled the suavest fragrance.

"O fair, O noble Queen," Gauthier said at once, "in every country, I have seen that love's perdition has its roots in those first attentions we call courtesy. Being people of vast intelligence, let us agree to love each other without making such a great pother about it. Thus we will arouse no suspicion; our happiness will be secure and permanent. Queens should behave thus or risk being interfered with."

"Well spoken," she said, "but I am new at the game; I don't know how to shape our course."

"Have you some woman whom you can trust implicitly?"

"Ay," she said, "I have a friend who came from Spain with me; she would lie on a gridiron for my sake, as St. Lawrence did for God's. But she is always ill."

"Capital!" said the rascal. "Then you often go to visit her."

"Yes," she agreed, "and sometimes at night."

"Ha!" said Gauthier, "I hereby vow to Ste. Rosalie, patron of Sicily, that I will build her an altar of gold in return for this good fortune."

"Jesus!" the Queen exclaimed, "I am doubly happy that so handsome a lover is so religious."

"Ah, my sweet lady, I have two loves today since I have a queen to love in Heaven and another here below. Nor, fortunately, are they incompatible!"

This charming speech moved the Queen to such immeasurable tenderness, that for a straw she would have fled with this artful Frenchman.

"The Virgin Mary is very powerful in Heaven," said the Queen. "Love grant that I be powerful like Her."

It was at this moment that Leufroid overheard them, having come to spy on them because a Sicilian courtier, piqued at the cursed foreigner's meteoric rise to favor, had sowed the seed of jealousy in his heart.

"Bah," he growled, "they are prattling about the Virgin Mary!"

The Queen and Gauthier laid their plans carefully; every precaution was taken to place two feathers in the royal cap. Gauthier rejoined the Court, made himself agreeable to everybody, and returned to Pezare's palace. There he informed his friend that their fortunes were made because, on the night of the morrow, he would sleep with the Queen. This swift success dazzled the Venetian. Like a good friend, he produced some costly perfumes, linens from Brabant and other precious garments for a queen's use, and gave them to his dear Gauthier so that the case might be worthy of the superbly mounted jewel.

"But, my friend, tell me: are you certain not to falter? Will you go full tilt, serve the Queen well, and give her such frolic in her messuage that she may cling forever to this master staff, like a drowning seaman to a plank?"

"On that head, fear nothing, my dear Pezare; I have the arrears of the journey and I will stave her hammer and tongs, as though she were a simple servant. Ah! I will drill her in the ways of the ladies of Touraine, who comprehend love better than all others, because they make it, remake and unmake it, in order to make it yet again; then, having remade it, still keep on making it, having nothing else to do save that which always implores doing. Now let us mark out our course. This is how we shall obtain the government of the island. I shall hold the Queen, you the King; we will play the comedy of sworn enmity before the courtiers and divide them into two factions under our command. Unknown to all, we will of course remain friends. Thus we shall discover and frustrate their plots, you by hearkening to my enemies, I to yours. In the course of a few days, then, we will invent some quarrel to set us against each other. We can base it on the King's high favor, which I will have obtained for you through the channel of the Queen. His Majesty will give you supreme power to my apparent injury."

On the morrow, Gauthier slipped into the friendly room (for the benefit of the courtiers, he had pretended to recognize the go-between as an intimate friend he had known in Spain) and remained there seven whole days. As you may imagine, the scion of Touraine served the Queen as a passionately adored mistress should be served. To her charmed senses he discovered so many virgin strands in amour, so many Gallic usages, turns and twists, blandishments and soothings that she almost lost her reason, and swore that only the French really understood the art of love. That is how the King was punished for seeking to keep her virtuous and yet turning tail too often, making his offertory too parsimoniously contingent, and stinting the straw with which her pretty kiln made bricks. This supernatural delectation affected the Queen so deeply that she vowed eternal love to Montsoreau, who had opened her eyes to the delights of the sport. It was agreed that the Queen's compatriot should take care always to be ill and that the lovers would confide in only one other person, the Court physician, who was devoted to Her Majesty. The medico happened to have vocal cords in every way similar to Gauthier's, so that, by a freak of nature, they had exactly the same voice, much to the Queen's amazement. He swore on his life to serve the charming couple loyally, for he deplored the sad neglect of so beautiful a woman and was delighted to know that she was used like a queen—a rare thing.

A month passed. Everything worked perfectly for the two friends. They evolved stratagems which the Queen put into practise and which tended to place the government of Sicily into Pezare's hands, to the detriment of Gauthier, whom the King prized for his deep wisdom. The Queen refused to hear of the Frenchman, protesting that she loathed him because he was ungallant. Leufroid dismissed the Duke of Cataneo, his chief minister. In his place, he appointed Pezare, who thereupon completely ignored his friend the Frenchman. Gauthier exploded, denouncing Pezare's treason and crying vengeance upon his betrayal of sworn friendship. This step immediately won him the devotion of Cataneo and his friends; they made a compact together to overthrow Pezare.

Now Pezare was a shrewd man, eminently qualified to govern states, which is characteristic of the gentlemen of Venice. No sooner in office than he wrought wonders in Sicily, improving the ports and attracting merchants there by the franchises and facilities he granted. He helped vast numbers of poor people to earn their bread; he held innumerable fêtes which drew artisans of all trades to the capital, as well as the rich and idle from every land, even from the Orient. The harvests, the products of the earth and other commodities were plentiful; galleys and ships came to trade from Asia, making the King the happiest and most enviable monarch in Christendom and his Court the most renowned in Europe.

Only the perfect coöperation of the two men could have brought about this flourishing state of affairs. They understood each other down to the ground. The one looked after the pleasures and personally catered to the Queen's delight; since she was being served after the method of Touraine, her expression was always gay and she communicated the flame of her happiness to all about her. He was careful, too, to keep the King amused, discovering new mistresses for him and casting him into a whirl of pleasure. His Majesty was much surprised at the Queen's amiability, for, since the arrival of the Sire de Montsoreau, he had no more touched her than a Jew will bacon. Thus occupied, the King and Queen abandoned the government of their realm to the other friend, who directed the affairs of state, ruled the establishment, managed the finances and kept the army in hand —all of which he did with great success, for he knew where money was, brought it into the treasury and prepared the ground for the vast enterprises mentioned above.

This splendid harmony lasted for three years—some say four, but the monks of St. Benoît never fixed the date, which must remain as obscure as the cause of the quarrel between the two friends. Presumably Pezare, a prey to the high ambition of ruling without control or even contest, forgot the services Gauthier had rendered him. Such is the way of courtiers. As Master Aristotle remarks in his works, of all human qualities, gratitude stales the soonest, though love extinguished is often very rancid.

Confident in Leufroid's tried friendship—the monarch called him his crony and would have given him his shirt, had the other asked for it—Pezare determined to get rid of his friend. He would apprize the King of the mystery of his cuckoldry; he

would show him what it was made the Queen so happy. Never
for a moment did he doubt but that Leufroid would begin by
chopping off Gauthier's head, according to the current Sicilian
procedure in such cases. Which would give Pezare all the money
he and Gauthier had been sending secretly to a Lombard in
Genoa. . . . This treasure was joint property, in consequence of
their brotherhood. It had been much increased on one side by
the magnificent presents Gauthier received from the Queen,
who owned vast estates in Spain and inherited others in Italy;
on the other side, Pezare had added to it by the King's bounties
to his faithful minister, who was granted certain rights over the
merchants and sundry other indulgences. The false knight, having decided to betray his faith, was very careful to aim the arrow
straight at Gauthier's heart, for the Frenchman was too clever
to be trifled with.

Accordingly, one night Pezare knew the Queen to be abed
with her lover—he adored her as though each night were the
bridal night, so skillful was she at the sport—the traitor promised to produce complete evidence of the case. His Majesty need
but look through a hole Pezare had pierced in the dressing-room
of the Spanish lady, who was always pretending to be at death's
door; to make sure of the view, they would wait until the sun
had risen.

On such nights as the Queen welcomed her lover between
sheets, which is certainly the best way to have one, the Spanish
lady usually slept in an adjoining closet. She was, by nature, fleet
of foot, lynx-eyed and sharp of hearing. Roused by the faint
patter of footsteps, she peered through the transom and saw the
King, with Pezare in his wake. In a trice, she had run to warn
the couple of this treachery. But the royal eye was already at the
cursed hole. Leufroid beheld—what?

He beheld that beautiful and divine lantern which burns so
much oil and which lights up the world—a lantern adorned with
the most magnificent baubles, flaming brilliantly and lovelier,
he thought, than all others because he had lost sight of it so long
that it looked like a brand-new one. But the size of hole prevented him from seeing anything else save a man's hand mod-
estly covering the lantern. Then he heard Gauthier's voice saying:
"And how is the little treasure this morning?"

A sportive expression, such as lovers use jokingly, because in all countries this lantern is the sun of love.

Therefore they call it a thousand pretty names, likening it to the sweetest things, as, for example, "my pomegranate," "my rose," "my shell," "my hedgehog," "my gulf of love," "my riches," "my master," "my pet." Some even dare to name it heretically "my god." Ask your friends, if you won't take my word for it.

At this stage, the lady motioned to them that the King was there.

"Is he listening?" the Queen whispered.

"Yes."

"Can he see?"

"Yes."

"Who brought him here?"

"Pezare."

"Bring the physician and get Gauthier back to his own room."

In less time than it would have taken a beggar to ask for a penny, Her Majesty glazed the lantern with cosmetics and swathed it in linen, until it looked for all the world as though she had a grievous wound and severe inflammation. When the King, infuriated by what he heard, broke down the door, he found the Queen stretched out on the bed, exactly as he had seen her through the hole, with the physician beside her, nose and hand bent over the bandaged lantern, saying in a voice no different from that His Majesty had heard:

"And how is the little treasure this morning?"

A cheerful, jocose expression, to be sure. But to address such whimsical phrases to a lady patient is part and parcel of a physician's bedside manner; doctors treat this luminous flower with flowery phrases. This spectacle made the King look as foolish as a fox caught in a trap. Her Majesty, crimson with shame, sat up and demanded what man dared intrude upon her privacy at this hour of the morning. When she saw the King, she said:

"Ah, My Lord, so you have discovered what I was careful to hide from you! Yes, you serve me so niggardly that I am afflicted with a burning evil, which my dignity will not allow me to complain of, but which requires secret dressing in order to ease the violent affluence of vital forces. To save my honor and your own, I am forced to come to my dear Doña Miraflor. She comforts me in my troubles."

Whereupon the surgeon proceeded to treat Leufroid to a lecture, interlarded with Latin quotations which he gathered like precious grains from Hippocrates, Galen, the school of Salerno and various other fields. He demonstrated how harmful it was for a woman to let the plot of Venus lie fallow; he expatiated upon the mortal danger menacing queens of Spanish temperament, whose blood was excessively amorous. He expounded these reasons with great solemnity of voice and feature, keeping a very straight beard and letting his tongue run loose in order to allow Gauthier time to regain his bed. The Queen adopted the same text to preach the King an interminable sermon. Then she asked him to lend her his arm, that they might leave the poor invalid who, to protect her from calumny, usually accompanied her back. As they passed the gallery where the Sire de Montsoreau lodged, the Queen said jokingly:

"You ought to play a good trick on that Frenchman! I wager he is with some lady and not in his room at all. All the ladies of Court are mad about him . . . some day he will be the cause of serious mischief! Had you followed my advice, he would not be in Sicily now."

Leufroid burst into Gauthier's room, to find him in a deep sleep, snoring like a monk in church. The Queen came back with the King, whom she kept in her apartments. Meanwhile she had found time to send a guard for the lord whose place Pezare had usurped. She breakfasted with the King, cajoling and cosseting him. When Cataneo arrived, she received him in the adjoining room.

"Set up a gallows on a bastion," she told him. "Go seize My Lord Pezare and make sure he is hanged instantly. Do not allow him an opportunity to write or say a word on any subject whatever. Such is our good pleasure and our supreme command."

Cataneo offered no comments. While the Chevalier Pezare was congratulating himself on his friend Gauthier's beheading, the Duke of Cataneo appeared, seized him and led him to the bastion. Looking up from there at the Queen's window, he caught sight of the Sire de Montsoreau conversing with Their Majesties and a knot of courtiers; Pezare concluded that he who kept the Queen occupied was better favored than he who managed the King.

"My friend," said the Queen, leading her husband to the window, "behold a traitor who was plotting to deprive you of

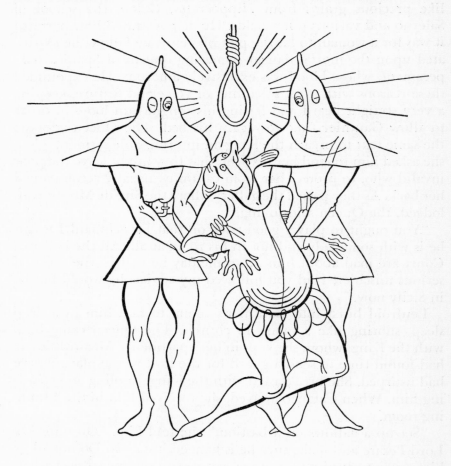

your dearest possession on earth. I will furnish you with ample proofs when you have leisure to study them."

Gauthier, seeing the preparations for the final ceremony, threw himself at the King's feet and implored the royal pardon for his mortal enemy. The King was much affected.

"Messire de Montsoreau," Her Majesty glowered at him, "are you so bold as to cross our good will?"

"You are a noble knight," said the King, raising Gauthier to his feet, "but you do not know what an enemy you had in the Venetian."

With the utmost delicacy, Pezare was strangled between the head and shoulders, after the Queen had established his treason by producing the testimony of a Lombard of the town concerning the vast sums Pezare had deposited in Genoa. All this money was given up to Gauthier.

As the history of Sicily records, this beautiful and noble Queen died in consequence of a heavy labor, giving birth to a son who proved as mighty as he was ill-starred in his undertakings. The King took the physician's word for it that the mischief caused by her hæmorrhages came from her excessively chaste life; he held himself criminally responsible for her death, made penance for it and founded the Church of the Madonna, one of the most sumptuous in the town of Palermo. The Sire de Montsoreau, who witnessed his remorse, pointed out that when a monarch went to Spain for his consort, he should realize that she required more devotion than most queens, because Spanish women were as lively as any ten other nationals. Gauthier added that if Leufroid wished a wife for show only, he should get her from the north of Germany, where the women were frigid. Eventually, the good chevalier returned to Touraine, laden with wealth; he lived there many long years, without ever referring to his happiness in Sicily. Once, he went back to the island to help the King's son in his chief struggle with Naples; but when, as the chronicles relate, this gentle prince was killed, Gauthier left Italy.

Beyond the lofty moralities contained in the title of this tale (where it is said that fortune, being female, always sides with the ladies and that men do well to serve them fitly) it proves to us that silence is the better part of wisdom. Nevertheless the monk who wrote this story would seem to draw still another lesson which is no less judicious: namely that interest, which makes so many friendships, breaks them too.

But from these three versions you may choose the one which best agrees with your point of view and your momentary requirement.

Of a Poor Old Man Who Had Various Names

*T*HE ANCIENT chronicler who furnished the hemp to weave the present story, states that he lived at the time when the affair occurred in the city of Rouen. It is, indeed, recorded in the municipal archives.

In the suburbs of this beautiful city, where Duke Richard of Normandy held his Court, an old man named Tryballot exercised the profession of mendicancy. People called him Le Vieux par Chemins. The phrase has nothing to do with *parchemin* or parchment, though our beggar was as yellow and dry as vellum; it means the Old Man o' the Roads, and he earned the title because he was forever on highway and byway, up-hill and down-dale, dressed in miserable rags, sleeping under the skyey roof. Nevertheless, people were very fond of him in the duchy; everybody had grown so used to him that if the month went by without his appearing cup in hand, people worried about him, and asked: "Where is the old man?" And the inevitable answer was: "On the roads; *par chemins!*"

This man's father, a very worthy Tryballot, had been a skilled artisan; his great thrift and order had enabled him to bequeath considerable wealth to his son. But the lad, who was exactly the opposite of his sire, squandered away his inheritance in dissipation.

What a frugal man the father was! On his way home from the fields, here and there he would pick up bits of firewood and branches that had been abandoned, adding, in all conscience, that a man should never arrive home empty-handed. Thus he kept warm in winter at the expense of the careless; and he did well. Everyone acknowledged what a fine lesson this was for the country. One year before his death, there was not a stick of wood to be found along the road: he had compelled the most heedless to turn economical and orderly. But his son, far from following this wise example, made ducks and drakes of everything. Anyhow, the father had foretold his future.

From the lad's earliest youth, when goodman Tryballot used to set him to watch the birds, who came to eat peas, beans and other seeds, and to drive these marauders away, especially the jays, who made a clean sweep of everything, he would watch them indeed. That is, he would study their habits and delight in observing with what grace they alighted and took off, how they winged away, laden with grain, and returned for more, what an alert eye they cocked at snares and nets. And their skill in avoiding capture drew roars of laughter from him; while old Tryballot flew into a fury when he discovered he was short two or three large measures of grain. But, though he pulled his lad's ears when he caught him playing the fool under a nut tree, the little rascal was always daydreaming; nor could any abuse prevent him from going back to study the industry of blackbirds, sparrows and other learned pilferers. One day, his father remarked that he did well to model his conduct upon them, for, if he continued to lead this sort of life, he would be compelled in his old age to pilfer like them, and would, like them, be pursued by justice. Which came true, since, as has been stated, in a few days he frittered away the crowns his sire had amassed in a lifetime of economy. His attitude towards men was like his attitude towards sparrows: he left his purse-strings open to anyone that cared to put his hand in, contemplating, the while, with what grace and what courtesy they begged leave to do so. When there was the devil to pay, Tryballot did not seem at all worried. He declared that, having studied philosophy in the school of the birds, he had no desire to damn himself for the goods of this world.

After having thoroughly enjoyed himself, he found that from among all his possessions he had retained only a goblet bought at the Lendit fair at St. Denis, plus three dice—ample equipment for drinking and gambling, especially as he roved about unencumbered with furniture. How different from the mighty, who cannot travel abroad without wagons, carpets, dripping pans and an infinite number of varlets. Tryballot would have liked to see his good friends, but he no longer met a soul he knew; this gave him leave to recognize nobody. Then, as hunger whetted his stomach, he decided to choose a calling in which there was nothing to do and plenty to gain. While pondering his problem, he remembered the grace of blackbirds and sparrows. So our excellent Tryballot selected house-to-house begging for his vocation, and, for his avocation, pilfering. From the first day, charitable folk gave him something, and he was content: the business was good, he risked no advances or commercial hazards but, on the contrary, enjoyed every conceivable accommodation. He practised his profession with such gusto that he was popular everywhere and received a thousand consolations refused to the rich. As the goodman watched the peasants planting, sowing, reaping and bringing in the vintage, he used to tell himself that they worked for him. A man with a pig in his larder owed Tryballot a slice of it, without even suspecting it. A man who baked a loaf in his oven baked it for Tryballot, without even knowing it. He took nothing by force; on the contrary, people overwhelmed him with courtesy while they bestowed their gifts upon him.

"Here, Old Man o' the Roads, cheer up! Are you quite well these days? Come along, friend, take this: the cat began it, you can finish it."

The Old Man o' the Roads was at all the weddings, baptisms and funerals, because he made a point of going wherever there was open or secret jollification and feasting. He observed the rules and regulations of his calling religiously: in other words he did nothing, since had he once been capable of working at the slightest job, nobody would ever have given him anything again. After gorging himself, this sage used to stretch out in a ditch or against a church wall and meditate upon public affairs. And, playing the thinker as much as ever the beggar, he would philosophize, like his sweet tutors the blackbirds, jays and sparrows. Need the poverty of his apparel exclude the wealth of his intelligence? His philosophy amused his clients; by way of thanks, he would treat them to the choicest aphorisms of his science. To hear him, slippers gave rich people gout; his feet, he bragged, were nimble because he received shoes ready-made to his size by the divine cobbler. Diadems caused splitting headaches from which he was exempt, being burdened by no chaplet or worry of any sort. Again, rings set with precious stones hindered the circulation of the blood. Though he covered himself with sores, as mumpers will, he was assuredly healthier than a child at the baptismal font.

Our goodman enjoyed himself hugely with his fellow vaga-bonds; very often he tried conclusions with them over his three dice, which he kept in order to remember to spend his money and always remain poor. Despite his vow, however, he was, like all members of Mendicant Orders, so opulent, that one Easter Day, he refused another old vagabond's offer of ten crowns in return for a twenty-four hours' rental of his privileges. Indeed, that same evening he spent fourteen crowns drinking the healths of the almsgivers because the statutes of beggary enjoin a mark of gratitude to donors. He was most careful to get rid of the commodity that harassed others, who, being too heavily laden with goods, aspire to evil; he was better off with nothing in the world than he had been with his father's fortune. As for patents of nobility, he was always on the high road to it, since he never dreamed of acting against his will and lived nobly without doing a stroke of work. Thirty crowns would not have got him out of his bed once he was in it. Each day dawned for him as for his fellow men, though his was a merry life, a life that not a few ancient sages had led before him, according to Master Plato, whose authority has already been invoked in these writings. At last, the Old Man o' the Roads reached the ripe age of eighty-two without knowing a single day that did not bring its tribute of money. What is more, his was the halest complexion and ruddiest color imaginable. He firmly believed that, had he persevered in the struggle for riches, he would have worn himself out and been laid underground many moons before. He was quite possibly right.

In his youth, he had the illustrious virtue of being a passionate lover; his plenitude in amour was, it is said, a fruit of his studies among sparrows and tits. Always he was ready to lend the ladies his assistance in counting the rafters—a generosity the physical cause of which lay in the fact that, having nothing to do, he was always prepared to do something. The washerwomen declared that, lather the ladies as they might, the Old Man o' the Roads was a better hand than they were at that game. According to gossip, it was these privy virtues that procured him the popularity he enjoyed in the province. Some say that the lady of Chaumont, curious to verify them, summoned him to her manor and kept him there a whole week lest he go begging. Terrified at the thought of getting rich, the goodman kicked over the traces and fled.

As he advanced in age this great quintessencer found himself disdained, although his remarkable amative faculties were in no wise impaired. This unjust revulsion of the female sex caused the first sorrow he ever suffered and precipitated the celebrated trial of Rouen, to which it is high time I came.

In his eighty-second year, old Tryballot, having met no indulgent woman, was compelled to remain continent for seven months—a situation which, as he later said before the Judge, afforded him the greatest astonishment of his long and honorable life. In this most pathetic state, while walking through the fields during the pretty month of May, he saw a wench who happened to be a virgin and a cowherdess. It was a sweltering day. The wench, oppressed by the heat, lay stretched out in the shade of a beech tree, her face to the ground, taking a nap, as peasants will, while her animals were grazing. Suddenly she was rudely awakened by the instrumentality of the Old Man o' the Roads, who had robbed her of what a poor girl can only lose once. Finding herself deflowered without notice or pleasure, she screamed so shrilly that the folk working in the fields came rushing up. These she immediately called to witness her plight at the moment when such destruction as is lawful only on a wedding-night was still visible in her. She wept and lamented, saying that the randy old ape might just as well have gone and abused her mother, who would have held her peace.

The peasants, enraged, brandished their hoes and were about to fall upon him when he explained that he had been forced to take his pleasure. They objected that a man could certainly take his pleasure without plundering a virgin. The case was obviously one for the Provost and the attacker would hang for it. Amid great clamor they led him to the jail at Rouen.

The wench, questioned by the Provost, testified that she had been sleeping to pass the time away. Truth to tell, she thought she was dreaming of her lover, with whom she had recently quarrelled because he had wished to take her measure before they were married. In this dream, by way of a joke, she was allowing him to put out a feeler and see the lay of the land, in order to convince him that their joint future happiness was incontestable: but, in spite of her protest, he was going further than she had allowed. Conceiving more pain than pleasure in it, she suddenly awoke in the grip of the oldster, who had leaped upon her as a gray friar leaps upon a ham at the end of Lent.

The trial caused such a commotion in Rouen that the Duke of Normandy, wildly curious to know if the thing were really true, sent for the Provost. Upon the latter's assurance, he summoned the old man to his palace and asked him what defence he had to make.

The poor goodman appeared before the monarch and naïvely exposed the misfortune which the force and will of nature had brought down upon him. Like the veriest youth, he was driven, he said, by highly imperious desires. Up to this year of grace, of course, he had had sweethearts of his own; but for the last eight long months he had remained necessarily continent. He was too poor to patronize the women of the town; the respectable women, who were once charitable to him, had grown disgusted with his hair, which turned feloniously white despite the verdant freshness of his love. Now the mere sight of this cursed virgin damsel constrained him to snatch at joy where it was obtainable. There she lay, stretched out under the beech tree, revealing the pretty lining of her dress and two snow-white hemispheres that had deprived him of his reason. The fault was surely the girl's, not his: virgins should be forbidden to bare the appurtenances that earned Venus the title of callipyge, to display them publicly and to entice passers-by. Finally My Lord Duke himself ought to know how hard it is for a man to hold a harrier in leash at high noon, since it was on the stroke of twelve that King David fell in love with the wife of My Lord Uriah; and surely where a Hebrew King and the elect of God had failed, a poor man, deprived of all joy and reduced to beg his bread, might be excused from succumbing? Moreover, Tryballot vowed that, by way of repentance, he was quite willing to sing psalms and strum upon a lute for the rest of his life, in imitation of the said King who had committed the fell crime of murdering a husband, while he, Tryballot, had ever so slightly injured a country wench. The Duke approved of this philosophy; he pronounced the culprit a man of great parts. Then he uttered a memorable decree. If, as this beggar said, he required indulgence so desperately at his age, he might lawfully prove it, at the foot of the ladder he must mount to be hanged, according to the Provost's sentence.

In this ultimate moment, when he stood between priest and hangman with a rope around his neck, if he could raise evidence of such desire, he should be pardoned.

When this decree became known, a tremendous crowd turned out to see the goodman to the gallows. There was a hedge of folk on either side of the street as if for a ducal entry, the bonnets outnumbering the hats by far.

The Old Man o' the Roads was saved by a lady who was curious to see how this precious violator would finish his career. Assuring the Duke that religion admonished her to give Tryballot fair play, she tricked herself out as if she were going to a ball, intentionally exposing two bulbs of living flesh so white that the purest linen neckerchief paled beside them. Indeed these exquisite twin fruits of love stood out over her corselet without a wrinkle; they were like two great luscious apples, whose tempt-ing beauty made your mouth water at the sight of them. This noble lady—she was one of those women who would rouse the male in any man—framed her lips in a provocative smile.

Poor old Tryballot came loping forward between the officers of justice; he wore a tunic of coarse cloth and appeared far more

likely to achieve a posture for rape after the hanging than before it. Very sad he was as he gazed here and there, seeing nothing but a sea of bonnets; as he remarked later, he would have given a hundred crowns for a glimpse of a wench tucked up like the cowherdess. Her full, white pillars of Venus, that had proved his undoing, he remembered still. They might yet save him. Ah no! he was an old man and the remembrance was not vivid enough....

But when, poised at the foot of the ladder, he saw the twin charms of the lady and the inviting delta over their confluent roundnesses, his rigidescent rodpiece caused his tunic to assume a very definite prominence.

"Eh there, quick!" he called to the officers. "Look and bear witness: I have won my pardon, but I cannot answer for the rascal."

The lady was delighted with this tribute which, she said, entailed a harder labor than his original offence. The guards, charged to corroborate the evidence, believed that Tryballot was the Devil himself, because never in their writs had they laid eyes on an "I" so perpendicular as the goodman's rod. He was borne in triumph through the streets of the town into the Duke's palace, where officers and others bore witness to the facts. In that age of ignorance, this singular adjudication was so much admired that the town voted the erection of a column on the spot where the goodman had won his pardon, and on it his effigy was reproduced in stone, in his exact position on sighting his honest and virtuous saviour. The statue was still there when the English captured Rouen; all the authors of the time relate the story among the notable events of the reign.

As the town offered to keep the old man supplied with wenches and to provide him with bed, board and raiment, the good Duke arranged matters by giving the deflowered maid a thousand crowns and marrying her off to the goodman, who, by the change, lost his names of the Old Man o' the Roads and Tryballot. The Duke named him the Sieur de Bonne-C—. Nine months after, his wife gave birth to a perfectly fashioned male child, alive, kicking and born with two teeth. From this union sprang the house of Bonne-C—, which, through false modesty, implored our well-beloved King Louis the Eleventh through letters-patent to change their name into that of Bonne-Chose. Our excellent King Louis objected to the then Sieur de Bonne-C— that in the Republic of Venice there was an illustrious house of Coglioni, who wore a trey of spheres *au naturel* on their coat of arms. The gentlemen of the house of Bonne-C— replied that their wives were horribly ashamed to be thus named at public functions; His Majesty rejoined that they would lose much by the change, because things take after their names. He nevertheless granted the letters-patent they asked for. From then on, the family was generally known under this name and spread to several provinces.

The first Sieur de Bonne-C— lived on for twenty-seven years; he had another son and two daughters. But he grieved at becoming rich and at being unable to beg in the streets for a living.

From this tale you may glean nobler lessons and loftier morals than from any you will read your whole life long—excepting, of course, these hundred glorious *Droll Stories*.

To wit: never could so magnificent an adventure have befallen the flabby, withered natures of the beggars at Court, the rich folk and others who dig their graves with their teeth, overeat, and drink countless wines that ruin their implements of pleasure. Hang-bellied gluttons loll and friggle on costly draperies and feather mattresses; the Sieur de Bonne-Chose roughed it. By the same token, had they fed on cabbage, they would have had diarrhœa.

Which may incite some of my readers to change their mode of life, in order to imitate the Old Man o' the Roads in his senescence.

The Inconsistent Sayings of Three Pilgrims

WHEN the Pope forsook his good town of Avignon to take up residence in Rome, certain pilgrims who had set out for the Provençal town were forced to cross the high Alps before obtaining the *remittimus* of their strange and sundry sins. All along the roads, and at every inn, there were brethren who wore the collar of the Order of Cain; they formed the flower of the penitents, every one of them a lewd fellow, burdened with a leper soul and thirsting to bathe in the papal piscina. They bore gold or precious things to redeem their baseness, to defray the cost of papal bulls and to reward the saints. Naturally those who drank water on the way to Rome changed their song on their return, and if the innkeepers offered them water, demanded the holy water of the cellar. . . .

Three pilgrims came to the town of Avignon—to their loss, since it was widowed of its Pope. As they journeyed down the Rhône valley toward the Mediterranean coast, one of the three, who had his ten-year-old son with him, parted company with his fellows, to rejoin them eventually at Milan, where he suddenly appeared but without the boy. They were delighted at his return, for they had feared that he had given up in disgust when no Pope was to be found at Avignon. That evening at supper they celebrated their reunion with a hearty feast.

One of this trio of roaming Romers was a citizen of Paris, the other came from Germany, and the third from the Duchy of Burgundy. The last it was, who had brought the youngster, doubtless in order to broaden his mind by travel. He held certain fiefs in the duchy, was a younger son of the house of Villiers-la-Faye (*Villa in Fago*) and was called La Vaugrenand. The German baron had met the Parisian just beyond Lyons; then, in sight of Avignon, both had accosted the Sire de la Vaugrenand.

In the Milanese hostelry, the trio let their tongues wag freely. They agreed to travel to Rome together for protection against footpads, nighthawks and other thieves who made it their business to ease pilgrims of their bodily burdens, ere the Pope eased them of their mental burdens. After drinking, they chatted on the more merrily, for the bottle is the key to conversation. And every man jack of them confessed that the cause of his pilgrimage was a woman. The maidservant who watched them drinking, informed them that out of a hundred pilgrims who stopped at this inn, ninety-nine were travelling for the same reason.

The three wise men then proceeded to consider how pernicious the female was to her mate. The Baron displayed the heavy gold chain he had under his coat-of-mail as a present for My Lord St. Peter; he went on to say that even two such chains could not atone for the enormity of his sin. The Parisian took off his glove and flashed a white diamond ring; he announced that he was bearing the Pope gifts worth one hundred times as much. The Burgundian doffed his hat, exhibited two magnificent pearl earrings for Our Lady of Loretto, and avowed that he would rather have left them round his wife's neck.

Whereupon the maidservant observed that their sins must have been as heavy as those of the Visconti. Each acknowledged having such wickedness upon his conscience that he had made a solemn vow never to wanton again for the rest of his life, however beautiful the woman might be and whatever penance the Pope might impose.

The maid expressed polite astonishment that all had made the same vow. The Burgundian announced that his vow had been the cause of his disappearance at Avignon; he had been terrified that his son, despite his youth, might wanton. Had he not sworn to prevent men and beasts alike from wantoning in his house or on his estates? The Baron asked for more details. The Burgundian nobleman told the following story.

"You are aware that years ago the good Countess Jeanne of Avignon made a law for harlots. By the terms of this law, they were compelled to live in a segregated district on the outskirts of town, in licenced houses with shutters painted red and closed.

Well, as we all passed through this cursed suburb, my son noticed the houses, the closed shutters and the red paint. His curiosity was at once awakened—you know what eyes these ten-year-old devils have for everything!—and he plucked at my sleeve without letting go, until I should tell him what these houses were. So to make him keep quiet, I explained that young lads had no business in such places and could enter them only at the risk of their lives. That, I said, was where men and women were manufactured; the danger, for anyone unacquainted with the task was indescribable; if a novice entered, flying chancres and other wild beasts would pounce upon his face. Fear seized the lad; he followed me into the inn with great trepidation, afraid to look at the brothels again. But while I was in the stables seeing about putting up my horses, my boy stole off like a thief. The servant could not tell me what had become of him. I trembled as I thought of the harlots, but I relied upon the ordinances that deny admission to such children. The rascal came back for supper, no more ashamed of himself than Our Divine Savior was in the temple among the doctors.

" 'Where have you been?' I asked.

" 'To the houses with the red shutters,' he answered.

" 'You little blackguard,' I said, 'I shall thrash you!'

"He began to whimper and sob. I promised that if he told me what had happened to him, I would let him off the whipping.

" 'Ha!' he said, 'I took good care not to go in, because of the flying chancres and other wild beasts. I only looked through the cracks in the shutters to see how men were manufactured.'

" 'And what did you see?' I demanded.

" 'I saw a splendid woman just being finished off; she only lacked one peg which a young workman was fitting into her with all his might. The minute she was finished, she turned round, spoke to her manufacturer, and then kissed him.'

" 'Get on with your supper,' I said.

"That very night I returned to Burgundy and left him there with his mother, for I was much afraid that, at the next town, he might want to fit his peg into some wench."

"Children often make answers of that sort," the Parisian cried. "My neighbor's boy revealed his father's cuckoldry by a naïve reply. One evening I was talking to him, trying to find out if he were taught religion properly at school.

" 'What is Hope?' I asked him.

" 'A big King's archer who arrives here when Father departs,' he answered.

"In point of fact, the Sergeant of the Royal Archers was named Hope. My neighbor was dumfounded at this remark. He looked in the mirror to make sure of keeping countenance; but of course he could not see his horns there."

The Baron observed that the boy was quite right in that Hope is a wench who comes to our beds when the real bonds of life fail us.

"Is a cuckold made in the image of God?" asked the Burgundian.

"No," the Parisian replied, "because God was too wise to take a wife. Thus He is happy through all eternity."

"But," the maidservant interrupted, "cuckolds are made in the image of God before they are hornified."

Whereupon the three pilgrims cursed women, accusing them of causing all the evil in this world.

"Their pods are as hollow as helmets," said the Burgundian.

"Their hearts are as straight as billhooks," said the Parisian.

"Why are there so many men pilgrims and so few women pilgrims?" said the German.

"Their cursed calix never sins," the Parisian continued. "Father or mother it does not know, nor the commandments of God or of His Church, nor any law, divine or human. The calix acknowledges no doctrine and hears no heresy; it is beyond reproach; it is all-innocent and forever laughing; its understanding is *nil*. Therefore, I hold it in just horror and profound abomination."

"I too!" said the Burgundian. "And I begin to understand the interpretation a certain scholar has taken of the verses in the Bible that tell of the Creation. This commentary, which we call a Noël in my land, serves to explain the imperfection of woman's vulva, which, in contrast to that of the other females, secretes such diabolical heat that no male can ever slake its thirst.

"Well, the Noël tells how the Lord God was busy manufactur-

ing Eve, when He heard an ass braying for the first time in His
Paradise. As He turned His head to contemplate His long-eared
Neddy, the Devil seized this moment to stick his finger into this
too perfect creature. He left a burning wound on her. The Lord,
however, took care to close it up with a stitch—which accounts
for virgins. By means of this frenum, woman was supposed to
remain closed and children to be manufactured as the Lord
made the angels, by a pleasure as far above carnal pleasure as
Heaven is about the earth. But the Devil saw this closure. Furious
at his discomfiture, Satan then pinched Lord Adam, who was
asleep, and stretched his skin out in imitation of his own diabolical tail. But as the father of man happened to be lying on his
back, this appendage came out in front. Thus these two works of
Satan longed passionately to connect, in obedience to the law of
similarities which God had established for the conduct of His
worlds. Thence rose the first sin and the sorrows of humankind,
for God, perceiving the Devil's handiwork, determined to see
what would come of it."

The anecdote done, the maid declared that they were quite
right: woman was an evil beast and she knew some of the species
whom she would sooner have underground than walking the
fields. For the first time, the pilgrims were suddenly struck with
the wench's beauty, and, in terror of breaking their vows, they
made hastily off to bed. The wench went and informed her mis-
trees that she was harboring infidels. She repeated all their old
saws about women.

"Pooh!" scoffed the landlady. "What care I for the thoughts
my customers have in their brains, so long as their pockets are
well lined."

But when the servant mentioned their jewels:

"This question concerns every born woman," she exclaimed
with evident feeling. "Let us go join issue with them. I'll take
the noblemen, you can have the townsman."

The landlady, who happened to be the most riggish female in
the Duchy of Milan, sped hotfoot to the room where the Sire de
la Vaugrenand and the German baron were sleeping. She first
congratulated them upon their vows, adding that women would
not lose much thereby. Next, she pointed out that, to fulfill these
vows, they should of necessity ascertain whether they could with-

stand the most exasperate temptations. Finally she offered to lie down beside them in order to gratify her curiosity, for she wished to find out whether she could do so with impunity. Parenthetically, she observed that this had never yet befallen her when abed with a man.

On the morrow, at luncheon, the servant had the ring on her finger; her mistress had the golden chain clasped around her neck and the pearl earrings dangling from her ears. The three pilgrims remained in Milan about one month, spent all their money there, and agreed that, if they had berated women so violently, it was because they had not known the Milanese.

On his return to Germany, the Baron made one pregnant observation; he announced that he was guilty of only one sin, that of being in his castle. The citizen of Paris came back heavy with experience and found his wife heavy with Hope. The Burgundian found Madame de la Vaugrenand so melancholy that, for all his proud vows, he almost died at the consolations administered.

Which proves that we must hold our peace in hostelries.

Ingenuousness

Y THE double red crest of my cock, by the rose lining of my sweetheart's black slipper, by all the horns of fond cuckolds and all the virtues of their blessed wives, the finest work of man is neither poetry, nor the painting of pictures, nor music, nor castles, nor statues, be they ever so beautifully moulded, nor galleys straining to the perfect tempo of a hundred oars, nor ships sailing home to haven. No: the finest work of man is children.

Make no mistake: I mean children up to the age of ten. (After that, they become men and women, and, grown reasonable, they are not worth the labor they cost—the worst are the best.) Behold them playing naïvely with everything, with slippers, especially the openwork variety, and with household utensils; note how they lay aside what displeases them, cry after what they like, ravage any sweetmeats and confectionery in the house, gnaw away at the pantry; consider how they are forever laughing as soon as their teeth are cut—and you will agree with me that they are delectable in every way. Besides, they are the flower and fruit: the fruit of love, the flower of life. So long as the hurly-burly of experience has not vitiated their intelligence, there is nothing in this world more sacred or pleasing than their sayings, naïve beyond the possibility of description. This truth is as obvious as the double haslets of a bull. You will never hear a man speaking as ingenuously as a child, because man's candor possesses some indissoluble ingredient of reason, whereas the naïveté of children is untutored, immaculate, redolent of all a mother's finesse. The following anecdote proves this conclusively.

When still Dauphine, Queen Catherine used to ingratiate herself with her royal father-in-law, who was grievously ill at the time, by making him occasional gifts, especially of Italian paintings. She knew how highly he prized them. Was he not a friend of Messire Raphael of Urbino, of Primatice, of Leonardo da Vinci? Did he not send them vast sums of money? Her family had the pick of these works, for the Duke of Medici governed Tuscany at this period. Through him, she obtained a precious canvas painted by a Venetian named Titian, Court Artist to the Emperor Charles and very high in his favor. The picture portrayed Adam and Eve at the precise moment when God allowed them to converse in His earthly Paradise. They were represented as large as life, in the costume of their period, which admits of no possible error, since they were clad in their ignorance and caparisoned with the divine grace which enveloped them. To execute such a work was a tour-de-force, because of the color, but Messire Titian excelled in just that talent.

The masterpiece was hung in the room of the poor King, who was then enduring the ghastly malady of which he eventually died. At the Court of France, the picture had enjoyed an enormous success; everyone wished to see it. But nobody was allowed to, until after the King's death, for, by His Majesty's will, it was left in his room as long as he lived.

One day, Madame Catherine brought her son Francis and little Margot to visit their grandfather. As children will, they began to talk at random. Now here, now there, the children had heard people speak of this picture of Adam and Eve; they had for a long time tormented their mother to show it to them. Since these youngsters sometimes cheered up the old King, Madame la Dauphine granted their request.

"You wanted to see Adam and Eve, who were our first parents," she said. "Well, here they are."

Leaving them to stare in great perplexity at Messire Titian's picture, she went to sit by the King's bedside. The invalid watched the children happily.

"Which of the two is Adam?" Francois asked, as he nudged his sister Marguerite.

"You dunce!" the girl said. "How can you tell when they have no clothes on?"

This reply, which delighted the suffering King and the mites' mother, was noted in a letter Queen Catherine dispatched to Florence.

Since no writer has brought it to light, it will rest enshrined, like a rare flower, amid these Droll Stories, although it is in no wise droll and there is no moral to be drawn from it—except that, in order to hear such charming infant speeches, you must first beget children.

The Fair Imperia Married

I

How Madame Imperia Fell Into the Trap She Was Accustomed to Set for Others

MADAME IMPERIA, the lovely lady who opens these tales so gloriously, for she was the pride of her times, was obliged to move to Rome when the Council of Constance was over. My Lord Cardinal of Ragusa loved her enough to toss his biretta over the windmills for her sake; he would not hear of having her anywhere except close to him. The old lecher proved magnificent beyond her dreams; he presented her with a sumptuous palace of her own.

At about this time, she had the misfortune of becoming *enceinte* through the Cardinal's offices. This pregnancy, as everyone knows, resulted in a pretty daughter who, the Pope said jokingly, should be named Theodora, as who might say *The Gift of God*. His suggestion was followed and the child grew up into a supremely beautiful woman. The Cardinal bequeathed everything to Theodora, whom Madame Imperia established in her mansion. She herself fled this priestly city as a pernicious place where children were begotten and where she had risked marring her svelte waist, her far-famed perfections, the lines of her body, the curves of her back, her flawless slopes and the serpentine charms which set her as high above every other woman of Christendom as the Holy Father is above any other Christian. But all her lovers knew that she was preserved from all harm by the aid of eleven doctors from Padua, seven master surgeons from Pavia and five medicos come from all parts to assist her in her confinement. Some even said that she had actually gained in supergracility and whiteness of flesh. A celebrated physician of the School of Salerno wrote a book on the subject, to prove how favorable a confinement was to the freshness, health, preservation and pulchritude of ladies. In this highly scientific treatise, it was clearly demonstrated to the reader that Madame Imperia's supreme loveliness lay in what her lovers alone might lawfully examine—a rare event, since she would not strip for the prince-lings of Germany, whom she called her margraves, burgraves, electors and dukes much as a captain ranks his soldiers.

Everyone knows that when she turned eighteen, the comely Theodora wished to atone for her mother's crimson career, to become a nun and to abandon her entire fortune to the Order of St. Clara. In this intention, she placed herself in the hands of a cardinal who was to imbue her with the ways of the devout life. The evil shepherd found the lamb so magnificently beautiful that he attempted to violate her. To avoid being contaminated by the wicked prelate, Theodora drove a stiletto through her heart. The tragedy, which was consigned to the history of the times, made a tremendous stir in Rome; and was bitterly lamented by everyone, for Madame Imperia's daughter had been exceed-ingly popular.

In deep affliction, the noble courtesan returned to Rome to mourn for her daughter. She was just entering upon her thirty-ninth year, the heyday of her radiant bloom, according to the contemporary authors; all her charms had attained the pitch of perfection, like a fruit in the flush of its ripeness. Very haughty, sorrow made her, and very harsh toward such as sought to dry her tears with words of love. The Pope himself visited her in her palace to offer certain words of admonition. But she would not take comfort, vowing, rather, to devote herself to God. Out of all the men she had ever known, what gallant had been able to satisfy her? Not one! Every single one of them had deceived her, too, even a priestlet whom she had adored like a holy shrine. God, for His part, would not do so.

This resolve spread terror through Rome, for Imperia was the delight of a vast number of lords. People meeting in the streets would ask each other: "What is the latest news of Imperia? How far gone is she? Will she deprive a hungry world of Love?" More than one ambassador kept his sovereign informed of the matter. The Emperor of the Romans was much distressed: had he not loved her to distraction for eleven weeks, and left her only when he was constrained to go to war? He still adored her

as much as his most precious limb, which, he explained to his
arguing courtiers, was necessarily his eye, because it embraced
the whole of his blessed Imperia. In this extremity, the Pope
summoned a Spanish physician and brought him to the comely
mourner. By various elaborate arguments, studded with quotations from Greek and Latin sources, the man of science proved
that her tears and lamentation were gradually impairing her
splendor and that sorrow opened the door to crease and wrinkle.
This proposition, confirmed by the doctors in controversy of the
Holy College, brought about the desired result. That very evening Madame Imperia opened up her palace.

Youthful cardinals, the foreign envoys, the wealthy townsmen
and the chief notables in Rome flocked to her side, crowded the
rooms and enjoyed a sumptuous entertainment. The common
folk lighted bonfires of thanksgiving. Everyone celebrated the
return of the Queen of Pleasures to her occupation; everyone
hailed the sovereign goddess of Amour. Craftsmen of every art
made much of her, because she spent large sums in building a
church over the tomb of her lost Theodora. (This tomb was later
destroyed during the pillage of Rome, when the traitor Constable of Bourbon died; the saintly maid had been placed in a
massive coffin of gold and silver which the cursed soldiers were
bent on looting. It is said that the building of the basilica cost
more than the pyramid erected of yore by My Lady Rhodopa, an
Egyptian courtesan, eighteen hundred years before the coming
of Our Divine Savior—which establishes the antiquity of this
pleasant calling, the costly price paid by the wise Egyptians for
their pleasure, and the gradual deterioration of everything, since
today, for a tester, you can get a chemise full of white charms in
the Rue du Petit Heuleu in Paris. Abominable, is it not?)

Never had Madame Imperia appeared so gorgeous as at that
first fête after her mourning. All the princes, cardinals and
others vowed that she deserved the homages of the entire earth,
which was brilliantly represented there by lords from every
known land. Thus beauty was triumphantly vindicated as monarch of all thing in all climes.

The envoy of the King of France, a younger son of the house
of L'Isle-Adam, arrived late, though he had never yet seen Madame Imperia and was most anxious to. A handsome young

chevalier, he was, and in high favor at the sovereign's Court, where he had left a fiancée to whom he was devoted. She was the daughter of Monsieur de Montmorency, a nobleman whose domain adjoined that of the house of L'Isle-Adam. To this penniless younger son of a noble dynasty, the King had entrusted certain missions in the Duchy of Milan. He had discharged them so ably that his master had just sent him to Rome, to advance the major negotiations which historians have cited so fully in their books. So if he had nothing of his own, the poor young gentleman could at least rely upon such a brilliant beginning. He was slight of waist but straight and firm as a column; he had dark hair, black glistening eyes and the beard of your true, seasoned diplomat, who will not grasp the shadow for the substance. But, concealing his strategic talent, he looked like a naïve child, with the gentle amiable air of a laughing maiden.

The moment this gentleman walked into her house, the moment she laid eyes on him, Madame Imperia felt herself stung by a sharp desire which twanged the lute-strings of her nature, made them throb, and produced a sound upon it that she had not heard for many a moon. She was seized with such a fit of genuine, unadulterated love at the sight of this youthful freshness that, but for her imperial dignity, she would have leaped up to kiss the tender, shining apples of his cheeks.

Now take heed of this: such women as we call modest, and highflown ladies with armorial bearings on their skirts, are utterly ignorant of the nature of man, because they cling to one man only (like that Queen of France who believed all men were malodorous because the King was). But a great courtesan like Madame Imperia knew men root and branch, because she had handled a great many. In her sanctum, all men were as bland as a hound friggling his dam; they flew under their true colors, convinced, as they were, that they would not enjoy Imperia's favor long. Their victim had often deplored this subjection; she frequently remarked that she suffered more grievously from pleasure than she did from pain. Such was the other side of the shield. You may be certain that a lover had often to part with a mule-load of gold to obtain a night in bed with her, unless her refusal drove him to cut his throat. What a treat for her, then, to gratify a youthful desire like that she felt for the little priest whose tale heads this collection. But because she was older than in those joyous days, love was more deeply rooted in her. The moment it permeated her, she recognized it as of a most fiery nature; she suffered in her epidermis like a cat that is being skinned. How she longed to leap upon this gentleman like a hawk upon its prey, to snatch him and bear him off to her bed! Though she was sitting on thorns, she restrained herself, and, with the utmost difficulty, kept her hand demurely over her skirts.

As L'Isle-Adam advanced and bowed, she reared her proud crest and showed the haughtiest features of her crimson majesty, as a woman will when love seethes in her heart. So marked was the gravity of her bearing toward the young ambassador that many thought she had a bone to pick with him, and they equivocated on the phrase, according to the custom of the times. L'Isle-Adam, confident in the love of Mademoiselle de Montmorency, bothered his head not at all about Imperia. Let her be solemn or vivacious, it was one and the same thing to him. He romped about like a goat let loose.

The courtesan, in a fit of pique, changed her tune. From solemn, she turned brisk and sprightly; she accosted him, softened her voice, sharpened her glance, tossed her head, grazed him with her sleeve, called him Monseigneur, found words as cockering as an embrace, ran her fingers lightly over the palm of his hand, and ended by smiling most gracefully upon him. Never suspecting that so unprofitable a lover could suit her (he had not a penny to his name!) and unaware that to her eyes his beauty was worth all the treasures in the world, L'Isle-Adam did not fall into the trap; on the contrary, he swaggered about with his hands on his hips. His disdain of her passion proved to be the spark that set Madame's angry heart ablaze. Do you doubt it? That is because you know nothing about her profession. In its function, Madame Imperia might be compared to a chimney. A prodigious number of happy fires had crackled there and deposited a burden of soot; in this state, a match was enough to ignite flue and all where one hundred faggots had smoked comfortably. She flamed within from top to toe in a most horrible manner; only the waters of love could quench the devouring element. And there was young L'Isle-Adam leaving the room without noticing her ardor!

Madame, in desperation, completely lost her senses from head to heels; she actually sent a messenger down the galleries after him with an invitation to be her bed-fellow. Never before in her life had she shown such cowardice for King, Pope or Emperor. On the contrary, the high price of her favors was in keeping with the servitude to which she reduced men; the lower she abased them, the higher she exalted herself. The head chamberwoman, an artful wench, informed the proud gallant that he would presumably enjoy a rousing reception, because Madame would undoubtedly treat him to her most delicate inventions in amour. L'Isle-Adam returned to the salons, overjoyed at this windfall. The whole company had seen Madame pale as the French ambassador withdrew: his reappearance gave rise to œcumenical gladness, since everyone was delighted to see Imperia returning to her sweet life of love. An English Cardinal, who had drained more than one big-bellied flagon and who had wished to try conclusions with the fair Imperia, accosted L'Isle-Adam.

"Belabor her manfully," he whispered in his ear, "and she will never again escape from us."

When, at his levée, the Pope was given an account of this night, His Holiness's sole comment was: *"Laetamini, gentes, quoniam surrexit Dominus"*—a quotation which the older cardinals abominated as a profanation of sacred texts. Whereupon the Pope called them severely to book, made the most of this opportunity to read them a lecture, and declared that they might be good Christians but they were poor politicians. Indeed, he relied upon the fair Imperia to pacify the Emperor, and, with this end in view, he used to syringe her with flatteries.

The palace lights out, the golden flagons on the floor, the drunken servants fast asleep under the tables, Madame went back to her bedroom, hand in hand with the love of her choice. How happy she was! Later, she confessed that she was so wild with desire that she could barely restrain herself from rolling at his feet, like a beast of the fields, and imploring him to crush her under him if he could. L'Isle-Adam slipped off his clothes and tumbled into bed as if he were at home. Seeing which, Madame vaulted over the daïs, trampling down the skirts that clung to her feet, and sprang to the sport with a frenzy that amazed her servants, who knew her usually as the most modest woman imaginable in the circumstances. The amazement became general throughout the country, for the amorous pair remained in bed for nine days, eating, drinking and playing a masterly battledore to a superlative shuttlecock. Madame told her woman that she had put her hand on a phœnix of love, since he rose to new life after every assault. This victory won over Imperia became the sole topic of conversation not only in Rome but in all Italy. The fair Imperia bested! Conquered, that proud courtesan who boasted that she yielded to no man . . . who spat on one and all, dukes included . . . who despised burgraves and margraves . . . who gave them the tail of her dress to hold, and vowed that if she did not walk over them, they would trample her down. . . . Madame also confessed to her servants that, in contrast to all the other men she had borne, the more she cockled this child of love, the more she desired to cockle him . . . that she would never be able to part with him, nor with his dazzling eyes that blinded her, nor with his branch of coral, for which she hungered and thirsted without surcease . . . that if he wished it, she would let him suck her blood, devour her breasts (the loveliest breasts in all the world!) and cut her hair (of which she had given but a single one to her dear Emperor of the Romans, who kept it next his heart like a precious relic) . . . that Villiers de L'Isle-Adam raised her to fever heat in his embrace . . . that he sent a triple flux of blood whirling through her heart in less time than it takes a brace of flies to know each other biblically . . . and finally that since their first ecstatic night, she knew her real life was just beginning. . . .

When bruited about, these reports made everyone very wretched. The first time she walked out, Madame Imperia informed the ladies of Rome that if this chevalier abandoned her, she would die a violent death, baring her body like Queen Cleopatra to the sting of asp or scorpion. To crown all, she publicly asseverated that she was bidding her wanton life an eternal farewell. She would show the whole world what virtue was by abandoning her empire for this Villiers de L'Isle-Adam, whose servant she would liefer be than the Queen of Christendom. The English Cardinal remonstrated with the Pope that this true love for one, in the heart of a woman who was the joy of all, amounted to infamous depravity; he urged His Holiness to issue a brief *in partibus,* annulling a marriage which struck at the heart of the fashionable world. But when the poor woman confessed the miseries of her life, her love emerged as a thing so touching and so awe-inspiring to the lewdest villain, that it silenced all clamor. Everyone forgave her her happiness.

One Lenten day, Imperia bade her people fast, commanded them to make confession and to return to God. She herself fell at the Pope's feet and there showed such penitence and passionate contrition that she obtained remission of all her sins, believing that the papal absolution would communicate to her soul that virginity she unfortunately could not offer her lover. It is impossible not to credit the ecclesiastical piscina with its share of virtue, for the poor youth was caught in a cage so royally gilded that he fancied himself in Paradise. He gave up the negotiations of the King of France, he gave up his love for Mademoiselle de Montmorency, he gave up everything in order to marry Madame Imperia, in order to be allowed to live and die with her. Such was the effect wrought by the learned ways of this great lady of pleasure once she applied her science to the profit of virtuous love.

Madame took her leave of lovers and admirers at a regal feast, given in honor of her wedding, which was a wondrous ceremony attended by all the Italian princes. She had, it is said, a million gold crowns, a sum so vast that far from blaming L'Isle-Adam, everyone congratulated him. Quite obviously neither Imperia nor her young husband gave their wealth a thought; the pleasures of love were manifestly their sole concern. The Pope blessed their union, remarking that it was a grateful thing to see a wild virgin returning to the bosom of God by the road of marriage.

In the course of the last night when all might lawfully behold the Queen of Beauty ere she doffed her crown to become a simple châtelaine in France, many a man thought regretfully of the merry, mirthful nights, the late suppers, the masked balls, the pleasant parties and the languid hours when each had emptied out his heart to her. Wistfully they conjured up memories of the ease and freedom they had found in this matchless creature, who appeared more tempting now than in the gladdest springtime of her life, for the white flame in her heart made her shine forth like a summer sun. Ruefully, they lamented the dismal fancy that made her wish to end her days as a respectable woman. To such mournful folk, Madame de L'Isle-Adam objected jestingly that, after twenty-four years of public service, she had earned the right to retire. Others protested that, however distant the sun might be, men could still bask in it, whereas she would never again show herself. In reply to this argument, Imperia promised that she would still have a smile to offer any lord who came to watch her play the rôle of a virtuous woman. The English envoy swore that she was capable of anything, even of pushing virtue to its extreme point.

Imperia left a present for each of her friends and large sums for the poor and afflicted of Rome; to the convent her daughter was to have entered and to the church herself was building, she gave the wealth she had inherited from Theodora and which had originally come from the Cardinal of Ragusa.

When the couple set out, they were escorted a long way by knights in mourning. The common folk, too, flocked out to cheer them and wish them happiness, for if Madame Imperia had always been hard on the mighty, she had never been anything but wholly compassionate towards the poor. This exquisite Queen of Love made a triumphant progress through all the towns of Italy, where rumor of her conversion had spread and where everyone was anxious to see that phenomenon, a husband and wife who loved each other. Not a few princes received the pretty couple at Court. It was but fitting, they said, to heap honor upon a woman brave enough to renounce her empire over the fashionable world and embrace the modest ways of respectable domesticity. There was, however, one evil-minded fellow, My Lord Duke of Ferrara, who said to L'Isle-Adam that his vast fortune had not cost him much. At this first insult, Madame Imperia showed all her loftiness of heart. She immediately gave up all the money she had received from her lovers and applied it to the ornamentation of the dome of Sancta Maria del Fiore, in the town of Florence. This turned the laugh against the Sire d'Este, who boasted of building a church in spite of his slender revenue. You may take it for granted that his brother the Cardinal reprimanded him for the *mot*.

The fair Imperia kept only her own personal wealth and what the Emperor had bestowed upon her through pure friendship after his departure. This still represented a considerable sum. Monsieur de L'Isle-Adam challenged the Duke to a duel and pinked his man. Thus neither Madame de L'Isle-Adam nor her husband could in any way incur reproach. This trait of chivalry procured her a glorious welcome all along the road homeward, especially in Piedmont, where the fêtes were splendid. The poems and verses composed in their honor—sonnets, odes and epithalamiums—have been included in several anthologies. But the best poetry proved trumpery beside her who, to quote Master Boccaccio, was poetry itself.

The prize in this tourney of fêtes and gallantry fell to the good Emperor of the Romans. Knowing what a crude blunder the Duke of Ferrara had committed, he dispatched a messenger to his old flame, charged with letters written in Latin by his own hand. He loved her so much for herself, he wrote, that he was delighted to know her happy, yet sad, too, that all her happiness did not proceed from him. He deplored losing the privilege of making her presents, but assured her that if the King of France received her coldly, he would deem it an honor to acquire a Villiers de L'Isle-Adam to the Holy Roman Empire. And he would give her husband such principalities as they might choose from among his domains.

The fair Imperia replied by acknowledging the Emperor's magnanimity but announced that even had she to suffer a thousand affronts, she was determined to end her days in France.

II

How This Marriage Ended

NOT KNOWING if she would be received, Madame de L'Isle-Adam did not venture to Court. She lived in the country, where her husband had founded a large establishment by buying the seigniory of Beaumont-le-Vicomte—a name which gave rise to the famous pun our beloved Rabelais cites in his most magnificent work. He also acquired the estate of Nointel, the forest of Carenelle, St. Martin and various other properties close to L'Isle-Adam, where his brother resided. These acquisitions made him the most powerful lord in the Île de France and Viscounty of Paris. He built a marvellous château near Beaumont (subsequently razed by the English) fitting it out with furniture, decorations, foreign tapestries, chests, paintings, statuary and curiosities belonging to his wife, who was a great connoisseur. Thus Beaumont rivalled the most sumptuous châteaux in existence.

The happy pair led a life envied of all; people in Paris and at Court talked much of the marriage, more about the good fortune of Messire de Beaumont, but most about the perfect, loyal, gracious and devout life of his wife, who from habit was still often referred to as Madame Imperia. No longer was My Lady proud, and sharp as steel; she possessed all the qualities and virtues of a respectable woman; she might have been a model for a queen. The Church loved her much for her deep faith. To resurrect a remark of hers from the buried past, she had never really been allowed to forget God, because she had frolicked plentifully with churchmen, abbots, bishops and cardinals who filled her couch with holy water and, under the curtains, wrought her eternal salvation.

497

The panegyrics heaped upon her bore such fruit that the King travelled to the Beauvais country just to have an excuse to view this paragon. His Majesty did L'Isle-Adam the honor of staying at Beaumont, spent three days there, and held a royal hunt with the Queen and the whole Court. Naturally he admired the manners of the dazzling châtelaine; the Queen, the ladies and the courtiers followed suit; Imperia was proclaimed as gracious as she was comely. First His Majesty, next the Queen, then all the company congratulated L'Isle-Adam on having chosen such a wife. My Lady's modest demeanor accomplished more than ever her pride would have. If there was anything imperious about her, it was her greatness of heart; her love for her husband was her only tyranny. She was invited to Court and everywhere else. Did she hide her charms under the vestments of virtue? They were none the less lovely for it. The King gave his former envoy the vacant posts of Lord Lieutenant of the Île de France and Provost of Paris; he also granted him the title of Vicomte de Beaumont, which established him as Governor of the whole province and assured him a high place at Court. But the royal sojourn also struck a blow at Imperia's heart and left a grievous scar.

A blackguard, jealous of this unbroken happiness, asked her jestingly if Beaumont had ever mentioned his early love for Mademoiselle de Montmorency. The latter, who was sixteen at the time of their marriage, was now in her twenty-fourth year. She loved L'Isle-Adam so passionately that she remained a virgin, would brook no talk of other suitors, and was dying of a broken heart. In vain she sought to banish the memory of her first love; nothing would avail. She was even now preparing to enter the Convent of Chelles. During six years of wedded bliss, Madame Imperia had never heard the name mentioned. Was this not proof positive that she had all her husband's adoration? Time had passed, brief as a day; it was as though they had been married on the eve; each night was as a wedding night, and if the Vicomte had business that took him away from his wife, he was filled with melancholy. Neither could bear to lose sight of the other.

The King, too, though he liked the Vicomte, made a remark that dwelled like a thorn in his flesh:

"You have no children?" His Majesty observed.

Beaumont started as a man starts when a probe finds his raw wound:

"Sire, my brother has, so our line is safe."

Now it happened that his two nephews died suddenly—one after a fall from his horse in a tournament, the other from an illness. Their father loved the lads so fiercely and grieved so mortally over their deaths that he in his turn died of despair. Thus Imperia's husband became the head of the house; the fief of Beaumont, the estates of Carenelle, St. Martin, Nointel and dependencies were joined to the seigniory of L'Isle-Adam and the neighboring forest land. Madame was then forty-five and so excellently preserved as to be still suitable to bear children. But she had conceived none! When she saw the lineage of L'Isle-Adam wiped out, she determined to obtain offspring.

If for the last seven years she had never once shown the slightest symptom of pregnancy, she believed it was because both she and her husband took too much joy in the business. A learned physician, whom she summoned secretly from Paris, agreed that this barrenness proceeded from the fact that My Lord and My Lady, always more lovers than spouses, baulked her pregnancy by their extreme pleasure. For a while, the blessed woman strove to curb her passion and to remain calm as a hen under the master cock. Had not the man of science pointed out that, in a state of nature, beasts never failed to breed, because the females employed none of the artifices, tricks, caresses and fiddle-faddle with which women season the olives of Poissy? That, Imperia commented, was why we called them beasts. But she promised to cease toying with the adored coralliform plaything and to forget the ingenious sweet manœuvres she had invented. Alas! all her resolutions were useless. In vain she kept as demurely rigid and quiet as that German woman who lay so still that her husband bestrode her to death. (He went, poor baron! to Rome, to seek absolution from the Pope, who delivered the celebrated brief in which he requested the ladies of Franconia to move slightly during the contact, thus preventing a repetition of the crime.) No, do what she might, Madame de L'Isle-Adam did not conceive and fell into profound melancholy.

She began to watch L'Isle-Adam, when he believed himself unobserved; she noticed how pensive he was and how he wept

that he had no fruit of their love. Soon the pair mingled their
tears, for everything was common to both in this perfect union,
and, since they were inseparable, inevitably they thought as one.
The mere sight of a serf's child was enough to plunge Madame
into the depths of grief for a whole day long. Her despair drove
L'Isle-Adam to give orders that all children be kept out of his
wife's sight. He would speak soothingly to her, too, telling her
for instance that children often turned out very badly—to which
she invariably countered that a child, made by such fond lovers
as they, would be the finest child in the world. If he suggested
that their sons might perish like his unfortunate brother's, she
assured him that she would not suffer them to stray from her
skirts, and that, like a hen with her chicks, she would always
keep an eye on them. In brief she found an answer to everything.

Madame next sent for a woman suspected of dealing in magic
and reputed to be very learned in these mysteries. This authority
informed her that she had often seen women who, despite their
studied efforts to copulate properly, still came off unsuccessful.
When, however, they had applied the simplest possible methods
—those of animals—their success was assured. Madame accordingly modelled her conduct upon the beasts of the fields; yet her
loins remained as firm, white and unalterable as marble.

Returning to the physical science of the master doctors of
Paris, she summoned a celebrated Arabian medico, who had just
arrived in France to propagate a new system of medicine. This
savant, reared in the school of a certain Averroes, pronounced
the cruellest sentence of all. She had, he said, been too open with
too many; for having yielded to their fancies, as she did in the
practise of love's sweet commerce, she had irreparably ruined
certain organs to which Dame Nature had attached certain eggs.
The latter, made fecund by males, were hatched in cover; thence
the young of all mammals emerged at birth—a statement confirmed by the hood certain children are born with. His theory
appeared so mammarily stupid, so absurd, so idiotic, so opposed
to Holy Writ, which establishes the majesty of man fashioned
in the image of God, and so contrary to the laws of reason and
sound doctrine, that the doctors of Paris laughed it to scorn. The
Arabian scholar left the University and his master's name was
never heard there again.

Madame stole up to Paris again for a secret interview with the physicians, who advised her to carry on as usual. Had she not had the beautiful Theodora by the Cardinal of Ragusa in the midst of her love-life? Did not the right of bearing children remain with women as long as the tides of their blood? The best advice they could give her was to strive to multiply the chances of conception. Their reasoning seemed so sage that she multiplied her victories; yet it was only multiplying her defeats, since she culled all love's flowers, but never a fruit.

Heartbroken, she wrote to the Pope, who was fond of her, and apprized His Holiness of all her sorrows. In a gracious homily written in his own hand, the good Pope replied that, where human science and mundane efforts failed, we should turn to Heaven and implore the grace of God. Imperia then decided to go barefoot with her husband on a pilgrimage to Notre Dame de Liesse, a shrine celebrated for intervention in like cases. Here she made a vow to build a magnificent cathedral in gratitude for a child. She bruised and cut her dainty feet, but conceived only a violent sorrow. So bitterly did she grieve, that some of her glorious tresses fell and some turned white.

Ultimately, the faculty of childbearing was withdrawn from her; this caused obscure thick vapors to issue from her hypochondriac regions. Her skin turned yellow. She was then forty-nine years old; she retired to her Château de L'Isle-Adam, where she grew thin as a leper in the lazaret. That her husband was still amorous and good as gold to her made the unhappy creature despair all the more; she realized that she failed in her duty because she had formerly been too free with men. In her own contemptuous words, she was only a cauldron to boil chitterlings in.

"Ha!" she said, one evening, when these thoughts tormented her, "in spite of the Church, in spite of the King, in spite of everything, Madame de L'Isle-Adam is still the wicked Imperia!"

She flew into furious rages at life's irony. Here was a handsome nobleman in the prime of life, enjoying everything man could wish for: vast wealth, royal favor, a peerless love, a matchless wife, pleasures such as no other woman could provide. Everything? No—one boon, the dearest to the head of a lofty dynasty, failed him: lineage! As she recalled how noble and magnanimous he had been towards her, how she failed in her duty by not giving him children and how she was henceforth unable to do so, she longed for death. Then, burying her sorrow in the depths of her heart, she conceived a devotion worthy of her great love. To put her heroic design into practise, she became more amorous than ever, took extreme care of her charms and applied the subtlest precepts to maintain her bodily perfections. She shone forth with incredible radiance.

About this time, Monsieur de Montmorency overcame his daughter's aversion to marriage; her alliance with a Sieur de Châtillon was much talked about. Now Madame Imperia lived only a few miles from Montmorency. One day she sent her husband out hunting in the forest; he had no sooner gone than she set out to call on his erstwhile fiancée. Arriving in the manor gardens, she walked about there; spying a servant, she sent him to ask his mistress to receive a lady who had a most important communication to make to her. Agog at the account the servant gave of the stranger's beauty, courtesy and escort, Mademoiselle de Montmorency hastened to the gardens. There she met her rival for the first time.

"My dear," said the poor woman, weeping to find the damsel as beautiful as herself, "I know that you are being forced to marry Monsieur de Châtillon, when you really love Monsieur de L'Isle-Adam. I beg you to have confidence in the prophecy I am about to make to you. I say that the man you have loved—he was untrue only because he was caught in a snare that would have trapped an angel!—will be delivered of his old wife before the leaves fall. Thus the constancy of your love will win its crown of flowers. Be brave enough to refuse this marriage they are arranging for you, and you will enjoy your childhood sweetheart. Oh, promise me to love and cherish L'Isle-Adam; for he is the most gracious of men; never cause him the slightest sorrow, and bid him reveal to you all the secrets of love invented by the fair Imperia. By practising them, you, a younger woman, will easily banish the remembrance of her from his mind."

Mademoiselle de Montmorency was so amazed that words failed her; she let this Queen of Beauty vanish, believing she had seen a fay until a gardener told her that her fay was none other than Madame de L'Isle-Adam. Though the adventure was inexplicable, Mademoiselle de Montmorency told her father that she would not commit herself on this proposal of marriage until autumn. Is it not Love's nature to marry Hope, despite the bitter pills this fickle and gracious companion gilds with honey? During the month of grape-picking, Madame Imperia would not let L'Isle-Adam leave her a moment; she called forth her most passionate delights so lavishly that, judging from appearances, she might have been seeking to kill him. Each night, it seemed to the husband that he had a fresh bride beside him. Awaking on the morrow, the good woman would implore him to store the remembrance of this perfection of amour in his heart. Then, to plumb the depths of her lover's soul:

"Poor L'Isle-Adam," she said, "we were rash to marry—a lad like you, just turned twenty-three, and an old woman close to forty!"

He protested that his excess of happiness made a thousand people envious . . . that at her age she had not her equal among the younger women . . . that, if ever she grew old, he would love her wrinkles . . . that even in the tomb she would be lovely and her skeleton lovable. . . .

His replies brought tears to her eyes. But once, she rejoined maliciously that Mademoiselle de Montmorency was very beautiful and very constant. These words forced L'Isle-Adam to confess that she hurt him by reminding him of the only wrong he had ever done in his life. But when he had jilted his first sweetheart, Imperia had already banished all love of the other. His perfect candor, and his loyalty in facing a subject from which many would have shrunk, moved Imperia deeply. She seized and pressed him to her:

"My love," she said, "for a long time I have been suffering from retraction in the heart. Already in my earliest youth, I was seriously threatened. Now the Arabian physician has borne this out. If I die, I wish you to swear by the most binding oath a knight can make that you will marry Mademoiselle de Montmorency. I am so certain of dying that I leave you my property only on condition this marriage takes place."

L'Isle-Adam turned deathly pale; he felt faint at the mere thought of an eternal separation.

"Ay, blessed treasure of love," she went on, "I am punished by God there where my sins were committed. The pleasures I feel so intensely dilate my heart; according to the Arabian medico, they have weakened the vessels, which will burst in the supreme throes of a moment of passion. But I have always prayed God to take my life now, at my present age, for I would not see my charms marred by the ravages of Time."

Then this generous lady was vouchsafed full proof of her husband's love. She alone knew what irresistible spells she wove in the ravishments, the glandogratifications and the unearthly blandishments of the conjugal bed. She knew, too, that poor L'Isle-Adam would rather have died than be deprived of the amative delicacies she concocted. But when she confessed that her heart would burst in the furious excitement of amour, she obtained the greatest sacrifice love ever called on man to make. Throwing himself at her feet, L'Isle-Adam vowed that to preserve her life, he would never ask for love . . . he would live content to see and feel her at his side . . . he would find joy enough in kissing her coif and grazing the hem of her gown. Imperia burst into tears.

"Dear love," she said, "I would liefer die than lose a single bud of your vine! I shall perish as I have lived. Heaven be praised, I have always been able to make a man bestride me at will without my having to speak a word!"

Now many years ago My Lord Cardinal of Ragusa had given Imperia a precious gift, which the old lecher called *in articulo mortis*. (You must excuse these three words of Latin; they come from the Cardinal.) It was a tiny bulb of thin glass, made at Venice, no bigger than a bean, yet filled with so subtle a poison that anyone breaking it between his teeth died instantly and painlessly. My Lord Cardinal had bought it from the Signora Tophana, the famous Roman brewer of poison. This bulb, fitted under the bezel of a ring, was preserved from any object that might break it by some thin gold plates. Several times poor Imperia put the glass in her mouth without being able to make up her mind to bite it, so blissful was the moment she believed to be her last. She would enjoy recalling all her erotic manœuvres and artifices ere she bit the glass; then, when she felt the most perfect of all pleasures, she promised herself to shatter the bulb.

The poor creature departed this life on the first day of October. The night she died, a mighty clamor rang through the forests and rose, resonant, to the welkin, as if the loves had cried aloud: *"The great Tunc is dead!"* in imitation of the Pagan gods who, at the advent of the Savior of man, fled into the skies, wailing: *"The great Pan is slain."* A cry, which was heard by some men who happened to be navigating the Ægean Sea, and preserved by a Church Father. . . .

Madame Imperia died without the slightest bodily flaw, so careful had God been to create an irreproachable model of womanhood. Her flesh, it was said, assumed a most exquisite tint, caused by the proximity of the flaming wings of Pleasure, who lay and wept over her corpse. Her husband mourned for her most sorrowfully, never for a moment suspecting that she had died to rid him of a barren wife. Nor did the physician who embalmed her breathe a word about the cause of her death.

Her admirable sacrifice came to light six years after the marriage of L'Isle-Adam to Mademoiselle de Montmorency, who witlessly told him all about Madame Imperia's visit. The unhappy man immediately fell into a state of profound dejection, dragged out a few listless days, and died soon after, unable to scatter the memory of such amorous joys, far beyond the power of a novice to restore to him. Thereby he proved the truth of a frequent saying, at the time, to the effect that Imperia never died in a heart where she had once reigned.

This teaches us that only such as have practised vice understand virtue properly; for, among the most respectable women, how many would thus have laid down their lives, in whatever high state of religion you looked for them?

Epilogue

HA, MY mad sweetheart, you whose task it is to make the house merry, what tricks have you been up to? Despite a thousand orders to the contrary, you have been wallowing in that slough of melancholy whence you fished up Bertha. And now you come back with hair dishevelled, looking for all the world like a wench freshly dragooned by a regiment of horsemen! Where are your pretty golden aiglets and their tinkling bells? Where are your filigreed flowers with their fantastical designs? Where did you leave your scarlet bauble of folly, adorned with priceless gewgaws and worth a minot of pearls?

Why shed pernicious tears that mar your night-black eyes? How much more pleasing they are when aglitter with the wit of tales!—so pleasing, indeed, that, for the sake of your laughter, popes forgive you your sayings, feel their souls caught between the ivory of your teeth, flush as the rosy dart of your sweet tongue draws out their hearts, and would cheerfully barter the holy slipper against the hundred smiles that grind your blood's vermilion on your lips. Fair, riant wench, if you would stay forever fresh and young, then weep no more. Dream, rather, of riding the flies unbridled, of snaffling your chameleon chimaeras with fragments of cloud-dust, of transmogrifying the stern realities of life into kaleidoscopic iridescences, caparisoned with roseate dreams, mantled with sky-blue wings, and luminous as comet wine.

By the Body and the Blood, by the Censer and the Seal, by the Book and the Sword, by the Rag and the Gold, by the Sound and by the Color, if you but once set foot again in that elegiac hovel where eunuchs crimp ugly wenches for imbecile sultans, I'll curse, I'll strappado you, I'll deprive you of roguery and love, I'll—

Pfrist! Here she is astride a sunbeam, holding a volume that is ready to explode with aery meteors! She sports within their prisms, gambolling so madly, so wildly, so daringly, so counter to all the laws of sense, direction and usage, so downright contrary to everything, that you must have known her for donkey's years if you would follow the silver facets of her siren tail as it frisks amid the artifices of these new peals of laughter.

Ye Gods! she has plunged helter-skelter among them like a hundred schoolboys falling on a hedge full of blackberries after Vespers. To the devil the magister! The book is finished! Out upon work! Tantivy, tantivy, my jovial friends, this way, this way!